# Praise for *Come In and Cover Me*

"Phillips's writing is . . . brimming with imagery. . . . Her greatest talent is her ability to create the world of the story. *Come In and Cover Me* moves us into the earth. The dusty landscape serves as both setting and metaphor, a beautiful but dangerous place where a sudden loss of footing can prove fatal."
—*The Washington Post*

"With a sure hand . . . Phillips weaves this strand of the supernatural through a compelling modern story of love and loss."
—*San Francisco Chronicle*

"As graceful and emotionally true as Phillips's debut—and, in its thoroughly researched reimagining of the American Southwest's prehistoric Mimbres culture and its leap into supernatural territory without once losing its credibility or riveting story line, surpasses it. . . . Amid a sensually sketched setting of rock formations, mesquite and juniper, narrow canyons, and night skies, Ren and Silas work side by side and try to bridge the growing distance between them. As the natural and supernatural worlds coalesce, both recent and ancient history become more insistently present, yielding an original and strikingly beautiful ending."
—*Elle*

"Long haunted by her dead brother, archaeologist Ren Taylor is being led to the find of her career by a ghostly woman who lived at the site of an ancient desert dig. Part love story, part field guide, this beguiling novel charts the excavation and restoration of a damaged soul."
—*Parade*

"Phillips makes Ren's story and even her ghostly visitors believable. . . . Silas and Ren's tentative romance is effectively drawn, revealing the omissions and commissions of nascent love and how people push away those they need most in times of crisis.
learn to pick up the broken pieces of li
thing new."

"A smart, engrossing ghost story . . . Haunting, compelling, and lyrical . . . A moving, well-crafted story brought to life through believable characters, vivid details, and honest prose. Phillips has provided the reader with a true find—an ending-surprising, satisfying, and memorable novel that illustrates the power of good storytelling."

—*BookPage*

"Moving."

—*Publishers Weekly*

"A lush, glowing, truly enjoyable work."

—*Library Journal* (starred review)

"Phillips handles Ren's communication with ghosts with enough delicacy to be persuasive, enhances the appeal of archaeology by personalizing its discoveries, and vividly illustrates the need to share oneself with loved ones."

—*Booklist*

## Praise for *The Well and the Mine*

"A quietly bold debut, full of heart."

—*O, The Oprah Magazine*

"When you close the book, you'll miss these characters. But *The Well and the Mine* doesn't just give you characters who'll stay with you—it gives you a whole world."

—Fannie Flagg, author of *Fried Green Tomatoes at the Whistle Stop Café* and *Daisy Fay and the Miracle Man*

"Gin Phillips has a remarkable ear for dialogue and a tenderhearted eye for detail; you can hear the pecans and hickory nuts falling from the trees and feel the stillness of a hot summer night. A whisper runs through the novel—the ghosts of places and people and luscious peach pies."

—*Los Angeles Times*

# come in and cover me

## GIN PHILLIPS

RIVERHEAD BOOKS

New York

**RIVERHEAD BOOKS**
Published by the Penguin Group
Penguin Group (USA) Inc.
375 Hudson Street, New York, New York 10014, USA

Penguin Group (Canada), 90 Eglinton Avenue East, Suite 700, Toronto, Ontario M4P 2Y3, Canada (a division of Pearson Penguin Canada Inc.) • Penguin Books Ltd., 80 Strand, London WC2R 0RL, England • Penguin Group Ireland, 25 St. Stephen's Green, Dublin 2, Ireland (a division of Penguin Books Ltd.) • Penguin Group (Australia), 250 Camberwell Road, Camberwell, Victoria 3124, Australia (a division of Pearson Australia Group Pty. Ltd.) • Penguin Books India Pvt. Ltd., 11 Community Centre, Panchsheel Park, New Delhi—110 017, India • Penguin Group (NZ), 67 Apollo Drive, Rosedale, Auckland 0632, New Zealand (a division of Pearson New Zealand Ltd.) • Penguin Books (South Africa) (Pty.) Ltd., 24 Sturdee Avenue, Rosebank, Johannesburg 2196, South Africa

Penguin Books Ltd., Registered Offices: 80 Strand, London WC2R 0RL, England

This is a work of fiction. Names, characters, places, and incidents either are the product of the author's imagination or are used fictitiously, and any resemblance to actual persons, living or dead, business establishments, events, or locales is entirely coincidental. The publisher does not have any control over and does not assume any responsibility for author or third-party websites or their content.

The author gratefully acknowledges permission to reprint lyrics from "Jungleland" and "She's the One" by Bruce Springsteen. Copyright © 1975 Bruce Springsteen, renewed © 2003 Bruce Springsteen (ASCAP). Reprinted by permission. International copyright secured. All rights reserved.

First Riverhead hardcover edition: January 2012
First Riverhead trade paperback edition: January 2013
Riverhead trade paperback ISBN: 978-1-59448-648-7

The Library of Congress has catalogued the Riverhead hardcover edition as follows:

Phillips, Gin.
Come in and cover me / Gin Phillips.
p. cm.
ISBN 978-1-59448-844-3
1. Women mediums—Fiction.   2. Women archaeologists—Fiction.   I. Title.
PS3616.H4556C66   2012
813'.6—dc23                    2011046842

PRINTED IN THE UNITED STATES OF AMERICA

10  9  8  7  6  5  4  3  2  1

for fred

*You are a gift to me.*

Whither thou goest, I will go; and where thou lodgest, I will lodge: thy people shall be my people, and thy God my God.

RUTH 1:16

# prologue

2006
*Crow Creek*
*New Mexico*

Ren stood perfectly still in the dark, listening. She did not know if she was alone. She'd been careful as she left camp, and she could still see the blowing slopes of tent canvas and the glow of the embers a hundred yards or so away. She knew that the others—the grad students and Ed and the engineer who'd driven down from Santa Fe and even the dogs—were asleep. But there were other things that sometimes crept up on her.

This is what she saw: her flashlight beam carving out a tidy circle of rocky dirt. The stars were legion, too bright. Juniper and piñon pines rose into the blue-black sky to her left and right. To the south, the cliffs were a wall of nothing. The moon was gone.

"Hello?" she whispered. She considered the silence. *"Marco?"*

She took two more steps toward the place the girl had shown her, just at the edge of the drop-off. Her nose was cold, and she buried it in the soft sleeve of her jacket.

*"Marco,"* she said again into the fleece. She did not have to be loud. If he were here, he would hear her.

Just behind her right ear, she heard his answer, singsong, just as it used to be when he dove away from her flailing arms in the swimming pool: *"Polo."*

"I thought you might be here," she said, not turning. He said nothing. When she spun around, quickly, hoping to catch him off guard, he had melted into the dark. She thought she could hear the drumming of his hand on his thigh—a repetitive sound that always drove her crazy—but it could have been the branches of the trees rubbing together in the wind.

The question, she thought, was whether Scott was the only one here with her. Was the girl still close by? Ren was on edge as it was—wired on too much coffee, anticipation making her mouth dry, trying to be quiet in case this turned out to be some ridiculous whim, impossible to explain away. She did not want any unknown visitors surprising her and making her yelp loud enough to wake the others. Respectable archaeologists did not yelp. Though respectable archaeologists also did not, as a rule, go digging under the cover of night.

Still scanning the darkness, she rigged her flashlight between two rocks; it shone on the spot she had marked with three sticks earlier in the day. The dirt was hard and cold. She had not brought her gloves. She swung the pickax, minding her own feet, chopping up hunks three or four inches thick. She would not go deeper than that so carelessly—who knew how shallow anything might be buried, and it was so hard to see. Something nearby howled. She switched to the trowel, dug another foot, feeling guilty for all the loose dirt she wasn't screening. She switched to the whisk broom just to make sure she wasn't overlooking anything. As she dug, she grew more certain that she was idiotic to believe that there was anything here to find.

But the girl had meant for her to dig here. If there even was a girl.

She moved the dirt, bit by bit. She was perhaps a foot deep now. The swishing of the whisk broom uncovered one, two, three rocks, none bigger than her hand. At the edge of the square hole she had made, a root protruded. So far, in this midnight excavation, she had discovered three rocks and a root. And now another rock—she could see only the smooth surface of it, still dirt-covered.

She tossed the broom to the side and used her fingers to rub off the dirt. She yanked back her finger at a flash of pain. Sucking on her finger, she tasted blood and dirt, but she kept her eyes on the rock. The flashlight beam was shining off its jet-black surface. Obsidian. She brushed off the rock with her uninjured hand and considered the fine edge. Honed sharp as a knife. Nature didn't do that—humans did.

She breathed faster and aimed the light at the edges of the hole she'd dug, taking more time now, checking every inch carefully. When she cleared off another half-inch of dirt from one corner of the hole, she could see the edges of more rocks. But these rocks were in a line, a close formation. It was the top of a wall.

She sat back on her heels and turned off her flashlight. She smiled, a little at first, then enough that she could feel it in her cheeks. She made a fist and hammered it against her thigh, silently, triumphantly, possibly hard enough to leave a bruise. *Yes. Yes. Yes.* The word echoed around her skull and flowed into her bones and warmed her fingers. There must be another room under her feet, a room that no one would have suspected from the unmarked surface. There was something here that she was meant to find.

"Yes," she said, quietly.

Just out of range of her flashlight beam, she thought she saw a thin shape dart past. The wind blew, and she smelled a sweet woody charred scent, like juniper set aflame. The small girl-shape skirted the edge of the light, spinning and teasing. She was too cheerful to be called skulking.

Ren lunged for the flashlight and tried to catch the shape. She was too late. There was no girl there, only a flutter of falling yellow leaves, reflecting in the light like wolf eyes, which was odd, because the only trees nearby were evergreens.

Ren went back to the dirt. She would cover up the obsidian and come back first thing in the morning, then run and wake up everyone as if she'd just been poking around. No one would know any different, other than her brother, Scott, and he wouldn't be saying anything.

# one

*Abandonment of sites, valleys, and regions has long been a topic of interest to archaeologists. Countless museum exhibits pose the question "Why did they leave?"... [In] all but the most extraordinary circumstances, abandonments probably involve some combination of "push" factors that negatively impact people's present circumstance and "pull" factors that suggest better opportunities elsewhere.*

—From "Abandonment and Reorganization in the Mimbres Region of the American Southwest" by Michelle Hegmon, Margaret C. Nelson, and Susan M. Ruth, *American Anthropologist*, March 1998

## 2009

Ren headed south out of Albuquerque. She could hear something metal rolling around in the backseat. Probably rebar. Possibly a tent pole. She'd forgotten to clean her boots, which were jammed under the passenger's seat; they were shedding flakes of dried mud on the floor mat. But these were minor annoyances, and she could shut them out.

He had called her a few hours ago, on her cell, and she'd nearly left it buzzing in her purse. Work calls usually came in through the museum line. She'd reached for the phone, flipped it open, not looking away from the computer screen: She needed another pair of seventeenth-century blacksmith tongs. The Valle de las Sombras City Museum had respectable collections of pottery and textiles, but it was the blacksmith forge out back that really brought in the paying visitors.

Ren Taylor, she'd said into the phone. Silas Cooper, said the voice on the other end. She didn't recognize the name. He explained that he did contract work in the southern part of the state. She could hear the wind blowing against the phone. He had to be in the field. She imagined him as about the age her father would have been, squinting against the dust in the air, dressed in the standard archaeologist's getup—khakis and a long-sleeved shirt, maybe a cap. He knew about her work at Crow Creek, he said, and she heard, tamped down, excitement in his words. *He's found something,* she thought, and she stopped imagining his wardrobe. She closed her laptop, spinning her chair toward the window.

*He's found something*—the thought circled through her head. A sparrow of some kind flew off the branch outside her window, and she watched it disappear into the sun.

I'd like you to come out to the site we're working on here at Cañada Rosa, he said. Come see what we've found. What is it? she asked him, hoping she already knew. He said she could judge for herself, but he thought he'd found some pottery that she might recognize.

The joy made her stomach knot.

It was nearly two o'clock when she hung up. She thought she could pack a bag at home and still make it to the site by dark. She grabbed her keys and passed the office manager and the PR director as she left her office. To both of them, never taking her eyes off the exit, she said, "I think we've found her again. I'll call from the road." The door swung closed behind her before she heard if they responded.

She'd jogged through her house, grabbing clothes and shampoo and boots and socks and her always-packed toiletry bag. She was back in the truck in less than ten minutes. She loved the frenzy of packing, loved locking up the house and cranking the truck and backing out of the driveway. It was always euphoric, this leaving, heading for open spaces.

The first two hours down I-25 passed flat and monotonous; it calmed her, even as she sipped gas-station coffee. She tried to exhale the excitement and breathe in only readiness. She did not want to be disappointed again.

She looked out at the mountain formations, like spines of stegosauruses, alligators, iguanas. There was a broad, flat hill like an oyster shell. She considered her hands, resting on the steering wheel. The scar on the top of her wrist was from a fall down a muddy slope outside of Tempe. She'd hit sharp-edged slate. That one she remembered. Her middle finger had a slice through the top knuckle. She had a vague memory of a paper cut from a file folder.

The asphalt road turned dusty and uneven as she turned off at her exit. A dented green sign with an arrow: Montpelier to the right. That seemed clear enough. She curved and clunked for several miles. Small dead and dying towns lay across her path. After a few twists of the road, she was at the start of the canyon, its dark walls rising up around her. She bumped violently down the road, not going more than ten miles an hour, the surface washed away in spots from flash floods past.

She stole quick glances at the jagged rock walls at narrow passes, automatically searching for signs of prior occupations. She caught sight of a small dark petroglyph—not so common in the area—along one flat wall. She slowed, rolling down the window halfway. It was a blanket pattern, from what she could see, an abstract design of lines and curves. Lovely. The Apaches had lived around this canyon, but their rock art tended to be painted red and was more sheltered than this wide-open section of rock. She guessed Puebloan, twelfth or thirteenth century.

She drove on. Where the canyon widened, the land was alive with willows and cottonwoods, cholla and prickly pear blooming all along the trickle of a creek. Silas Cooper had told her the water ran from a warm spring at the mouth of the canyon. It had been a long, dry summer, and now in August most of New Mexico had faded to various hues of tan. She hadn't seen color like this on the whole trip down: bright purples and hot pink from the cactus blooms, rich, deep greens of the dense cottonwoods. The creek snaked back and forth across the road—she lost count of how often she'd crossed it. Her windows were splattered with water.

It was disorienting, all this green.

He'd told her that the bunkhouse would be the first building she saw after she passed through the gate marked "Montpelier Box Ranch." The iron gate was open, and she drove through, scanning for the house. She saw it almost immediately, a small rectangle pressed against the sheer drop of a cliff. Tin roof, pine porch. The Black Range loomed close by to the west. To the east, the San Mateo Mountains.

She circled behind the building, past a Jeep parked facing the cliff, and pulled in behind a black Dodge, angling into the shade of one of the wild walnuts. Ed Ripley's truck, she felt sure, and the sight of it relaxed some of the tension in her shoulders. It had been at least two months since she'd seen Ed. He had that same truck fifteen years ago when she met him on her first dig—she'd been in a crowd of khaki-wearing undergrads and he'd been silver-haired and dapper. He wore a white linen shirt every day, and it never showed dirt or sweat. He looked almost fictional, like someone who would have searched for King Tut. Only he wasn't an archaeologist, technically—he'd moved to New Mexico and developed a taste for amateur archaeology after retiring from some vague career in Washington. There were rumors of FBI or CIA.

She jumped from the driver's seat, landing softly, immediately feeling the dust and sand slide into her sandals. Voices were coming from inside the screen door. A black-and-white spotted dog—part Dalmatian and part some kind of hound—appeared from under one of the trucks and trotted toward her. The dog sniffed at her hand just as the screen door opened.

"That's Zorro," said Ed, moving into the sunlight. His white hair—no black in it at all now—was cut close to the scalp. His clothes looked fresh-pressed. He was with a younger man whom she guessed to be in his early twenties. Too young to be Silas Cooper.

Ed held out his arms. She grinned and half-jogged over to him, hugging him tightly enough to feel his shoulder blades.

"Ah, it's good to see you, Ed." The scrape of his beard against her cheek was comforting.

"Ren, we've been eagerly awaiting your arrival," he said in his Walter Cronkite voice. All of Ed's sentences seemed to come from the nightly news. "This is Paul. He's the grandson of the ranch owner. He's been helping us out. Thinks he wants to be an archaeologist when he grows up."

The young guy held out his hand. Maybe not even his twenties, reconsidered Ren. His cheeks and nose were red, and his hair was sun-bleached, but the rest of him was a dark brown.

"Nice to meet you," he said.

The screen door swung open again. The dog still at Ren's feet spun and headed toward the man who walked their way. His green T-shirt was untucked, and his dark hair was wet. He was a few inches taller and maybe a few years older than she was.

"Ren?"

She nodded and shook his outstretched hand. She could feel his calluses. "And you must be Silas. Good to meet you."

"Sorry it took me a second—I was just grabbing a shower." He reached down and rubbed the dog's head. "Any trouble getting here?"

"None. Good directions."

"Glad to hear it," he said. She noticed his hair hadn't been cut recently, and he had the beginnings of a beard. One knee was skinned up, with the scab hardened. He had the hard calves and thighs of a runner. "And glad you could come out on such short notice. Braxton—he's the ranch owner—wanted to be here to meet you, but he's not back yet. He bought this place a couple of years ago when he realized what was on it."

"And what exactly is on it?" asked Ren.

"Oh, I'm not going to just blurt it out like that with no drumroll or anything. I've got to set it up. Zorro, you're an idiot." The dog had arranged itself on his foot, and Silas reached to scratch its ears. "But I'll show you something later that'll curl your toes."

Ren considered his forehead and his slick, messy hair while he was focused on the dog. He looked up from the dog, caught her eyes again. Half a second of a smile.

"Professionally speaking," he said. "We were just about to make some dinner. I'll catch you up on everything while we eat. Glad you made it before the sun set."

"Is it too late to see the site?"

"Yeah. Sorry, but you don't want to get stuck up there in the dark. I'll take you first thing in the morning." He took a step toward her Land Cruiser. "Need help with your stuff?"

She didn't, and they all walked together to the bunkhouse, the dog weaving around their feet. Silas held the back door for her as she stepped into the ranch house, Paul and Ed behind her. The windows were wide, letting in plenty of light, and the ceiling fans whirred over an open den with two worn sofas and speckled white tile. She stepped into the kitchen, which had steel counters piled with loaves of bread and bags of junk food.

"We had college volunteers here over the summer," Silas said, lifting a red plastic cup off the counter. It read "SC" in black Magic Marker. "The last group left a week ago, and we've been living on the leftovers."

He motioned to two doors on the closest wall, then pushed one door open. "There's a bathroom here, between the bedrooms. This one's yours—my stuff's in the other one."

Ren looked from Paul to Ed. "Just two bedrooms? Did I kick someone out?"

"Nope," said Ed. "I've got a cot set up in my tent, and I like the view out there. Paul and I have been outside all summer."

"They didn't actually offer me a bed," said Paul.

"You kidding?" asked Silas. "You have to earn a bed."

"Couldn't you sleep at your grandfather's?" asked Ren. "His place must be close."

"Just up the road," said Paul. "But, you know, I have to earn a bed."

"He idolizes us," said Ed.

Ren noticed a screened porch with a row of tables. Silas followed her gaze. "And that's where we do the lab work," he said.

She scanned the brown bags and cardboard boxes she saw stacked and piled in corners. "Is it in there?" she asked.

"I told you she wouldn't wait," said Ed.

Silas looked over at the porch, then back to Ren. "Don't you want to at least put your bags down? Eat a hot dog or two?"

"He thinks he's being funny," said Ed.

"Show me," said Ren.

Something shifted in Silas's eyes, and Ren could see the same excitement she had heard on the phone. It had been lurking there, underneath, pressed down under introductions and luggage.

"Show me," she said again.

He headed toward the back porch more quickly than she'd expected. She dropped her bag where she stood and followed him. In the lab, breeze blowing through the screened windows, Silas reached for a cardboard box on top of a file cabinet. He lifted the lid and pulled out a convex piece of ceramic bowl. It was roughly a trapezoid, grayish, with a good section of the rim showing. Maybe eight inches wide at its widest point. Three thick black lines ran under the rim, and two shapes converged into the white space. One shape, filled with diagonal lines, could have been a wing. But it was another curved triangle that made Ren's breath catch. For a moment she could only think *Yes yes yes yes*.

When other words came to her, she pointed to the shape. "It's a beak. Part of a parrot's head and a beak."

"Yeah."

"It's her."

"I think so, too. We've dated another room at the site to being about the right time period."

She passed the sherd back. "You could look at the beak and know to call me?" she asked. "You knew it was her?"

"I told you I was familiar with your work." Silas replaced the box on top of the cabinet.

There had been a year or so when she had spoken everywhere, when she forgot which microphone she was standing at and all the audiences looked the same. The bowls she'd discovered, really, were the draw, but since they kept silent, the glamour rubbed off on her. The find at Crow Creek was in all the daily papers, not just the academic journals. Three twelfth-century Mimbres bowls found— arguably the biggest ceramics find in half a century in the South- west. And she could persuasively argue that these bowls pointed to one artist, a mysterious figure who could add a personal touch to a scientific story. *Smithsonian* magazine did a feature story; *Time* and *National Geographic* each ran a column-long piece. Ren was at first flattered, then overwhelmed, and finally relieved when it was over. The attention only distracted her from the artist.

Her artist. She'd been here in this canyon. Silas insisted on going to start dinner before Ren could ask more questions, and, despite her impatience, she knew he was right to give her a few solitary minutes. A single sherd. She shouldn't get too confident. She should focus on asking the right questions and listening to the answers. And then she could get her hands in the dirt tomorrow, and she would see what the dirt could tell her.

She unpacked efficiently, lining up shirts, socks, and underwear in the dresser drawers. She could hear footsteps outside, heavy steps, and branches rustling. She brushed her hair until it was smooth and straight and her hands were steady.

Ed and Paul were sharpening green branches when she stepped onto the front porch. Silas stood a few yards away, adding a log to a small fire. Adirondack chairs and brightly colored foldable chairs were scattered along the porch and into the dirt yard. Ed flicked his eyes away from Paul briefly to smile at her.

"Seriously, he was this tall," said Paul, one foot propped on the porch. "Have you ever seen a jackrabbit that big?"

"I've seen ones that'll look back at you at eye level." Ed had a calm, serious newsman's face to match his newsman's voice. "There've been documented cases of jackrabbit skeletons up to four feet tall."

"He's making that up," Ren said. "You can tell when he's lying, because the left side of his mouth crooks the slightest bit."

"Documented cases," said Ed. A long shaving of wood fell to the ground with a flick of his pocketknife.

"The dreaded jackalope," said Silas, approaching with a pack of hot dogs. He'd sliced a slit into the side, and grayish juice dripped into the dirt. "Sticks ready?"

"Almost," Ed said.

"You know what you call a giant jackrabbit in Las Vegas?" asked Paul.

Silence.

"A blackjack-alope."

"Did you make that up by any chance?" asked Ed. He handed a stick to Ren, one to Silas.

"Yeah." Paul nodded proudly. "Pretty good, huh? I got a bunch of 'em. What about a seven-foot jackrabbit that plays basketball?"

"Shaq-alope," said Silas. "You're well on your way to that postgrad degree, m'boy. Now, all of you grab a dog and start cooking. Buns and assorted condiments over there. We got Italian sausages, too. And bratwursts. Popsicles in the freezer for dessert."

"Impressively phallic," Ren said.

Silas gestured toward the sharpened branches. "Help yourself to a pointy stick."

They stood as they cooked the hot dogs, then pulled folding chairs into a wide ring around the fire. They settled their drinks on flat sections of ground and balanced plates on their laps. Silas slid his shoes off, resting his heels on top of them. Ren noticed the lines and curves of his feet.

The sun had started to pinken the sky. Ren looked toward the deep green line of cottonwoods growing along the creek she could no longer see.

"I got one," said Silas. "What do you call a giant jackrabbit that causes cavities?"

Ren chewed, blackened skin crunching softly against her teeth. "A plaque-alope," she said after a moment. She swallowed. "What about a giant jackrabbit you can land a plane on?"

"Tarmac-alope," said Silas.

"You guys got skills," said Paul.

The wind kept shifting, blowing smoke into their faces. Ren's eyes watered, but there was something comforting about the smell and the thickness of it. They ate quickly, licking their fingers.

"So fill me in," said Ren, when the urge to know overwhelmed the pleasure of the fire and the easy silence. "On this place. On where you found that sherd." *On how you found her again when I couldn't,* she wanted to say. She had assumed if her artist showed herself again, it wouldn't be to some stranger. She felt somehow rejected, although the giddiness over the find had mostly tamped that down. The dead were so fickle.

"He's a storyteller," Ed said approvingly.

"Oh, no need for the whole spiel," Silas said, shrugging. "So Chaco was about two hundred miles north of us here at Cañada

Rosa. And the Mimbres River Valley is about fifty miles to the east."

Ren leaned forward. By the turn of the first millennium, the city of Chaco had been the epicenter of the world in what is now modern-day northern New Mexico and beyond. The first city built of permanent masonry, made to last. Homes and storehouses and public areas were impressively constructed. A few well-to-do elites ruled the common masses. It was a center of power.

Their neighbors to the south were a quiet bunch of egalitarian farmers. The Mimbres people had no impressive structures like Chaco—they built with mud and river cobble, not a right angle in an entire site. No one talked about their architecture—they talked about their pottery. It was stunning, one-of-a-kind. And very valuable. It was also typically buried with the dead, which had not turned out so well for the dead. Ren had a snapshot on her desk— the work of some local paper—of a pothunter surrounded by piles of dirt, a bulldozer in the background. The pothunter was holding a Mimbres bowl in one hand and, with the other hand, tossing a skull over his shoulder.

The boy popped the tab on another beer. Ren wondered if he was old enough to drink.

"So you have these two ways of life spreading out," Silas continued, "one from the south and one from the north. Cañada Rosa is an intersection point of the two worlds. We're the frontier. We think we've found your lady's work up at the Delgado site, which was occupied off and on for about six centuries. We've got four hundred and eighty rooms there, spread over sixty acres. Just a fraction have been touched."

"You have a large Mimbres site?" said Ren, straightening in her chair. "Untouched?"

"That's the beauty of this place," said Silas. "It's the land that time forgot. Or that time didn't want to take the trouble to find. As you may have noticed, it's hard to get here. Even harder for bulldozers. The canyon was spared from massive destruction partly because of the inaccessibility. And it's on the edge of the known Mimbres world. Pothunters and looters didn't think to look here.

"This was life at the boundaries. Far away from the center. And the question I'm trying to answer is, what did people do when they abandoned their center? Did they create a new thing altogether, or did they cling to old habits?"

Silas's arms hung over the sides of his chair, relaxed, as he turned to Ren. "Now. Your turn to tell me about Crow Creek."

She glanced toward Ed. "Ed told you about it already, right?"

"Ed told me some. And I saw your presentation in Albuquerque last fall. You never called on me to ask my question."

"What was your question?"

"Tell me the story, and then I'll ask you."

She told him the version she told everyone. She had told it enough by now that the words left her mouth as smooth as a recording. All emotion—shock joy relief—had detached itself and sunk deep down somewhere inside her rib cage.

"Some well-informed rancher down along the Gila—Crow Creek is a little offshoot—noticed rows of rocks and knew enough to know they could be fallen walls," she said. "So he called the university. I'd just finished up my dissertation, had applied for a few openings, and my doctoral adviser called me and asked if I wanted to take a look. I did, and when the principal investigator had to get back for the fall term, I took over.

"Some of the crew stayed on with me, including Ed." She smiled at him across the fire. "I'd sort of harassed him into coming out in the first place. We'd found a few large sherds that seemed very interesting. Mimbres pottery, clearly, classic black and white, but the slip was wrong."

"Slip?" asked Paul. He was only a shape in the shadows. "These guys have mainly taught me how to dig big holes. We haven't gotten to pottery definitions yet."

"He idolizes us," said Ed.

"The slip is the coating on the ceramics," Ren said. "It's put on before you fire or paint the piece. In the north, they polished the slip before they painted the piece. But the Mimbres polished the piece after it was painted. The sherd we found had a polished slip. And the designs had diagonal hatching."

Ren paused and looked across at Paul's silhouette. "Hatching is a pattern of lines filling a shape. Northern groups—ones connected to Chaco—were known for diagonal lines. So the slip and the hatching were northern, while the overall style was southern. It was odd. Why was someone making bowls with both northern and southern elements?

"Still, we weren't finding anything significant. We were thinking about packing up. But then we moved to one of the smaller blocks, at the edge of the site. When we got to the bottom, we found a small storage room. We struck a stash of stuff: six parrot effigies, none bigger than a man's fist. They'd been painted in detail, although the shape of them wasn't exactly anatomically correct. Larger-than-life beaks, big eyes, short tails."

She took a breath. "And we found three perfect bowls—a complete set nesting inside each other. With the same traits as the sherds we'd found. One had a ring of parrots. Scarlet macaws. The others had parrots in the center of the bowls. On each bowl, the parrots were drawn very distinctively: Their beaks are too curved. Their wings are partially extended and diagonally hatched. Their claws are pronounced."

"Whole bowls?" asked Paul. "I thought whole bowls were practically impossible."

"Yeah," said Silas, slowly. "And she found three of them."

"It's one artist," said Ren. "I know it is. The work is too idiosyncratic. The pieces are Style Three Classic Mimbres Black-on-White, dating somewhere after AD 1100. We know it all came to an end around 1150, so the artist must have lived in the first half of the twelfth century. Assuming the Mimbreños assigned the same gender roles as other Pueblo groups, the artist was a woman. So maybe this woman moved from the north to the south. Or maybe the daughter of a northern woman is copying her mother's style. But it's one woman. I know it. One set of hands made those bowls."

She brushed nonexistent crumbs from her hands. She needed to stop talking. There was a temptation, always, to try and convey why this mattered, why the idea of one artist was so compelling. But she couldn't put words to it. Surely no one wanted to disappear. An archaeologist sought out those who couldn't tell their own story, and then, bit by bit, she tried to tell it for them. The Mimbreños were unusual for actually painting images of their world. They illustrated people and animals and insects—small snapshots of their lives. But for all the thousands of stories they may have painted into their pottery, no one knew how to read them. The meaning was missing. No one even knew what the people called themselves—*mimbres* was the Spanish word for "willow," a label attached long after the culture had died out. *Mimbreños*, the Willow People.

But this artist was one person, one woman who would have felt the sun on her face and known the smell of her paints and laid her head on her mother's lap when she was small. The discovery of the bowls felt to Ren like a personal plea. She could bring this woman, piece by piece, back from the dead. She could make sure she was remembered. She could save her.

"And now it looks like she might have been here, too," she continued, "fifty miles from Crow Creek. Or her work was taken here."

"Our preliminary data suggests populations were migrating from up to seventy-five miles away. Maybe further," said Silas.

"So why did the artist come here?" Ren asked. "Or, if she started here, why did she move there? What does it mean?"

She didn't expect an answer, and no one offered one. You assumed the dead wanted their story told, that they wanted their lives to be known and remembered and understood. You had to assume that. Only occasionally did Ren allow for the possibility that they were happy sleeping, that they didn't want to be known, that they didn't need their stories told by people who dug in the dirt. That maybe it was the diggers who needed the stories.

She looked down toward her feet, and the fire in front of her was all shining embers. Red and orange flashing. A long time ago her mother had a ruby ring that had fascinated Ren. It was huge and almost definitely fake. Ren would sit at the kitchen table as her mother cooked and just hold the ring in her hands, watching the light reflect off the stone. Not only off it but inside it. She imagined that if she were very, very small and could climb into the ring, she would hear a sound like wind chimes as the light moved through the ruby. She thought maybe there were, in fact, little creatures inside the ring that sunbathed in the red light and warmed their hands in the sparkle. She would tell this to her mother, and her mother would ask her what the creatures were called and what they looked like. One afternoon her mother came home with a set of wind chimes as a surprise. Ren walked out onto the porch with her mother's cool, soft hands over her eyes, her mother nudging her forward, and before her mother told her she could look, Ren heard the sound of rubies.

When she raised her head again, the fire was dead. Ed and Paul had melted away. She and Silas were left. He gave no sign that time had passed. Colors were always a problem: She could make herself forget conversations and feelings and entire months and years, but colors rose up clear and bright from the past. Still, she did not remember often.

"I told you that I wanted to ask you a question," Silas said, head back, either resting his eyes or looking at stars.

She straightened in her chair. "Sure."

"I've seen your map of the site. That room where you found the bowls was way off from the center. It looks like the room itself wouldn't even have been visible from the surface. What made you dig there?"

She looked at the sky herself, away from his face. A falling star streaked down.

"I was lucky."


The bed was not comfortable. She could feel a broken spring gouging her back whenever she rolled over. The pillow was thin foam, and she had to fold it in half to make it acceptable. She tried moving the pillow altogether, lying flat on nothing but mattress. She dropped the pillow over her face, huffing into its bleached cotton. She thought about the dead, about the Mimbreños' burials with a single black-and-white bowl over the faces. Everyone equal in death. Such fair-minded grave diggers—not like those in Chaco, where the rich were showered with trinkets and the common laborers earned nothing but stooped spines and brittle bones. She wondered if her artist had been loved and celebrated when she was put into the dirt. She wondered who had laid her in the ground and if she was out there in this canyon somewhere, the dust of dead flowers mixed with her bones.

She slept in bursts and dreamed in disjointed fragments that she wouldn't remember in the morning. Once she woke to the moonlight streaming in the window and the sound of wings hitting the screens. Probably a moth. She blinked and rolled onto her back. She could hear the night sounds clearly—wind through the trees and against the tin roof, chirping tree frogs, a single owl.

She heard humming and, still not quite awake, tried to place the song. The humming was slightly off-key, as usual, and she wished he would sing the words. One phrase floated past, and she snagged it: *With her hands on her hips and that smile on her lips.*

Springsteen. But the name of the song wasn't coming to her. She frowned, not opening her eyes. He only did this to her to wake her up in the middle of the night.

A rattle and clank outside. Probably raccoons in the recycling. Wait, she nearly had it. She hummed under her breath, tapping a rhythm on the sheets with one finger. *And her eyes that shine like a midnight sun . . .*

"She's the one," she sang aloud, softly, opening her eyes.

She could see a silhouette at the foot of her bed. Hands clasped behind his head, face tilted toward the ceiling, knee bobbing up and down furiously to his humming. His arms were thin and boyish, more elbows than biceps.

The bed was perfectly still.

❖   ❖   ❖

From where she sat, feet tucked under the sofa cushions, Ren watched her mother struggle with the pie in the fireplace. Ren's brother—sprawled across the green recliner—tried to balance a battery on his knee. The battery wobbled, and her brother slammed his hand down, trapping it.

Ren's stomach itched, and she reached under the leg of her leotard. It was hot pink and she loved it. With a few good swipes she could feel the scabs peel away from her belly—quick and satisfying.

"Stop scratching," Ren's mother said. She faced the fire, but she could hear the scratching. "You'll make them scar."

Her mother, Anna, kept her hair pulled back, safe from sparks. This was a new thing: The front of her Levi's stayed hot to the touch, and her face was always slick because it was too hot, really, for a fire in early fall, but she still needed to practice.

Frontier women used to bake pies in the embers. Those women fluffed eggs in iron skillets and browned biscuits and crisped fatty bacon in the fireplace, and Ren's mother needed to be one of those women by the end of the week. She knew all the history—the people at Litchfield Farm had given her thick books and thin pamphlets—and she'd ordered her muslin dress and leather lace-up boots, but she still had to master the cooking before she could start playing her part as an innkeeper. It amazed Ren that someone would pay her mother money to pretend.

"I'm hot, Mommy," Ren said.

Her mother wiped the sweat from her own forehead before running her hand along her jeans and then resting the back of her hand on Ren's forehead. "You really should go upstairs where you can feel the air-conditioning," she said. "You probably still have some fever."

"I don't want to be by myself."

Anna studied her daughter's face. "Leave that one on your forehead alone. It's bleeding you've scratched it so much. I'm going to tape mittens around your hands."

Ren sat on her hands. She had tiny flakes of skin and scab under her fingernails.

The embers on top of the pie pan were orange and bright, and Ren wanted to string them on a necklace. She watched the fire and her mother's sweat-shiny face. She was waiting for the pie to come out, to see if this one would be liquid as milk or gloppy like pudding or maybe perfect and solid. She liked the pie required by this new job of her mother's. She liked the fire and the wide dress.

Her brother, Scott, did not watch the fire or their mother. He had fit the new battery into place. He watched the blink-blink of red, green, yellow, blue on his new game. The game would flash a color, and Scott would have to press that same color. Then two flashes of color to remember, then three. Then it got harder. Blue. Blue green. Blue green yellow. Blue green yellow yellow. Blue green yellow yellow red green blue. Scott's memory was not good, and the toy squawked at him every few seconds when he remembered wrong. He let Ren play only when their parents made him, because he was nine and she was four and he could pin her arms behind her back with one hand. So she watched the colors and memorized them, pushing imaginary buttons on the sofa cushion. Red blue yellow green green yellow red.

The room was too warm, but she sort of liked it. Not too close to the fire, Ren. Don't scratch, Ren. Don't spill your juice, Ren. Don't run around, Ren. She did not move. She watched. Mommy bending and head tilted and looking back at her and smiling. Scott, his back to her, muttering under his breath because the toy was smarter than him. This was her first clear memory.

She liked songs that told a story. Scott would teach her good new ones sometimes.

"Repeat after me," Scott said. *"Young teacher / the subject / of schoolgirl fantasy."*

He sang it almost in tune with his average-but-pleasant voice, and Ren mimicked him. Her voice was pretty and much better than his—he told her that sometimes. He specifically called it "pretty."

*"Young teacher / the subject / of schoolgirl fantasy,"* she sang. She included the strange pauses.

Their mother's voice rang from the kitchen: "Don't teach her that one."

"It's got literature in it," Scott called back.

"Shut up, Scott," said their mother.

It was two days before Ren's eighth birthday, and she had been promised a Wonder Woman birthday party, complete with a costume. Her mother loved parties. She liked to do research. She had spent time with comic books and had even gone to the library, and she now knew that Wonder Woman's mother was named Hippolyta. She was going to wear a white toga and a gold laurel crown to Ren's party. And a name tag that said, "Hi: My name is Hippolyta."

Ren was already wearing her Wonder Woman costume, which her grandmother had sewn. (She was disappointed because her costume was not a leotard like the real Wonder Woman's—it had a blue skirt down to her knees.) Ren was pulling at the elastic waistband as she swept up raisins from the kitchen floor. The raisins were there because Sunday was pancake day, when her father tossed interesting things into a massive bowl of batter. Sometimes blueberries and chocolate chips and bananas and marshmallows, but today it had been raisins. Ren and Scott had ladled the batter onto the griddle, and it had dripped everywhere and then they both complained about having to clean up.

Neither actually minded cleaning, but each was convinced that the other one was managing to clean less. They demanded equity.

Scott threw a raisin at her, and she deflected it with her magic bracelets.

"You don't have on magic bracelets," said Scott.

"They're invisible," she said.

"No, her plane is invisible," he said. "You don't even know *that*?"

"Keep sweeping, Ren," said her mother. "Scott, you're supposed to be wiping the counters. I am confident that Ren is wearing magic bracelets."

"They can be invisible if I want them to be," Ren said. "And also I can fly without the invisible jet." She had never thought it was fair that Wonder Woman couldn't fly. There were no rules to this. She would be whatever Wonder Woman she wanted. She would swoop down on Scott as he threw the football in the backyard, and she would lift him up by his T-shirt and drag him over the treetops, where his feet would scrape the branches. He might cry. She would let him fly, too, if he cried. They could do the backstroke through the air and maybe have a pet bird they would put on a leash like a dog. They would need to avoid telephone wires.

She looked down at her wrists, and this time she could see the magic bracelets shimmering like glass.

She sat in her own room, her back to the door, listening to murmurs of conversation from downstairs. Her cheeks felt dirty and sticky from tears, and her lips were salty and her eyes were swollen, but she wasn't ready to go wash her face yet. They would feel so guilty if they opened her door and saw how hard she had been crying. She considered that scenario, then stood and walked over to her bed. She lay on her belly and pointed herself toward the door, face in her hands. It was a better pose.

She had called Scott a jerk, and her mother told her to apologize. But she didn't apologize. She said she hated him—he'd been saying her feet were too big for her body and she would grow up to be seven feet tall, and his delivery was so good that she believed him—and her mother told her to apologize for saying *that*, and then Ren had said, "You always pick his side. You're a bad mother."

She had not meant for those words to come out, and she didn't even mean them. But her mother's hand came down with a smack on the countertop, and she said, "You will go to your room. Right. This. Minute. I don't want to look at you right now, Aurenthia Leigh Taylor. And you will not come down until you apologize to me and to Scott."

And Ren had raced up the stairs, happy to escape. Now she felt a niggle of guilt and shoved it down. She and Scott always had to apologize if they called each other a jerk. Or an idiot or a moron or a butt. But now she had decided to wait out her mother. She would stay in her room until her mother or father came to check on her.

Then they would see her puffy face and feel terrible. She could see it all like a movie in her head. She would pack her red overnight bag and put on her coat, and she would head out the front door and down the street. Mommy and Dad and Scott would stand at the door, begging her to come back. But she would leave and head to downtown Indianapolis. She would stand on a street corner and play the drums, and people would give her money so she could buy an apartment and groceries. She would learn to play the drums. Or she would live in the branches of a tree where she would build a nest like a bird. She would eat fruit and nuts and the free mints they gave you at restaurants.

She was hungry. She could hear everyone talking at the kitchen table—she heard Scott's snorting laugh—and she hated them all.

Aurenthia Leigh Taylor. She hated her stupid, hard-to-say name. They all called her Ren, which sounded like "hen" or "pen" and made her think of barnyards. Scott called her Ren-tin-tin and barked at her. Her mother insisted she should be proud of her name, because she was named after her great-grandmother. Ren wished her great-grandmother had been named Danielle. She hated her great-grandmother. She hated them all. She hated herself for hating them. She watched the splatter-paint patterns her tears made on the pillowcase.

She heard Scott's footsteps outside her door. Before he even knocked, she slid under her bed, buried her face in the carpet smell. He opened the door, and she could see his Tretorns.

"Marco," he called to her, even though he surely knew where she was. "Marco."

She kept silent.

"Marco Marco Marco Marco Marco Marco Marco Marco," he said, like a ball bouncing against the gym floor. Super-annoying.

She gave in. "Polo."

His head appeared under the bedspread. "Come downstairs with me."

"No."

He held out his hand, palm out. He smiled, and she could hear nothing but sweetness in his tone when he said it again: "Come downstairs with me. There's cookies."

She held out her hand and followed him.

# two

*[We] argue for the reconceptualization of frontiers as socially charged places where innovative cultural constructs are created. . . . Some archaeologists are beginning to consider frontiers as interaction zones where encounters take place between people from diverse homelands.*

—From "Frontiers and Boundaries in Archaeological Perspective" by Kent G. Lightfoot and Antoinette Martinez, *Annual Review of Anthropology*, October 1995

In the still-dark morning, Ren woke to the creak of Silas's bedsprings and his feet hitting the floor. She heard him pad into the bathroom, then the sound of running water. When she stepped into the kitchen a few minutes later, still smoothing her ponytail, he was there. He offered her a coffee mug before she said a word. He apparently made a habit of handling breakfast—he heated up the electric griddle, and Ed and Paul called out their requests for fried eggs as they walked in through the screen door. Ren forced herself to eat one egg scrambled on toast, knowing she'd need the fuel for the rest of the morning. She was aware of the others chatting, scooting chairs back for coffee refills, checking backpacks. Her mind and her stomach were too unsettled to enjoy the food or conversation.

Ed and Paul were taking forever to finish their last bites of runny yolks. The sun was over the horizon, the pink streaks in the sky already fading.

"Go on and take Ren up, Silas," Ed said suddenly. Or maybe not suddenly—she hadn't been paying attention. "She's been twitching to get up there."

Silas was drying his hands as he turned to her. "Suits me. You ready?"

She was. They walked down the main road, passed a flattened scorpion, rubbed Zorro on the head when he came running, then rock-hopped over the creek Ren had driven through the day before. After one more creek crossing, they reached a wide-open stretch of dead grass to their left, which gave way to a steep, rocky incline. A thin path zigzagged up the hill, past stones and cactus and occasional bushy juniper.

"Elk trail," Silas said, starting toward it. "Watch the poop."

They walked steadily, Silas setting a quick pace that Ren matched. The air was still cool, but the sun was bright and her thighs felt a pleasant pull with each step. It had been a year since she had last done real fieldwork. She'd spent a month near Farmington the previous summer, and since then she'd spent only a day here and there at various sites, checking and authenticating ceramic finds. She'd missed the physicality of a dig. She'd missed the intense awareness that came from being outdoors, the consciousness of your own body and its specific place in the broader surroundings. A lack of attention in the office meant a missed deadline or a late meeting. But here there were cactus spikes and sidewinders, dehydration and spiders and gorges and uneven ground ripe for turned ankles and lost footing. There were scorpions and coyotes and bobcats and the boarlike javelinas. When she first met Ed, he spent an entire lunch insisting there was such a creature as a vinegaroon, a type of what he called whip scorpion that sprayed acetic acid. She didn't believe him for days: That was before she learned that his encyclopedic insect knowledge rivaled his talent for straight-faced fibs. Now she'd seen vinegaroons—not actually toxic—along with black widows and giant centipedes and one bark scorpion. It made you feel more real, the nearness of disaster. There was an intimacy created with the ground around you, with the sounds in the air, with your own skin and muscles and hands and feet. It made you see things more clearly. And, really, if you kept your eyes open, if you saw the right things— the snake sunning on the rock, the slick spot of gravel in the middle of the path—you were safe. But you had to know how to let it all seep into you until you could feel a nearby snake in your fingertips, without even looking.

Silas paused, looked back over his shoulder as he stopped. She shuffle-stepped to keep from running into him. Her hand landed on his shoulder blade.

"You're fast," he said. They resumed the pace. "Paul and Ed are always bitching at me about racing to the top."

"I like to get where I'm going," Ren said.

They hit a plateau, then the path curved around the edge of an overhang. Rocks shifted under Silas's foot as he stepped, and a sprinkle of stones fell into an arroyo below.

"When I see a hill, I want to run up it," he said.

She waited for the rest.

"There was this hill way behind our house when I was growing up, back behind my dad's tool shed," he explained. "It seemed huge at the time—Mount Everest. This was when I was really small, before I'd started school. My dad could jog up to the top without even breathing heavy. Every chance I got I'd slip away from Mom and head to that hill so I could stare up at it, kind of study it, and then take off as fast as I could to the top. It was more dirt than grass, and sometimes I'd slip and slide all the way back to the bottom. Even when I made it, I'd get my hands and knees bloody. But I was fascinated by the thing."

"And you still are?" she asked.

"There's something about hills," he said.

She tried to imagine him small and uncoordinated. "Did your parents try to stop you?"

"Oh, Mom did. Dad was always impressed by bloody knees. He said it meant I had character."

They were nearing the top, and for a while there was only the puff of breathing and the soft crunch of rocks and dirt.

"So when will you have to go back to your day job?" Silas asked. "I know you're not a fancy-free new Ph.D. anymore."

"Are you kidding? This artist is what got me the director's spot at the museum. If the board thinks there's a chance I can get out of here with more bowls, they'll let me stay here until Christmas. Well, not until Christmas. But I have some leeway."

She was in no hurry to get back. Not that she disliked her job. Her first couple of years at the museum had been intensely satisfying: She'd spent every spare moment cataloging the Crow Creek finds. There had been intense days and nights of sitting at a table, sifting through sherds, trying to fit pieces together, making sure each artifact wound up in the right bag with the right label. She selected fragments to ship to labs in hope of more information on clay and geography and time periods. Pulling things out of the dirt was the fun part—the hard data took much longer to unearth. The museum board had given her the time and the resources to continue her analysis on Crow Creek, had given her a place to showcase the results. They paid her salary. They occasionally let her take time off to chase after pottery. In return, she managed the very self-sufficient staff, planned exhibits, and strategized how to bring in more visitors. It was not a bad trade-off. Still, she preferred the sun and sky to fluorescent lighting and e-mails.

"And what about you?" she asked. "Why are you here?"

"It's this place." He took several steps, watching the trail, then glanced back toward her. "The unclaimed space. The outer edges. Not northern, not southern. Somewhere you could shed your skin and create a whole new existence. I want to know how it all came together. And it's a nice thing to get paid to play in the dirt. Braxton—the guy who owns the place—has the money to fund this himself. He set up a foundation, just for his own curiosity as much as anything else. Last year, when he asked me to work out here full-time, I didn't exactly argue."

"It is a pretty nice gig."

"He and my father grew up together in the middle of nowhere. I've known Braxton forever. So there was a little nepotism involved."

"Sounds like the work here isn't close to done," Ren said.

"We can't even begin to guess how much is here. Sites are scattered all over the canyon. When the populations at Chaco and the Mimbres River Valley were exploding during the tenth and eleventh centuries with all the rainfall, we got people trickling into the canyon. But by 1130, when the massive drought hit—and everything started falling apart—we really started seeing some action. The tributaries of the Rio Grande were drying up, but our spring-fed Rio Rosa held steady. Even during a drought, we're getting two thousand gallons per minute from an aquifer that taps into a Pleistocene lake bed. It must have been very tempting here."

They'd made it to the top, and the land was flat and brown.

Nothing but juniper—great bushes of it towering over their heads. Ant piles like mounds of kitty litter were scattered across the landscape. And cholla, much of it dead, with the look of Swiss-cheese driftwood.

"We had this college kid last year," Silas said. "No attention span. We warned him and warned him about the cholla, but he was always horsing around. One day he was talking to the kid behind him and ran straight into a cholla—smack into it, head to toe. Hugged it like a brother."

"What did you do?"

"Went looking for the pliers."

Away from the water source, it was one endless tan-and-brown landscape up here, broken only by the occasional burst of dark green. Silas pointed out sites previous groups had excavated, most still marked by rebar planted vertically in the ground, physical reminders of grid points.

They kept walking.

"Here," he said. "There's where we found it. Feature Forty-eight."

There was a dead juniper in the center of the site, dense and wide and low to the ground, the smallest branches like gray toothpicks. The rooms seemed to spread from the juniper. Here, by her feet, was the only feature actually excavated. The entire hole was less than three meters across. Only dirt and the round circle of adobe at the hearth remained.

"I'm going to sit here for a while," she announced. "You don't need to wait."

The beginning of a question flickered across his face.

"Really," she said, before the question took form. She tried not to sound like she was dismissing him. "You don't need to wait. I'd like a little time to take it all in. But thanks."

He nodded once. "*Bueno*. The guys will be up shortly. We're working on the next-closest block. I'll be three juniper bushes over."

She stood by the excavated room, her shadow pointed straight ahead, shadow hat blanketing one stone. She knew people who loved the exactness of this, the mathematical precision of breaking a site down into a grid of square meters. Identifying each tidy square on the X and Y axis—this would be 500 N 1001 E. She remembered Ed staring out at Crow Creek four summers ago, saying every new site was like beginning a game of Battleship.

She did not see this as mathematical. She did not want to think of grids or meters or tape measures and string. She stared over the landscape, blotting out the rebar, the silver buckets, the folded blue tarp, the wooden frame of the screen already set up on the sawhorses. A branch behind her brushed the back of her knee. Beside her right foot was a string with a level, looped carelessly, tossed there probably the last time someone measured the depth.

She started with the dead juniper bush in the center. It would have been gone—she erased it, then erased the other bushes. The stones ran in curves and uneven lines, mazelike, wrapping under and around the other dead junipers rising out of the dirt and dry grass. The stones were walls, some obviously caved in, but an aerial map to what was below. There were a dozen rooms that she could see—uneven rings of stone, some with slight depressions. Not all of them connecting. Here she had a T-shaped room block with three rooms across and three down.

She stared until her vision blurred. The lines of rocks shifted. They rose from the ground, forming sun-baked walls. The walls wavered, unsteady, perhaps shoulder-high, more mud than stone. The flat roofs were rough with sticks and adobe, and the rooms themselves melted into the ground. It was architecture the color of dirt, springing from the ground as inevitably as shrubs and rocks. The adobe room blocks always made Ren think of prehistoric Legos, almost-cubes and almost-rectangles making almost-straight lines.

No people. They should have been climbing up ladders, chatting on the rooftops, bringing water from the creek. But she could never see the people at first. They hid and refused to come out of the dirt until she cajoled them. A movement to the left caught her eye, and without thinking she turned her head and focused on it. The image shattered. She could never hold on to them if she looked too hard.

She gazed down again into the room they'd already uncovered at the edge of the T. Neat walls dropped about eighty centimeters down to the original floor, which was slightly uneven with adobe wash. She lowered herself into the hole, landing on the protective yellow interlocking pads that covered most of the floor. She pressed her hands flat against the walls, feeling one large flat stone under her right hand. It was a smooth river rock, carried up from the creek to help anchor the walls: Ground rock had obvious striations that showed in the sunlight.

The river rock felt flat and cool as marble against her skin. Patches of adobe along the wall were solid as concrete. This was essential, getting the feel of the site on her fingers. It was how she always started. An invitation. A summons. Her mind stubbornly turned to her father, as it sometimes did at the touch of dirt.

Her father would fill the back of his truck with small trees planted in burlap sacks, solid bags of dirt and bark, blocks of pine straw, endless flats of flower after flower, each one no bigger than Ren's longest finger. Sometimes on Saturdays she would shimmy into the center of it all, tucking herself against the cab of the truck, the metal hard against her tailbone. She liked riding in the back with the flowers.

She was allowed to help him plant after he carried all the sacks into someone else's yard. He carried them one by one, sometimes two by two, across his forearms, and his knees bent with the weight. Sweat would drip down his face, and when he took off his head-band, he would wring the sweat out of it in a steady stream. He laid the sacks in complex configurations, and Ren pictured old-timey soldiers hiding behind the sacks with rifles. After the last bag was on the ground, he would raise his arms to shoulder length, bend his elbows, and twist back and forth. His back cracked like fireworks. Then he would reach to the sky, reach to the grass, and sigh, "Ahhh." Ren could tell that all the weight he'd taken into his bones carrying those sacks had shot out through his fingertips and disappeared into the air. Then he'd tell her it was time to dig. She loved the first handful of cool dirt as she scooped out a hole for each petunia, but most of all she loved watching her father force out his pain into the sky and the ground.

She would start with this room block, of course. But her artist could be anywhere. The sherd could have been brought over by a friend or neighbor. Or maybe the pot had been traded and her art-ist had never set foot on this site. Or maybe there was a treasure trove of artifacts within meters of where she stood.

She felt light-headed, which she took as a good sign.

It wasn't even nine a.m., so she could get in nearly a full day of digging. She turned in the direction Silas had pointed, and she could see clouds of dirt rising over the brittle shrubs. She headed toward the clouds and soon could hear the murmur of voices. As she drew closer, the voices grew more distinct and there was a metallic undercurrent—the shaking of the screener, the rattle of rocks against the wire mesh. When she rounded a clump of juniper bushes, the three men were only ten feet away. Silas was scribbling onto his notepad, and Ed was sifting a bucket of dirt through the screener. Paul was down in a room, only his shoulders and head above ground. He straightened, holding something in one glove.

"Silas," he called. "Deer?"

Silas let the notebook fall to his side, walked over, and took the small bone from Paul's hand.

"No—wild pig. Probably a chunk of a scapula—see that curve?"

They hadn't seen her yet, and she stepped back into the shade of the bush. Paul kept digging, and Ed screened. They must have been near an ash pit, because they both found bone after bone.

Silas put down his notebook altogether and knelt near the edge of the pit, just out of the way of the rolling waves of dust pouring over and around Paul. He reached in occasionally, noticing a flash of white in the turned-up dirt that Paul missed. But mainly he sat on his haunches while Ed and Paul brought him bones, holding them out like offerings for him to interpret. Deer ulna, coyote joint, bird and rabbit and elk, vertebrae, piece of skull, toe, he called, handing the bones back before he'd finished speaking. He called their names with one quick narrowing of his eyes, easy and smooth as exhaling.

She watched him interpret the bones. This was what they did: try to rebuild lives out of broken pieces, bits of trash, gnawed bones.

It was difficult to hear over the screening. Paul held up a wriggling centipede nearly as long as his arm, and Ed said something that ended with "three feet long in my shower."

"Fourth deer vertebrae in the last five minutes," Silas said, as Paul held out another gray chunk.

She remembered the excavation of a huge ash pit in the Mimbres Valley. It had been like working in a crater full of printer toner, and she hadn't known any of the other archaeologists. Their first morning they'd all dipped their fingers into the black ash and drawn designs on their faces, like prehistoric warriors. She'd turned her face into a Mimbres bowl, and the others had reached to touch it. She'd felt their fingers on her face, and they had all belonged to one another absolutely. The dirt could make you belong so easily, so quickly.

She left the shade, although it was tempting to stay on the outskirts a little longer, to watch the gears and cogs turning so smoothly between them.

"You're fast," she said to Silas, nodding at the foil envelope packed with bones at his feet.

"Hunted a lot growing up," he said, tipping his hat back to meet her eyes. "I'm not much of a geologist, but I do okay with bone."

Soon Silas took Paul's place digging, and Paul moved over to the screen. Ed blew his nose, took off his gloves, and walked over to Ren. He tipped his head at Paul.

"That kid's a hard worker. And smart. Good attitude. You'll like him."

"I already like him. Is he even old enough to drink?"

"Apparently he manages just fine."

"Apparently."

"And listen to you, ready to check his ID. You don't look so different than you did when you bopped in with that college group a few years ago."

She cut her eyes toward him. "Fifteen years ago, Ed. But you get points for flattery."

"Only then you had that guy following you around. What was his name? The one who gave you that big rock?"

"He hadn't given me a big rock then," she said.

"No big rocks from anybody else yet?"

She lifted her hand and wiggled her bare fingers.

"That one looked like a football player," Ed said. "Not much of a neck."

"Hey, look!" called Paul. "I found a pretty big sherd. Maybe Socorro." He jogged toward them.

Ed held out a hand, took the sherd, pursed his mouth, and spat on the pottery, rubbing with his thumb until the surface was clearer.

"Tularosa?" he asked.

"Yeah, Tularosa," Ren said. "Nice job, Paul." She reached for the sherd, holding it between her thumb and forefinger. There were certain oral elements to fieldwork: If you wondered what sherd you'd found, you spat on its surface. If you wondered whether you'd found bone or wood, you laid the bone on your tongue. Bone would stick, and wood would not.

"It was packed in a clump of dirt," said Paul, words coming quickly. "And if I hadn't been scraping it pretty gently, I'd probably have broken it. But I saw just the edge of it, and see how it's a piece of the rim?"

"Definitely the rim," said Ren.

"I'll go show Silas," Paul said, already moving.

Ed stepped closer to Ren, and she was reminded of how he had a way of edging into your personal space that was comforting rather than intrusive. He leaned in to her in a way that felt like a confidence.

"You think we'll find her?" he asked. "Your artist?"

She answered without editing her thoughts. "Yeah."

"If we do," he said, "the hordes will descend. Journalists. Tourists, maybe. Universities wanting a piece of it. It'll be bigger than last time." He swiped at his nose. "A lot of people wouldn't have called you here. A lot of people would assume you'd steal the spotlight."

"I know. Did you tell Silas I don't care about the credit?"

"I didn't tell him that. He didn't ask."

She nodded at Silas, who was peering at Paul's sherd. "You like him."

"I do."

"I've never heard of him."

"I don't think he publishes much. He doesn't teach. He likes the data, likes digging it up and teasing out the patterns, but he doesn't care which journal it winds up in. But he's like you out here. You both walk around a site with a look on your face like a kid at Christmas. You're filthy and you've got bugs in your mouth and blood oozing out of a cut, and you feed off every second of it."

She considered this and felt pleased by the assessment. When Ed returned to screening, she veered off toward Silas, who was kneeling at the edge of the hole. She looked at the walls of the room. "You don't think this room is Mimbres, do you?" she asked. "Too much rock."

"Yeah," Silas said. "Northern influence. They didn't have good rock to work with. This tiny river rock is like trying to stack ball bearings."

She was studying the lines of the wall when she felt his finger on the inside of her knee. But not his finger—the leathery tip of his glove, barely skimming her skin.

"What's that?" he asked.

She had a thin red scrape from the top of her knee to mid-calf, like a mark from a teacher's grading pen. His fingertip followed the path of the scratch, not touching any longer.

"I don't know," she said, watching his hand in the air. She stood up and brushed her hands against her shorts.

Silas offered to pair up with her on the T-shaped room block while Paul and Ed finished the room with the cache of bones. She and Silas spent the rest of the day working on the room that had already been started. The first ten centimeters were hard-packed, but the second and third layers were soft as beach sand. Silas dug, and Ren screened. She liked the feel of the dirt under her hands, so she screened and sorted bare-handed. She dumped each bucket onto the screen and spread it with her hands, feeling the silkiness of the dirt, the roughness of the rocks, the curves of broken roots. A breeze blew steadily.

They found a dozen small black-on-white sherds. Silas found a serrated stone blade, and Ren found a perfect projectile point. He took her back to the bunkhouse a different way, following a steep path through an arroyo. The descent looked vertical from the top. Ren watched Silas start down. He held a bucketful of bagged artifacts in one hand. He skidded, and she frowned, but he rode out the skid, skiing smoothly down the gravel.

"Okay with this?" he called back. "It's much faster than the way we came."

She took a breath and a sideways step. She lost traction immediately, but, like him, she leaned back, balanced with her arms, and relaxed into the slide. She careened downhill, riding the rocks. The lack of control was thrilling.

She reached the bottom of the arroyo right behind him. He watched her jog down the last few steps and grinned as she came to a stop. The edges of his two front teeth were slightly jagged, serrated like the stone blade he'd found.

❖  ❖  ❖

That afternoon they finished up lab work, scrubbing pieces of stone and sherds with toothbrushes and water, then leaving them to dry in the sun. Bone and charcoal, which could be weakened by the water, were not cleaned. They remained in tightly wrapped foil packets. Once dry, artifacts were sorted into clean paper bags, labeled based on their type and location, recorded in a thick plastic binder, and tucked inside cardboard filing boxes. These bits of pottery, worked stone, and remains of meals would, at some point, be unpacked in a different lab room and organized more thoroughly.

Her hands and arms gritty from splashes of dirty water, Ren headed to the swimming hole Silas had mentioned on their way back from the site. She took a bag with shampoo and conditioner, a towel, her water bottle filled with lemonade, hiking down the main road to the creek. It was a narrow creek, and even the swimming hole was only four feet or so across. She set down her bag and stripped down to her bathing suit, walking close to the water, past fat black ants patrolling the shore. Carefully, she stepped off the bank—dried grass and leaves sticking to her feet—down into the slope of mud and moss leading to the creek bottom. The water was up to her waist, cold. Almost unpleasant.

She sat down and leaned back into the flow of the water, feeling pebbles from the small of her back down to her thighs. She let the current support her. She and Scott used to see who could stay at the bottom of the pool the longest, sunk like a stone: The seat of her favorite purple bathing suit—with the fringe along the neckline—was always rubbed furry from the rough concrete. Sometimes they would toss some toy or bracelet into the pool and race to find the sunken treasure, or they would invent dives and floats, or they would play Marco Polo until she screamed because Scott always eluded her and usually dunked her two-handed like a basketball just to add insult to injury. Her mother could catch Scott because she had been on swim teams and still leaped and dove like a seal, and she would grab his ankle and pull him under and Ren would splash him in the eyes as he went down.

Now she dipped deeper. She washed her hair in the rushing water, suds swept downstream almost immediately. She shivered— her teeth were chattering by the time she pulled out her soap and started rubbing her arms and legs. She thought of calling the office. She thought of the smell of juniper. She shivered again. As she rinsed, she clenched her teeth and tried to block out the cold. Block out the day, block out herself. There was only the water and the cool air, her clean skin and wet hair. The feel of the pebbles against her thighs. The pull of the current. She relaxed into it, feeling the water lift and stroke each strand of hair.

When she stood, water running off her, she did not fight against the cold anymore.

Their feet had stirred up this dirt and walked through this water. Here. Soft breeze and willows bending and dried bits of grass on feet.

From her first dig when she was twenty-two, these were what had appealed to her: the constants. The scenes, the land, the chemical compositions—the moments—that remained the same now and a thousand years ago. There was a power to the constancy, to the connection through distinct, holdable physical things. It was a rock that astonished her at first. She'd been shoulder-deep in a room, and a piece of river cobble had fallen from the side of the wall, landing right at her feet. Someone, not Ed, had told her to toss the rock out of the hole. She'd reached to pick it up, and the same someone had yelled out, Wait, is it already drawn on the map of the wall, and she'd said yes. And he'd said, Okay, toss it. She wrapped both hands around it, and somewhere deep in her chest it struck her that other hands had wrapped around this same rock and fit it into the wall in the first place. The rock joined her hands to that set of unknown hands that had first placed the rock, and the simplicity of it had floored her.

She'd chosen to specialize in ceramics because pottery intensified the connection to those who came before. The ceramics talked to her far more than a rock could. Each piece had a language, a message in pictures and design, or at least in form and composition. The pottery spoke with the voices of its makers. And she was eager to listen. If she decoded the right signals, she imagined she could disappear—for even a second—into those other lives, cross over the rock or the adobe floor or the ceramic dust and find herself living as another self, in another time.

She reached into the water and came up with two handfuls of rocks, smooth and cool in her palms, then let them fall back into the water one by one. She could feel a pressure behind her eyes. This was when she could see things—when she got outside her own skin. And somehow also more deeply in her own skin. She opened herself and felt sun and air on her face. She sank into the sound of water.

When she turned back toward the path, the landscape shifted. A thick wall of trees appeared where there had been a dirt path. A new grove of piñon stood in the distance. Swirling around her feet, the creek was deeper and wider. She could see it branch off, foaming, where seconds before there had been only dry land. She saw the imprint of bare feet in front of her. She heard a girl's laughing and saw a flash of brown skin and bare feet and dark hair disappear into the trees.

Then the forest was gone, along with the footprints. The creek had calmed. It was a beginning.


The next day they began the serious digging. The soreness never sank in on the first day of a dig. And in a few days it would be gone. But now Ren's body complained about the new routine. The entire length of her spine felt the strain of bending over the dirt, of scooping and shoveling on her hands and knees. The weight of the buckets pulled on her fingers and shoulder joint as she walked, and if she carried two full buckets, that ache spread to a strain across her shoulders.

Clouds of dirt flew when Silas dug. He made soft grunts as he swung the pick. His rhythm seemed effortless, and when he stopped and laid the pick on the ground, Ren was surprised—and gratified—to see him breathing heavily. He rolled his shoulders one at a time.

"Feeling it?" she asked.

He winced as he stretched his arms overhead. "Like a wet sponge."

"Oh."

When she took her turn hacking at the dirt, Silas stood, waiting for the buckets. A fringe of the juniper peeked around his knees and thighs, past his shoulders. He had a habit of breaking off tiny pieces of juniper and crushing them between his fingertips. She could smell the strong woody smell when the wind blew just right.

Paul and Ed joined them later in the day. They chipped in with carrying buckets, chattering as they carried.

"What did the Apaches make tiswin beer out of?" asked Paul.

"Juniper, I think," said Ed.

"Silas, what was tiswin beer made out of?" Paul called more loudly.

"Sprouted corn," answered Silas, without looking up.

Ren screened the buckets of dirt. Since the dirt was no longer soft, she wore one glove—Ed told her she screened like Michael Jackson—so she would have protection against the sharp rocks but could still feel the texture of the dirt. Her hands felt as if they would crack like arid earth.

"I thought they made something out of juniper," yelled Ed. More softly, he said, "You've got to at least try to stump him."

"Turpentine," Silas called back, before Ed stopped speaking.

Later in the afternoon she hit a root, long dead, and pried at it, then hacked at it with the pickax. She splintered it but couldn't detach it. She paused to readjust her grip and catch her breath. When she looked up, Paul was kneeling, eyeing the root she'd been attacking. He flexed his biceps.

"Very nice," she said, straight-faced.

"Can I interest you in two tickets to the gun show?" he said, deepening his voice. She thought it might be a movie reference.

She handed him the ax.

"Or one ticket to the ax show," he said in the same voice. He rolled his sleeves up even higher. "I'm all about manual labor. It gives me a little something for the ladies."

She vaulted out of the pit to give him room. "Girls do like muscles."

"Yeah?"

"Oh, yes," she said, dislodging some sort of gnat from the corner of her eye. "I would have noticed those muscles when I was in college."

"Don't get any ideas, son," said Ed, rummaging through the supply bag. "She's a long way from college now."

"I can't imagine why you don't date more, Ed," she said.

She turned back to Paul, shaking her head sadly. "But it wouldn't have worked out between us. You're a nice boy. I would have eaten you for breakfast."

The boy blushed, actually blushed underneath his tan, and she arched an eyebrow at him. He ducked his head and started chopping at the root.

The truth was she did like nice boys. And she had eaten them for breakfast. Spat them out and left them bruised and battered. But even though that was the truth, when she said it to Paul, it was not real. It was only dialogue.

Later, as they began packing to head back to the bunkhouse, Ed and Paul bickered over when chilies arrived in the Southwest. Paul thought they had come up from Mexico at the same time as corn and squash.

"Hey, Silas, when did New Mexico get chilies?" called Ed.

"When the Spanish came," said Silas. He'd been chasing a paper bag that was blowing across the site.

"Told you," said Ed.

Later that night they sat on the porch, watching the darkening sky over the mountains. A jackrabbit bounded across the field near the grazing horses.

"So you know how some of the Mimbres pots have people with parrots perched on their heads?" asked Paul in the silence. "What's the deal with the parrots?"

"It taught good posture," said Ed, unblinking, as if he were staring into the cameras, announcing a traffic jam on I-10.

"It depends on what we think pottery means," Ren said. "I mean, there were, in fact, parrots. The Mimbreños traded for parrots from northern Mexico. But are they drawing these pictures the same way we would take a photograph—to capture what actually existed? Or were the images just symbols—representations of an idea or emotion, or some historical allusion? An expression of faith?"

"So we don't know?" Paul asked.

"The only people who know for sure are long gone," Ren said.

Paul frowned. "How many licks does it take to get to the bottom of a Mimbres bowl?"

"That doesn't even make any sense," said Ed.

Paul rocked back on two chair legs. "Silas, how many licks does it take to get to the bottom of a Mimbres bowl?"

Silas had not been in a storytelling mood tonight. He had stayed quiet, sitting away from the rest of them, close to the fire. Zorro had fallen asleep on top of his feet. Silas didn't answer Paul, who waited for a moment and turned back to Ren.

"I like the animal hybrids on the pottery," he said. "Macaw heads on women. Bear heads on turtles."

Ren nodded. "Turkey men. Macaw women. Maybe that's where the jackalopes got started."

"I think I saw a bear-elk the other night, by the way," Paul said. "Body of a bear and the head of an elk. Better than Bigfoot."

"People have made a lot of money off Bigfoot," Ed said.

"I like money," said Paul. "I should license it."

"It'd sound scarier in Latin," said Ed.

"Okay," said Paul agreeably. "So 'bear-elk' in Latin is . . . Who knows Latin?"

"*Ursa-cervus,*" Silas said.

Ren turned. "You can translate 'bear-elk' into Latin?"

He looked over, smiling, finally, at her, then not smiling, just looking. She looked back. She blinked. Before she blinked again, they both looked away. Paul said something else she didn't hear. She could feel Silas's eyes on her again; then she heard his chair creak and his feet slide against the dirt.

"Night, everybody," he said. She turned then to say good night, and she saw his hand raised. She thought he might pat her back or squeeze her shoulder. But he brushed one knuckle along the line of her jaw, so brief she didn't register that it had happened until after the crunch of his footsteps had faded.

When she looked back toward the fire, she saw Ed watching her. She didn't recognize his expression. She thought he might tease her or tease Silas, but he kept quiet; his silent, speculative gaze unsettled her more than the touch of Silas's finger.

That night Scott woke her by leaning in close to her face, his nose almost touching hers—it was a trick their old terrier used to do when he wanted to be let out in the middle of the night. She opened her eyes and stared directly into Scott's darker brown ones. He seemed solid in the moonlight. She shoved at him and felt nothing but air.

"Go away, Scottie," she said. "You're not the one I'm trying to see."

Back in the days and weeks and maybe months right after the accident, she could feel him behind her without turning her head. The air felt different when he was nearby. For a while he was next to her bed most mornings. He seemed to be around every corner. Then, over time, she didn't see him as often. Eventually he stopped speaking, but he never stopped singing to her. Sometimes she couldn't make out the words, but she always recognized the tune. He sang the same music he had taught her.

He used to come to her in the in-between times—when she was rubbing the sleep out of her eyes in the morning; when she was staring at her bedroom wall, bodiless and mindless, forgotten homework spread over her bed. He came to her as she paced the empty house in the long afternoons before her parents came home.

Ren rolled back over, and Scott was still standing by the bed. The bad thing about these nighttime visits was that her mind was open and relaxed whether she meant it to be or not. She could never be sure which song might slip under her skin and where it might go. She hoped he'd stay quiet.

She sighed. "I really need to get some sleep. Really. Go haunt someone else for a while."

Sometimes if she closed her eyes fast enough, she would feel only annoyance with him. She could pretend she would see him in the morning, eating breakfast and piling folders in his book bag. And if she was lucky, she could fall back asleep without feeling anything else.

# three

*If art is intended to communicate with others, artists are additionally constrained by the necessity of producing images that can be "read," or understood by an appropriate audience.*

—From "Picturing Differences: Gender, Ritual, and Power in Mimbres Imagery" by Marit K. Munson, *Mimbres Society*, 2006

For the first week, Silas drank his coffee black. On the seventh day, he was making his lunch while she fixed her coffee. He layered thin slices of ham, sprinkled them liberally with salt, then added the top piece of bread. He finished with one more shake of salt, straight on the bread.

He glanced at her cup as she poured in the cream.

"I'll take cream, please," he said.

"You drink it black."

"Not really."

"You've drunk it black every day for a week."

"Black coffee is manly," he said, folding foil around his sandwich. "It makes a statement. I like the *idea* of black coffee."

"You're not drinking an idea."

"Exactly," he said.

She added sugar to her own cup. "If you want to prove your manliness, there are ways other than coffee."

"There are," he said slowly.

When she looked up from her coffee, he seemed closer somehow, although she was sure his feet hadn't moved. The smile flickering around the corners of his mouth was both amused and challenging, and possibly other things. This was where she should say something clever. Or laugh it off. Clever would be better. But nothing came to her, and he filled the silence himself, his voice all easiness and self-mockery.

"It has a certain romanticism to it," he said. "Black coffee. Out here in the prehistoric ruins. Wild animals gnashing teeth."

She passed him the cream. "You really don't like black coffee?"

"Not really."

He was impossible to decipher. "Seriously?"

"I have a variety of coffee moods."

They walked through the front door, stepped off the porch, and Silas headed toward what had become their favorite folding chairs in the yard. She held her cup to her lips, lingering on the porch as Silas settled in his chair. She watched his shoulder muscles shift under his T-shirt as he stretched. She watched him close his eyes.

The door swung open behind her. Ed sipped his own cup of coffee—black. She had no doubt that he did actually drink it black. She'd been with him for months out of her life—a month during that first summer, three months at Crow Creek, and plenty of shorter digs in between—and every morning she'd seen him with his ink-black coffee.

"Morning, Rennie," he said. He was the only one outside her family who had ever called her Rennie, and he seemed to have divined the name from thin air. She had certainly never told him.

When she looked up, he was looking at Silas, not at her. She wondered if he had followed her own gaze.

"How long will you stay?" he asked, surprising her. "If we don't find any more traces of her?"

"I think I could swing another two or three weeks. I don't know. I've put off calling the museum. But I'll have to update them soon."

"It might not be her."

"It might not be."

He looked at the mountains. "If you had to go back, we could handle this, you know. Call you back if we found anything."

"You trying to get rid of me, Ed?"

"Never. But I don't want you to worry that finding the Crow Creek artist depends on you staying. If you have to leave, we'll keep looking."

She had a second of doubt, a flash of thinking he really was trying to get rid of her, which made no sense at all. There was no one she was closer to in the world than Ed.

"Hey, Ren," called Silas, still stretched out in his chair with his eyes closed. "I left my sandwich in there. I was thinking, you're a woman; I'm a man. Go fetch it for me, huh?"

"Shut up, Silas," she called back.

He smirked, never opening his eyes. She wasn't even sure he knew Ed was there.

"Ed, go get my sandwich," called Silas, who apparently did know they had company.

"You just wait there for it, Silas," said Ed. "Just keep on waiting."

Ren waited to see if Ed would say more about her leaving. But he only took a sip of his coffee.

"Remember that excavation along the Gila a few summers ago?"

he asked. "With that older archaeologist who fell hard for that big blue-eyed grad student? He kept offering to rub her feet?"

"The really well endowed grad student?"

"Yeah."

She pretended to think. "The one who turned out to be a lesbian?"

Ed smiled. "Yeah. Yeah. That was a good dig."

And just like that, he was the Ed she had always known, the man who could name every insect in water, land, or sky. The man who could tell a tall tale like he was giving the weather. At times over the years she could almost imagine this was her father. A father she saw occasionally, who treated her with affection and professional courtesy. It was an appealing vision, a scenario in which fathers were without personal lives or expectations and existed only to be charming and kind and fatherly for as long as their presence was appreciated.


She'd walked past the swimming hole, farther into the canyon. The dirt road stayed close to the creek. Two sets of deer tracks crossed her path: The splayed, rounded toes of a buck smudged the pointed, compact prints of a doe. She turned a corner in the road, and the air changed: It sparkled around her, bits of light blinking past her face and hands and around her knees. She'd reached a huge cottonwood, towering, with thick green branches. The tree was snowing cotton bits, and the fading sunlight caught them, spun them glittering in the air.

She walked to the trunk and ran her fingers along its alligator bark. The trunk was thick and ropy, immense. She stood still, wind blowing, caught in its snow globe.

She heard breathing just behind her, low to the ground. Animal panting, like a dog needing water. She looked behind her, expecting to see Zorro wagging his tail. Nothing.

She stayed still. Again, the sound of panting, this time farther away. There was the sound of feet moving through leaves so loudly that they must have wanted to be heard. She looked and saw no one. The footsteps grew faster.

She did not know if she wanted to see whoever was moving through the woods. She made herself control her own breathing—deep and slow. She needed to see whatever or whoever was willing to show itself. She walked slowly back to the creek. For a while, the sounds stopped.

As she stepped through the creek, she watched the rocks—burnt orange, pink, black, deep gold, pale yellow, chocolate. Ferric oxide in the reds, limonite in the yellows, manganese in the blacks. When she reached the other side, she knew she was not alone anymore. She looked up and saw a man hunched in the tall grass with his back to her. He was strong and lean, and his hair was long down his naked shoulder blades.

It was only a flash, lasting maybe five seconds. She saw his black hair and an expanse of skin and a carcass at his feet. It was skinned and glistening—a deer, probably. She saw a small mass of what she thought were intestines in a clump of weeds. The man had a blade, a sharpened rock, in his hand, and he was cutting strips of meat, sawing along the whole width of carcass. He pulled off a strip maybe two feet wide and three feet long, the right size for jerky.

The meat was steaming slightly, and Ren thought she could smell blood. It was surprisingly pleasant. The man had blood streaked up to his elbows. He turned in her direction, pausing, looking at the creek but not at her. She thought he was coming to the water to wash. She looked at the dead thing and breathed in the blood.

Then he was gone and only the smell lingered.

She waited for several more minutes and saw nothing else. She tried to clear her head of the smell and make sense of what she'd seen. The man was obviously not her artist, and she couldn't see how he would have anything to do with pottery. But she was glad to have seen him: He'd been part of this place. If he was here, others might be, too. She only needed to keep looking.

They'd all taken a long lunch break, because Ren felt she couldn't put off checking in with the office any longer. It was the second time in her two weeks at the canyon that she'd driven off the ranch to the asphalt highway, watching her phone screen until she picked up reception. She'd answered e-mails, pulled off on the side of the road, windows rolled down to catch a breeze. As soon as she closed her phone, the whole conversation—her whole life on the other end of the phone—caught the wind and floated away.

She'd been pestering Silas to take them up canyon to a previously excavated site called Apex, and he'd finally agreed. A jagged hill rose out of the flat ground, with edges of rock obvious along the outline of the hill. Ren could see the rocks were walls embedded along the peak. She could count room blocks, but they were packed in tightly, a prehistoric tenement apartment building. The families had built right on top of each other, all the way up the rock face. It was clearly Northern Puebloan.

"We've got six-foot walls, collapsed architecture, rooms—as you can see—all the way up that slope," Silas said. "Obviously these guys were worried when they built here. You can see for miles and miles here, all across the canyon, so no one can sneak up on you. The other side of this hill is a sheer drop—absolutely no way to approach from that side."

"Think they were afraid of the neighbors?" asked Ren.

He shrugged. "I think they were afraid of everyone. These guys got here around the beginning of the thirteenth century. The world was a dangerous place."

Ren cocked her head and squinted against the sunlight. After the fall of Chaco, the city's residents had spread into surrounding valleys, uprooted and unsure. The population had fallen into valley-to-valley warfare. Chaos and violence. In the Gallina Highlands, outside of Albuquerque, studies of human remains had suggested that sixty percent of adults and nearly forty percent of children had died violent deaths in those years after Chaco fell. Beheadings and dismemberments with dull flint knives; quick, brutal deaths during hand-to-hand fighting over land and food and survival.

"What's wrong with the name Anasazi?" asked Paul.

Ren and Silas turned. Paul looked slightly surprised they had heard him.

"I mean, the northern groups, the ones with Chaco, they were the Anasazi, right?" he said. "From all the movies and books? You say Northern Puebloan, but it's the same thing. Why don't we call them Anasazi anymore?"

They were walking around to the back of the cliff, watching the cliff swallows darting through its shadows. The back was unassailable, as Silas had said, a vertical wall of rock where nothing but birds and bugs could find footholds.

"It's offensive to some people," said Ren. "*Anasazi* is a Navajo term, meaning ancient enemies. It's a little, oh, negative. Some of the tribal groups prefer 'Ancestral Puebloans,' but it doesn't exactly roll off the tongue. 'Northern Puebloan' works."

"Cities of gold, weren't there?" pressed Paul. "Treasure? Mass human sacrifice? Some of it has to be true."

"Not so much," Ren said.

"A little," Silas said.

She rolled her eyes.

"No cities of gold," said Ed. "But it's hard to believe Chaco controlled hundreds of miles just with charm and good looks."

"So maybe it was just the possibility of withholding food surpluses," said Silas. "If you don't do what we say, you won't get food. But judging by what we've seen of their plazas and where there've been traces of human blood and remains, it was more than that. If you bucked the system, you got taken there and beaten in public. Humiliated." He pointed a dusty finger at Ren. "Then, possibly, you were cooked. And eaten."

She frowned. "They haven't found that many boiled human bones. We don't know that they were eaten."

"Just how many boiled human bones would you say are required?"

"It's a very Hollywood kind of explanation."

"It was not a nice place," he insisted. "Or, rather, maybe it was, but it was also ugly and brutal. And beautiful. Chaco made beautiful buildings, and they also probably ate people occasionally. Life is blood and death and fear and joy and fierce architecture, man."

They walked deeper into the canyon, wading through the creek, only the soles of their shoes getting wet. The pebbles crunched under their feet. Ren was feeling irritated. Something about Silas's tone was getting on her nerves.

"You should get that on a bumper sticker," she said.

He stepped onto the shore and motioned toward the hillside rooms. "That's always what life is. *Esta casa es su casa.*"

"Another good bumper sticker," said Paul, still splashing through the water.

"This house is not my house," said Ren. "My life is not blood and death and fierce architecture. And it may not be what life at Chaco was. You talk about it—joke about it—as if it were fact."

"Oh, no," said Silas. "Not fact. I'm very stingy with what I consider a fact. I believe in margins of error."

She shook her head. "Violence is not inevitable. It's not a given, not at Chaco, even. I mean, we don't know that the Mimbres were anything but peaceful agrarians."

"There've been references to fighting on Mimbres bowls," he said.

"I know that." She stopped, and so did he. "That doesn't mean they weren't peaceable people."

"And it doesn't mean they were." He licked his lips and rubbed a hand over his chin. At first she took the pause as a reluctance to argue with her. Then she looked at his eyes and saw only pleasure.

"Look," he said, "you're trying to say that where we have gaps in our knowledge, there is nothing. We know the Mimbreños were farmers. We know that they were artists. So they are defined only by what we know. They are nothing else. I'm saying they can be anything until it's disproven. They are everything that's possible all at once. All those possibilities are out there, all existing at the same time, a million different variations floating around until we can prove they are not the case."

"'I am large, I contain multitudes,'" said Ed.

Ren exhaled. "Now you're quoting Whitman at me, Ed? Are you saying you agree with Silas?"

"I find it interesting," Ed said. "The idea that we are not filling a blank space. We're not creating a people, creating a history. It all exists—we're just trying to choose which reality is the correct one."

"But only one reality is correct," said Ren. This seemed inarguable. She turned back to Silas. "The others are false. We just don't know which ones. We do not know that the people at Chaco were cannibals. You should not say they are cannibals when there is not substantive evidence. You're saying, I think, that until we have proof either way, they are both. They both are and aren't cannibals. The Mimbres were both peaceful and warlike."

"Exactly," said Silas, sounding satisfied. His face was lit up like he'd just found Atlantis at the bottom of the creek bed. "We can't know the reality, not for sure. There are always other possibilities. And I'm not sure reality is as concrete as you make it out. I think it can be, even in our current time, more complex. An entire person, much less an entire civilization, is not just one definable thing."

"If we're not out here searching for one empirical truth, then what's the point of being out here at all?" she said. "If we can't know anything, what's the point of trying?"

"Because it's fun. Because it's what we have. But it's a puzzle we're trying to fit together knowing that we'll never have all the pieces. We can't avoid the blank spaces. They're a part of it."

"I have to believe the pieces can fit together," she said. "We owe them that—to tell the truth about them."

Paul had been listening carefully. "Do you believe there's a truth?" he asked Silas.

"Several of them," said Silas. He looked back to Ren. "But don't you think my way is less limiting?"

"I think your way is ridiculous," she said, and he laughed.

If they were going to get any work done before sundown, they needed to get back to the site. When they turned back and stepped in the creek, Ren looked down at a school of minnows veering around her boot. She was not thinking about the relative sanity of his idea. She was thinking of what Ed had said about Silas not wanting to teach. The way he looked when he argued reminded her of professors, the good kind, at least—the look said if you don't challenge me on this, you're a boring sort of person.

She'd never wanted to teach, herself. She didn't particularly enjoy being questioned.


The planks of the bench were poorly spaced, and she could feel the edges of the wood biting into her thighs through her cotton skirt. It had been silly to wear the skirt. Still, she had been covered in dust for weeks, hair either clean and wet and plastered to her head or dry and dirty and pulled into a ponytail. Her face stayed clean for minutes at a time. So it was only natural that for this one afternoon when they made the trip to Truth or Consequences for supplies and a good dinner, she would want to look like a woman, not an archaeologist, to look feminine and attractive to the extent that a skirt and lip gloss and eyeliner could signify those things.

"Like the skirt," Silas had said to her as they got in the van, not looking at her, and she had the unexpected thought that he seemed a bit shy. But then he turned his head and waggled his eyebrows, lecherously, goofily, and she was at a loss.

They'd been in T or C for only half an hour. Ed and Paul had each made a quick phone call, then headed to the grocery store to start the shopping. Silas was walking—pacing, really—along the sidewalk behind her as he took care of his own phone calls.

She was editing copy for an upcoming exhibit, which was not an efficient process by phone. Three short-lived desert colonies had coalesced in various bends along the Rio Grande during the late 1800s, and her first draft of exhibit copy was more than ten thousand words. The office manager, Sally, was reading the problem paragraphs aloud. Too much talk of spirituality. Not enough on agriculture. She needed to do this right, needed to prove that she could do her job long-distance. The museum board's patience wouldn't last forever.

She glanced at Silas, who had called his parents. He was speaking to his father, whom he called "sir," and asked about a fence Silas had apparently fixed on some recent visit. He nodded at the phone frequently. Then his mother took the phone, and he teased her about something to do with watching *Jeopardy!* She made him laugh. He told her he had a book he wanted to bring her the next time he came. When he hung up, he looked over at Ren, phone still open in his hand.

"Still the office?" he mouthed.

She nodded, rolling her eyes.

"My brother's next," he said. He punched in numbers and said, "Hello, young man," into the phone.

She tried to focus on the next paragraph Sally read. But she was aware of Silas asking someone named Skillet to record a game, because apparently football season was starting in two days.

She hung up just as Silas was sliding his phone into his pocket.

"I'm done. You need to make more calls?" he asked. "I can wait. Or go on inside while you finish up."

"I'm done, too," she said.

He cocked an eyebrow. "Just the office?"

"I'm a conscientious worker."

A pause, then a grin. "No boyfriends to call? No ex-husbands? Current husbands? Boy toys?"

This, she knew with unusual certainty, was a joke but not a joke.

"If you wonder about my personal life, you could just ask me," she said.

He looked surprised, and she watched the possible responses play across his face. His expression shifted from amusement to self-consciousness and then something that she would almost swear was embarrassment.

"Well, then," he said finally, exhaling a short laugh. "Grocery shopping it is."

She had not meant to chastise him. She didn't want him backing away from her. She wasn't sure what she wanted, but she knew it wasn't distance. At least not right now. She stood and put a hand on his arm as he started to turn. He stopped moving.

"And you had no girlfriends to call, either," she said, voice light. "Unless Skillet is a girl."

"Skillet is not a girl," he said, and she couldn't look away from his face.

She took her hand off his arm and stepped off the curb. "Skillet is a friend I used to play pick-up basketball with," he said from behind her. "The name's because when he shot, he sizzled."

At the restaurant, the tamales were hot and perfectly moist, and when Ren finished her helping, she peeled the strips of leftover breading from the corn husks and dropped them into her mouth bit by bit. When she wiped her hands, she could feel the cornmeal under her fingernails.

"The bulldozers would turn up the bowls in a cushion of dirt," said Silas, ripping a tortilla in half. "Along with turning up the bodies, of course, because that's where the bowls were. The landowner and Gardner would split the profits. Before the burial laws were passed, Gardner raked in the cash. Even reputable museums bought from him."

Silas was describing Bob Gardner, the best-known pothunter in New Mexico during the seventies and eighties, whose construction business had served as a front for large-scale bulldozings of archaeological sites. A landowner could find a pot, call up Gardner, and he'd send out the appropriate number of men with the appropriate number of bulldozers.

"I was twenty," said Silas, "doing an internship up at the Museum of Fine Arts in Santa Fe, and my boss wanted to go see Gardner about a cylinder jar he'd heard about. He told me I could come. A maid let us in the house, and when we walked into the living room, there were Mimbres bowls everywhere. Everywhere. In the entranceway, on the coffee table, on the shelves. On the mantel there was this one spectacular polychrome—a red-on-white-with-yellow misfire—with an image of a warrior. I bet it was worth more than any piece we had in the museum. And next to the mantel, there was a jaguar pelt stretched across the wall. I'd never seen a jaguar in the wild. It's been illegal to hunt them for as long as I can remember. Then Gardner walked into the room, using a cane. He told my boss he'd sold the jar already, and we sort of lapsed into silence. So I asked him if that was a jaguar pelt on the wall.

"He said he'd bagged it himself, and he asked if I hunted any. I said yes, but that I'd never seen a jaguar. He told me they weren't easy to come by."

Silas sipped his beer, setting it back on the table with a soft clank. "I said, 'Aren't they an endangered species?' even though I knew they were.

"And he said, 'Everything has to die sometime.'"

He glanced around the table. "And that, in a nutshell, was Bob Gardner."

"Not a good man," said Ren.

"No," said Silas, "he was not. Although I think sometimes the old-time pothunters get a bad rap. It wasn't always good versus evil. Some of them really loved the pieces and did what they could to preserve the pottery. They were in it for the art instead of for the money."

"They kept it for themselves," said Ren. "Whether it was the money or the art."

"Didn't you manage to direct some of Gardner's pieces to the T or C museum after he died?" said Ed.

Silas nodded. "A few."

"How'd you get them?" asked Ren.

"His housekeeper knew of some smaller pieces he kept in storage. He hadn't made arrangements for them."

"How did you know about them?" she asked.

"I went out to his house after he died and asked her if there were any pieces unaccounted for," Silas said. "We drank a few cups of tea and talked about her two daughters in high school. One was hoping to be an engineer. It was a nice afternoon."

Ed snorted. "Silas flirts with women, men, cats, dogs, sometimes lizards."

"And houseplants," added Paul.

"I do not," said Silas, with some dignity. "I am not attracted to houseplants. And I did not flirt with that woman—I talked to her. Nicely."

"You flirted with that geologist when she came out to the canyon," said Paul. "She was in her sixties."

"I did not flirt with that geologist. That's ridiculous."

Ren thought he sounded annoyed now. She watched his face, although he wasn't looking at her.

"You don't even know when you're doing it," said Paul, and it occurred to Ren that Ed had grown quiet. "It's like breathing. You can't help it."

She remembered that when Scott was in middle school, her parents had devoted entire dinner conversations to trying to teach him when a joke was no longer funny. To explaining how to read your audience. But the more Scott wanted to impress someone, the more he beat a dead joke into the ground.

Paul turned to her. "Ren, he flirts, doesn't he?"

And now they were all looking at her. She held her glass in front of her mouth, not drinking. "I hadn't noticed," she said.

Silas was folding his napkin. Paul kept looking at her. Ed did not.

"But I'm not a houseplant," she added.

"We're just giving him a hard time," said Ed, a little loudly. "It's not like we've seen him with a constant stream of women coming through the canyon."

"Hence the houseplants," said Paul.

"Enough," said Silas, flatly, and everyone became interested in their napkins. Ren watched him in her peripheral vision, and he did not move, not even a jostle of his knee or the twitch of a fingertip.

She wanted to say something very quickly, something utterly fascinating. "Paul," she said, "when did you get interested in archaeology?"

It was sufficient. They moved on. She and Ed and Paul chatted easily enough until the waitress brought the checks. Eventually Silas picked up his beer again and nodded his agreement at a comment or two.

Until they pulled off onto the dirt road into the canyon, the ride home had been almost completely silent. Ed loved to drive, even on these roads, and Paul sat beside him. Ren and Silas sat in the backseat, seat belts buckled, jerking forward and back as the tires hit ruts and rocks. Ren pressed her cheek against the cool glass to watch the sky in early evening. She had a takeaway sack of tamales still warm against her foot. Her forehead smacked the window as Ed drove through the creek, and she pulled back slightly. The sky was deep and rich just after sunset, tactile as velvet or raw silk. She saw a small movement along the edge of the road.

"Jackrabbit," she said, pointing.

"The bunnies love running across the road this time of the day," said Ed, taking a quick look. "It's suicide alley."

Silas was removed in a way she was coming to recognize. He was transparent at times, and at other times he completely disappeared. One second he could be joking and holding court, filling up the car or the porch or the open air with the force of his presence. Then that very presence that drew them all to his every word would collapse like a star turned—what did stars turn into? Supernovas—no, black holes. In any case, he would be gone, vanished into his own head. He'd been gone ever since the restaurant. She disliked feeling him turn inward. She herself was skilled at not getting caught in her own head.

Another creek crossing. Then another. The water was solid black, reflecting nothing, and even though she knew its shallowness, Ren could not shake the feeling that each time the wheels tipped into the water, they were all plunging into an abyss.

She wished this were not an excavation she cared so desperately about. To get involved with someone on a dig risked the entire project—all the drama and emotion of the personal contaminated the professional. She'd seen it happen to others, but she had never been tempted. She resented the timing of the temptation. This dig, more than any other, she did not want to risk.

She looked over at Silas. She enjoyed how his mind worked and the length of his eyelashes. She thought about houseplants.

"I can't believe you wouldn't do a shot of Jäger with me," said Paul to the car in general.

"It's like drinking motor oil," said Ed.

Paul swung one foot onto the dashboard with a thud. Ed swatted it back to the floor.

"I spent some time at El Barrio Inglés in Roatán, Honduras, on this ethnographic research project," said Silas.

Ren thought she could hear the slightest rustle of cotton against upholstery, the sound of them all settling back against their seats, anticipating a story. They could all surely feel the shift in his mood, the energy radiating outward once more, the light turned on.

"My dad had ordered me not to go, and I was in a rebellious phase," he continued. "He said I should wait and go on a project where someone could watch after me. He said I'd get my head cut off and stuck on a stick. My dad hadn't really traveled much. And I was looking for any chance to prove that I was tough enough and good enough. I was supposed to be looking at how native diets had changed from historic times to present times."

Ren wished he would say more about his father, and at the same time she wondered why he bothered to mention his father at all. The reference had been unnecessary.

"Anyway, they don't like outsiders too much in the barrio," continued Silas. "I had a contact who was supposed to hook me up with the locals. It turned out he looked like a very tan Andre the Giant, and he took me on this never-ending tour of the surrounding hillsides. He didn't even bring water the first day. The second day he did the same thing, letting me get a feel for the land, he said, and this time I brought my own water and kept my mouth shut. I thought maybe it was some sort of test. Either that or he really was going to kill me and hide my body in the underbrush. The idea of my head on a stick did occur to me. On our way back to town the second day, he said, 'So what are you going to do here?' I told him I needed to ask people some questions about what they ate. He said, 'Then what?' I told him the answers would tell us if their diet was healthy. He shook his head and said, 'No—what are you going to do after you ask the questions?'

"I thought about it and told him I didn't really have anything planned. He said, 'Do you like rum?'

"The next morning he had a few dozen kids and adults show up. I talked to them, and then he and I drank rum—*ron*—for the next forty-eight hours. We set up a game of bowling with the empty rum bottles and a mango, and we actually had enough bottles for all ten pins. Let's just say that scenario does not have the appeal that it once did."

Paul craned his head toward Silas. "Why a mango?"

The Jeep lurched into the creek again. Paul braced his hands on the dashboard, and Ren grabbed the door handle.

"You can always use the satellite phone at Braxton's, if you want," Silas said quietly into the dark. He didn't turn toward Ren, but he was clearly talking only to her. "He likes the company. And he should be back this week."

She frowned, knowing he couldn't see.

"Okay," she said to him, considering what he might mean. "I'm not really big on talking on the phone."

"It's not that you need to use the phone," he said quickly. "It's not like I'm the phone police. But my parents are older, and they get nuts when they think I've disappeared into the wilderness. Sometimes people like to know you're okay. And you've dropped off the face of the known world for weeks."

The Jeep jerked hard to the right.

"Okay," she said, rubbing her neck.

"In case anyone will worry," he added.

She nodded. He waited, expectant. She let her head fall back against the seat.

"No one knows I'm here," she said.

"What?"

She knew how it sounded. That's why she avoided the subject—if she opened the door, people expected explanations. There was no point.

"I mean, people at work do, obviously," she said. "But no one will worry. No one knows I'm gone."

He nodded, his shadowed profile unreadable. Paul and Ed were quiet in the front seat.

She nodded, hoping he was satisfied.

"You do have family out there, right?" he said. "Parents still around?"

"I have family," she said, and her tone must have successfully conveyed her lack of interest in elaborating. He didn't speak again.

Another lurch of the Jeep. In the pitch dark, with the ground and the sky shaking with every turn of the wheels, her thoughts wandered to Scott coming home from high school. Their parents were leaning against the kitchen counters, her mother cooking, her father talking, and Ren listening. She'd been in fourth grade. She could feel crumbs on the bare soles of her feet, so she rose to her tiptoes on the yellow linoleum, using one foot to scrape the crumbs off the other.

"Hey," she called, when Scott walked through the door.

"Hey," he said, dropping his book bag on the floor.

Anna, stirring green beans, turned her cheek for a kiss when Scott reached for a glass. "Hi, Mom."

"Good day?" asked their father. Harold had changed from his work jeans into soft, frayed khakis and a Pacers T-shirt with the lettering nearly worn off.

"Fine."

"You have any homework?" asked Anna.

"Not much."

Ren saw the mark on Scott's arm before her father did, and she was deciding whether to mention it. But her father didn't hesitate. "What's that on your arm?" he asked.

"Nothing," said Scott, grabbing his left forearm with his hand. He wore short sleeves, and his hand couldn't quite cover the ink.

"Someone wrote on you," Anna said, turning. She'd left the pots to simmer. "Who would write on your arm?"

"It's girl writing," announced Ren.

"What did a girl write on your arm?" asked their father.

Instead of answering, Scott started backing toward the kitchen door, slowly, arm covered. The family advanced equally slowly.

"Nothing," Scott said.

He turned to run.

Harold reached quickly, wide, strong hands grabbing. Scott looked over his shoulder, grinning, and feinted to the left. But their father had an endless reach—he caught Scott's shirt and reeled him back. Chaos broke out. Anna reached for Scott's arm, too slow, and he twisted away from her. Harold hauled his son closer, into a bear hug, his weight slowly pushing Scott to the ground. Once his knees hit the floor, Harold flopped on his side, taking Scott with him, horizontal now.

There was the sound of laughing and breathing, and shoes scuffing against linoleum.

"What does it say?" asked Anna, on the floor herself, reaching again. Scott wriggled and balked, red-faced, chuckling at them all and at the fingers Ren kept poking into his underarms.

"Stop it!" he gasped. "Dad, it's like having a house dropped on me! Get off me!"

They were all on the floor now, Harold with his hands on Scott's shoulders, one calf braced across his son's thighs, pinning him with sheer weight. Anna had caught his left arm under her leg and was using both her hands to pry away his right hand.

"Help me, Ren," she ordered.

Ren stopped poking at Scott's underarms and added her small fingers to the struggle, pulling at Scott's thumb while her mother worked on his four fingers. Scott gave in with an "Uncle!" and a long laughing wheeze. His hand dropped to his side, Harold suspiciously eased his weight off his son, and they all stared at the writing.

Ren renewed her giggling, but her parents only stared, foreheads wrinkling.

"What's that mean?" asked Harold.

The message read "Scott is a QT" in curlicued writing with emphatic flourishes.

"What's a cut?" asked Anna. "A quit?"

"No," said Ren, smirking at Scott. "I mean, I haven't done this since, like, third grade, but you read them like letters. Read it aloud and say the letters."

Scott rolled his eyes at her.

" 'Scott is a cue-tee,' " Anna obliged. "Oh, 'Scott is a cutie'!"

She looked delighted with herself. Scott stopped trying to look offended.

They lay still, side by side, flat on their backs, like they'd all been making linoleum angels. The floor was cool, and crumbs stuck to exposed skin in constellations. Harold and Scott breathed hard, chests like bellows. Anna rested a hand on her husband's chest, and her long, pink-tipped fingers rose as he inhaled. She stroked Scott's hair, once, twice, and Ren tried to maneuver closer to draw her mother's touch.

"Who thinks you're a cutie?" asked Harold.

"Nobody." Then, after a long wait, "Elizabeth Roberts."

"Do you like her?" asked Ren. She tried to imagine a fourteen-year-old girl in love with Scott. She was not in love with any boys.

"She's okay," Scott said.

"You could have just showed us," Anna said. She'd moved her hand to Ren's shoulder, lifting the hair off her neck with gentle sharp nails. The other hand she left on her husband's chest. He'd captured her hand with one of his own.

"Yeah," said Scott. "I don't know why I thought you might harass me."

"So is she a cutie?" asked Harold.

"Does she know how to spell?" asked Anna.

No one seemed to want to expend the energy to stand, so they stayed on the floor until Anna said she thought the beans were burning.

It was Ren's favorite memory. She wished she could cut it from her head like a tumor. She wrapped her arms around herself and pressed against the cold, hard side of the Jeep, absorbing the jolts into her body.


They were always in the heat and the light, and sometimes Ren craved shade.

More than a month in the canyon, they had opened a dozen rooms, and still no sign of her artist. She had driven back to Valle de las Sombras twice, rushed through her to-do list, then returned. What they'd found seemed to back up Silas's original theory: Northern and southern groups had been here at times, separately, but there was no evidence of the kind of intermingling that distinguished her artist.

She knew the pace of these things, the slowness and the monotony. You had to get through the first layers—the real answers were usually at the lower depths. Once in a while the secrets came to the surface early on, offered up as gifts by tunneling rodents or erosion. And sometimes one well-placed blade shone sunlight on a revelation. But most of the time the truth was doled out piece by piece, after many hours and many square meters. Level by level, if the ground was kind, you learned its story.

The ground was not being kind. She had spent weeks thinking it was on the verge of telling her something: Now she was beginning to wonder if instead of being perceptive, she'd only been desperate to believe something was here. The evidence pointed to repeated migrations and abandonments, as Silas had said, but there was no combined culture, no hybrid of north and south. No artist.

She kept hoping, but it was getting harder.

They had developed a routine. At the hottest part of the day, Silas and Ren sat under the juniper while they ate lunch and jotted notes with dry, filthy fingers. Since two people could fit in a single pit, they had split into groups again. Ed and Paul were working at a room block a few hundred yards away.

The heat sucked the pleasure out of the sandwiches and granola bars. They ate quickly. The water, though, they savored, passing a bottle back and forth. Neither one of them was willing to stand up to get the other water bottle. The ice had melted long ago—which Ren was thankful for, because Silas had a habit of crunching ice steadily and loudly between his molars—but the water still felt cool.

Silas lay on his back, hands cushioning his head, elbows jutting. He pressed the water bottle against his cheek.

"I feel like a ripe tomato," he said sleepily.

She looked at him, eyebrows raised.

"That's right," he said. "A ripe tomato."

They were close enough that she could hear him breathe.

"Why did you leave Indiana?" he asked. He made occasional forays into her past, scouting out the territory. He pulled back when he sensed she was about to close up; then he'd approach from a different direction. She enjoyed observing his strategy.

"I wanted to see something new," she said. "I liked the university."

He shot her a look that told her he found this answer to be lacking. "That's what you tell someone during a job interview. Give me a real answer."

"That is a real answer. I felt like I needed space."

"From what?"

"Doesn't every eighteen-year-old want space?"

He gave her another look. His hat was tipped back, barely hanging on his forehead. "You get home much?" he asked.

"Enough."

"Family still there?"

"My mom is." She had decided to give him small pieces, just broken-off tidbits. She wanted to give him enough to keep him from thinking that there was something wrong with her.

They'd taken off their boots and socks to shake out the sand. Their pants covered their ankles, but their toes pointed and flexed in the open air. Silas propped one foot on top of the other leg, ankle against kneecap.

In the beginning she wished they had met at some dinner party, in line at a coffee shop, at a conference. That would be simpler. There would be no professional ethics involved, no chance of ruining the project. But if they had met over coffee, she would not have witnessed him chanting his litany of bones as they were pulled from the earth. She would not have seen him show Paul how to create an obsidian dart point with a chunk of limestone. She would not have known how his mind absorbed and tabulated as he looked over a room block.

The flaw in her earlier concerns about getting involved with him was that they were already involved. They had hardly touched, but that had not decreased the intimacy. Instead they sat in the sand with this tight cord of anticipation strung between them, rib to rib. It thrilled her and worried her: She didn't know when it had attached itself, and she didn't know how to cut it, even if she wanted to. She didn't know how quickly he might be able to cut it.

"Did you sneak out?" he asked.

"What?"

"Of your bedroom. When you were a teenager. Climb out a window, shimmy down a tree, scale a wall, have a boy throw rocks at your window. Something like that."

She turned her head toward him but closed her eyes against the sun. "Did you throw rocks at some girl's window?"

"No. I'd shine a flashlight under Hannah Hightower's window, and she'd come out the back door to meet me."

"And then what?"

"We sat in the garage, and I'd see how far she'd let me get my hand up her thigh."

"How far did you get?" She pictured a bleached-blond girl with heavy makeup hiding acne.

"I hadn't exactly honed my skills then."

"Good for her," Ren said. She allowed the girl clear skin.

"Hannah was a good girl."

She opened her eyes. "Good girls don't let you slide your hand up their thigh?"

"Yes," he said. "They do."

She kept silent.

"I thought I would love Hannah Hightower forever," he said. "That lasted for a few months. I think I thought the same thing about Jennifer Bixby in third grade and Kathy Wolfson in seventh grade. Which was weird—I don't know how I got to be a romantic. Mom and Dad weren't exactly touchy-feely about love and romance. I mean, Dad would kill the extra puppies with bricks to their heads sometimes. But I really wanted to love someone forever."

"No luck?" she asked.

"When Hannah and I started having sex, I felt like it was love. But we lasted long enough that I got past the hormones. I could see how I'd been crazy about sort of an imaginary Hannah. When I calmed down, I could see the real Hannah. She was good to me. But if I was honest, when she talked I had trouble listening to her. On some level I was always wondering who else was out there."

"So you broke up?"

"After senior year. In as friendly a way as possible. But it shifted how I thought. I let go of that teenage idea of there being 'the one.' You know? I think loving someone forever is probably a choice, not some meeting of souls."

She raised herself up on her elbows, squinting.

"I wish we could rush the lab," she said. "It'd be great to get a couple of definite dates. Do you have any favors you could call in?"

She looked over and noticed that the wet sweat pattern on his T-shirt looked like a tulip.

"You didn't answer my question," he said.

"Which question?"

"Did you ever sneak out?"

She watched him watch her and took her time responding. She did not want to search her head for an answer. She wanted to enjoy the warm ground under her palms.

"I never snuck out."

"What were you like?"

There had been silences at home that lasted for days. Her mother and father had blank, smooth faces like masks. Sometimes her mother would tell her to do something—go pick up the shoes she'd left by the door or go put her cereal bowl in the sink—and there would be a pause at the end of the command, like a place where Ren's name should have gone. "Go answer the phone. . . ." Pause. Nothing. Sometimes she suspected her mother had forgotten her name.

"I liked Guns N' Roses," she said.

He accepted it. "I lived on a ranch outside of Silver City," he said. "We'd drive up and down Highway Ninety, and eventually we'd wind up at the Dairy Queen. We talked and drank tall boys. We'd see how long we could hold our breath before we passed out."

"You'd actually pass out?"

"Well, yeah. Sure. After two minutes. That was my record. Dad told me I should be able to make two and a half—mind you, he didn't know about the beer part of the evenings, only the breath holding—but Mom told me I would kill myself."

She never had to ask questions. He offered up whole pieces of himself as if they were unbreakable.

"We went to Allison Shum's basement and pretended to audition for MTV," she said.

She had been something of a star at those slumber parties because of her talent for remembering lyrics. Scott had taught her. He had loved music—real music, he always said. He loved Springsteen and Dylan. He had tight, neat rows of cassettes lined up against his walls like dominoes. She liked the clicking sound they made when they rubbed against one another. He had carefully alphabetized them, and she liked the B's best: *Back in Black*, *Band on the Run*, *The Beatles*, *Beggars Banquet*, *Between the Buttons*, *Blonde on Blonde*, *Blood on the Tracks*, *Born to Run*. Each case held a tiny picture that she could pull out from under the shiny plastic. She would study those pictures—cheekbones and squinting eyes and clouds of hair—most of them just blurry enough to leave her looking for more. These were the men who made Scott's music.

She loved those men, too. When she tried to talk about songs in kindergarten music class, no one else even knew who Bob Dylan was.

Still, she was not allowed inside Scott's room when he was not there. Once she had unraveled some tapes, leaving shiny piles of ribbony spools all over the carpet. She didn't even remember doing it, but Scott had told her the story plenty of times. So his room was officially off-limits. Sometimes when no one was looking she would scan the hallway, then go bounce on his bed with one quick, serious leap and retreat. Sometimes, if he was in a particularly good mood, he would let her come in while he was there, and sometimes he would even play what she requested on his boom box. When she was inside, he sat on his bed and she sat cross-legged on the carpet, back against the bed. The carpet was green and yellow, thick and rough. She imagined grizzly bears would feel like Scott's carpet. It scratched her cheek when she tried to lie down on it.

She realized Silas would never know the girl who had daydreams about carpets. He would never know her at ten, when she'd eaten grass because that stupid Elliott Nash dared her. And she'd never see him fifteen and drunk and trying to make himself pass out. He would never hear her mother squeal as her father ran his finger up the back side of her knee. He would never know her as a girl with a big brother and two parents. And maybe that was as it should be. She didn't really know that girl, either.

"I chewed my nails," she said.

Her nails had bled, the skin of her fingers white and soaked and sad. That was after the accident. She didn't think she'd chewed her nails before the accident. She had hated the sight of her hands. Her mother had beautiful hands. They were piano player's hands, artist's hands, even though her mother was neither of those things. For a while, the weeks after the accident, her mother would wrap two slender fingers around Ren's wrist and lift up her mangled fingernails. She would make a *tsk*ing sound with her tongue, and Ren never knew whether the sound was annoyed or sympathetic. After a few months, her mother did not notice Ren's hands anymore.

When Ren was little, her mother's hands were cool on her forehead. Her mother would rub her feet—and Scott's feet, too—with deep, long strokes. Her mother could curve her fingers and make an alligator shadow puppet with chomping teeth.

Ren did not tell Silas any of this. She said, "I chewed my nails even though my mother didn't like it. I think I disappointed her."

When she had been silent long enough that it was obvious she was done talking, he sat up and leaned toward her, slowly. His hat fell to the ground. She forgot about the pleasure of the fine, taut string stretched between them. She could smell sweat and dirt, but when he touched her face with the whole of his hand, she could smell juniper on his fingers. She ran her tongue along the rough edges of his teeth, and he made a sound she enjoyed. He tasted of salt.

# four

*It seemed a daunting task at first to interpret the very
subtle indications. To the untrained eye, much of the
site appears to merely represent nothing more than the
rocky terrain. . . . But with training, the . . . evidence
became observable as [a] long-abandoned home.*

—From "Rebuilding an Ancient Pueblo: The Victorio Site in
Regional Perspective" by Karl W. Laumbach and James L.
Wakeman, *Sixty Years of Mogollon Archaeology: Papers
from the Ninth Mogollon Conference,* 1999

They had a couple of hours left before they needed to head
back to the bunkhouse. Silas had gone to find Ed so he could
take a photo of the floor level for this last room.

Ren stared at the mountain of sifted dirt looming over the
screener. Kissing Silas had blown her concentration. He'd pulled
away from her, touched her jaw, and said they should probably get
back to work. So they had. But then they had spent a reasonable
portion of the afternoon staring at each other's mouth. And that
was exactly why she should stick to digging and screening and note-
taking instead of sliding her hands under a man's shirt and cataloging the feel of his teeth at her neck and the dusty salty taste of his
mouth.

It was a distraction. She reminded herself that the artist should be the most important thing. For all she knew, he fell in love on every dig. Or he spent his free time chatting up housekeepers and geologists. She was the only woman in the entire canyon, and their bedrooms were next door to each other. For all his words about himself, she had no idea what he really thought of her, what he really wanted of her. She was, she acknowledged, the low-hanging fruit.

And yet.

She lowered her head, rubbing at her face with both hands. The dirt coating her palms smelled almost pleasant. Complicated. She thought of his hand on her face. She could smell the detergent on her long-sleeved shirt. And she could smell juniper.

When she lifted her head, the pueblo was all around her. A living, thriving pueblo. As solid-seeming as Scott perched on the edge of her bed.

The sun was higher in the sky than it had been a few seconds before, and she squinted against the light. The ground was green, not brown, with patches of thick, tall grass swaying. Stalks of corn grew in the distance.

The air was cooler, and it felt moist. Ren crossed her arms over her chest and stood.

The even expanse of dry land that had seemed so wide open now felt hemmed in by the low buildings dug into the dirt, rising, squat and steady. The flat roofs came to Ren's eye level and above. The ends of horizontal wooden beams—vigas—protruded from the walls in straight rows just under the roofs. The flat tops of the structures were punctuated by ladders rising from the interior rooms and by the shapes of women working and children playing.

She felt the relief, nearly overwhelming—finally the ground was opening up to her. She wouldn't let herself acknowledge it. If she got back in her own head, she'd lose the vision. She breathed in the juniper, still heavy in the air, and her eyesight sharpened.

Two women were sitting on the nearest roof, crushing something on a grinding stone. Ren could see the muscles working in their tanned, bare backs—one had loose hair falling around her shoulders, and the other had thick circles curved around her ears. She could hear them laughing as they dusted powdery meal into brown bowls. One of them raised a hand and gestured toward a little boy playing. There was a jangle of a bracelet—shell or maybe bone. Ren hadn't noticed the boy before, but there he was, aiming a pointed stick toward a circle drawn in the dirt.

She turned and surveyed the landscape. Other children were scattered around the cubical buildings. A little girl was coming around a corner, carrying a basket bulging with wood. Her mouth was wide open as she called something, but the specific sounds were blurred.

She heard footsteps. An older boy with his own stick joined the smaller boy at target practice. Before they threw a single stick, both boys looked up, squinting in Ren's direction. They held their pose, frozen deer, for a full second. Then they went back to watching their target halfheartedly. Heads tilted down, they cut their eyes toward Ren.

She frowned, taking a step back, nervous. Then she turned around, looking behind her. And she saw whom they were watching. Past a nearby plaza and another block of rooms, a woman was approaching. She was tall, with broad shoulders. Ren thought of a story about Lozen, sister of the Apache chief Victorio, who had killed an antelope as it stampeded through camp. She had jumped on the galloping antelope's back and slit its throat with a knife.

The woman walking toward Ren was strong and straight-backed.

She looked as if she could kill an antelope with one smooth move-ment of her arm. Her black hair was loose and wet, clinging to her bare shoulders and fanning across her naked chest. A thick mark of red—closer to berry than blood—was painted across each cheek, highlighting her wide, dark eyes.

She wore a band of fur low on her waist. Hanging from the fur were red and yellow and blue strips that shifted against her thighs as she walked. Feathers, Ren realized. Macaw feathers. And then the woman's bearing made sense—she was someone who had power. Only a person of power would have these feathers at all, much less wear them to simply walk to the creek and back. Only someone of power would make these boys stare without staring.

The woman drew closer, taking long, easy strides that covered ground quickly. Her feet made no sound. Ren stepped toward her, trying to memorize her face, her skirt, the lines of her arms and hands. She noticed the woman had lines around her eyes—she was not as young as Ren had first thought. Small straight scars marked her arms like scattered sticks, none of them even an inch long.

Before she reached Ren, the woman veered toward one of the taller structures and reached for a middle rung of the ladder. She called to someone inside, patting the wall with her hand. Ren noticed that the women on the roof next to her were above a room that had already been excavated. The woman with the macaw apron was maybe ten feet to the east.

In that moment of calculation, the woman reached the top of the ladder, the bottoms of her feet coated with dust. She stepped onto the roof and everything vanished.

Back to nothing but flat land and shrubs and lines of stones on the ground.

Ren walked to where the woman had reached for the ladder. She stood on one of the stones that had formed the wall. She felt slightly dizzy.

"Ready?" asked Silas from behind her. "It'll be dark soon."

She turned, and he saw something on her face.

"What?" he said.

"Have you found any macaw feathers here?" she asked. Casually, she hoped, although she was aware that the question was bizarre.

"No."

She took a breath and pointed to her feet. "I'd like to open up this room."

She could hear Ed's voice and Paul's laughter headed in their direction. She waited.

"You saw something, didn't you?" Silas asked.

She swallowed. "What do you mean?"

"I assume you saw something— or found something—on the surface that caught your attention. Show me."

They were both standing still, feet slightly apart, waiting for her answer, when Paul and Ed found them.

"Ready?" asked Ed. His T-shirt read "I Make Stuff Up."

Ren still didn't say anything.

"I need someone to hold the tarp and even up the shadow if I'm gonna take this photo," added Ed. "The wind's really picked up."

"I'll hold the tarp," said Silas, shrugging. "Then I want you guys to give us a hand for the rest of the afternoon. Ren wants to see how much of this room we can take down."

She moved the tools and their backpacks to the other room while Silas and Paul wrestled with the tarp in the wind, and Ed tried to catch the right light. The tarp kept billowing, letting sunlight into the shadows exactly where the hearth lay, ruining the shot.

The rustle of the tarp quieted, and Ren felt Silas behind her again.

"I don't have any problem with going with your gut," he said. "We've got the entire canyon and the entire history of existence to work with—you need a little gut to find what you're looking for. This room's as good as any other."

"I could be wrong," she said. Even as she said it, she pictured the feathers attached to the dark pelt and knew that she was not.

"Sure you could," said Silas. She couldn't help but notice that he was staying several inches away from her. He hadn't joked, hadn't smiled, hadn't given her even a sideways look that hinted at the memory of skin against skin. He was being completely professional. That was good, she told herself.

Paul was nearly as efficient with the pick as Silas was, and dirt flew as the ground dropped by inches. They checked at each level, looking for signs of artifacts, but the first forty centimeters went quickly. When the number of sherds increased—finally, they'd reached the dirt that had been lived in and lain in and worked in—they switched to trowels.

"What are we looking for, exactly?" asked Paul. "I know Silas wants pieces of corn. But I don't get the feeling we're looking for corn."

"No, I'm the corn guy. She's onto something else," Silas said, face totally hidden by the shadow of his hat's brim. Finding two pieces of corncob in an ash pit the week before had been like striking gold. Unlike wood, which could be collected and burned long after it was dead, corn plants lived for only a year. Their carbon traces could be analyzed more reliably. Charcoal, corn, the right kind of tree rings—those would get him within a couple of years of a specific date of occupation. The real story of the canyon would be told by bits of corn.

"I'm looking for feathers," said Ren. "Maybe a feather apron."

"Well, that's specific," said Ed.

"Yes, it is," said Silas. He wrinkled his forehead—he had one vertical line between his eyebrows—but he didn't seem to be frowning at her. More like he was trying to read very small print.

She didn't want to lie. She could just say she saw a small bit of feather, maybe, right at the surface, mostly decomposed, and it blew away before she could look at it. She could say she thought she saw something—anything, really—and maybe that would be enough to buy her time. Maybe they would just hit something soon and she wouldn't have to say anything at all.

"She gets feelings sometimes," said Ed, before she could speak. "That's how it works."

Maybe Silas would have said something else, but Paul spoke first. "How would feathers last this long?"

"They're slow to decompose," said Ren quickly, encouraging the thread of conversation. "But we'd have to get lucky."

"Like a roof cave-in or a piece of pottery collapsed over the feathers," added Ed. He was working with just his hands, running his gloves over a pile of loose dirt. "So the space under it would be protected, and you have little treasure troves of sealed-off space. Little time capsules."

Ren's fingers twitched, watching Paul and Silas in the dirt. Every swipe of their hands, every scrape of the trowel, could leave them holding her apron. She did think there was an apron. It could be something else, but the image that had stayed etched in her mind was of that apron. She thought that must mean something.

"Can I switch out with you?" she asked Paul.

The light had started to fade, and she told everyone else they could stop and leave her to dig by herself, but they all stayed with her. And just when she thought they would have to call it a day or risk being stuck on the mountain in the dark, she saw a flash of pale red in the dirt.

She reached for the whisk broom. It could even make dirt interesting, brushing out lovely islands and continents from nothingness. The broom could sometimes let you see anything you wanted to see, but she was not hallucinating now. A piece of the adobe roof had fallen over this red bit of feather. It was a protected space, just as she had wished for, just as Ed had described, and she could see Ed and Silas exchange a look.

She made short, firm strokes, brushing away until the outline of the adobe fragments was clear, with a small bit of feather protruding. She tossed the whisk broom off to the side and lifted the pieces of roof. The frail, wispy tips of the feathers sprang into the open air for the first time in centuries. The garment wasn't whole, but six feathers were lying together, some still attached by what had once been buckskin straps. The pelt the straps had hung from was partly decomposed, with a few patches of disintegrating fur visible through the dirt.

"Rabbit, I think," Silas said from behind her.

They did not have time to uncover the apron fully, and none of them wanted to risk damaging the find. They barely had time to speak. They covered the apron with a few shovelfuls of dirt for protection from the elements, anchored the tarp over the hole, and headed back down the mountain. All of them were too focused on their footing in the near dark to discuss what they'd found.

"Who would wear that?" asked Paul, when they were back on flat ground. "I mean, was it actually worn?"

"Maybe something ceremonial," said Ed. "Ritualistic."

"Maybe," said Ren.

She did not want to say anything about the apron or the woman

until she could sort her own thoughts. Macaws were certainly ceremonial. Images on Mimbres ceramics showed women holding the
birds, sometimes with a curved stick presumably of some proce-
dural or training importance. Women could have trained the birds,
cared for the birds, handled the birds in spiritual observances. A
single feather was considered a sign of prestige in burials, on the
same level with turquoise or shells or copper bells. To wear macaw
feathers was surely a mark of importance, of accomplishment, of
skill or uniqueness.

Who was this woman who clothed herself in such importance?

And where was the artist? Ren had not come here to find this
straight-shouldered woman striding around the canyon, leaving
wide-eyed boys in her wake. She had come here to find a woman
who painted ceramics.

Ceramics filled with parrots.

The sun dropped out of the sky just as they all stepped off the
slope and onto the main road. An early owl hooted, close by. They
scattered when they reached the screened porch, headed for show-
ers and toilets and changes of clothes.

Propping her flashlight against a wooden shelf, Ren stepped into
the outdoor shower first. The concrete floor had soaked up the day's
heat, and she curled her toes against the rough surface. The pine
walls came up to her nose, leaving a clear view of the house, the yard
and the path to the shower, and the mountains. The floor was cooling, slick with water, and her skin was cooling as well. She closed
her eyes, leaning forward and bracing her hands on the shower wall,
the lukewarm water hitting her shoulders, her arms, her face. When
the chill bumps started rising on her arms, she adjusted the temperature knobs and got down to the serious business of cleaning.
The water ran brown, opaque, down the drain. Digging left a coat

of grime—gray dust covered her skin and her hair, had worked its way into her nostrils and ears and the corners of her eyes. She could taste it, dry and bitter, in her throat.

She washed her hair twice, and her eyes slid closed again as she ran her fingers along her scalp, sluicing out the water. When she opened her eyes, she saw Silas walking toward her, headed toward the sink by the shower. She rinsed once more, and when she opened her eyes again, he was turning on the sink faucet.

"Feel good?" he asked, looking straight at the sink. He filled his hands with water and splashed his face.

"Good," she said.

"You ready to talk?" he asked.

"Talk?"

"You can parrot things back to me all you want—no pun intended—and I'm still going to ask you questions."

It was difficult, Ren thought, holding a serious conversation while naked, separated from him by a pine wall. She wondered if he could see only her eyes or if the view included her whole face or bare shoulders.

"Questions?" she said.

"Funny."

"I'll talk, Silas," she said. "I'll answer your questions, for whatever good it does. I'll come find you after I've put my clothes on."

"Clothes?" he asked.

She watched him leave as she wrapped a towel around her hair. He would ask her about the feather apron, and she would tell him about the parrot woman. He would not believe her because seeing ghosts was crazy. But she would still tell him the truth, because it was the only explanation she had, and some part of her—a part she didn't want to probe too much—wanted to share it with him. She would tell him the truth about the parrot woman. Other things she would keep to herself.

Sometimes her mother used to send Scott to wake her, and that was always less pleasant than her mother's tentative "Good morning" from the bottom of the stairs. On the morning of the accident, her mother called once, twice, three times—a hint of a threat in the final call—before Ren rolled out of bed, landing on her knees. It was October 5, 1984, the first date ever push-pinned into her brain instead of floating away like all the days before it. It was two months before she turned thirteen. She rested her head on the edge of the bed. One eye open, the other one closed. She thought of it as half sleeping. She pushed herself to her feet finally, stumped to the bathroom, and clomped down the stairs to the kitchen a few minutes later. She heard the Sex Pistols screaming in Scott's room as she passed it.

"You left your music on," she said to him as she walked past the kitchen table. He was slumped over his cereal.

"No, I didn't," he said.

"Did. I heard it."

"You were dreaming."

"Mom, he left his music on."

Her mother pretended not to hear her.

They ate cereal silently. She was pouring a second bowl when he stood and grabbed his book bag, kissing their mother's cheek. He said "Bye" to them all as the door swung shut behind him, and she didn't answer, although her mother and father did. She heard the door slam. She did not see him get in his car, arrange his book bag on the front seat, or drive away. But she knew he must have done those things.

That afternoon, she didn't see his car when she walked up the driveway. That was normal: He usually hung around with his friends after school and got back home long after the bus dropped her off at the end of the block. She opened the front door and walked into the den to see both her parents sitting on the couch. They weren't touching at all. Her father sat perfectly straight, both feet on the floor, his chin touching his chest. Her mother had her hair twisted up like she wore it for work, but she had on jeans. Her mascara was smeared down her cheeks. They were slow to look up when Ren asked why her father was home so early.

When they did look at her, she could see the mascara tracks went all the way to the collar of her mother's shirt. She had the sudden thought that one of them had cancer. Her music teacher had cancer the year before and wore a butterfly scarf around her head. Her parents must have planned to tell her about the cancer together, she thought, but it didn't make sense that they would tell her separately from Scott.

"We have to tell you something, honey," her mother said. "Come over here and sit with us."

Ren watched her mother's wet face and thought her father probably had the cancer.

When she got to the sofa and sat on the very edge, her mother laid her hand on Ren's head, too heavily, oppressively. Ren fought a flinch. Her mother didn't say anything, just left her heavy hand on Ren's skull.

"Harold," she said finally.

Ren heard her father swallow and felt the couch shift as he leaned toward her. "It's Scott," he said. "He had a bad accident on the way to school."

She was so surprised she couldn't make her brain work. They should be at the hospital if Scott had an accident.

Her father put his hand on her shoulder, and she slumped with the weight of both parents' hands. She wanted to stand. She did not move.

"He was. He was." Her father started and stopped. A third time: "He was. He never felt anything probably. He just went to sleep and never woke up. The other car ran a red light and hit him and it was very, very fast."

He kept talking, but the sleep part confused her.

"Is Scott dead?" she asked.

Her mother started crying, and her father said "shhhhh," but Ren didn't know which one of them he meant.

"He is," Ren said, answering her own question softly, in case her father had been talking to her.

People came over that afternoon and night—aunts and uncles and grandparents and friends from church. Some handed over things wrapped in tinfoil and then left, but some stayed. Her grandfather wanted to build a fire, because fires were comforting, even though it wasn't cold enough. Her grandmother dusted the shelves.

Her mother kept her hands on Ren for a long time. On her head, on her back, through the crook of her elbow. She escaped the weight of her mother's hand eventually. When she walked to her bedroom, she could hear the whir of Scott's tape player running wordlessly. She had told him so. She considered turning it off but didn't.

They had left her at school all day thinking he was still alive.

That night her grandmother sat on the edge of Ren's bed and pulled up the blankets. Her grandmother had squishy, wormlike veins on the tops of her hands that Ren liked to flatten—they sprang back quick as sponges. She experimented with the veins as her grandmother told her that it always took time for people to understand when someone was gone. She said that Ren's feelings were frozen and they would start to thaw out later. She heard her grandmother whisper to her mother at the doorway, "She doesn't understand. She doesn't know it's real yet."

It did not feel real. It was not a death—it was a vanishing. She never saw his car again. She never saw his book bag again. They didn't think she should go to the funeral, and she believed them when they said she would feel better if she remembered Scott alive instead of remembering his coffin. During the funeral she stayed with Allison Shum and played Frogger.

For a little while Scott's room remained with its treasure trove of music, and she would visit the treasure. She liked to look at *Born to Run*: Scott had been trying to do that Springsteen thing with his hair for a year, and he'd never gotten close. His hair was perfectly straight and always fell neatly into place no matter how much he wanted it wild and disheveled and curly. She had told him he needed to use curlers, and he wouldn't, but she thought they should have curled his hair for the funeral, because he would have loved for everybody to remember him looking like Springsteen. She wished she had thought to tell her mother that.

She couldn't believe that a plastic cassette tape could last longer than a human being.

They did not like finding her in his room. It was not healthy, they said. It was a few weeks, a month, maybe, after the accident—"the accident," that was what her parents said when they spoke of it at all—when they found her there for the last time. She heard them whispering in the hall. The next day her mother carried empty boxes and garbage bags into Scott's room, and bit by bit his room was broken down. The boxes and bags with bits of his room in them were carried to the attic. The next day, a large white truck came and collected his bedroom furniture. It would go to people who needed it, her mother said. Her father came home with a desk the next day, and Scott's room became an office. A strange, bare office that no one ever worked in. There were no pictures on the wall. There was a typewriter on the small wooden desk. Next to the desk, a round end table tilted to one side. The wheels of the desk chair snagged in the carpet and would not roll.

So Scott's room vanished. They gave her his tapes in three big boxes. All the little hard cases, tapping and sliding against each other, unimaginable riches. She had never wanted anything more than she wanted Scott's music. They told her she could sort through them and keep the ones she wanted, but she couldn't stand to throw out a single one. She spent an entire afternoon unpacking them and arranging them into towers, skyscrapers of cassettes lining her wall just as they had lined Scott's.

By the next day, the tapes made her sick. Looking at them, she felt her stomach shrivel and knot. They were alien things in her room. When she tried to slide *Born to Run* out of its slot in the stack, she could not stand the sounds the cassettes made rubbing against each other, talking to each other in clicks and clacks that she couldn't understand. They did not belong to her. She still could not throw them out, but she could not listen to them and could not look at them. She climbed on her desk chair and hid them one by one on the top shelf of her closet. Stacks from the shelf to the ceiling. Then she started lining them along the back of her middle shelf. She buried them under two old T-shirts, a pair of matronly shorts, a robe her grandmother had bought her, a black-and-yellow sweater her grandmother had knitted for her, a raincoat she'd never even considered wearing. She hid the extras under her shoes, in the dark recesses of the closet floor, where belts and scarves and single socks had fallen and where no one would want to explore.

Sometimes she wondered if Scott ever knew she had his tapes. He probably did. Because after he died, another unexpected thing happened: He did not go away.

The day after the funeral, he woke her up, singing "Lily, Rosemary and the Jack of Hearts." Face smushed in the pillow, T-shirt bunched above her hips, she was struck first by the fact that he wasn't tickling her feet. That was always how he woke her up, and he wouldn't stop until she'd twitched and seized her way off the bed. She slept on her stomach, arms and legs stretching to the four corners of the bed like she was being drawn and quartered. He had always made fun of her for that. But he didn't touch her feet at all this morning, just sang, which made her frown as she pushed her hair out of her face and stretched, still belly-down. Then she remembered why he couldn't touch her anymore.

He sat on her bed, one leg on the floor and one tucked under him. *"Lily was a princess, she was fair-skinned and precious as a child . . ."*

She sat up, fully alert. It was the most awake she'd ever felt in the morning.

The wreck could have been a dream, she thought. She pushed herself farther against the headboard, blinking at him.

He kept singing.

"Scott?"

"Morning, Renny-ren-ren."

The wreck had not been a dream. She knew it had not.

She could still be asleep. This could be the dream. She scooted closer to him, raising her hands to press her palms to his cheeks.

He pulled away slightly.

"Are you a ghost?" she asked, because if this was a dream, then it didn't matter if she sounded stupid. "If I touch you, will my hand go straight through you? Can you walk through walls?"

It took him a moment to answer. "You can touch me."

She did, both hands firm and focused on his upper arms, testing. It was the only time she could ever touch him after he came back. When she was grown, she wished she'd touched him differently. Touched his hair. Hugged him. She wished she had used the touch for affection instead of fact-finding.

"You were having a nightmare," he said.

"I was?"

"You were making that whining sound in your sleep. The scared-cocker-spaniel sound."

"I was not."

"Were, too."

She considered. "But the nightmare wasn't that you died?"

"No. That really happened."

She moved closer to him. She had a vague, fading memory of being chased. Claws and wings. "I don't remember," she said.

"You don't have to remember," he said, and he started singing Dylan again.

The water in the shower ran clear; soap and suds and dirt and grass vanished down the drain. Scott belonged to her. She had the right to share him or not, and she had never wanted to share. But the woman in the feather apron belonged to this canyon. Ren could not claim her for her own, and she did not feel that it was her right to keep her from Silas, who had lived and breathed the canyon for much longer than she had. She had screwed everything up by not keeping her distance properly—if she disliked him, if she hardly knew him, she could have avoided his questions. She could have sidestepped and deflected until he backed off, like everyone else always did. But she couldn't do that now—it would be unfair. It would be a lie. She would tell him what he wanted to know, and that would be that. She would be a freak. And he would be gone.

She found him sitting by the creek half an hour later, far away from the house and the others. She had seen his flashlight bobbing in the dark and had followed, but the flashlight was nowhere to be seen now. The moonlight was gentle and kept her from walking into trees. The grass crunched under her feet, brittle, and the willow branches whispered in the breeze, rustling like silk. Small winged things chirped from the trees and the undergrowth.

"Sit with me," he said.

"I can't see the ground," she said. But she followed his voice and sat, bending her knees. The edge of her shorts skimmed the denim over his thighs as she settled.

On and on, the creek gargled.

"The thing is, there's a mystical side to this," he said.

How like him to start an interrogation by answering rather than asking. She smiled in the dark. "Yeah."

"One time here in this canyon we found a burial," he said. "My trowel went right through the wall and scraped the edge of the skull. At that second when my trowel hit, there was this hum in the air, and then movement everywhere. A black cloud. Bees. Everywhere I looked, there were bees. There were three of us there, and none of us saw where they came from, but there were bees down in the pit, all around our faces and hands, brushing against our ears and necks and every square inch of skin. Not stinging at all, just hovering around us. I looked down at my hand, and it was like I had a black glove on. Then they were gone. Twenty seconds, maybe, of bees everywhere; then they disappeared as fast as they'd come."

He let his knees fall apart slightly, and she felt the warmth of his leg against hers. "Tell me what you really saw at Crow Creek, Ren."

That was not what she had expected. She had not prepared that story.

"That comes first," he added. "Whatever happened here, I'm not going to understand it until you tell me about Crow Creek."

The moon was almost full, the shape of a rabbit clear and nearly complete in it. This close to him, she could see Silas's face. He always wore his hat during the day, and his face seemed naked and vulnerable out in the open.

"I told you part of it," she said. "I wasn't lying."

"But there's more. It doesn't make sense unless there's more."

"Yeah," she said. She saw no reason to prolong it. He deserved these answers. He would not believe her, of course. But she would try. And if he walked away from her, there would be an advantage to that. Everything would be much easier.

She remembered the girl's face and focused on it, closing her eyes so she could see it better.

"You can take it or leave it, but this is what happened," she started. "We'd been at the site for three weeks. I was sitting on the side of a hill that led down to the creek bank, and a little girl passed by me on her way to the water. She wore a string apron, and she had thick black hair down to her hips. I knew she didn't belong—or that I didn't belong—one or the other."

She opened her eyes and looked at him, trying to gauge his response. He faced the water and said nothing. She continued.

"She was maybe twelve years old, with narrow little shoulders and dusty feet and ropy muscles like kids who stay in the pool all summer. She waded into the creek up past her waist, so her hair was floating around her like a veil skimming along the ground. She had something in her hand, behind her back, that I couldn't see. She stumbled, and she must have dropped it because she bent over suddenly, looking in the water. I scooted closer and watched. She reached down again and again, feeling around. When she bent over, more hair would drag through the water, and it had to be blocking her view. She'd toss it over her shoulder, but it would fall down again. Hair everywhere. Then she came up with a rock about the size of her hand. It was thin, thinner than your finger, black, with a sharp edge. I worried she would cut herself accidentally. She turned toward me but didn't look at me, standing still in the water with the sharp edge in her hand, pointed right at the skin of her throat. I thought I could see her pulse.

"I stood up then, worried, about to say something, anything. To stop her. Then she grabbed a chunk of her hair right above her ear, held it out away from her face, and started hacking at it with the rock. It fell into the water, and she grabbed another handful. Hair everywhere. There was black hair falling in strands and clumps, drifting all around her like seaweed or snakes or something alive, floating and swirling and then finally washing downstream. It happened very fast. Like I was imagining it all. At the end she stood there with her little bare head, shorn like a sheep, with pink skin showing through in places. And she smiled a huge smile."

Ren stopped, remembering.

"Her jaw was square and her cheekbones were sharp and her eyes were bright," she continued, then paused. She tried to hold on to both faces—the girl and the woman in the macaw apron—and compare their eyes. She'd thought the girl's eyes looked wet, glossy, like stones in the river. Were the grown woman's wide, dark eyes those same eyes? She didn't know.

"There was this look on her face of, oh, at first I thought happiness. But now I'd say it was satisfaction. She had done something important. So she walked to the edge of the creek, stepped out, and started climbing up the hill. She walked so close to me I could have touched her, and then she knelt down at the top of the hill about ten feet behind me. She looked straight at me then, and tossed the hair-cutting rock behind her, like she was showing me. So I dug there, where the rock landed. By myself at first because none of it made any sense. I couldn't tell anyone I wanted to dig there because an imaginary little girl told me to. But pretty quickly, I realized there was a hidden room there—a few rocks from the wall were right under the surface, and once I found those, I had a reason to suggest we dig there. And you know the rest."

Silas rubbed his palm across his jaw, back and forth. His beard rasped against his hand.

"Do you see ghosts lurking around sites often?" he asked with no trace of sarcasm.

"No," she said. "Almost never."

"But you don't act like you were very surprised to see a little girl who died in the twelfth century."

"Not totally shocked, no."

He studied her. "So why do you think you saw her?"

She shrugged. She had never figured out the answer to that question.

"Sometimes knowledge comes out in strange ways, you know," he said. "Your mind puts together connections in ways you don't understand."

"Right," she said, exhaling. He was trying to make it all logical, sensible. He had reached some sort of limit, maybe, on just how much he was willing to accept. But he was still here. Still next to her, still listening. That mattered.

Meanwhile, the weight of talking about this, of shaping it and lifting it up and passing it along so carefully to Silas, had exhausted her. She was ready to let the subject float away into the dark. She had seen people, specific individuals, twice before she saw the girl at Crow Creek. Not counting Scott. She'd seen a gray-haired man shaping a dart point near Casa Grande, and she'd seen a woman crying in Mesa Verde. In both cases, she'd been feeling, not thinking—absorbing the strong breeze or the baking sun—then suddenly someone was there who had not been there a second earlier. At Crow Creek she had been focused on the shine of the water, on the fast-moving currents, when the little girl appeared.

These ghosts wanted something from her, she assumed. She was trying to guess what it was, trying to help them. She did not know why they appeared to her. She did not know why she could hear inarticulate sounds but not their actual words. She did not know what the hair or the feathers or the pottery meant. And she didn't know what song Scott had been humming by the window this morning, with sunlight and tiny floating particles raining down on him. She did not know if she should invite Silas into her room tonight, and she did not know what she would say if he knocked on her door uninvited.

She had to tell him about the woman in the macaw skirt, of course. When she finished, he had only one more question for her: "Do you think the girl you saw then and the woman you saw today were the same person?"

"I don't know," she said. "There was maybe twenty years' difference in their ages. It's possible."

He was quiet after that. She found it hard to remain still. He was not acting like he thought she was insane. When he stood and held out his hand, she let him pull her to her feet. She was eye level with his chin. He held her hand as they made their way out of the willows and back into the open moonlight.

It occurred to her that some men were attracted to crazy women.


She did not have to invite him. He stood halfway in her room, one hand still on the door. He was only a step away from the bed, which took up three-quarters of her pine-paneled room. Her jeans were in a pile on the floor, and her pullover hung on the doorknob. She'd been reading, and her T-shirt was bunched around her hips, under her red flannel sheets. Looking at him, she rubbed her thumb against the sheets, which she thought were somehow sexy and comforting at the same time, and surely if any sheets could send the image she wanted these would be those sheets because they said she was neither Madonna nor whore but someone in between and she'd nearly packed the light blue sheets but thankfully had not brought them because they lacked all allusions to whores and when he looked at her she forgot her sheets.

"I missed you," he said.

She wondered if he'd knocked and she'd forgotten that already.

"Hi," she said.

"Can I come in?"

"Yes."

"Can I sit down?"

"Yes."

"Chatty, aren't you?" he said, sitting, his hand flat on her sheets. Then, before she could say anything, "Are we going to do this, Ren?"

"You're in my bedroom," she said.

"That doesn't mean we're going to do this."

"You're in your boxers," she said. They had a pattern of what she suspected were beagles. She would remember to make fun of them later.

"That still doesn't mean we're going to do this."

She pulled back the sheets, not too far, just enough to make the invitation clear. Now he could see where her T-shirt had ridden up, exposing the tops of her thighs and her black panties—utilitarian, but still black.

"Oh," he said, closing the door behind him. He walked toward her, and she scooted toward the middle of the bed, putting down her book. She was sitting with her back pressed straight against the headboard.

"I missed you," he said again.

"We said good night about fifteen minutes ago," she said. He was playing with the edge of her shirt, the backs of his fingers lightly rubbing against her thigh, sliding down toward her knee. She felt the touch more because his hand was hidden under the sheet.

"Yeah," he said.

She picked up his hand—the one not teasing her thigh—and raised it to her jaw. She tilted her face into his palm. He smelled like soap now, the barest trace of juniper still underneath. His white T-shirt had a hole at the neck.

"Come here," she said, her hand sliding to his wrist, pulling him toward her until she could feel his heat and his weight. He slid his hand down her leg, wrapped it around her ankle—still under the cover of sheets and blankets—and pulled her under him smooth and fast. She heard her book hit the floor, his elbow sharp against her side, and he said her name into her mouth.

THEY CALLED HER VILLAGE Women Crying, although this was not because of any particular sadness. Her mother said that long ago there had been no people here—not a single footprint along the wet mud of the creek, not a single room shaped from sticks and water and earth. Instead of people, there had been a crowd of yucca, a field of them, too many to count. They had grown there without anyone's help, but still they looked like a planted field, like laid-out rows of corn or squash.

By the time the people came, the yucca had died some time before. And so they stood sadly, collapsing in on themselves, woman-shaped and gray, loose hair blowing. Women Crying. But the sound of the village's name was a liquid sound, like water pouring, so there was a pleasure to saying the words.

That was only one of her mother's stories. Her mother had the gift of seeing the patterns in things. She saw the images in the clay, and then she would paint the clay so that its true stories were revealed. The gift of seeing patterns ran through the blood from mother to daughter, and her mother said the gift was strongest when it was poured into a single daughter, an only daughter. Sisters diluted the gift.

She was her mother's only daughter. She had three brothers—once four brothers—but they did not touch the clay.

Her mother's hands smelled of clay, rich and wet and restful. The clay was always in the lines of her knuckles, under her fingernails. She would say that to have clean hands, to wash all trace of the clay from yourself, was an insult to the earth and to the spirits. Around her throat, her mother wore a piece of turquoise, a piece of the sky from the previous lower world that ants had carried with them as they emerged into this world. The mother valued the necklace, but the daughter adored it. She would sit in her mother's lap and roll the stone between her fingers.

Her mother finally let her try her own bowls. The first ones she attempted—all of them patted and kneaded with hands too little to grip a grinding stone—had exploded. Three bowls destroyed. That was because she had not added enough water to the powdered clay. How small was she then? So small. Years before Non came.

Her mother had been patient with the first two shattered bowls, but she was not patient when the cracking of the third pot echoed through the air. (There had been whole pots in between broken ones, nicely shaped smooth bowls, as long as her narrow feet, and it was probably those whole, satisfactory bowls that dried up her mother's patience.) A cold hard look, no fondness in her eyes—her mother did not have to speak. She closed herself off, making invisible walls go up in front of her eyes like frogs did. Her mother never needed to yell—the walls in front of her eyes were enough.

So she did not explode another pot. She paid very close attention to the feel of the clay in her mother's hands, rolled it and pressed it in her own hands, feeling how it stuck to her skin, but not too much—it must not stick too much. It needed the correct balance of slick and slide and stick. Add the water splash by splash to the powder and watch the color of the clay darken with the water. (This moment of darkening reminded her of how Spider Woman took great handfuls of the dirt itself—black, red, white, and yellow—spat on them, and with this wet clay made the First People. The colors of the clay could still be seen in hair and eyes and bone and teeth and skin, all brought to life when Spider Woman blew on her first clay dolls.) She learned how much water to add by the feel of the clay in her hands. After the water came the temper, the pieces of the present needed to anchor the idea of the clay. She crushed broken bits of pottery on the grinding stone, smashing them fine as salt, and added them to her clay, smooth and cool as river moss. Pound and mash and smooth and stroke and smooth and mash.

Then, for a small bowl, big enough for only powdered herbs or a drink of water, she would measure out a clump that filled both of her hands without spilling over and roll it into a long worm, then start the coiling, making the worm curl around itself, laying one rung flat on top of the next until the entire worm was asleep, neatly wrapped.

Her mother roasted rabbits stuffed with sage and saltbush, and the two of them could eat an entire rabbit. (All rabbits and deer and fowl came from her mother's brothers, since her father had died in her eighth year. One of the big cats on the ridge had knifed his leg with its claws before many spear points killed the cat. Her father's leg filled with thin clear liquid and thick yellow liquid and swelled as wide as a fat turkey before he died.) She and her mother would sit on the roof, pulling the rabbit apart, snatching their fingers back from the hot meat, pulling it from the bones in hot, dripping strings. And then for hours her fingers would taste of salty juice and clay, and she could see her mother's lips shine with fat.

In the blurry sharp memories of early childhood, she recalled the dripping fat and burning-hot meat as being familiar. Treasured, but as reliable as finding a painted beetle in the low shrubs by the creek. She could walk through the creek a dozen times a day and see no beetles, but sooner or later, inevitably, she would see a round, yellow back with black paint marks on it. She would grab it and let the bug crawl across her palm. No matter how many trips she made without seeing one, if she waited long enough, a painted beetle would come. And so would rabbit meat.

By the time Non came, beetles were much more common than rabbits. The rain dances were even more common, and the men would grow hoarse singing for the crops to come. Sometimes, as with corn, the singing and dancing would take days at a time, an elaborate courtship to woo each ear.

The dances. Her feet knew well the feel of the plaza stones, smoothed by years of pounding soles and smacking hands. Because she was her mother's daughter, she had been asked to perform at an early age. She had been a cloud girl, face painted with white clay, only eyes showing through, hair powdered white, blossoms from the cottonwood tree woven in a belt around her waist. She had danced to welcome the first rain of summer, her feet hitting the stones like raindrops, while the rattle of gourds and shells brought thunder and lightning. There were handfuls of meal thrown over her and the other cloud girls, sprinkling down, sticking to the bottoms of her feet. (It brought good luck, her mother had said, to eat the

cakes made from the meal off a cloud maiden's feet.) One fall
she had been the moon—always a role for a girl who had not
yet come of age—wearing a blanket of yellow that scraped
the ground. Her feet were painted white, and crescent moons
were painted on both cheeks. This was a dance of harmony,
where the small moon and a tall sun and many stars would
move in circles, their paths looping around each other but
never touching, as with the sky. The sun lifted his face
proudly, but the stars hid their faces, always looking down, so
the eagle feather points on their heads could shine. Six dancers, a dozen dancers, then—as more and more stars joined
in—twice that many moving around the plaza. Then would
come the Bitter Spirit, which always sought to break circles.
The spirit was always male, and he would leap onto the plaza,
body painted dark red, with a gourd snout filled with sharp
snapping teeth, and horns curving from his head. No matter
what the red spirit did, the sun and moon and stars must stay
on course, must not be frightened out of their paths, or bitterness would replace harmony in the seasons to come.

There were patterns to the dances, as intricate and subtle
as the patterns in the clay. You could not always see the design
when you yourself were stomping your own rhythm on the
cold plaza stones. But she was a part of it, even if she could
not see it.

Seeing the patterns was only one part of her gift, her
mother told her. You had to bring them to the surface. You
had to show others what you could see lurking in the clay.

# five

*We know relatively little about the social contexts reflected by the burials and secondarily by the pottery contained in them.... Hereditary elites should be set off from nonelites by the presence of certain emblems or badges which, varying in form among societies, should be recognizable by their exotic materials, large labor input, and visual distinctiveness.*

—From "Social Organization and Classic Mimbres Period Burials in the SW United States" by Patricia A. Gilman, *Journal of Field Archaeology*, vol. 17, 1990

The wind outside was whipping through the trees, and Silas listened to the whistle of the air as he stared at the rise and fall of Ren's rib cage. Her head was on his shoulder, hair spread over his chest, and he'd lost all feeling in his arm. He wasn't ready to move it yet.

He couldn't sleep.

There was a soft thud outside the window, and he listened for any animal sounds—snuffling or pawing or grunting. Ed's and Paul's tents weren't nearly as sturdy as the walls of the bunkhouse. But there was no sound of life beyond the bed. He considered that if he needed to scare away a wild thing, his gun was in his own room, with the bullets in the bedside table: He spent days and nights by himself in strange, untraveled nooks of the state, and the pistol was a precaution. Right after college, when he had long hair and an earring, he was slightly concerned about running into cowboys, but now he worried only about wild animals.

The birds were starting to stir. He and Ren needed to be awake and ready to head up the mountain in no more than three hours. He tried to close his eyes.

He had felt her certainty yesterday when Ren asked to dig in a different room. He knew she had seen something. He had seen it in her face. He felt the same certainty when she told him about her daydream of the Mimbres girl—he knew it cost her something to share it. And because she'd shared it, he knew she must feel something for him. Plenty of times since she'd come to the canyon, he'd felt like he'd said something ridiculous, done something ridiculous. Touched her leg the first day she was here, for instance. Stupid. But last night he had known it was the right time to knock on her door.

Certainty. As Ren's leg slid against his, he wondered if he'd been sure about her from the moment he'd seen her speak in Albuquerque. She'd been wearing a brown skirt and heels that showed off the muscles in her calves, and even a sedate paper reading couldn't hide the excitement in her voice.

He did not trust certainty. It did not last.

She had held an apple in one hand at lunch yesterday, waving it as she said that of course the first thing to do when butchering an animal was to remove the intestines. He wondered if she normally fell for academics who debated in faculty lounges and hypnotized grad students.

"I don't flirt," he whispered. In case she was asleep. "Ed's been teasing me about that for months, ever since some waitress gave me a free coffee."

Ren pushed herself more tightly against him.

"Sure you do," she said sleepily, her hair dragging along his skin. She turned toward him, and he took the chance to move his arm. He could see the white of her teeth as she settled onto the pillow.

"Well, with you," he agreed.

"I get the feeling you've had practice."

"None," he said. He considered. "Like pick-up lines. I've never had a good one. Once I went up to this cute girl sitting by herself at a bar, and as I was saying hello, I spilled my drink on her table. A full beer. It was pouring into her lap, and all I had in my hand was a slice of pizza. So I started sopping up the beer with the pizza, and she said—before I'd ever even said my name—"You're pathetic." So I walked back to my own table. That's how smooth I am."

"Why did you have pizza in a bar?"

He ran his tongue along his front teeth. "I have no idea."

She propped herself on her elbow and traced one of his eyebrows. He leaned in to her touch.

"You share every single thought in your head," she said. "You think it, and it just falls out of your mouth. You'd think that would make you easy to figure out."

"Oh, I can be easy." He kissed her shoulder. "But in my vast experience, women like the unpredictable."

"Maybe."

He lowered his face close enough that he could feel her breath. His eyes were millimeters from hers. His vision blurred.

"You have one giant cyclops eye," he said, unblinking. He ran his hand down her side, pausing at the curve of her hip. "And many other fine parts."

She stroked her palm along his triceps. "I appreciate your parts as well."

He drew back, allowing both of her eyes to come into focus. He felt deeply tired and deeply content.

"So who does that skirt belong to?" he asked.

She sat up. "That's what you want to talk about? You want to talk work?"

He tried to read her face.

"She's not my artist," she said in a rush, dark eyes shining. "I don't think. There's no reason a woman couldn't be both a potter and a macaw handler, but if we agree there were specialists who crafted the most impressive pottery—and what we found at Crow Creek definitely counted as impressive—then I don't think she would handle macaws, too. It makes sense that both roles were too important for one person to do both."

"What if the skirt was a mark of prestige?" he asked. "Not a mark of her role."

"So they give a master artist a skirt of macaw feathers as a gift?"

"Maybe," he said. "A gift from someone of power? As a tribute to her own skill? Or was it unrelated to anything she did? Was her husband or mother or father someone who worked with macaws? Because, again, we haven't found any macaws here."

She shifted positions. "You actually believe I saw her, don't you?"

"I do," he said. "I believe you saw something. But can I make a suggestion? For now, can we try to analyze this based solely on what we've found? I feel the need to narrow it down a bit. What would you think if you'd found that skirt yesterday with no context other than the archaeological record?"

She kicked off the covers, and he lifted his head to look at her legs. The planes of them, the curve of muscle, the inside of her thighs soft. Strong.

"Valuable. It must have belonged to someone of importance," she said.

"And I would tend to think it didn't come from this area, since we haven't seen other feathers," he said. "I'd say it was made somewhere else. Which might make it even more valuable."

"No one would leave that apron behind," she said softly. "You wouldn't cave in a room around it like it was a broken jar or a heap of ash. It's too precious. You'd take it with you. If you could. Or."

She breathed the end of her sentence rather than speaking it. He heard the words anyway.

"You'd bury it with the owner," he finished.

"We've got to get back to the site. We've got to take down the rest of the level." She sat up, her feet hitting the floor.

"I know," he said, wrapping his fingers around her wrist. "But we can't go in the dark."

"I know," she said. She fidgeted, swung her legs back onto the bed, her feet landing near his head. "I know. But she's under there, isn't she?"

"Come here," he said, holding out his arm. She turned herself around, her head fitting against his shoulder.

Normally burials took place under floors, or sometimes in the fill of a collapsed room. Those were the traditional ways to honor the dead, to aid their journey. It was the routine, the way of taking time and care with those lost. What Silas didn't say, didn't see any need to say, was that sometimes the routine was shattered. Theft or war, invasion and panicked departure. No time for thought or effort. Sometimes things were lost or left behind in unexpected ways.

❖ ❖ ❖

Paul and Ed were ready to leave early. The exhaustion hadn't hit Ren yet, although neither she nor Silas had drifted off for more than a few minutes. She could feel the adrenaline pumping, shoving away the need for sleep. It was a buzz from Silas and the feather apron and the potential of the burial. Anticipation.

It was not altogether a pleasant anticipation.

They walked, single file as always, up the elk trail, first Ren, then Silas, then Paul and Ed. It had been a mostly silent walk up the hill—the possibility of human remains had dampened the usual chatter. She didn't look at Silas, didn't touch him. He had not touched her in any way with the others watching. He had not put a hand on the small of her back or rubbed his leg against hers under the table.

As they approached the site, they could see the flap of the blue tarp from across the plateau. It had pulled partially free from the rocks they set on the edges. They squinted from the dust in the air and the sun in their eyes, and they walked toward the flash of blue.

Before they could see what lay under the apron, they had to move the apron itself. It was a slow process of frequent photos and small movements, lifting and scraping and brushing. When the apron was free, Ren and Silas used trowels and a flat piece of cardboard to scoop up the apron, cushioned with plenty of extra dirt. Silas lowered the cardboard piece full of dirt and feathers, inch by inch, into a large box for safe transport. His arms were taut: She could tell he was trying to avoid a single tremor, a single jolt.

The wind again—she kept noticing it. It blew hot and hard, lifting Silas's hat from his head but not quite dislodging it. His shirttails blew in the air behind him.

Ren allowed her focus to return to the dirt and to Paul. He was as eager as she was to find something, and she recognized in him the same desperate, hopeless desire she'd felt on her earliest digs: a craving to accomplish something important, to play a major role, even knowing you were too raw, too ignorant, to be trusted with the big jobs. So she'd told him he could start the digging. And she wanted to be sure he was keeping it gentle. She could see the nerves in his movements, in how his fingers shook occasionally. She'd been like that, too, the first time Ed let her uncover a collared adobe hearth. The boy deserved to play his part. She wanted him to know that she acknowledged he was a part of this. He mattered. It was important to know you mattered.

It was slow work, and the shadows shortened as the morning passed. The wind almost seemed to be helping, blowing the dirt up and out of the hole. The thick dust rose and spread like a nimbus cloud over their heads. They widened the hole, making it easier to maneuver. All four of them could fit into the pit at one time, their shoulders and heads above ground level. Paul and Ren worked at the east wall, while Silas and Ed worked at the foot of the west wall.

Paul was lifting a bucket of dirt to ground level when Ren caught her breath.

"Here," she said. Her hair was blowing into her mouth; she whipped it back over her shoulder without touching it.

Silas stepped over a half-full bucket and leaned over her shoulder. She brushed the dirt away from the very center of the grayish bowl. Only a small segment was exposed, but the few inches were enough to show the outline of the kill hole. That jagged hole meant the bowl had been placed over the face of the dead: The hole was punched to let the loved one's spirit escape.

Even the wind was quiet for a moment. All talk had evaporated.

Ren had always wondered if that was something as shallow as ingrained etiquette—speak softly when you walk through a graveyard—or if it was something more fundamental, some fear or acknowledgment of the inevitable, bones calling to bones. The probable body in the dirt made them step back slightly. As much of a sway as a step.

Paul swallowed and opened his mouth; Silas laid a hand on his shoulder.

"Shhh," he said, softly, leaving his hand in place. Paul seemed grateful for the direction. Ren could remember that sense of not knowing how to act with a burial bowl—giddiness over the find warring with discomfort over the corpse.

After that second—two seconds, three seconds, four seconds—of stillness, Ren took the first step out of the pit, allowing the others room to move. Ed was already reaching for his camera, and the others cleared out of the space. Ed snapped photos from every angle; then he and Ren stepped back into the pit, reaching for brooms. Ed and Ren worked with quick flicks of their wrists to brush back the dirt from the bowl. They squatted on the balls of their feet, leaning onto their toes, touching the ground as little as possible. They pressed themselves close to the dirt walls, trying to avoid where the body might lie.

It did not take long. Soon the clavicles came into view. But one bone did not mean a body. Once Ren had felt confident she had found a burial at a site in the Mimbres Valley—she'd unearthed a toe bone, then, at the appropriate distance away, two leg bones, parallel. She'd stopped digging, called for photos. But a little more poking and prodding revealed that the tibiae were only two random leg bones, perhaps from some grave disturbed long ago, but lacking all requisite bits of torso and arms and head to create a proper body.

Since then, she liked to uncover the better part of a skeleton before she declared a set of bones to be a burial.

They found the hip bone next, only a few sweeps away, surfacing wide and curved in the dirt under Silas's broom. As they continued to take away the dirt, they revealed the entire outline of the body, lying on its back with knees drawn to the chest. It was surprisingly small, as bodies always were once they were condensed to a pile of bones.

Only the back of the skull could be seen. The bowl, facedown, shielded the woman's face. No, Ren reminded herself—they didn't know it was a woman. She couldn't be certain of that. But she felt certain. She couldn't shake the sense that she'd seen this face, seen the slashes of red paint on the cheeks and the proud tilt of the head. As she stared at the unseen face, she heard Silas say that the pelvis seemed to indicate a female. She felt comforted by the clinical, concrete feel of the pronouncement.

"She has a broken wrist," said Silas, gesturing. "It's healed crooked."

Ed pointed to a yellow-white circle of bone lying under the radius and ulna. It was not a bone that belonged with the arm bones. "Bracelet," he said. "That's a bone bracelet, not human bone."

"Yes," said Silas, appreciatively. "Nice catch. Old Eagle Eye Ripley does it again."

Ren had cleaned off the bowl, though its edges were still lodged in the soil. It had a long crack down one side, and a piece of the rim had broken off. The kill hole had destroyed a couple of centimeters, but otherwise the vessel was intact.

Ed picked up his camera again. More photos, this time of the exposed skeleton and the uncovered bowl. The sun had inched higher, and the shadows from the walls were infringing, so Ren and Silas held the tarp to even out the lighting.

There was barely room for them to stand without touching the skeleton, but they all climbed into the hole again as Ren knelt. She skimmed her fingers over the bowl, barely touching it.

"Go on," said Silas.

She fit her fingertips under the edges of the bowl, testing its solidity. She lifted it slightly, then with more confidence when it remained steady in her hands. She raised it into the air but did not look up. Bowls could give a glimpse of life as it had been; they reflected back once living loves and thoughts and hands and feet and faces. The bowl was only a route to the people themselves. So before she glanced at the inside of the bowl, she looked at the woman's face and acknowledged her, acknowledged that she mattered.

The skull was filled with dirt, eyes and nose and mouth packed solid. The jaw was askew. A few strands of hair remained beneath it, and a few of those strands were braided through with feathers. A dull red, an algae-colored green, a yellow that almost matched the dirt. Tattered feathers with no segments bigger than a fingernail.

As Ren bent closer, the wind swirled into the pit, mingling the feathers with strands of Ren's hair. She did not move away.

"You want me to take that?" asked Ed, on his knees, reaching down.

She didn't look up. The wind snatched Ed's straw hat from his head, tossing it out of the hole and toward a cholla.

"The bowl, Ren?" he said. "Careful."

Ren looked toward him, then glanced at the bowl she was holding. It had slipped her mind for a moment. Ed had one hand waiting under the bowl, just in case.

The inside of the bowl was a complicated image, small details jumping out from the larger shapes. Black lines zigzagged against a white background. One figure covered most of the bowl. It could have been a man or a woman—there was no hairstyle or clothing to give any clues—but the smooth white oval of a head was dominated by two diamond-shaped eyes. The two shapes were filled with smaller and smaller concentric diamonds, tapering down to a solid black triangle in the center. No nose. A straight line for a mouth. The arms sloped down, and the hands were raised, palms up. The torso and lower half of the body bloomed into a bird's tail, with a great fan of feathers spreading across half of the bowl. Black feathers and white feathers and feathers with diagonal lines. The same kind of hachure Ren had mentioned from the Crow Creek bowls. They were bold, geometric feathers shaped like the blades of a fan. The design was closer to the half-circle of a peacock's tail than a parrot's tail, but the effect of half human, half bird was unmistakable.

Silas studied the bowl over Ren's shoulder.

"Her hands," he said, pointing to the design. "Or his hands. They have long fingernails. I've never seen that."

"I think they're talons," said Ren. The three men, as if a string were attached to each of their necks, looked down toward the skeleton's hands.

Ren laughed. "Not so literal. I didn't mean the person actually had talons. But I think the artist was very clear on the connection to birds."

Ren finally passed the bowl to Ed. She clambered after it, holding out her hands again. She was not ready to let it go.

"We'll have to walk up to Braxton's to call the medical examiner," Silas said. He hoisted himself from the pit and wiped his dirty palms on his khakis. "I saw his truck at the house this morning."

"Medical examiner?" Paul asked. He'd been studying the diamond eyes, his own eyes a few inches from the pottery. "For someone who's been dead for a few hundred years? Or a few thousand?"

"Procedure," said Ren. "They have to come out to confirm that this isn't a murder. Or, at least, that even if it was, it was a murder from several centuries ago."

"How do they do that?" asked Paul.

"They'll ask Ren or Silas if this is a body from several centuries ago," said Ed.

"Then what?"

"Then we cover her back up," Silas snapped. "Let her rest again. Just pretend it's your great-grandmother we dug up—what would you want us to do?"

"Okay," said Paul quickly, quietly.

Silas's mouth was tight. "There's a difference between a piece of pottery and a person."

"I know," said Paul. He looked confused and uncomfortable. "I'm sorry."

Ren suspected he wasn't sure what he was apologizing for. She wasn't quite sure, either. But Silas nodded. He rubbed the bridge of his nose.

"You guys can start on the next room block while I make the call," he said, the sharpness not quite gone from his voice. "I need a walk anyway. Then we'll drive the truck up so we can bring the bowl down."

He turned to Ren. "You still haven't met Brax. Walk with me."

She looked from the bowl to him, then back to the bowl.

"If you don't mind," he added.

He seemed edgy, and she suspected he wanted to talk through what they'd found. She wasn't quite ready to leave. She ran her finger tips along the rim of the bowl, reluctant to let go. She took a last look and offered the bowl to Paul, whose eyes widened as he felt its weight in his hands. Her eyes stayed on it for a long moment after her hands had let go. Finally she broke her gaze and moved toward Silas.

"Don't drop it," she said to Paul, partially joking.

He did not smile. Ed suggested he sit down so the bowl wouldn't have as far to drop.

Silas and Ren headed toward the elk trail and the main road up to Braxton's.

"You okay?" asked Ren, as a hawk dipped toward them.

"Fine."

"All right, then."


Silas did not want to talk. He wanted to watch her walk in front of him—her windbreaker was gone, and if she leaned forward, he could see the concave small of her back—and think of something other than a broken wrist rising out of the ground. It was one thing to sit by the creek at night and listen to a pretty story about friendly ghosts roaming the hills of the canyon. It was another thing to dig up a friendly ghost and see its bones scattered in the dirt. Scattered right where Ren had said to dig.

He hadn't been lying when he said he believed her about the visions. In his experience, plenty of people had dreams and hunches and maybe helpful hallucinations. She was a creative type. If she liked to reconstruct the past and occasionally got lost in her own imaginings, so be it. It was sort of charming, and it was particularly charming when they were lying in bed out of breath. He had had no issues with ghosts last night. But this morning had left him feeling uneasy.

He didn't like finding bones.

When he talked to student groups, he always started with the same line, which he thought he might have plagiarized from some long-ago *Introduction to Archaeology* book: "Archaeology is more than a study of the past—it's a chance to add a new page or a new chapter to the human story." That was what he did. He imagined cities from ruins; he imagined lives from corpses. He gave stories to bones.

But staring at the bones themselves, naked, exposed to the air and the sun and clinical study, he did not feel like he was giving anything. He was taking away. Taking away rest and shade and quiet, and throwing a blinding light on it all. The sight of a burial always left him wanting to apologize, to push dirt back over the bones with his bare hands. He hated this, hated it more because of the inevitable thrill: It was an exciting discovery, an entire skeleton, particularly one with an entire bowl. The giddiness never really quit warring with the guilt.

The bones were slightly yellow, smooth as river stones. A bit porous. When he'd pressed his mouth to Ren's neck the night before, her head thrown back, his beard against her skin, he'd felt her hard clavicle under his cheek.

His mother used to tell him that he managed to see even his strengths as weaknesses. And this was certainly one of his talents: reading the bones themselves. Interpreting power and status and health and age and success and love from the contents of graves. How much time and thought was taken with a body? How much labor was required to dig the grave? What valuables were left behind? Those were clues of status. The teeth could tell you what they ate; the curve of the spine and shoulders gave clues as to what kind of work they had done; multiple bodies gave hints of family ties.

Bodies were often found below living areas, and not even the most precise dating could answer the fundamental question: Were they buried before or after a family stopped sleeping or cooking or working on that same floor? How much crossover was there between the dead and the living? This woman's body was in some-one's home, in what seemed to be a storage room. Her loved ones had buried her, placed the bowl over her face, and then, above her head, inches away from her, in the adjoining rooms or even in the same room, the family had continued. The graves could have been a sign of ownership, a claim of possession. Our space. Our people.

There were things you could know about the living from how they treated the dead. "Everything has to die sometime," Bob Gardner had said. A man who stole bowls from corpses, who had his men till up their bones and rip the burial adornments from their faces, to be sold to men in suits and women in heels who would place the sacred things on marble mantels and shelves with flawless recessed lighting.

Silas had seen Bob Gardner bared like the pelt on the wall, and he'd been horrified by the man. And yet he looked at himself and saw a man who could lift a bowl off a dead woman's face and con-sider how best to analyze it. For posterity, for knowledge—those were the words they used. He did not think the dead woman would know those words.

He and Ren had descended the elk trail without a single word. The main road opened up in front of them, the creek splashing against the stepping-stones a few feet away. Ren stepped into the middle of the creek, both feet on one flat rock. She turned to face him.

"Yes?" he said. The tips of her boots were getting wet.

She reached her hand toward him, and his hand rose up. She slid her straight splayed fingers into his hand, palms not touching, like they were starting a game of "This is the church, this is the steeple." Then she pulled. Hard.

He yelped, taking a step at the last minute so he wouldn't fall into the water. He landed on the edge of her rock, toes on, heels hanging over the water. She scooted backward, offering slightly more rock to stand on.

"You think too much," she said.

If he stepped off, he wasn't sure that even his ankles would get wet. But he jostled on the rock with her, both of them off balance, chests pressed together. He snaked an arm around her waist and pulled her hips against his. She kissed him, eyes open, and he thought she would push him into the water, which would be okay, but he was taking her with him.

She did not push. She took her time, sliding her hand down his back, under his khakis. He tilted to one side, one arm windmilling, and she laughed against his cheek.

He had to admit—she'd broken his train of thought.

When they leaped to the other side of the creek, his mind had cleared somewhat. The bones seemed slightly less vivid in his mind. And so what if they had found the apron and the body right where she had suggested? She had seen something on the ground. She had processed something he had not. Or she had gotten lucky. It was impossible to feel anything alarming as he watched her now, flushed and dusty and smiling, her hand brushing against his as they walked.

"That bowl was made for her," Ren said.

He took a moment to catch up with her thoughts. "Are you that sure?"

"Yes," she said. "My artist knew the woman buried under that room, and she made that bowl for her specifically."

"But you still feel sure that the woman we just found isn't your artist?"

"The bowl looks like it was intended as a burial bowl. The artist could have painted her own burial bowl, I suppose. But there's nothing in the design to suggest the woman depicted is an artist. Nothing to designate her as a potter. No tools buried in the grave. A family member of the artist's, though? A friend? Someone loved and respected? That feels right."

"Mother and daughter?"

"Maybe. I'd lean toward believing that mothers passed along pottery-making to their daughters. And on and on through generations. I don't see how parrots would fit into that scenario. But it could be the artist's mother."

"What about a gift simply as a gesture of respect to someone important?" he asked. "The skirt certainly implies importance. Maybe the artist and this woman weren't particularly close."

"Those lightning bolts around the edges of the bowl—we sometimes see those painted on animals the Mimbreños considered dangerous or worthy of respect. So that fits your theory," she agreed. "But there've been exceptions to the trend of one bowl per burial. Jewelry, shells, tools. If this woman was so powerful, so respected, wouldn't she have had more tributes?"

"Not necessarily. These aren't a materialistic people."

"They've found up to seventeen bowls in one grave. Finding multiple grave goods with the burial would lead me to believe this was about honoring accomplishment. But there's such detail in that bowl. It feels personal to me. I think it speaks to love, not power."

"Hard to tell the difference sometimes, isn't it? But okay. We think there's a connection between the artist and the bird woman.

Could be power. Could be love. Could be something else that we haven't thought of."

She nodded. "But regardless, they knew each other well enough that the artist would design a bowl for the woman with the parrot feathers."

"What if the bowls were made here?" he asked. "What if they were transported down to Crow Creek at some point, but the manufacturing site was here? What if the artist started here?"

"The clay from the first set of bowls came from along the Gila," she said. "It matched beds we found a couple of miles from the Crow Creek site. But that doesn't mean this bowl wasn't made here. It would make sense that the artist was trained by someone from the north or had spent time with Northern Pueblo people. This canyon is certainly a logical intersection point. If she lived at Delgado, she could have seen northern-style pottery being made by the next-door neighbors."

Silas rubbed his chin. "We'll get the clay tested and see if what we found today came from local banks. For now, let's say we have an artist who moved from the Cañada Rosa to Crow Creek. Or maybe vice versa."

"If she learned here, it makes sense she started here," said Ren. She couldn't help picturing the ragged-haired girl at Crow Creek, so young and sure. But there was no proof that the girl was her artist. The artist could have grown up playing in this canyon, splashing in this creek.

"We can't back that up," said Silas firmly. "It's still pure conjecture. Logical, but pure conjecture."

"I thought you were the one who didn't believe in fact. Who thought there were endless possibilities."

He tipped his head at her. "I never said I didn't believe in fact. I said

I was careful about it. Data is fact. What we find is fact. The skeleton and that skirt and the bowls are facts. It's the interpretation that veers off into the land of conjecture. I like to be clear about which is which."

She shrugged her acceptance. If he needed her to stick with hard fact, she could do that. "At some point, the artist either leaves here or comes here. All we know for sure is that she was both here and at Crow Creek. And the parrot woman was here. Surely you're willing to concede that the woman worked with parrots now. That skirt. Plus the feathers in her hair."

Silas stopped. They were at the bottom of the short, steep hill leading to Braxton's house. The Manor, as Ed called it.

"There are no macaws here," he said. "Not a single skeleton of a single macaw. Not a single feather of a single macaw. Other than on your girl there. She was not handling parrots here. There is no evidence to support that."

They started up the hill.

"Then what do you think she was doing?" Ren challenged.

"I don't know. But here, at this site, I do not think it involved parrots."

"You think she handled parrots somewhere else?"

"That's more likely."

"So maybe the parrot woman came from somewhere else, and then moved here. Without her parrots. But the people here still knew her history and buried her accordingly."

"Maybe."

"The parrot woman starts out somewhere else, then comes to the canyon," said Ren. "My artist moves, too, toward Crow Creek or away from it."

They were halfway up the hill with still one curve to round before they could see the house full-on.

Silas slowed his steps. "Is it a more direct link than that?"

"They came here at the same time?" she suggested. "For the same reason? They knew each other *before* they came here? A family who traveled together? Part of the same clan?"

"Any of the above."

She lost her footing for a moment on a patch of gravel, then jogged to catch up to him. "Could it be as simple as drought? A mass movement here at the same time?"

"Could be," he said. "I hope it was. The broader the movement, the bigger the implications."

They had reached the house.

It was not a particularly large house, only one story, adobe, with a red tiled roof. It was as much glass as it was adobe, with wide blocks of windows. Braxton had built his home on an overlook with the valley spread out beneath it. From the vantage point, the green of the willows and the cottonwoods and lush grass by the creek dominated the landscape. The walls of the canyon caught the sun, and the shades of gray and pink, peach and tan—rhyolite in all its tones and moods—shimmered. The dryness muted everything slightly; in wetter years, Silas had seen these greens much deeper, the earth much richer. But the muteness only made the view more of a watercolor, soft and blended and fantastic.

"It would be huge," Silas said, as they approached the front door, "if we could track a migration so specifically. I've got a web of data with northern and southern groups coming and going, but with very few specific dates. If we can track one group of people and know where they came from and when they arrived here, that could anchor the whole map of the canyon."

Braxton had heard their voices through his open windows, and he appeared at the front door just as they stepped on the porch. He clapped Silas on the shoulder and held out a tan hand for Ren to shake.

"I wondered if you were avoiding me," he said. Braxton's hair was still black, falling over his forehead, and his eyes were nearly as dark. The lines around his mouth and eyes were deep, deeper still when he smiled.

"I wondered the same," she answered. "Thank you for letting me come here. For letting us do this."

He waved a hand curtly, shaking his head. Silas had gotten the same response every time he'd tried any expression of gratitude.

"Come in and have some tea or a beer and sit on the back deck with me. After you do whatever it is you need to do. Phone, Silas?"

"Human remains," said Silas. "Just need to call T or C."

"You do that, and I'll fix Ren a drink," Braxton said. "I know Silas won't touch anything serious this early, but maybe you'd like a Corona?"

"Iced tea would be wonderful," she said.

"Damn teetotalers."

"It's ten-thirty," said Silas, looking over his shoulder as he stepped into the shadows of the house.

"You're archaeologists, for God's sake. Didn't anybody ever tell you you're supposed to drink all the time?"

After he made his call, Silas poured himself a glass of tea. He made his way to the deck, which jutted into empty space and hovered over the valley. Ren was nodding at something Braxton said.

"He's going to call me back," Silas said. "In a meeting. I was thinking I'd pull up some articles on macaws while I'm here."

"Fine, of course," said Braxton. "Help yourself to the computer." He turned to Ren. "Satellite connection. Only place in the canyon with access."

"You don't mind being so removed from everything?" she asked. "An hour away from the grocery store? Half an hour from neighbors? No newspaper, no cell phone?"

"I grew up in the wilds of New Mexico a good sixty years ago. Lived about a mile away from Silas's dad, by the way. Not many amenities. Then I moved away, of course, and did a little of this and that."

"By 'this and that,' he means pushed the right buttons on the stock market until it poured out money like a slot machine," said Silas.

"Yes," said Braxton. "Like a slot machine. I was in New York for a while and spent a dozen years in Boston. I miss restaurants and music and good coffee shops. I miss seafood. But look at this place. Sometimes I sit out here in the mornings and I think I can feel myself evaporating, spreading out over the valley and drifting down."

"Like dust," said Silas.

"You lack poetry, Silas Alan Cooper. This place makes you want to be absorbed by it. I never wanted to be absorbed into Boston."

"It's like stepping into a magic wardrobe and winding up in Narnia," Ren said. "Time moves differently here."

Braxton smiled. "Silas loved that book when he was a kid. Is that the one with Turkish delight? He was obsessed with figuring out what Turkish delight was."

Ren chuckled. "He was?"

Something on her face made Braxton's eyes widen slightly, and he glanced quickly at Silas, then back at Ren.

"It's a jelly made of starch and sugar," said Silas.

"Let me tell you something," said Braxton, leaning toward Ren and brushing his fingers against her wrist. "Silas wrote a little song about Turkish delight. He used to carry around an out-of-tune banjo when he was just a tiny thing. He wrote songs about Turkish delight, about a deer named Wild Bill, and, as I recall, about a girl named Mohawk."

Braxton sat back and turned a pleased face toward Silas.

"Thank you very much," said Silas. "That was very helpful."

"I also seem to remember you setting 'The Love Song of J. Alfred Prufrock' to music," Braxton added.

"It makes a good fight song," Silas said to Ren.

"That wasn't so long ago," Braxton said, rubbing a hand along his cheek. "When was it? After your grad work? You were visiting with, ah, Tina."

Braxton was not subtle. He had paused, belatedly, before Tina's name. And as he said it, he looked uncomfortably at Silas, then stared intently at the wall. That led to another pause when it seemed obvious that Ren would ask who Tina was.

Instead, she started describing the bowl and the feather apron they'd found. The moment passed by.

"So just how big is this?" Braxton asked. "This artist's bowl you've found? This body underneath it?"

Neither of them answered. He watched their faces, and his breath hissed out. "That big, huh?"

Soon Silas and Ren said their good-byes. They trotted down the hill with shuffling steps. Slowing down took more effort than speeding up. As the ground evened out and the path opened onto a horse pasture, Ren slowed to a walk, and Silas matched her pace.

"A girl named Mohawk?" she said.

He shrugged. He could see only two horses grazing, but the others must be behind the trees.

"Sing it for me?" she asked.

He kept his eyes on the horses. "I was married."

"You were?" She stopped.

He felt a relief at announcing it, and an annoyance at himself for feeling relief. He did not do well with secrets. He liked things out in the open. For weeks he had considered telling her about his ex-wife, thinking Ren would ask about past relationships at some point and give him a good opening. Braxton had done him a favor by mentioning Tina, and even then Ren had remained oblivious. She had less interest in personal history than anyone he'd ever known. He suspected, if it were up to her, they would confine their conversation, their relationship, to these specific days in this specific canyon. She seemed to have no history of her own, and he mostly liked the challenge of unraveling her, layer by layer. There was a thrill to her opaqueness: She was open to interpretation.

"When I was twenty-nine," he said. "For five years. Tina. She was an anthropologist."

She laughed and started moving again. "We're an inbred kind of bunch, aren't we?"

She had no more questions, of course. He put his arm around her shoulders, and her hair fell over his arm, soft. They walked on.

If Silas was to ask himself why he married Tina and not someone else, he would point to one particular moment: him sitting in a library cubicle, fighting off a headache, with a small-print book on his desk and fluorescent lights beating down on him from the particleboard ceiling. A paper airplane sailed over the wall of the cubicle and hit him on the cheek. He unfolded it, leaning his chair back on two legs to scan the library. He saw no one, but the paper read: "Catch me."

He was in graduate school by then, and they'd already had a handful of dates when she'd launched that plane from behind the nonfiction stacks. He saw a flash of her jean jacket between the shelves and stood up, walking as quickly as possible. When he rounded the corner of the stacks, she was disappearing down another aisle. He had a clear view of her ponytail. He took off running. When he caught up to her, his arm curving around her waist, Tina laughing up at him silently, he thought she was much prettier than he had realized. He felt like he had never really looked at her face before, and he felt off balance.

It had seemed like a sign at the time.

They married just as he started his dissertation. It lasted five years, and they were not a bad five years. But he was gone a lot, and she was gone a lot. There were no more paper airplanes. He never actually finished the dissertation. He got caught up in fieldwork, project after project, and never seemed to find time to sit at his desk long enough. He felt more comfortable in the field, loved the ebb and flow of site work, the reading of signs, the predictive leaps, the pieces eventually sliding together. He had told Tina once that he felt intimidated by his profession, meaning not the work itself but the rituals of scientific one-upsmanship. He disliked conferences. He disliked that when you asked a question after someone's presentation, the point was not to get an answer but to convey the superiority of your own incandescent intellect. He felt unsure of how to ask a question when he simply wanted information. He never felt unsure as he looked over a prehistoric site.

Tina said he needed to work on self-esteem issues and recommended a book with "embrace" in the title. When he thought of her now—when he thought of any of the women in his past—his lack of recall bothered him. Nancy Turner in the eighth grade with her red-brown curls that went in every direction, twisted into a braid when she ran the mile at track meets. Hannah Hightower, whom he dated all through high school, the first girl he slept with. A handful of girlfriends in college. Liz, the nurse he'd dated after his divorce. Gina, the banker who loved the Celtics and cursed like crazy when she was mad. At various points, each woman had felt integral. His head had been filled with her. And then, after it ended, he could not imagine having been with her. Now, at forty, he remembered more specific conversations with his favorite history teacher than he could remember with Hannah Hightower. A perfect image from watching the 2000 NCAA basketball championships—Mateen Cleaves driving the hole with a sprained ankle—seemed clearer to him than any moment in his marriage. The women drifted away or he drifted away, but after some point of intersection they spun off in their own directions, leaving only the smallest traces behind: the citrus smell of Nancy's red hair, Hannah's laugh, Tina's small feet in his lap as he rubbed her arches.

Migrations and abandonments.

When Braxton first invited him to the ranch and he first tromped through the canyon, it had been out of fashion to talk about different groups of people coming and going. The popular notion had been that every group of people was shaped and transformed by the environment around them. Each group had a specific territory, a permanent landscape.

Silas was not sure that he believed in permanent landscapes. He was not sure he believed in one perfect match. Regardless, nothing had been permanent here. Ever-shifting groups came through this canyon, staying for a season or a year or a decade. They came because of water or game or enemies chasing them from a former home. The prehistoric world had been a web of connections: Trade routes allowed for an exchange of food and trinkets and materials across hundreds of miles. Parrots came from Mexico. Mollusk shells from the Gulf of California were shaped into smooth bracelets and worn by women in this canyon. You could trace the networks of connections by the objects you found.

Groups moved among one another, young couples intermarrying, because in a world full of small villages—maybe four or five families living as a group—the gene pool needed livening up frequently. So you had women moving for men, men looking for women, traders selling their merchandise, entire villages uprooting in search of food or water. Of course, there was conflict, a stronger group wiping out a weaker group for a prize section of land. The losers scattered. Or at times groups merged for the greater good.

It was a world of movement and change, souls shifting and drifting and severing ties to place after place. Amid all the paths crossing and families pulled together and apart, most things were left behind. There were no wagons, no pack mules, no wheelbarrows. No wheels. When these people moved, they brought what they could carry. Stone tools and tanned buckskin and a sharpening rock could be packed in a burden basket with a copper bell and a child's doll. What they chose to take with them, what strained their muscles and bowed their shoulders, were the treasures they couldn't bear to lose. If you didn't love it or need it, you left it somewhere along the way.

The medical examiner acknowledged that a prehistoric body had been found. Silas and Ren agreed that they would keep the bowl to study at least temporarily—they would contact the local tribes, who would probably want the bowl back in the ground with the body. But she could examine the bowl herself until they heard from the tribes. Silas wrapped up one of the sherds from where the kill hole was punched to be sent for an analysis of the clay.

They found nothing else around the body. After one last round of photos, they backfilled the room, dumping shovelful after shovelful back into the hole. Even through his gloves, even with his already concrete calluses, Silas ripped blisters into his palms. He poured peroxide on them at night, savoring the sizzling sound.

"Your hands are frothing," she said, as she sank onto the bed. "Does it hurt?"

"No." He frowned. "Not at all. Which sucks, because I feel more confident about it if it hurts. You have any rubbing alcohol?"

"Masochist."

"I do have a bit of a puritanical streak."

She shook her head. "I have no interest in pain."

"Coward."

She was still watching the peroxide bubble on his skin. "I have not noticed this supposed puritanical streak, by the way."

He looked over at her thighs.

"It comes and goes," he said.


*She lay next to him and traced the ridges of his chest, finger sliding up and down over skin and muscle. Wearing a path over the bands of muscles covering his ribs. Hills and vales, she thought. Pectorals. Ribs. Abdomen. Ribs.*

*"What are these?" she asked once.*

*"Ribs."*

*"No, the muscles."*

*He shrugged. She traced, eyes shutting.*

*"They're the part of you that would make barbecue ribs," she said.*

*"Yeah," he said.*

*"I like this." He ran his hand down her shoulder blades, pausing flat and warm at the small of her back, stopping at the curve of her hips.*

*"The dip of my back?"*

*"It's not a dip. It's a reservoir." He traced the curve of it, the thin hardness of her spine and the soft flare. "It's geography."*

*He talked another language when he slept. He fell asleep quickly, effortlessly, while she had to coax sleep to come. But his sleep was rarely silent.*

*"Snee," he said, rolling over, one arm falling hard across her hip.*

*"Snee," she agreed.*

*"You're a Volkswagen flip-top."*

*She liked to repeat his words back and see if he would agree with them. "A Volkswagen flip-top?"*

*"You are," he insisted. "You are, baby. Man. You're a baby man."*

*"Baby man?"*

*"Shaped like a baby. Built like a man."*

Weeks passed. If Ed or Paul noticed where Silas was sleeping, neither commented on it. During the day, everyone stayed focused on what else the ground might offer up.

Sometimes at night Silas could tell that Ren wasn't sleeping, would know when he shuffled to the bathroom after midnight that she was still lying there awake. Her breathing was too shallow, and there was no sleep in her voice when she answered his hello. She would curl against him when he came back to bed, smiling against his shoulder blade. Sometimes in the mornings he would not remember her insomnia, but sometimes he would, and he would try to be quiet and let her steal an extra half-hour of sleep.

One of those mornings while she slept, Silas found Ed on the porch when he walked outside to sip his coffee.

Silas sank into the chair next to Ed.

"Morning, Silas."

"Morning."

"Ren still asleep?"

"I think so. I don't know how anyone who hates mornings so much can manage to do this every day of the week."

"Stubbornness," said Ed.

"Probably."

"If I had a daughter, I'd want her to be just like that one," said Ed. "Smart as a whip, never complains, never takes herself too seriously, kind, generous, willing to try anything."

"You don't have to sell her to me," said Silas. "You're preaching to the choir."

"I think the world of her, is all."

Silas was amused. "Are you asking me what my intentions are, Ed?"

Ed turned to him and held his gaze. Silas had never noticed that Ed's eyes were gray. A pale silvery color that seemed clear as glass.

"No," Ed said. "I'm not. What I am telling you is that as much as I adore that girl, I wouldn't want to fall in love with her."

Silas frowned.

Ed didn't break his stare. "There's something broken in her."

Silas hoped, weakly, that Ed was making some sort of joke, even though it was clear he wasn't. "What are you talking about?"

"You'll make up your own mind," Ed answered. "But I've known

her for nearly twenty years now, and I've seen the men who follow
her around, and I've seen how she looks at them. Something's
broken."

Silas's expression didn't change. "In what way, Ed?"

"I don't know. I don't know why she is like she is, but she's got
some limits."

"I know you mean well, Ed, but ..."

"I don't mean anything. It is what it is. And I hope you'll act like
we never had this conversation. I don't want to hurt Ren. But I see
how you look at her."

He left then, and Silas didn't go after him. He let his coffee grow
cold between his knees. He wanted to work up some anger at what
Ed had said, to deny it or disprove it or at least to laugh it off.
Instead he thought of all that Ren had not said, of the avoidances
and silences and nonanswers. She left nothing about herself unpro-
tected. But that did not have to be brokenness. He wanted to
believe it was no more than reticence.

He didn't like to talk when they were finished, lying wrapped
around each other and trying to catch their breath. He would talk
plenty before and during, telling her how she felt and what he
wanted. Where he wanted her mouth and hands, whether he wanted
her bent over or flat on her back or on her hands and knees. But
when they were finished, he would keep quiet. He kept his eyes
closed and memorized her touch. Her palm skimmed over the
planes and curves of him, over his breastbone and paying careful
attention at his ribs, rising and falling, a wave washing over him. If
he lay alone in bed after she went to take a shower or get a drink, he
could feel the undertow of her fingers.

When she was under him, her lips parted and her eyes nearly
boiling over, he sometimes thought she wanted him to sink into

her, into her skin and bone. Or maybe she wanted to sink into him. Yes, that was how she looked at him—as if at any moment she might leave her body behind, burst out of it and show herself as some new being altogether. She seemed, looking into his eyes, just on the verge of showing him what was under her skin.

# six

*The past speaks in a loud voice.*

—From "The Role of Adaptation in Archaeological
Explanation" by Michael J. O'Brien and Thomas D. Holland,
*American Antiquity*, January 1992

It's raining its brains out," Silas said, staring out over the dirt, now wet and shining. Raindrops tapped a light rhythm on the tin roof, and the willows by the creek were bending in the wind.

Ren smiled. They had woken to the sound of the rain when the sky split open in the middle of the night. It meant a lost day's work at the site, but they had a table full of bags to clean and record. It did not need to be wasted time. Still, here they were on the porch in the late morning, watching the ground drink up the water. The land wouldn't swallow it all—rivulets were streaming across the hard dirt like rain tracks down a windowpane. There was no sun in sight.

Silas was lying at her feet, his arms cushioning his head, because he said he could hear the rain hitting the ground, that it vibrated though the porch floorboards.

"Comfortable?" she asked.

"Like a ripe sponge," he said.

They were alone. Paul was listening to headphones at the kitchen table, and Ed was on the sofa, reading a thick hardback mystery. Ren had been in the canyon for two months. She would have to go back home soon, at least for a couple of weeks.

She did not want to leave, for more than one reason, but for now it was the pottery that gnawed at her. She had missed something. It was there, in the clay and the paint, something that had been shown to her and she had still not seen. Folding her legs under her, she lifted the bowl from its box padded with Bubble Wrap and frowned.

"It's not a magic eight ball," said Silas.

"It sort of is," she said.

"You've stared at it for weeks, and it still hasn't given you the answers."

"That doesn't mean it won't."

She knew every detail on this bowl, every crack and every indentation. Every slight smudge of a line. She had photos of the other bowls she'd found, but it was a different thing to hold this piece in her hands, to fit her palms where the maker had fit hers. Still, feeling it and seeing it only scratched the surface of what it had to tell her. There was the forensics of it, the science of its construction. Clay—maybe from somewhere along this canyon—had been ground into a powder; then water had been added to make it pliable. The clay itself was a clue. To keep the piece from cracking under high heat, temper—bits of stone, crushed pottery, or sand—had to be added to the clay. The temper was a clue. The slip—Mimbreños usually used fine clay that fired white—was a clue. The pigment—hematite-based, iron-laden and dark—was a clue. A sign.

One quick glance told Ren how the piece was made. The artist had rolled out ropes of clay, coiling the ropes around a base, then scraped and smoothed the coils. And the images were visible enough. They were the slipperiest clues, the ones that couldn't be tested and measured. She turned the bowl in her hands. The lightning bolts she knew. And the drawing of the feathers was not unique—straight-lined and geometric. Aerodynamic like an airplane instead of a living bird. It was the eyes that fascinated her, those diamonds inside diamonds with their solid black cores. Those symbols, too, she had seen before, although she had never seen them used as eyes.

The kill hole was small and tidy. Most people thought the hole was punched into the bowl to allow the spirit to escape. Possibly the spirit of the person, possibly the spirit of the bowl. But the hole was crucial to the burial process, to the rebirth process. Spirits had particular opinions about how they liked to conduct their business. Ren wasn't sure they ever really left the ground, though, that they weren't waiting, waiting to rise to the surface when the dirt was disturbed. Maybe they never wanted to escape.

Sometimes the absence of a thing held its own meaning. There were few signs of violence on Mimbres pottery. The archaeological record showed no signs of war, and ceramic images backed up the theory of a fundamentally peaceful people. They did not paint war because they did not know it, or perhaps because they did not want it. Or both.

Another standard absence: For all the imagery of animals, Mimbres artists rarely painted any elements of landscape. Ren saw no sign of place on the bowl she held—no trees or grass or creek or canyon. They were a people who were a part of the land, who lived off it and lived in it. They built their homes into the ground itself, forming the walls from mud and water. And for all their comfort with the earth around them, they did not paint it.

She scanned the landscape—lovely tans and browns and moss greens, all deeper in the rain—and remembered that this land was saved because it was unreachable. If these ridges and valleys had been an easier walk, an easier drive, the bowl sitting beside her would probably be in some private collection by now, the woman's bones tilled back into the soil.

She looked down and noticed Silas had one bare foot dangling off the porch. The rain had covered his toes like dew. He was asleep.

Along with strange absences in the pottery designs, there were strange inclusions. Water animals—fish and turtles and water birds—showed up much more in Mimbres art than made sense for a people who lived in a dry land. But maybe that was because water was a highly prized thing—sacred, even. Perhaps artists' heads were filled with visions of what they couldn't have. They also admired symmetry—an odd thing, really, in a world dominated by chaos and weather and uncertainty. Even their walls were uneven. If life was utterly without pattern, they nonetheless created a perfect balance in art.

These bowls could no doubt hold longing. They could hold all kinds of emotion. Artists loved exaggerating the length of a heron's neck, stretching it into ridiculous loops and curves. The artists' amusement was as thick as the paint. They combined animal bodies to comic effect. And there was something like awe when they drew the curve of the moon into the body of a rabbit, an animal intrinsically linked with the celestial body.

There was a famous Mimbres bowl filled with an image of a potter. It was a meta-bowl, a bowl drawn inside of a bowl, with a human figure that blended into the outline of the bowl. The hands were different, the nose was different, the geometry was different—the artist of that bowl had a very different style from Ren's artist. But she suspected the intent was the same: An homage. A tribute. A remembrance. The potter's bowl was a burial bowl, and no one

disagreed that the dead face it covered was likely the face of the potter herself.

What did Ren's artist feel for the woman she painted?

A sudden movement from Silas caught her attention. He'd
jerked in his sleep, throwing his arm over his head. She looked
down just in time to see his hand knock his empty coffee cup off
the porch. His eyes popped open as the cup fell into the dirt with a
loud crack. It hit a rock—the one rock in all the endless dirt—and
shattered.

She shook her head, ready to tease him. He was, for the most part,
quite athletic, but he had a definite clumsy streak. As she opened her
mouth, he swung his legs off the porch and reached out to pick up
the broken shards. She leaned forward to help him, still smiling;
then she stopped moving altogether. Her smile slipped away. Silas's
wrists turned and flexed as he collected the handful of pieces. She
felt the rush of a new thing, spreading warm under her skin.

The last man before Silas had arms twice as big as hers, with
wrists and ankles that seemed solid as biceps and thigh. Silas's wrists
looked breakable. She was mesmerized by the fragility of his bones.
She could see the wide muscles in his back shift, the hard lines of his
forearms, unyielding—head turned away from the rain, he reached
for the last shard—and yet his wrists could break like coffee cups.

She worried he would cut his fingers.

What Ren did all day, every day, for the last fifteen years, was
read signs. You could see a drought in the tree rings. Hearths
indicated rooms of habitation. The lack of domestic features, especially in a long room, could mean a storage space. Interlocking walls
meant rooms were built at the same time, as opposed to one of them
being added on at a later date. Red-on-white instead of black-on-
white meant a misfire, too much oxygen in the pottery-firing blaze.

Wolfberry preferred disturbed soil, so it could be an indication of caved-in rooms.

An awareness of the pleasing shape of a man's foot, the uneven edges of his teeth, the size of his wrists—she suspected what it meant. It was steadying to focus on the pottery.

As Silas settled back by her feet, she picked up a photo from the chair next to her. She'd taken the photo years ago—it was one of the nested bowls she had discovered at Crow Creek. She called it the twin parrots. It was a bilateral design with a zigzagging black-and-white border. One parrot was in each lobe of the design. The complicated border had two of the same diamond-in-a-diamond symbols that served as the woman's eyes in the newest bowl.

Ren turned the photo in her hands, then reached into a manila envelope to pull out another photo: This bowl she called the practice bowl. It was only six inches across, and Ren hadn't mentioned her unsubstantiated guess to anyone, but she suspected this was one of the earlier bowls the artist had painted. It felt less confident, less complex. There were three thick lines around the rim of the bowl, framing a parrot in the center of the bowl, perched on what seemed to be a branch or a stick. It was a small parrot, maybe three inches tall. Disappearing behind the border, the stick was only partially shown, an outlined shape with what could be leaves or twigs sprouting from one end. The bird's claws wrapped around the stick in two smooth lines.

Ren stared at the two smooth lines. The odd thing was the intersection of the claws and the branch. The claws were off-center from the bird's body. Why would there be such deliberate skewing of anatomy, not in a way that seemed artistic or surreal but simply sloppy?

Ren put down the photo and looked again at the bowl in her lap.

Her gaze landed on the curve of the parrot woman's wrists, palms up, the white bracelets on her arms. The angle of wrist and arm made something prick at Ren's thoughts, an unease, like seeing a familiar face but not remembering the name. She lifted the bowl closer, inches from her nose. The talons on the woman's hands were painted as slightly curved triangles on the tips of the fingers; the fingers themselves were thick and unjointed. They looked more like a stick figure's hands.

Stick.

She felt her body thrum under her skin. She flexed her legs, her muscles suddenly aching to move. Without the shoulders and head and body, the top half of the woman's hand and arm could look very much like a branch. The fingers could look like a tuft of leaves.

Her hands clumsy, Ren grabbed the practice bowl photo again, scraping her knuckles against the wooden bench. She squinted at the abstract lines drawn under the bird's body: It could be a hand. And if so, those weren't the parrot's claws. If that was a hand and an arm, the two white circles in the photo were bracelets just like the shell bracelets worn by the parrot woman on the bowl in her lap. And just like the shell bracelet they had found in the parrot woman's grave. The repetition of the diamond design—in the border on the twin parrot bowl and as the eyes on the newly discovered bowl—could be dismissed as a coincidence. But the bracelets added up to something more. Back when she was crafting bowls at Crow Creek, the artist of the bowls had seen a parrot held by someone with two bracelets on her arm.

The photo fell to the ground, landing next to Silas's shoulder. Ren saw a sharp white flash from the corner of her eye, like the sun glinting off a body of water, like a lightning strike or a tree caught fire, but when she turned, there was nothing but hard rain.

"The artist knew the parrot woman at Crow Creek," she said.

Silas opened his eyes and sat up quickly, leaning back on his palms. He cocked his head, and she showed him the bracelets, holding up the photo next to the bowl itself. She explained the similarities, the way that the branch could just as easily be an arm.

"It explains why the claws are so misaligned," he said. "I think you're right. It's an arm, not a branch."

"It's the parrot woman's arm."

The lines on his forehead deepened. "Maybe all parrot handlers wore bracelets."

"But you know we've seen several images of parrot handlers with no bracelets."

"Just because other artists chose not to paint them doesn't mean there weren't bracelets on other handlers."

"She knew her at Crow Creek," she repeated. "The artist who painted the woman buried up on Delgado saw that same woman handling parrots at Crow Creek."

"I'm not ready to agree to that," he said.

Part of her was glad that he said it, glad that the force of her belief would not sway him. Glad that he had his own force that she would have to navigate. But another part of her thought that he was so clearly wrong, that she could feel the truth of this in her bones, that she was inhaling it in the damp air.

She put down the bowl, carefully, slowly sliding it into its padded box. She opened the screen door and set the box against the wall inside. The door swung shut, and she turned back to him, toward the ridges of the canyon.

"Ren?" he said, when she did not say anything.

It was too small here on this porch. Everything was out there, out where she couldn't see it, beyond the gray haze of the rain. She did not want to stare at the bowl anymore. She knew what it had been trying to tell her. Anything else she needed to know was out under the sky, where the parrot woman had come to her and where she had seen the pastures shift to forests and dry land turn into creeks.

Her tone was playful when she spoke, as if the last five minutes had not happened.

"Want to play in the rain?" she asked.

"Not particularly," he said slowly, confused.

"Come on," she said, and stepped off the porch into the down-pour. She was soaked before he could answer.

"Are you serious?" he asked, standing in one easy movement. "You can't even see where you're stepping. You'll slice your feet to pieces."

Blinking water out of her eyes, she smiled. He did not. He reached for her, leaning off the porch, and she backed away.

"Come on," she said again, a giddiness, a need to move, running through her. "Let's find out what the view's like from the site."

He was not catching her mood at all. "We'd kill ourselves getting up there. Come back up here and dry off."

"The answers are all up there," she said, turning away from him and starting to run. She ran through the dirt yard, now mud, splashing through small streams and large puddles. The rain was coming down in curtains, heavy as the thick cotton of her mother's old-timey costumes, falling down on her shoulders and head. Wet and cool. It was not completely unpleasant with the still-warm air. Her hair grew heavy and slapped against her cheeks, and she was glad she had on shorts, because wet denim would have slowed her. She did not have on shoes, though, and she could feel the rocks cut into her feet, just as Silas had warned her they would. Still she ran, and rain bathed her face.

She crossed the creek, hopping, trying to avoid the sharpest stones, and then she could hear Silas behind her.

"Ren! Stop, goddamn it! Ren!" He called her, and she kept running, on the balls of her feet now, minimizing the amount of skin that touched the ground.

She was at the elk trail, where there was nothing but stone and gravel and cholla. She knew that if she misstepped onto the cholla, the pain in the soft undersides of her feet would be unimaginable. She began the climb up. She could feel the cuts in her feet more intensely, but there was an ecstasy to this. The water was running off her like it was running off the ground. She would not absorb it—she cast it off. She could not see more than a few feet in front of her, and she was wrapped up in the soft, heavy sound of the rain.

She missed a step, didn't see the dark crevice open in the ground. Her toes caught, and she turned her ankle. She cried out but didn't stop. Her thighs hurt, and the bottoms of her feet were slick and sensitized.

"Ren!"

Too fast. She was going too fast, and the gravel was slick, and when her foot didn't find a grip, she slid off to the side, out of control. She tried to steady herself, but her hands only scrabbled against the rocks, breaking one nail off below the quick. Her left foot wedged against one large flat rock and stopped her skidding, and she stood, starting upward again. She was inches from the ledge, maybe thirty feet from the ground.

"Ren!"

He called and called, her name ringing off the rock, and then he stopped calling. It was the silence that finally slowed her. She heard her own panting breath and nothing else, and she felt the forward motion drain from her muscles. She stopped. A stab of pain shot up

her leg from her right foot. She had made it only to the first shelf of
the elk trail, looking over the rocky bottom of the arroyo, but still
endless zigs and zags from the plateau of the top.

The euphoria started to evaporate. When she turned around,
she saw Silas walking back down the hill, facing away from her. She
kept her eyes on him, catching her breath and waiting for him to
turn toward her.

"Wait," she called, after she'd watched him take ten or fifteen steps.

He kept walking.

"Silas," she said, not quite yelling, just wanting him to come
to her.

He stopped and turned.

"What the hell was that?" he asked, and she could hear the anger
in his voice.

If he would come closer, she could answer him, she thought. But
he wasn't moving. So she picked her way down the trail, trying not
to limp, ignoring the pain in her feet. He let her come.

When she was close enough to see the water dripping into his
eyes, he spoke again. "I don't know why I'm still here. If you want to
fall off the mountain, go ahead. I'll be back at the bunkhouse."

He turned and started back down the hill, and she stumbled
after him. It wasn't only anger in his voice, she realized. She had
frightened him. Frightened him so that his jaw was clenched.
Frightened him so badly that he would hardly look at her.

"I had to get out," she said.

He kept walking.

"It's all up there, Silas. I know it is." She hoped he didn't notice
that she was putting all her weight on her left leg. "I couldn't just sit
there. Can't you feel how close we are?"

"You're trying to tell me you ran up a mountain barefoot because you're excited?" He stopped and shook his head. "This wasn't excitement. This was something else."

Her breathing was slowing, and her head was clearing. He had his tennis shoes on, which she knew must be ruined. She felt a pang of regret for his shoes. He must've stopped to grab them, she realized, which would explain why he hadn't caught her sooner. She had seen him run, and he was much faster than she was. At least he was standing still now, listening to her.

"I just wanted to get out in the rain," she said. "I'm sorry."

He wiped the rain from his eyes. He reached for her arm, looping his fingers around her wrist lightly. She had felt his fingertips biting into her hips, smiled against his fingers as he rubbed her cheek raw with his stubble, but now he seemed afraid to touch her.

He pulled her toward him slightly, looking down. "Let me see your feet," he said.

She felt a sudden internal pressure against her ribs, and she thought it might be strong enough to crack bone.

She had been sitting on the bed, putting on her sandals, during the last fight she had with Daniel. It was like him to start a fight while she was sitting down, using his height over her. But she hadn't blamed him, really, knowing he was trying to use whatever he could to even the balance between them.

He wanted something from her, she knew he did, and she was annoyed with him for wanting. He was blond, with long limbs and a wide chest with perfect lines of muscle. For the two years she was with him, she was always thrilled when Daniel undid the first button, then the second, then the third, on his shirt. He was not too handsome— she did not like too handsome—but his torso was flawless.

He loved her, she knew he did.

She sat on the bed, trying to work a prong into a hole, the sandal strap unyielding, and he said, "Will we just do this forever?"

And she thought, Crap. I want a cappuccino even though it has too much sugar but I could get it with skim milk and if we do this now I won't have time to get coffee before my meeting and I thought we just had this conversation last week and I do still love his shirt unbuttoned like that.

"Do what?" she said. Even two years after the discovery of the bowls, they were still running tests on the hundreds of sherds found around the Crow Creek site. The lab had singled out three particular sherds that they thought she should look at just in case they came from the same artist. She knew she shouldn't get her hopes up.

He had some sun on his face from their long run earlier that afternoon. "Did you even hear what I said?"

She immediately knew he was not asking if she had heard his question. He had been talking before the question, taking long strides across the hotel room as he rolled his sleeves up his forearms. She needed only to grab hold of what he had said.

He did not like her pause. "You didn't."

"I did, too," she said, thinking. "You were saying how you could get hardwood floors."

"I said since you like hardwood floors, if we turn the upstairs bedroom into your office, I could take out the carpets and put down hardwoods for you. I could do a lot to that room."

"Right," she said.

"Some men like mysterious, complicated women," he said. "I don't. You won't tell me anything. You don't even hear me sometimes. How can we get married if you're not even here?"

He had not given her a ring yet. The only one who ever had given her a ring, John, had talked much less than Daniel. She wanted to say, Daniel, of course you like mysterious complicated women, you ass. If that's what I am. You obviously like whatever I am, because you're still here, aren't you?

But he wasn't an ass. He was kind. Kinder than she was.

"I want to be married to you," she said. And she did. As long as he didn't talk about it too much. But he was kind. And thoughtful and perfectly smart, and she would surely be foolish not to be in love with him.

"I'm always the one who brings it up," he said.

"What do you want?" she asked.

"I don't know," Daniel said. "But you're not giving it to me."

She respected him for that answer. John would never have said that. He was the first one she let herself stay with, and he was the one she had hurt the most. He had large hands that were always warm. With him, she knew she was giving him nothing, only complaints, and yet he never would acknowledge that he was being shortchanged. Argue more with me, she would say. You agree to everything. Aren't you ever mad at me?

"Sure," John would say, agreeably.

She believed he had not been mad at her. He loved her. And it drove her crazy, the obligation and the boredom and the guilt of it.

She had been twenty-one when she met John, and she should never have taken that ring. She figured that out only later.

"I love you," she said to Daniel that day, and she meant it. "I want you. I want to spend my life with you."

She was considering, as she waited for his reaction, that the artist might have made some of the plainer brownware they'd found, but there was no way to confirm it. The brownware had no paint, no brushstrokes to compare. But she was interested in the question itself of whether this artist worked solely on the artistic pieces or also on undecorated functional pieces.

Daniel finished buttoning his white shirt and covered up his beautiful chest while his green-blue eyes watched her, and she could see the need in them. If he grabbed his things and stormed out and told her he never wanted to see her again, she would still have time to get her cup of coffee. But if he stayed and kept talking, she would have to make do with a Diet Coke from a vending machine.

"That's not what I want," he said, and sank down next to her on the mattress. "I mean, it is, but only partly. But sometimes I feel like I should leave just so I could see if you'd come after me."

She wrapped her arms around him. The fact that all the bowls were parrots made her believe that the artist herself had chosen the design. It was possible she had been told to paint the parrots, but Ren didn't think so. She believed there was a personal connection, at least a preference. And she liked the idea of the woman bent over her clay, considering all the ways to fill the blank space, feeling a flash of satisfaction when she hit on the right image.

Daniel didn't leave, of course. She always did the leaving. It was another month before she knelt beside his chair and said she thought she was being unfair to him. She had learned that a man liked it better if she was below him when she said it was the end of things. She liked to sit close, kneeling, not touching, because she had found that touching could make it worse for him. He would jerk away from her hand on his knee or arm. She would position herself on the carpet, off to the side, so he could stand and leave whenever he liked. If he did not stand and leave, if he wanted to convince her, she would stand and let the veil fall away so he could see how she had already left the room, already left him, and that this conversation was only a courtesy. And then he would leave and he would hate her at least for a while.

The day she ended things with Daniel, he asked why she'd stayed with him.

"Because I loved you," she said.

He didn't comment on the past tense. "No, you didn't," he said.

Daniel hated her permanently. At least she assumed that he did. He never called again, never e-mailed, never responded when she left a message saying she still had some of his clothes and his bike helmet. She was always stunned by the depth of what he seemed to feel, of what all of them seemed to feel.

The rain had slackened. She looked at Silas's mouth and his breakable wrists. He was standing close to the edge, and she had a clear image of him windmilling his arms, teetering, then disappearing off the ledge. If he slipped, it would be too fast for her to do anything but grab for empty air. He would hit the stones in the arroyo below, spines of cactus in his arms and cheeks and fingers, and she would be too far away to do anything but call for him.

This was what Daniel had wanted from her: fear. But she couldn't have summoned that, even if she had wanted to. She never feared the absence he would leave behind.

"I'm going to have to head back to Valle de las Sombras for a while," she said, as if this were a normal conversation not taking place in the middle of a downpour. She tugged him closer to her, farther away from the ledge. "Next Monday or Tuesday, I'm thinking. For a couple of weeks."

He tapped his left shoe against the ground, knocking off a clump of mud. He looked only at his shoes. He didn't pull away from her, but she could feel the tension in his arm. Maybe it was only anger on his face, after all. Maybe his attachments flared fast and bright and faded quickly. That girl Hannah Hightower or his anthropologist wife. Maybe he'd looked at them with the same softness on his face. Maybe he'd told them all the thoughts in his head without them even asking.

"I'm sorry," she said.

"That was insane," he said, his voice as hard as she'd ever heard it. "You could have killed yourself."

She tightened her hold on his arm. "I know. I don't know what to say except I'm sorry."

"You can say you will not do it again."

She took a long time to answer, making sure she meant it. "I won't."

He pulled his arm away from her grip, gently. He rubbed his palm over his chin, and water misted off his beard. "So," he said, "you want some company when you go home?"

"Yeah," she said. "Yeah, I do."


*"Tell me when something's different," Ren said to him. "Tell me what's different than it was with the others."*

*"Everything that's different?" he asked.*

*"Yeah."*

*"Than with all the dozens of women before you?"*

*"Screw you," she said, and brushed the back of her hand against his jaw.*

*"Nobody's ever liked me not to shave before," he said. It struck him as the safest answer. Her own reserve had tempered his need for full disclosure. He did not want to scare her off. Or bore her. He would make her laugh and keep her reaching for him at night, and the rest could come later. "I mean, the stubble thing."*

*"I like it," she said.*

*"I know."*

He was sore from the day, from holding his neck too long at one angle.

*"I need a new body," he said.*

*"I like the one you have."*

*"But it hurts me." He looked back at her, pulling one elbow behind his head. "What if I could have a body that was totally painless, but it was, um, pear-shaped? Wouldn't you rather me be pear-shaped and not be in pain?"*

*"No," she said, running her palm over his hip bones, the flat of his belly, hard thigh muscles.*

He fidgeted again, making the mattress squeak.

*"My shoulders hurt," he said. "And my knees and my neck and the place where my left leg connects to my hip."*

*"Okay, you can have a new body," she said. "A fat, pear-shaped one. Fine."*

*"Thank you."*

Ren came within inches of stepping on a little brown grass snake on her way to Santina Canyon. It had blended perfectly with the sand, and only when it moved did she jump back.

The snake slid past her foot as silently as a ribbon falling through the air, making quick looping curves through the sand. It was perfectly harmless. Silas had tried to get her to take his gun with her—he said hiking alone without it was dangerous—but she didn't want to carry it. Still, she should have been more observant. She had been too lost in, well, not even thought. Lost in non-thought, in blankness. It could be comforting.

You could walk right past Santina Canyon and never know you'd passed it. Silas had shown her the way during her first week at the site—a path that seemed to dead-end into a rock wall actually dead-ended into the hidden entrance to the canyon. Someone— probably a long-dead someone—had carved footholds and hand- holds into the twenty-foot sheer wall, and the first chamber of the canyon appeared huge and solid around a corner just a few steps from the top.

Ren had hiked this canyon a handful of times, most of those with Silas. Going up the wall was satisfying and fairly quick, although going down would take more concentration. She slung her pack over her shoulder and reached for the first hold, moving steadily until she got to the top and needed to push off with her arms and reach with her left foot to cross over to another rock for- mation. A gap between the two rocks showed the gravelly ground below, and it was impossible not to dislodge a few pebbles that clat- tered to the ground in slow motion. It was a gap just large enough for a body to fit through, and Ren always tried to keep her eyes focused on her handholds.

Once the climbing was done, the base of the canyon opened in front of her, with a network of narrow pathways. The paths branched off and inevitably came back together into wide, round areas with towering walls, natural amphitheaters, little Roman Colosseums carved out of rocks. It was an alien world, harsh and sharp, but the colors of it were soft. Rose and tans and golds and yellows and pale pink—the colors of rose gardens, not rocks. It was lovely and claus- trophobic, and only the bright blue sky above kept it from over- whelming her. But she liked to wander through the maze of it all—about two miles before it emptied into an unexpected meadow—and feel the quietness of the stones.

Sometimes she thought that complete silence sharpened her vision, in the same way that she sometimes thought the steady rhythm of hiking might open her mind to potential ghosts.

Sometimes she wondered if she really ever saw anything at all.

She had just turned thirteen when her mother started taking her to church. It was a few months after the accident. Her father stayed home. Ren and her mother sat in the fifth pew from the front, behind the lady in the green furry hat. The hat covered the lady's eyebrows completely. At the front of the church, behind the pastor, behind the choir, a stained-glass window showed Jesus on a throne. His hands were extended, palms up. His face was kind but strong, not pale and emaciated like other Jesuses she had seen. She liked this Jesus. She liked the pastor, who would talk about grace and mercy and faith and salvation, all beautiful words that she liked to roll around her mouth. He gave a sermon on the gifts we receive from God. He meant abilities, not actual presents. These gifts were manifestations of the Spirit, and they were different for each person—the gifts of wisdom or faith or healing or prophesying or interpreting or miraculous powers—but they were to be used for the common good. She liked this. She looked up the word "manifestation" when she went home and decided Scott could be one.

She did not look for solace in church the way her mother did. Her mother needed to know that there was something after death; she needed to be reminded of it, promised it, convinced of it. Ren didn't need convincing. So she looked at the stained glass. Jesus and his throne were in the center of the window, and they were the simplest part of the design. A ring of disks surrounded the throne, framing it in vivid blues, reds, and yellows with the sunlight streaming through. There was a different image inside each perfect circle, and they reminded Ren of foreign coins that someone had melted into glass. There were angels and unrecognizable beasts and horses and doves. There was a bird with the head of a blue-eyed man. There was a blood-colored horse with the golden head of a lion. There was a woman with the wings of an eagle.

She would stare at Jesus and imagine him coming to life, stepping from the window into air, floating over the heads of the church members. She would reach up, and his robe would brush against the tips of her fingers. He would look down at her and put his hand on her head.

This fantasy had many endings, depending on the Sunday. Sometimes Jesus would lift a hand and the window would vanish. A great gleaming round doorway to another place would open where the window had been. The doorway would shine with something soft like candlelight and a strong sweet wind would blow. The doorway did not lead to heaven. It led to another world, and anyone who wanted to walk through it could go, but the catch was that Jesus would not tell you anything about the other world. It was a blind leap. Ren always chose to go—sometimes she was the only one in the whole church to go. She would discover that the world on the other side of the window was full of warriors and sorcery and magic.

On some Sundays no doorway was revealed. Sometimes Jesus set the church aflame, and fireballs rained down from the arched ceiling. Ren would save her mother by dragging her out of the church, dodging the falling fire, and pushing her mother into the safe open air. Then Ren would save others, lowering them out the windows and heading back for more. Sometimes Jesus would take the rainbow light from the stained glass, leach it right from the window itself, and let it pour down on Ren. She would feel the warm light soak into her skin, and everyone would look at her and know that she was chosen.

One Sunday, the stained-glass Jesus moved. Actually moved. It did not happen as Ren had imagined it. It started with only a twitch of his finger. It was no fantasy, not at all like her daydreams—the movement of his finger was as concrete and undeniable as the rustle of the pastor's papers on the lectern. Ren looked up at her mother to see if she had noticed Jesus, but her mother was staring straight ahead at the pastor. Ren looked back at Jesus's fingers—they all moved this time, beckoning to her. Come. Come here. Come to me. She looked to his face, to his kind mouth and sharp cheekbones, but he showed no expression. Then one of the brilliant circles—the one with the winged woman—flew out of the window, sailing like a Frisbee into the crowd, then shattering against the back wall of the church. A round hole was left in the stained glass, and behind the hole there was only blackness. A cold wind blew from the empty space. Jesus blinked. He did not meet Ren's stare. The circles began to break free, one by one, spinning in the air, sunlight still inside them. They smashed and turned to dust over the pews, over the gray marble floors, over the suit coats of men, and over a furry green hat. The glass broke hard against wood and skin, shards flying, blood-red and eye-blue, but no one made a sound. No one screamed. No one ran. No one even looked away from the pastor.

It was the lack of reaction that made Ren realize she was wrong, that nothing she was seeing was really happening. She squeaked, but she held the small sound inside her mouth, the way dogs could sound during thunderstorms. She was breathing heavily, pulse knocking inside her throat, and because of either the squeak or the breathing, her mother looked down at her and frowned. Ren lowered her eyes. She could see amber-colored pieces of glass by her feet, with the red tail of a horse in one of the pieces. The pieces had swirls of color like gasoline in rain puddles, and the swirls were moving. The air was frigid from the wind blowing through the empty circles in the window. Ren shivered and tried to control her breathing. She closed her eyes and squeezed her numb hands together.

She could feel a small thin cut on her thumb, along the lines of her knuckle.

When she looked up, the circles were back in the stained glass where they belonged. Jesus was still. She did not trust anything she saw anymore, though. She did not know what was real and what was only falling glass. She refused to go inside the church again. Her mother did not argue with her.

At one of the larger amphitheaters, she found a flat rock almost perpendicular to another tall rock. Both were slightly warm from the sun. She sat down, hugging her knees to her chest, leaning back against the L shape of the rocks. This close to the rocks, she could see the striations in a single broad boulder, dark pink bands and yellow stripes, swaths of color side by side.

She pulled off her shoes and socks, checking the bandage wrapped around the ball of her right foot. She'd been afraid she needed stitches, but the gash was healing up nicely. She pulled off her hat and sat on the rock, lifting her face to the sun.

She heard the tune to "Just Like a Woman" before she saw Scott. He cast no shadow, so she could only tell he was getting closer by the song growing louder. Then she saw him from the corner of her eye, just his legs and feet at first, until she turned her head and looked up at his face. He smiled and sat beside her, on the edge of her rock chair, making no sound other than his song.

"I wondered where you'd been," she said. "It's been days." She always saw him more often when she was on-site. At home, in her flat-roofed bungalow, she sometimes went weeks without hearing the hum of his voice.

"*. . . just like a little girl,*" he sang. He added an instrumental "da-da-da-da-da-da-da-da-da-da" at the end.

"You could have asked for a better voice if you were going to haunt me." She shifted on her rock, crossing her legs and facing him.

He never aged. His hair was always the same length—a little too long, flopping over his eyebrows, shaggy over his ears and down his neck. He still had an awkwardness in the slump of his shoulders. His legs seemed to be in his way. His face was perfectly smooth. He always looked just as he had when he left her.

"Do 'Dark Eyes,'" she said.

It had been her favorite Dylan song to fall asleep to. Before the accident. She once upon a time had a favorite Dylan song for each of a wide range of activities. She liked to lie awake to "Ballad of a Thin Man." She had selections for brushing her teeth, for jumping on her bed, for drawing on her notepad, for remembering.

Scott obliged, leaning in, eyes too sincere, arms thrown out with jazz-hand palms. She giggled, tempted to touch him, knowing better than to try. She covered her mouth with her hand as she laughed, a gesture she did not use anymore. All the girls in sixth grade had covered their mouths demurely at the first sign of giggles—it was a tic that her mother had loathed. Her mother said if you want to laugh, laugh. If you want to be mad, be mad. Don't cover it all up like you're ashamed of feeling something. Put your hand down, Ren, put your hand down. Let us see you.

"Sing it for real, Scotty," she demanded, behind her hand.

He sat straighter, looking toward the ground, not her. "*I live in another world, where life and death are memorized / Where the earth is strung with lovers pearls and all I see are dark eyes.*"

His hair caught the sun, gold for a moment, as Silas had said hers sometimes did. She'd always coveted Scott's hair. When he'd run, when he'd chase her—back when she was half as tall as he was—and she was slow to turn away, she would see his hair rise and fall in a single short sheet, thick and straight. She'd loved to touch it, thread her fingers through it, when he hugged her good night.

His eyes shifted to hers again, and she missed him. She missed sharing a look with him when their parents' backs were turned—she missed him kicking her under the table. She missed how he would pick her up in a fireman's carry and walk through every room of the house, nearly banging her head against doorways.

A story her mother told her: When Ren was nearly three, she hit a rebellious stage. Prior to that, she'd been consistently adorable, and Scott was fed up with it. He got spanked, got sent to his room for talking back, got lectured on saying "Thank you" and "Please," and Ren got nothing but cuddled. But when she learned to scream "No" and throw herself on the ground and dig her fingers into the carpet for leverage, she started getting her bottom slapped and her hand popped and her blanket—she called it a bah—taken away. Scott was delighted at first. He would appear when he heard a tantrum and prompt, "You should spank her, Mom. Or take her bah away. You should take her bah away."

And they would take the blanket away, and she would cry. And he would laugh. Then the laughing would stop. He would start saying, pleading, "I'm gonna give her the blanket back, okay? She's been punished enough, okay?" And he would pat her head like she was a terrier, kiss her cheeks, hold her in his lap while she yanked at the holes in his jeans.

It's only a story—Ren doesn't remember any of it. It is not that they were particularly close. They were not friends—they were brother and sister. It was something not as smooth as love between them. Maybe they didn't even like each other. She had certainly hated him at times, hated him for always doing everything faster and smarter and better and first. But he knew her when things were still right. He knew her when their parents were right. He knew her when she was right. He was the only one who could see what happened, how things had changed, only he was dead by then. But he still remembered. He was still right, the only right thing left. She loved him for that.

"*Some mother's child has gone astray, she can't find him anywhere,*" he sang. "*But I can hear another drum beating for the dead that rise / Whom nature's beast fears as they come, and all I see are dark eyes.*"

She felt a chill, a tremble along the surface of her arms and shoulders. "I do love your voice. I always did. It has character. And feeling. Dylan doesn't have a very good voice, either."

He frowned at her.

"Well, he doesn't, technically."

He leaned one shoulder against the wall of rock, draping an arm over his folded knee, looking up at her. Once upon a time, he would have tickled her next. That look of affection had always led to bottom-of-the-feet attacks.

"Silas is getting gas for the trucks, and I told him I wanted to take the afternoon to hike," she said. "We're all going home for a little while to catch up on phone calls and e-mails and sleep and stuff. Then we'll come back."

He looked puzzled.

"I have real work to do that pays me money. But we'll come back before the month's over." She rubbed a popped blister on her palm. "So do you like him? Silas?"

Scott tilted his head, fondness back on his face. Fondness and something more painful.

"I like him," she answered. She looked at her brother, smiling as his silky hair brushed against rock. "Is he a good man?"

She couldn't read his face.

"I think he is," she said. "I think it's different this time, Scott."

He leaned forward, his forehead nearly touching hers. His eyebrows were in disarray.

"Could you maybe find some of his dead family members and pump them for information?" she asked.

Sometimes when he came to her, time seemed to waver. She could almost see it quiver, like heat waves rising off asphalt. It was as if she had a fever that crept up degree by degree, not noticeable at all when he first appeared. But the longer she looked at his face, the less steady the rest of the world seemed. Now her head felt fuzzy. She did not know if he had been beside her for minutes or hours. Her fingers felt thick and swollen, as if the circulation to her hands had been cut off. She rubbed at her temples again, and when she looked up, he was gone. Her cheeks felt like they might have blistered. She reached for her hat, and her fever lifted slowly.

She took a long swallow of warm water and reached for a bag of peanuts in her pack. She heard a noise behind her. She thought Scott had come back, and she half turned.

It wasn't Scott. There was a rustle of bright feathers, and a movement of legs. The woman stepped onto the rock, her sandaled feet a hand's length from Ren's hip. The yucca cords between her toes were dusty and starting to fray.

Ren looked up, recognizing the woman by her skirt but wanting a better look at her face. The woman's torso was solid and strong, a small wrinkle of fat or muscle pressing against the band of the feathers. Her two bracelets were fixed in place around her forearm. The undersides of her small breasts lay flat against her rib cage. Her chin was sharp, and there was no paint on her face this time.

Then there was heat against Ren's back, so much heat that she was afraid her skin would scorch. She spun on the rock and saw a fire in the open dirt, between the clumps of rocks. There was too much smoke for her to see it clearly—her eyes burned. But it was roaring, burning fast and hard.

A young woman, slender with long legs, was sitting near the fire, cross-legged. She was sweating from the heat of the fire, beads dripping from her forehead into the dirt. She was hunched over a bowl. Her knuckles were scabbed over in places, freshly bloodied in others. She held a stripped piece of yucca in her hand, and the end of the plant was in her mouth. She chewed contemplatively, large eyes glancing at the older woman, at the sky, at the high walls of the canyon. Ren could see her face. It was the girl she had seen cut off her hair in the river. She was several years older, in her late teens or perhaps early twenties, with her hair thick and long again.

This was unusual, this crowd of ghosts dropping by for social calls.

The girl wore her dark hair in a loose braid, and the apron around her waist was more standard than the older woman's. A braided brown belt—plant fibers, probably also yucca—held a bundle of cords in place. The cords were tucked between her legs and hung over the belt at the small of her back, arcing and spreading across the dirt like a drab tail. As plumage went, it paled in comparison to the parrot skirt's brilliant rainbow.

The unfinished bowl in her lap explained the heat of the fire— finished and dried pieces must be in the blaze, baking, layered between broken bits of pottery. The fire was piled with enough fuel to suck up all the oxygen, leaving not the slightest draft of oxygen to tinge the black color of the paint.

The end of the yucca brush had grown pliable enough, apparently, because when the girl pulled it from her mouth and nudged it with the pad of one finger, she seemed satisfied. Holding it between her thumb and two fingers, she dabbed it in a small clay jar, then pulled the brush across the interior of the bowl in a long movement followed by several shorter dashes.

Her eyes did not leave the bowl once the brush touched the paint. A frown line appeared by each eyebrow, making an upside-down V over her nose as she concentrated. She did not look as if she smiled easily or often. Her face was harder than it had been when Ren had seen her at Crow Creek.

The older woman stood, legs apart, watching the younger girl. Ren scooted toward her, across the rock, trying to read the woman's expression. Her face was soft, fond, proud. Ren could see the wrinkles around the woman's eyes, deeply set, plus laugh lines etched around her mouth. It was a mouth that had smiled often. This woman certainly was old enough to be the young woman's mother.

The older woman looked down at Ren sharply, holding her gaze for a moment, and Ren was sure the woman could see her.

But the parrot woman looked away and called to the girl—Ren couldn't really make out the sounds, much less the words—stepping nimbly from the rock and pointing toward the bowl being painted. The girl shook her head, and the woman mouthed something more emphatically. The girl gestured for the woman to go away. The girl did not look away from her bowl, and Ren couldn't tell if she was angry or amused.

The parrot woman did not step away. But she did stop speaking. For a moment, the girl painted silently, and the woman stood by her side, watching. Then the woman raised her fingers to her mouth, squashing her lips together, making them flat and wide. She rolled her eyes and in general made herself ridiculous. She seemed to have a problem with some part of the bowl.

Ren rose from her rock and walked toward the painter. She took a wide route around the fire, still flinching at the heat, and came up behind the girl. She could see the head of a parrot taking shape in the bowl, and the last pull of the brush had finished the beak. It was a style of beak Ren recognized instantly.

She heard the clap of the other woman's hands and jumped. The girl looked up quickly, nearly smudging the paint.

A parrot flew down, from a tree or a rock or from thin air, Ren wasn't sure. The woman held up her arm, and her two bracelets rattled against each other. The parrot landed between her elbow and her wrist. Ren again noticed the small scars along the woman's arms.

The woman whispered in the parrot's ear. It squawked twice, then ducked its head.

"Ly-nay," it called out. "Ly-nay. Ly-nay."

Apparently, Ren thought, she could hear words if parrots spoke them.

Now the girl laughed, showing white teeth, with the bottom row slightly crooked. It was a short, quiet laugh, let out on an exhale. Ren suspected the parrot had said her name.

"Non," said the parrot next, and the older woman tipped her head in acknowledgment. She turned her head to the side, mimicking the pose of the parrot.

"Non Non Non Non Non Non Non Non," chattered the parrot, steady as an alarm clock. "Ly-nay. Non."

Then the woman—Non, Ren assumed—placed two fingers under the bird's beak, lifting its head. She said something to the girl, jerking her head toward the parrot, holding her forefinger close to her thumb.

"You think she drew the beak too big, don't you?" Ren said.

Both women looked toward her. The woman made a shuft-shuft sound to the parrot, and it flew to a tall basket Ren hadn't noticed among the rocks. The girl, Lynay, stood, carefully placing the bowl on the ground, and Non held out an arm toward her. Arms linked, they took a step toward Ren.

Ren took a step back, bringing her closer to the heat of the fire. It was still bright daylight, but somehow the older woman's face seemed cast in shadow. She knew they could see her. They were looking right at her, still walking toward her. If she backed up more, she would be in the fire.

They were only ghosts. They were only shadows that she could see when the light fell just right, and they would be gone soon. But she was afraid nonetheless. She was not used to this attention. She assessed the dead: They did not assess her. When she met the stares of Lynay and Non, she felt less substantial.

Lynay showed her crooked teeth, opening her mouth to speak. But the older woman placed a hand on the top of her head, and Lynay closed her mouth. They both stopped moving. All the women, living and dead, stood still.

"What do you want?" Ren asked. She was pleased that her voice sounded strong and sure.

"You will lose him," Non said. The smoke circled her hair.

"What?" said Ren. The fact that the woman answered her and that she answered in English kept the meaning of the words from penetrating. They were only sounds.

"You will lose him," Non repeated calmly. "There is nothing you can do."

THE PARROTS CAME FIRST. They were splashes of paint in the air. Lynay had never seen one until the day that Non came, announced by the parrots. They came as a pair, circling, and Lynay called to her mother and asked what they were, knowing they had too much red and blue to be hawks or eagles, were too big to be firebirds or jays.

This is what Lynay noticed about Non: The air around her vibrated, as with heat. Years passed before she realized that not everyone found Non beautiful, that it wasn't something undeniable like small feet or long hair. Non made no noise when she walked. Her thighs were long and muscled like a large cat's. Her teeth were large, and she was missing none of them. When her wide mouth smiled, her teeth formed a white wall.

It was not unusual for a woman with sons of the right age to make the journey to find suitable women. It was a helpful bargaining piece for a man to have his mother with him, to have some visible sign that he was of a good family, that he had connections of his own. It meant something to the women of a place to know the beginnings of a man who would be climbing down their ladder, laying his sleeping mat next to one of their daughters'. Of course, many men came by themselves, small clouds of dust announcing they were coming to Women Crying.

What was unusual about Non arriving, other than the parrots, was that she came alone with her sons. The traveling groups were usually larger. Mothers needed someone to accompany them on the way back to their own people if their sons did indeed find women. No mother would stay with her sons. But obviously Non intended to do that.

She came with her bright waving apron and her hair threaded with red and blue and green feathers and her jangling shell bracelets and a basket on her head and one on her back. She came with two boys and two parrots. After a few seasons, she would have only one of the four left to her.

The men and women of the village, the older ones who always knew of things without being told because the wind brought all secrets to them, whispered that there had been trouble, that Non had been someone of considerable power in a large place farther north. But the water had gone dry, and even Non and her parrots and all the power their feathers brought could not make the water return. The elder men and women said Non had a daughter and the daughter had been chosen for one of the blessing ceremonies, the killing ceremonies, and Non had turned dark after that. She refused to intercede on her village's behalf anymore. She had closed the door on top of her head, so she would no longer listen to the will of the Creator. But because of her power, her village was afraid to punish her. Instead they asked her to leave, which she was quick to do. She headed south with her sons.

Now the elders in Lynay's village were forced to decide whether to welcome this woman or to turn her away. Either decision had certain dangers.

Here was the essence of Non's power, as Lynay knew on

that very first day: She charmed the parrots, and the parrots charmed the earth into blooming. Lynay had known colors as long as she could remember. She tried to capture the colors even in black and white, capture the movement of water and the blue of sky, but these birds were made of the most fundamental colors—sky, blood, sun. And this woman who could touch the birds also had her hands on all the rest. Lynay loved her immediately. She hungered for her attention, for the touch of her hand, for her strong-toothed smile.

The day that Non came. Lynay always came back to it. It was the best of days, before she had lost anything, with everything laid out before her. This was the day that shaped all that followed. It was a sharp point inserted, and the rest of her life flowed around it, shifting and molding to accommodate the edges of the one day.

Her mother was still with her on that day. And she saw her man that day, the first and the best of them. Non's son. He was not a man then, not quite yet. His arms were too long and his waist too thin. She could see the stark lines of his ribs and thought he needed to eat, thought Non and the two thin boys must have stopped because they needed food, although later she realized that the boy was thin because he was always moving, running, throwing. She had drawn close to look at Non, but she could tell that the boy liked her, because he would not look at her while she looked at him. Still, she could feel the brush of his looks like blades of grass on her skin. She had no eyes for him at all. She had eyes only for his mother, who she thought had risen from the earth or from the trees.

Later she had eyes for him. Later the softness in his eyes

made her lower her head to his hip bones and taste his skin. Later she would long to feel his hair drag along her shoulder blades and to feel his body press her into the earth.

Later still, she would press flowers over his closed eyes, flowers over his closed lips.

Perhaps that is how it happened. Perhaps that is the pattern hidden under the surface, waiting to be revealed.

Or perhaps she never really loved him. Perhaps she never even noticed him that day. Perhaps he accepted her later only because his mother pressed him to do so.

When things are written in the sand, the wind blows them away. And Lynay's story was written in the earth, hidden in the fickle dirt. So every piece of her story could be blown this way and that, a thousand different directions. Countless possible patterns.

What is true is the bones that lay in the earth. The bones of her man, the bones of her children. So perhaps the best story is the one that is the most pleasant to hear, the story that gives her back something other than bones. We'll say he had loved her from that first moment when she was smitten with his mother, had memorized her wide dark eyes and the fragility of her face. Her small face was far more delicate than her broad, strong shoulders and jumping-leaping legs.

This is what she remembered as her first conversation with him:

"Why did you come here?" she asked, fingering a bone bracelet that shattered only days later, when she went climbing to fetch sage.

He did not meet her eyes. "She said it was necessary."

"Will you stay for good?"

"If no one argues. At our old home, no one could argue with her. She hopes it will be the same here."

"You mean because she has power over the birds?"

He shrugged his bony shoulders, still not looking at her. "She does not have power over them. They share the same power. All the women in our family have it."

"The women in our family are makers," she said.

His eyes widened and met hers.

"What are you called?" he asked, and touched the cool hardness of her bracelet. She did not move her arm.

Or maybe that wasn't her memory at all. Depending on how the bones scatter, a different story is told. This also could have been their first conversation.

Non was surrounded by the elders, only the blue-red-yellow tips on her head showing. The boy was standing by himself, and no one noticed when she approached him. He was bouncing, up and down up and down, on the balls of his feet. This made his head swing forward and back, like a woodpecker's.

"She is your mother?" Lynay asked.

He stilled but did not look at Non. "Yes."

"Where did you come from?"

He lifted his chin and jerked his head to the north. "A long way. Over the mountain. Twelve days' walking. We were very strong and fast."

"She raises the birds?"

His chin was still lifted as he spoke. "They come when she calls. They follow her even when she doesn't call." He was bragging. "When we left, dozens of them came after us. They pulled free of their tethers, and she had to sing them back to their pen. They covered the pen with five cloths so that the birds couldn't see her leave."

She did not like this boy. He thought his mother's importance was his own. He was only a duckling tottering behind her.

"Do they follow you?" she asked. "The birds?"

He looked away and focused on his mother and the group of elders.

"My mother shapes the clay," Lynay said. "She is the maker here, and no one else has the skill. She's teaching me."

Of course the elders let Non stay. She could bring blessings to the village if she chose, and they needed more water. For as long as Lynay could remember, it had grown drier and drier, the creek shrinking smaller and smaller. Rain was a loved one who visited rarely. The most powerful songs and dances had not lured it home. The last crop of squash had been small and withered, growing like old men's toes on the vines.

And even if Non did not have her power anymore, or even if she chose not to intercede for the village, her boys were fast and strong and intelligent. They would be fine additions. They could work hard in the fields, run fast to catch the hard-to-find game. The older one—the one whom Lynay would choose—seemed serious and quiet at first, while the younger one could not stop smiling. He existed only on the edge of Lynay's days and nights. He was no part of her story.

Or perhaps she liked him better. Perhaps he ignored her and the lack of attention was more attractive than his brother's attentiveness. Perhaps she settled on her owlet only as a second choice, trying to make his younger brother jealous.

Non soon noticed this girl with clay on her hands, noticed the girl was always following her, either with her feet or with her eyes. The others in the village noticed as well and smiled or shook their heads, and even Lynay's mother noticed, although she was not offended. She was at first nervous that this new woman with the straight shoulders and strange tones of the north in her voice would be offended by a girl always lurking around. When Non, unexpectedly, welcomed the girl's company, Lynay's mother was proud and pleased by the attention shown to her daughter.

This is how Non first addressed Lynay:

"Do you want to come closer?"

Lynay could only move her head in an unsteady way. She had been watching Non feed the parrots nuts and chokecherries. The bracelets on her arm clicked together as the two beaks reached for food. Non was often alone—no woman came to grind corn on her rooftop or to weave strips of yucca by her side.

"What are their names?" asked Lynay.

"They haven't told me," said Non. "But I call this one, the female, Early Waking. I call this one, the male, Empty Stomach."

It had taken Lynay days of watching before she could tell the birds apart. Empty Stomach was the fatter of the two, and she thought she understood how he had earned his name.

Standing next to Non, Lynay had never been so close to a living bird, not one so still and quiet, where she could learn all the lines and curves of it. Their eyes were perfect circles like bowls, and the colors in the feathers shifted like wet paint in the sunlight. They had patterns of dots around their eyes like ants walking. Four curving toes on each foot, with skin more like lizard than bird.

"Would you like to feed one?" Non asked, and her voice was different from her face. Her voice was gentle, easing into the ears and pooling somewhere in Lynay's throat. She found it difficult to speak with Non's voice in her throat.

"Yes," Lynay said.

"Hold out your hand and keep the palm flat," said Non, and dropped four piñon nuts into her hand. Lynay watched Empty Stomach's eyes, how the dark circles inside the yellow swelled and then retracted, pulsing.

Non began to show Lynay the ways to avoid sharp beaks and curved claws. She showed her how to call the parrots, how to win them over, how to be quiet and calm and let them learn to trust her.

Lynay started making small parrots out of clay, playthings only. Her mother did not object; rather, she called them clever and correct. By "correct," she meant that Lynay had captured the thing well. It was easy to shape a piece of clay to look like a parrot, but it was another thing altogether to capture what made a parrot a parrot. This basic parrot, in Lynay's mind, was about the movement of feathers and the brightness of color and sharp eyes and beak. That had to come through in the paint and the clay. She wanted to capture the softness of the feathers at Early Waking's throat and the lushness of her tail. She wanted to capture that the beaks looked like stone, not like living matter. And yet the beak and claws were always moving and reaching, always grabbing and pulling with the parrot in tow behind.

She was captivated by the birds.

It was Lynay's thirteenth summer when Non came with her two boys. The next summer was the summer that Lynay's mother lost her breath altogether. First she was too weak to reach for the clay. This was a very bad thing, because no one else among them shaped and painted the clay, and her mother had not yet taught her everything. Her mother could not be taken yet. The wise one came and laid his hands on her head, her heart, her belly, to see where the illness was centered, but he could not feel the place of attack. Her mother grew weak until her arms could not lift a water jar and her fingers could barely curl around a bowl. As her mother grew stiller, Lynay also turned immobile. Her mind could not spit out the thoughts that would tell her legs to walk or tell her body to lie down and sleep or tell her mouth to chew. She sat by her mother, and that was all. But by the end all her mother would drink was willow tea, and for some reason this request, this longing for the bitterness of the tea, loosened Lynay's feet from the ground. She and only she would brew tea. She thought of nothing but tea.

There was a skill to making it. She looked for tips with swollen buds and cut them off into lengths as long as from her elbow to her wrist. The buds held the strength of the tea. She ground buds and stems into a pulp, then left the willow mush soaking in boiled water. When the water was cool to the touch, Lynay would strain it through a tightly woven basket, letting it trickle into her mother's favorite drinking bowl, which was smooth and worn and easy for her mother to hold with two hands. She was careful with the straining, catching every bit of twig and greenery, and only a dusting of pollen floated to the top of the willow water. Her mother would drink it down, not very fast, over the course of an entire afternoon or a long uncomfortable night, and Lynay would watch her throat work.

Lynay could never again stand the taste of willow tea after those months.

The tea and all the months of praying and chanting did not work. Her mother went into the ground and on to the next world. Lynay picked the burial flowers. She chose the burial bowl, an old favorite of her mother's that captured the patterns of the wind, and she handed it over to the wise ones, who would place and punch the hole into it that would allow her mother's spirit to escape.

Her mother had told her that makers had been touched by the finger of the Creator, that his fingertip had rested on the top of Lynay's head as she was born and had left the indentation of her soft spot. That was why makers could see the patterns in things—the Creator had commanded the door on top of their heads to open wide so that his voice would be heard. His voice would sound inside their heads, and all manner of other things would pour inside—the way the ripples spread through the water, the lift of a hawk's head, the endless mica bits in a woman's eye, the whorls of a footprint. These things would all come out in the clay.

Lynay did not want to keep her door open. She did not like the sad voices in her head and the pictures they painted. She wanted silence in her head—it was too full. She did not want to let anything in anymore. As she walked down to the water three days after her mother was put in the ground, she remembered what Non had told her of parrots. Their feathers held their power, and if they were killed in a respectful way that pleased the Creator, those who took the feathers would then hold the power. The feathers were plucked from both the wings and the tail, and the power was plucked off along with them. The parrot would go into the next world as something other than a parrot. Its being had been changed. Its gifts had been taken.

Perhaps she could cut off her own gift. Perhaps she could deplume herself and change her being. Close her door.

She walked down to the water and found a sharp rock. Non found her, hair jagged, as she walked back to the village. She had felt relieved from the weight of her hair. Free. Non knelt beside her and called her a word in the language of the north: *multa*. Warrior girl, she said. And then Non brought her back down to the water and washed off the loose hair, passing her palms over Lynay's scalp as the water flowed over it and pretending she did not see Lynay cry. Lynay did not cry in front of anyone else.

"You cannot close the door," Non said. "It always breaks open again. Eventually. Or you will break open yourself."

No one mentioned her hacked hair, not even the sharp-elbowed boys who kicked dirt as you walked past, and she suspected Non had something to do with this circumspection.

Here was one question Lynay would have liked to ask the stars themselves—if her mother had lived, would Non have held so much space inside her? After Lynay's mother was gone, Non expanded and filled her whole chest and heart. Until Lynay's man carved out some space for himself in her chest.

Lynay's brothers were already joined to women, and her grandmother had died many years before, so Lynay lived alone for a short period of time in the two rooms she and her mother had shared. She visited Non often, and on one of these visits she saw the two bowls Non had brought from her home in the north. They were not everyday bowls, so they were not left on the roof filled with corn or beans. They were kept inside the storeroom, resting in their carved-out spaces in the floor.

Lynay had come into the room to fetch a scraping tool for Non, and when she saw the bowls, she yelped loudly enough for Non to hear, then bounded up to the roof, breathless. Why had Non not shown her these treasures before? Non said it had not occurred to her—these bowls were certainly no better than the ones Lynay and her mother had created. And in fact she found Lynay's art to be more striking.

Better or worse did not matter, Lynay had answered. What mattered was that she had never seen bowls like these. They held unknown stories. She nearly slid down the ladder back into the storage room and began acquainting herself with the bowls. She stared at them for hours, running her fingers over them and memorizing their feel.

The first thing she noticed about the bowls was the slight shine to them, unlike the finish of her own bowls. And, of course, the designs on the bowls were different. The mountains and the lines of the land looked foreign to her, and even a heron diving for fish had a strange shape.

She asked Non about how the bowls were made, though Non did not know much about the art of seeing and making. But she had watched the women in her old home work on the bowls, and she had an idea about the shine. She described what she had seen the northern women do, and Lynay listened and considered. Then she walked to the river to find the kind of stone Non had described. She chose a stone, returned to her roof, and selected an unfinished bowl. She slowly polished the smooth sides of the bowl with the hard bit of cobble rock, and Non was right—the rock added a pleasing sheen. Lynay thought it sharpened the patterns.

On a different day, Lynay asked Non about the designs she didn't recognize, the diagonal lines that filled in spaces. Non used her finger to draw slanted lines in the dirt, like a crooked ladder.

"This is what you find unusual?" Non asked.

"Yes," Lynay said. "It's a pattern I haven't seen before."

"They say that it eases the passage," Non said.

Lynay studied the lines and knew they looked like the ladders that led from the insides of rooms to the outside world. But she could not make sense of Non's answer.

"What passage?" she asked finally, as much as she wanted to act as if she understood. She did not want Non to think she was slow.

"You always have a meaning behind your pictures," Non answered. "You tell me how important it is for the patterns to be made clear. You want the meaning behind the pictures to leave the piece of clay and enter the thoughts of those who look at the bowl. How can your ideas leave the bowl if they have no way to climb out?"

Lynay absorbed this idea. She began painting crooked ladder rungs across bird wings or angry skies. She imagined the feel of the ladder under her feet as she climbed out of her room in the morning, as she felt the first rays of morning on her face. She wondered if that was what her mother felt when she took her first steps into the next world, if perhaps the next world was even brighter and warmer.

The summer after her mother died, Lynay joined hands with Non's older son. The rest of the people called him Restless One, but Lynay never used his public name. She always called him Little Owl, as his mother did, because of a tuft of hair on the top of his head that never lay flat. When he woke in the mornings and peered around blinking, hair pointing to the sky, he was an owlet. She laughed aloud at him that first morning when they woke together, understanding the name fully for the first time.

She ran her hands over his hair as the light came down on them from the roof opening. Dirt rose from the floor and danced in the brightness, floating.

*"The golden light appears in the east,"* the people in the square had sung on their joining day. *"The birds call a greeting. The sun lifts its head from the earth. Man and woman answer. As one, they lift their heads from the earth."*

Lying on their mats, he would argue with her, mock fierce, telling her to call him Panther or Deer or Eagle, to talk of speed and strength. He was not an owlet, he would say, and she would insist that he was, even as he slid a hard thigh between hers, as he flipped her onto her back and his chest and shoulders blocked out the morning sun and dancing dirt.

That piece of the story has fallen out of place.

First there was the joining, with their bare feet on the cool stones of the plaza. Even over the scent of the flowers across her shoulders, she could smell the juniper on him, and when they returned to her rooms—their rooms—she understood why. He had covered the floor with juniper leaves, plucked the needles neatly off the hard branches. As they knelt, she felt the needles press into the skin of her knees, and, deep inside the bone, she felt the leftover childhood pain from when a rock shifted and she slammed her knee onto hard earth. She was wincing at her knee when his mouth found hers. The juniper soaked into their skin as they moved over and under each other. She had always loved the smell of juniper.

# seven

*Scanning the landscape of the North American South-west, even an untrained eye notes the . . . abandoned dwellings. . . . It is tempting to see these sites as the products of collapse or of a disaster of some sort. Otherwise, why would people move away? Although both collapses and disasters have occurred, movements were not always predicated on failure. Movements were also effective strategies.*

—From "Abandonment Is Not As It Seems:
An Approach to the Relationship Between Site and Regional
Abandonment" by Margaret C. Nelson and Michelle Hegmon,
*American Antiquity*, vol. 66, 2001

It surprised Ren how easily Silas fit into her house, setting up his computer on her dining room table, stacking his books on his side of the bed, laying claim to her Little Bighorn coffee mug. Ren left for work in the mornings, and he took his coffee to his computer. The first two days back in town were hectic at the museum, and she didn't get home until long after dark. He did not seem to mind. Both nights she found him typing at his computer, glasses perched on his nose. His backpack stuffed with papers blocked her way into the hallway, and he'd left books on the kitchen counter.

She found his socks in the bathroom, and he'd finished off the orange juice without telling her. He was not particularly messy or inconsiderate, but her house felt disordered and unfamiliar. She was not sure whether this was good or bad.

The second night he cooked an enormous vat of macaroni and cheese with chunks of Brie embedded in it. They ate it straight from the pot as they finished a bottle of cabernet. She fell asleep still tasting butter and cheese and wine.

The third night she arrived home thinking about corn. She was organizing an exhibit on the role of corn in pueblo culture. *The Gifts of the Corn Mother,* she thought she'd call it. She'd have the ceramics and the grinding stones and the tapestries all resting on a sea of corn kernels, reds and yellows and browns. Pretty as gemstones. She wanted the colors of the harvest, the feel of living corn infusing every display. She saw corn flickering under the surface of her driveway, her tin mailbox, the deep red of the front door, and the dead beetle by the welcome mat.

Corn. When she had first come to the museum, she had organized a couple of exhibitions based on the Crow Creek finds. She'd hardly slept at all, laboring over each piece. Since then, other exhibitions had come and gone, and all of them had to be devised and crafted and overseen. The work didn't exactly keep her awake at night, but she didn't mind it. At times she welcomed getting lost in the details.

Only when she closed the door and tossed her keys in the woven basket did she realize that the house was too quiet. Silas's computer was closed and unblinking on the dining room table. She called his name, wandered through the house, and looked in the backyard. The silence unnerved her, even though until the last few days, it would have been reassuringly normal. She stomped down the tendril of unease. He had left his truck back at the canyon, so he couldn't have gotten far. She called his name again, and she found herself walking more slowly, turning corners carefully, watching.

No answer.

She'd laid out the parrot woman's words in one corner of her mind, spreading them out neatly. This gave her a space where she could move and rearrange them like puzzle pieces, trying to decipher them. Trying, really, to disarm them, to render them, through sharp analysis, harmless. She had not been successful so far. But she had been reasonably successful in barricading them off.

Finally she noticed a note on the stove, which informed her that Silas had walked to the bookstore and planned to be back by six p.m. Her watch read five-thirty. She briefly considered driving to the store and giving him a ride home, but she decided instead to take a bath. He would be fine. She would not let herself see a trip to the bookstore as a supernatural danger. She would not give the words that much power. And in the rush of work, she hadn't had the chance to enjoy the luxury of indoor bathing again. She missed soaking until the hot water cooled.

Waiting for the tub to fill, she considered her face in the mirror. She was thirty-seven. The bathroom lighting was gentle. The only lines she could see on her face were the faint ones around the edges of her eyes and fainter ones on her forehead.

Lighting would be another issue with the corn exhibit. The MR16 halogen lamp hadn't been warm enough. The corn storage jars, so intricate and eye-catching, had seemed washed-out. An amber filter might help.

A soft slight bird's foot spread from the edge of each of her eyes. But these lines in her face were not always there. She could still make them disappear altogether when she rubbed in moisturizer slowly—gentle strokes with two fingers—and then the face in the mirror was the same face of a decade ago. She could see that younger version of herself whenever she wanted. It still existed, ready to rise to the surface at a touch. Then a tilt of her head, a shadow, and there she was at twenty. No time had passed at all. And it was during these moments, the moments when she saw no evidence of the passage of time on her own face, when it seemed most surprising that she would be gone in thirty or forty or, if she was lucky, fifty years. She had lived thirty-seven of her allotted years, and she did not feel thirty-seven years closer to death. All day she studied the ruins of civilizations, of families and bodies and babies—she had picked up an infant femur accidentally in a bucketful of dirt, had run her fingertips along the holes in skulls—and still she found it difficult to believe death was coming. She could see her other selves just underneath her skin—the teenager with eyes that dropped to the floor too easily and the college student who only looked forward and the youngest member of the team, hungry-desperate. They all waited, and they watched her in the mirror.

The hinge on the bathroom door creaked, and the door swung wider. This was not unusual: The foundation of the house had settled, and the door was loose in its frame. Still, when she saw the movement from the corner of her eye, she turned toward it quickly.

Nothing there. She'd half expected to see feathers or clay-covered hands, and there was both dread and excitement to the thought. It wasn't fair, she thought, that when she'd finally come face-to-face with the girl she'd spent years trying to find—a girl who'd called to her clear and loud across centuries—Ren hadn't had the chance to bask in the joy of seeing her face. Of seeing the hands that had shaped the bowls. Instead, the parrot woman's words had overshadowed the sweet solemnity of the artist's face, the grace and quickness of her hands.

She closed the bathroom door. There had been a time when a shifting in the air was an unmistakable sign of Scott's arrival. Once he joined her when she found a caterpillar lying on the sidewalk with green blood oozing from its side. He came only when she was alone.

For a while, she felt guilty for not telling her parents, but she didn't think they would believe her. She thought her mother would cry, and she was tired of watching her mother cry. And then silence seeped into the house, and it did not occur to her to speak. Her parents did not play on the kitchen floor anymore. When they spoke to her, they said nothing. She couldn't stand the pain of their faces, so she stopped looking at them. Scott had left a hole in the house, and many other things fell into it.

She turned thirteen . . . then fourteen, fifteen, and sixteen. They must have been forgettable birthdays, because she could barely remember them. Scott still came to her during those years, but less often.

Then toward the end of tenth grade, without warning, she realized something: She had missed things. She realized this when Andy Layton asked her to the spring dance. She hardly knew Andy Layton—she hardly knew anyone anymore. She said hello and held long conversations, shopped at the mall with gaggles of girls, went to parties when invited, but she knew none of these people.

Andy Layton was in her homeroom, and she knew he was popular and supposed to be handsome. He played football and scored many points. He had a jaw like a cartoon character, and his teeth were too white. He smiled and she winced. She had no idea why he had asked her, but she said yes because it seemed the easiest answer to give. Then she considered the phenomenon for the rest of the day, all through biology class and French verb exercises and a lunch of rectangular pizza. She had never gone on a date with a boy. She had never kissed one. She had never snuck out at night, had never tasted beer, never smoked a cigarette. She heard girls talk about it all, but she hadn't listened with any real interest.

After school that day, she drove home, thinking. She had not been pretty as a child. She hadn't been ugly, but her features never came together in a way that brought out smiles from strangers. Then sometime before the accident she hit a phase where she grew lanky and angular and her head did not fit her body—she thought it wobbled weirdly on her neck—but she didn't care very much. Her own looks had never struck her as a particular pro or con. Then Scott died and she stopped caring about most things.

So Andy Layton asked her to the dance. As his date. She shut herself in her bathroom at home and stared at herself in the mirror, at this girl who was going to a dance with a boy who had teeth like lightbulbs. Her once not-blond-not-brown hair had turned dark honey with gold streaks, mysteriously sunlit even though she never spent time outdoors. She had her father's olive skin, smooth and ever tan. She had brown eyes, not dark chocolate like Scott's, but clear like the brandy her father sipped from dinnertime to bedtime. Her nose had always been too big for her face, long and straight, but now it seemed to have reined itself in, and it sat tidy and proportional in the middle of her face, just as it should. But her mouth looked larger, wider, so she smiled carefully. It was a fine smile—more lips than teeth—which she could extend into a wide grin that crinkled her eyes.

She felt her jaw, the slope of her neck, then ran her hands down her sides. Her lankiness had turned into long, strong lines, but she could feel how her hips flared under her hands. She lifted her shirt and stared at her belly, which seemed flat and reasonable and didn't make an impression on her one way or the other. She took off her shirt, along with her jeans, then, after a pause, her bra and panties. She climbed on the counter, standing on her knees. She was soft and rounded—she cupped her breasts with her hands, contemplating their weight and wondering if they shouldn't angle more upward. They fell slightly when she released them, and she shrugged. She'd gained some weight, no doubt, but it seemed to be mainly in these breasts and hips and—she skimmed her hands along the inside of her thighs—maybe wider thighs. She had hair in all the usual places.

The body seemed good enough. The face she was a bit more intrigued with. It was still her face, but it had moved on without her permission. She was not beautiful, and there was no one feature that seemed remarkable, but taken as a whole, her face had become striking. She looked slightly feline and exotic and—she narrowed her eyes—grown. She had turned pretty.

The boys didn't notice that she'd missed things; they noticed she'd turned pretty. Andy Layton kissed her the night of the dance, and she let him, though she didn't let him do more than that. She did not enjoy being intimate with his intimidating teeth. A few months later, she let Sam Norman kiss her more thoroughly, and she enjoyed it immensely, although she never lost her fear of where his hands were traveling. Neither boy commented on any lack of expertise. She was more afraid of being found out as a fraud, as a freak, than she was afraid of the kissing and the handling and the quest for zippers and buttons. But she monitored their hands and stopped their quests that year. She was still learning, still trying to find her spot in this new time with this new face. And those boys didn't spark anything in her.

She went to slumber parties. She tried beer and learned to like wine coolers. She snuck out to meet boys and sat in dark cars. She never got drunk, and she never fell in love. But she learned to fake it. No one ever knew she'd missed things.

Staring at herself now in the mirror, she thought she looked a little too alert. As if she'd had too much coffee. She took several deep breaths and stepped into the tub and paused, one foot and ankle stunned by the heat. It occurred to her that the blood of the caterpillar she'd found—with Scott looking over her shoulder—could not have been bright green. It must have been red. Maybe the caterpillar itself was bright green.

She lowered herself into the water, and the heat blanched the memory completely. Soon she sat with her eyes closed, head tilted back against the tile wall. She had one arm under the water, the other hanging over the edge of the tub. She thought only of the contrast between the almost scalding water—she had a waterline of pink meeting white across her belly—and the chill of the porcelain tub. The porcelain was ice against her neck, but she could feel beads of perspiration on her lip. She skimmed her hand over the water, nothing but fingertips submerged, marveling at the pull of the water, the urge to immerse her hand.

She focused on her fingertips. She thought about the caterpillar and tried to sharpen her memory. The right answer was in there. The past was solid, weighable as cement. You could pull it out if you wanted to, but it was done and over, and could be wrapped up and stored without fear of it ever changing.

She heard Silas come in through the front door and called to him from the bathroom. She sank lower into the water and waved one dripping foot at him.

He smiled as he slipped through the door, eyes settling on what the water concealed. "Need company?"

"Not this time," she said. "I'm stewing myself. Five more minutes."

He swayed toward the tub, but he turned and left without more than a friendly leer. She could hear him clanging in the kitchen.

She took longer than five minutes. He walked in again and said that if she was getting clean, he probably should, too. He pulled his gray T-shirt over his head, his back to her. He faced the mirror over the sink and rubbed his face. He'd kept the beard and mustache he'd accumulated over months at the canyon, although he'd mentioned shaving them. The hair was dense and starting to curl and not at all unpleasant against her skin.

"Hand me the shampoo?" he asked.

"Shampoo?" she repeated. But she handed him the bottle.

He cupped his hands and brought the water to his face, rubbing palms and fingertips in circles over his forehead and cheeks and chin. He reached for the shampoo, and Ren sat up, propping her elbows on the tub.

He poured a small dollop into his hand, then began working it from his sideburns down the line of his jaw.

"You use shampoo on your beard?" she asked.

He turned to her, foam-faced. "Heck, yeah. It's hair."

"And your mustache."

He shook his head once, not enough to disrupt the lather. "I don't think of this as a mustache."

"Then what is it?"

"It's an element of my beard. It's part of a broader expanse."

"Huh."

After he had scrubbed to his satisfaction, she told him to give her another five minutes. He closed the door behind him. She dragged both hands slowly through the water again, letting them float on top of the heat. She dipped herself low enough that the ends of her hair, hanging loose from a plastic clip, were dark and drenched. She did not linger longer. She slipped on the T-shirt he had left discarded on the bathroom floor. When she found him, he was sitting on his side of the bed, reading glasses on, flipping through a stack of loose-leaf pages.

He looked over the edge of his glasses as he put down the paper. She came to him, still tinged pink, and took off his glasses. When she touched him, the heat of her skin rubbed off onto his.

Later they brought in grilled cheese sandwiches and tomato soup and ate carefully on her white sheets. She liked lying with him in her own bed. Other parts of the house felt crowded from his clothes and books and stacks of things, but the bed felt warm and cozy. He found a basketball game, then two basketball games, and he flipped back and forth between them. She moved her dishes to the ground and turned so she lay on her side with her feet by his head. She was digging through the bedspread and sheets, pulling them from their moorings, trying to get to his feet.

"I like your feet," she said.

"I know. You ever go to a Pacers game? You must have grown up liking the Pacers."

She'd won her battle against the sheets. His toes flexed in the air, and she traced one finger down his arch. He jumped.

"You should watch the Suns with me," he said. "You'd like the Suns."

She pressed just under the ball of his foot, hard enough to feel the muscle yield. He made a pleased sound.

"I've always liked Nash," she said.

"We had a hoop off the side of Dad's tool shed and a dirt court. Dad used to shoot with me back before my brother, Alex, was old enough to play. Or not really shoot. Dad never cared for playing basketball, but he'd stand under the net and toss the ball back to me. He'd do it for an hour sometimes—back when I was nine or ten, I didn't exactly make many shots. But he'd just feed me the ball, over and over and over, and congratulate me when I made one."

"That's a very patient dad," she said.

"Yeah," he said. "Sometimes. The last time I remember him spanking me was when I was eight years old and he asked me to put the ball up in the shed. But I didn't. I didn't feel like it. I took it into the house and bounced it around—moron that I was—and launched it right into a porcelain lamp. Dad took me to my room and beat my butt until there were welts. It took three days for the marks to go away. Of course, he felt worse than I did. He said losing your temper was a weakness, and he had no patience for weakness. He never spanked me again."

She sat up, one hand still resting on the top of his foot. "That's harsh."

"Nah," he said. "He hated that loss of control—that's why he never did it again."

"You're not at all mad about it? Even now?"

"No," he said, and the tone of his voice made her think he didn't really understand the question. She must have looked skeptical.

"Dad's parenting was sort of like raising puppies," he said. "Show them who's the alpha dog. And don't overpraise them. He pushed us hard, and it made us better."

"I'm not sure I think it's possible to overpraise an eight-year-old."

"You know," said Silas, blinking down at her, "in biblical times, if a woman uncovered a man's feet and lay down by them, it meant that she was offering herself to him. It's how Ruth gets Boaz to marry her. Although there's also some thought that uncovering feet was only a euphemism. Maybe she wasn't anywhere near his feet."

She raised an eyebrow. "You're a biblical scholar?"

"My dad sort of was."

"I thought your dad owned a ranch."

"That, too. He has many sides." He wiggled his toes. "Come up here, Aurenthia. *Ven aquí.* Come lie next to me."

Even shortened, her name was barely palatable. Renny-ren-ren, Renny-Penny, Renny-Skinny, Scott would call her. Nonsense words that for some reason used to embarrass and infuriate her—she thought she remembered biting his arm once in blind rage. Scott could make her cry just by saying her name over and over until it became meaningless.

When Silas said her given name, she wanted him to repeat it. *Aurenthia.* He said it with the same easy lilt she admired in his bursts of Spanish, syllables rising and falling and blurring at the edges. Her name was a new word altogether.

*She felt his stubble against her forehead, occasionally swapped for the softness of lips. He spoke against her eyebrow.*

*"I wonder how long before you'll be completely bald," he said. He wrapped his hand in her hair, twisting, using the rope of it to pull her head back gently. He studied her exposed face.*

*"I'm not going to go bald."*

*"No?"*

*"No. No women in my family have gone bald as of yet."*

*"Good. I'm not going to go bald, either."*

*"I got that feeling." She threaded her fingers through the thick, dark*

*hair at the nape of his neck, then skimmed her hand over the shape of his skull.*

*"I'd still love you if you were bald," he said, "but it would be an adjustment."*


*"Did something happen with your family?" he asked, her cheek on his chest, his hand in her hair. His voice was soft and careful. "You've clearly declared them to be off-limits for conversation, and I can't help wonder why."*

*Her fingers ran up and down his arm lightly, distractingly. "They're not off-limits," she said. "Almost all my family still lives in Indiana. Nothing exciting."*

*"Your mom and dad still together?"*

*The rhythm of her fingers stopped, then started again. "Dad died of a heart attack when I was in college."*

*"I'm sorry."*

*She nodded once.*

*"Any siblings?" he asked.*

*"No."*


The girl, Lynay, had followed Ren back to her house. This had certainly never happened before. Only Scott had appeared to her when she was at home, alert, and looking straight at him. He was familiar and comforting. She did not know what this girl was, exactly.

As invasions go, it was a quiet one. Lynay showed no inclination toward conversation. She seemed to want only a solitary place to do her work. It was like having a mouse in the house—there was nothing inherently frightening about the girl other than the suddenness of her appearances. If she would announce herself before she entered a room, Ren thought, they could have coexisted pleasantly. Because at first Ren was mostly curious, intrigued by the girl following her home like a lost puppy. She was somewhat flattered. She felt a kind of protectiveness for her young artist. She thought that the girl's presence promised something—maybe an intimacy, a confidence.

There was no sign of the parrot woman. Her presence would have felt like a very different kind of invasion. Because the words were still there, hanging in the air without any explanation. If ghosts intended to make announcements, Ren thought they should at least be more specific about them. But the girl might know what the words meant. She might be able to decipher them.

On her fourth day home, the morning after she'd taken her bath, Ren turned the corner into the kitchen and saw the girl sitting cross-legged on the floor by the kitchen table. She was rhythmically scraping the outside of the bowl with a chunk of sandstone. Ren had watched other women—living women—do this occasionally. The junctures between the coils were weak, always the most fragile part of the structure. So the inside of the bowl had to be scraped for practicality's sake, and often both sides were scraped for art's sake. The bowl in Lynay's lap had already been scraped smooth on the inside.

She had thin hands with long fingers, and she worked steadily, soothingly, as if she were rubbing skin and muscle rather than clay. Some of the scabs on her knuckles had peeled away and oozed thin blood. Clay was soft as it was molded, but once it hardened, it was not kind.

"Nice of you to visit," said Ren, forgetting the growling in her stomach.

The girl was back to pretending that she was unaware of Ren's presence. Her hair was pulled into an intricate knot, whorls twisting around her ears and neck with no visible means of support. Her hair did not move. Her breasts were bare, obscured by her arms. Her legs were folded under her, but she had leggings on, dark webs of crisscrossed strips of cloth. Her head was at an angle, with the curve of her neck and the strong line of her jaw and chin exposed. There was no softness to her face, just smooth skin stretched over perfect bone, large eyes intent, and she was lovely in a way that left Ren unsettled. She was glad that Silas was in the shower. But maybe that was no coincidence—maybe the girl did not care to appear in front of Silas.

Ren took a step closer. "I think you have to admit you can see me, since you're sitting in my kitchen."

Lynay kept working her clay. In more scientific terms, silica and aluminum. Ren loved to watch it under a microscope, where the molecules ricocheted and slid, spastic and frantic. Disconnected but trapped.

"What did she mean?" she asked the girl.

No answer.

Ren frowned. "The parrot woman. Non. She said I would lose him."

The girl ran the tip of one finger down the curve of the bowl, testing for unevenness.

"Silas?" pushed Ren. "She meant something will happen to Silas?"

Ren's cell phone rang, and the girl was gone. Ren cursed at herself for asking the question—asking the question acknowledged that she somehow believed the parrot woman. Which she did not. She did not. She worried about leaving Silas alone in the house all day, worried about occasional catches in his breathing at night, worried when he winced as he stood up, worried about him walking to the bookstore, for God's sake. But she would not explore her reasons for worrying. She rolled her head from shoulder to shoulder, considered the empty tile floor, and turned back toward the smell of coffee.

The next day, Lynay appeared on the brick hearth of the fireplace, where seconds before there had been only air. Her hands were gray and wet. She was shaping a jar. The clay had smeared not only on Lynay's hands but all the way along her arms, up to the elbows. She looked like she was turning to stone.

Ren sighed and stood. She walked to the fireplace and sat at Lynay's feet on the braided wool rug. It was rough against the soles of her feet, but she felt guilty sitting on a soft sofa while the dead girl sat on hard brick.

"So don't you do anything other than make pottery?" asked Ren. She was more prepared to make conversation than she had been the day before—she had used the past twenty-four hours to consider her options. What she needed, she had decided, was the right kind of small talk. The kind that was appropriate for dead prehistoric artists. (No weather, no sports. Movies and television were out.) She needed something light, something nonthreatening that wouldn't frighten Lynay away. She would work up to the more important questions slowly.

It also had occurred to her that she should not waste the chance to answer questions she'd wondered about for years. So she chose a practical line of questioning. She smiled at the girl and kept her tone friendly.

"Do you take care of kids and cook and clean and all that business?" she said. "I mean, did you? I notice I don't see you making stew or tanning a hide or carrying water. I don't see any reason you couldn't be tanning a hide in my living room. It's just as easy as molding the clay. You know, or you could be cooking. Do you cook?"

She stopped, aware that she was babbling.

The girl's dark eyes flickered to Ren's face so briefly that Ren wasn't sure she had seen them move. She felt a shiver along the tops of her arms, a physical thrill at the possibility of response. Of two-way communication, however subtle. Then Lynay raised her eyes again, holding Ren's gaze before looking down. Her hands slowed.

"Why do you make these bowls?" Ren asked softly. She felt a twinge of discomfort, a different kind of gooseflesh on her arms, and she knew what it was about the girl's prettiness that felt wrong. There was pain etched into it, in the way she held her mouth and the dullness of her eyes and the small lines across her forehead. Suffering. The suffering intensified the allure of her face, making it sharper and deeper but also, Ren thought, making it into something that should not be observed.

"Why?" she asked again.

Lynay set the not-solid jar on the floor. One side of the jar crumpled, slack. She raised her wet hands to her face, and held up two fingers on each hand, a sign, in Ren's mind, for either victory or peace. The fingers were slick and smooth, and the lamplight changed the tone of the clay slightly, making it less grayish and more honey.

Lynay dragged her fingers across her cheekbones, leaving clay marks from the bridge of her nose to her hairline. She lifted her fingers and pressed them under her ears, tracing the line of her jaw. She made a sharp finishing motion—a flick into the air—when the tips of her fingers came together at her chin. Her skin was smooth and dark and almost perfect other than a thin scar on her forehead.

The lines of clay gave her face the shadowy variegation of a pelt, part raccoon or bobcat.

Lynay held her hands out to Ren, palms up. The clay on them was still smooth and shiny, and her hands were their own creations. The marks were beginning to dry on the girl's face, seeping into it, forming small lines as it hardened.

"You love it," said Ren, understanding, watching as the girl's skin drank up the clay. The next thought that crossed her mind was that she had chosen the wrong word, that this girl did not love the clay so much as she needed it.


Silas was surrounded by paper. He'd requested that some articles be mailed to him and had downloaded a stack of others. He sifted through old site reports and obscure journal articles, following up with calls to universities and museums. He wanted to know more about macaws, more about hypothetical trade routes or migrations in the area between Crow Creek and Cañada Rosa. He wanted a context.

Meanwhile, he waited. Discoveries did not usually come with shock and gasps, despite the periodic appearances of bowls or bodies. It took days and weeks and sometimes months for lab work to come back, to connect the dots among soil samples and charcoal pieces and bone and ceramics. There would be analysis of the architecture, of the sediments and deposits in the dirt itself, the stratigraphy of the trash heaps. Instrumental Neutron Activation Analysis required a thin section of a sherd to identify the elements in clay— a step toward locating where a ceramic piece was made. That would help determine where. The when would come together from an intricate web of ceramic cross-dating and chronometric dates. The data points on his graphs did not come from ghosts, which were altogether too insubstantial to leave a mark. As long as they fit the data, he had no issue with Ren's phantoms. But they had no more influence on his conclusions than a cloud or a gust of wind.

He wanted to map the canyon, to lay out the years and the people as accurately and thoroughly as a street map of Silver City, from major intersections to tiny offshoots that dead-ended after a few yards.

Parrots did not fit his map. He needed to draw them in correctly, or everything else would be thrown off scale.

His father taught him to shoot, gave him a .22 on his twelfth birthday. He was allowed to deer-hunt when he was sixteen. Rifles were for hunting, his father said, and pistols were not. If Silas wanted a pistol, he could wait until he turned twenty-one and buy his own.

Silas's friend Jim had a father who gave him a pistol before he got his driver's license. When they were both seventeen, Silas and Jim would pass afternoons driving along the beaten-up road to Kingston, playing the radio, windows down. Jim drove an old Buick with burgundy upholstery and kept his pistol in the glove compartment always, although he didn't show it off. It lay there as unused as the state map beside it.

One Saturday, with empty road behind them, they saw a blue Ford pickup coming from the other direction. Jim said, "Oh, shit," under his breath. Silas hadn't known that Jim had been running around with someone else's girl, but the cheated-on boyfriend was behind the wheel of the blue truck. The truck passed, then brakes squealed and the truck spun in the middle of the road behind them, changing directions. Silas could hear the engine roaring. Jim had the gas pedal on the floor, but the truck kept gaining, pulling close, ramming the bumper of the Buick. The jolt made the car jerk and wobble. They headed off into an open field, clouds of dirt flying up from the tires. They hit a ditch or a rock or something—Silas couldn't remember. But the Buick wouldn't go forward, and they couldn't back up because the truck had pulled in close behind them, doors opening before the engine turned off.

Silas watched the truck through the rearview mirror from the passenger side. One guy came staggering drunk out of the backseat, weaving toward the car. Likely because it was closer, the drunk guy came to Silas's window. Three more boys—all older than Silas and with slouching shoulders—stayed by the truck. The drunk one slammed a flat palm against Silas's window and said, "You get out of the car."

Silas cracked the window, and the flat palm slammed against it again. "Get out of the car, motherfucker," the guy said.

Jim wasn't saying anything.

When the truck had started chasing them, Silas had been nervous. When they drove off the road, he had been scared. His mouth had been dry, he remembered that—the need for water. And when he saw the drunk boy's face at the window, he was completely terrified. He'd never taken a real adult punch. But the second slap of the drunken palm shifted something. It steadied him. His door was unlocked, and he made no move to lock it. He opened the glove compartment—not hurrying, reaching calm and steady—and showed the pistol. He did not touch it; he only showed it. And then he looked in the boy's bloodshot eyes.

"You go on and open that door," Silas said. "You go on and open it."

The boy held up his hands, backing away. He and his friends climbed back into the truck, and they all drove away. Silas sat in the car, listening to Jim freak out, and he felt something new, something satisfying. He would feel it again when he was grown, once he learned the ground and the bones and the ways a village could disguise itself underground. But driving back home after making that drunk boy back down, that was the first time he felt like he was someone who could do things. Someone who could take care of himself and maybe other people, too.

It hadn't lasted. He got home, walked through the door, and announced something like, "I am a tired Spanish donkey." Or possibly "I'm a tired mechanical monkey." This was a habit of his mother's—inventing nonsense phrases—and his father usually ignored her when she did it. But it drove him crazy when Silas joined in. Before Silas closed the door behind him, his father strode from the kitchen and snapped, "Talk like a normal human being."

Even as he'd rolled his eyes at his dad, his confidence evaporated. That sense of himself as competent and smart and brave—gone. He hadn't even told his father the story of the drunken chase until years later. But that sweet feeling of sureness, it was lodged inside him as vivid as a childhood smell—bacon cooking, cut grass, his mother's jasmine hand lotion. The memory of it filled his head. He thought that the most you could hope for, really, were moments of such true certainty. Most of the time, inevitably, you screwed up. You struggled to tolerate yourself. But sometimes you got moments where you felt good and strong and sure, when the right words were waiting on your tongue, when you knew the answer without thinking.

He called Ren at work on Friday.

"I'm willing to acknowledge that there could have been one parrot on the site," he said without a hello. "Maybe even two. We wouldn't necessarily find a trace of one or two parrots. But I still find it highly unlikely the parrots were trained or raised en masse."

"Okay," she said slowly. "So why would there be only one parrot?"

She had stopped herself from saying "Why was there only one parrot?" She was willing to make her questions more conditional. She could give him room to explore this for himself.

"It was a pet," said Silas. She noticed he did not say "could have been." He said "was."

"A pet," she echoed. She considered the macaw appearing from thin air, landing on Non's arm. Chattering to Non and Lynay. It was a bird that seemed to have a degree of charm. She had done her own reading: Scarlet macaws were easily tamed, good company, and not prone to bad behavior, unlike the military macaw and the thick-billed parrot, which also showed up on pottery.

"The birds were usually sacrificed when they were around ten to thirteen months," Silas said. "There've been very few remains of older birds found, but it's likely they were pets. Maybe they'd learned to speak and were highly valued because of it. It would make sense."

"So the older birds weren't sacrificed?"

"Not from what I can turn up. I guess if they made it past the proper ceremonial age for sacrifice, they were home free. I haven't found a lot—some of the notes from the older sites just don't have the detail. But it appears that the older birds hadn't been plucked, and they didn't have a left wing missing."

"Because you don't pull the plumage off something you love," Ren said. "You don't use his body for rituals. You bury him like a family member."

"So I'm just saying if you're right and the parrot woman had the macaw with her, he could be a pet. And that still wouldn't point to any raising of parrots at the Delgado site."

"Agreed," she said.

She could hear him smile on the other end of the phone.

The next afternoon, Saturday, Silas got a call that made him jump onto the sofa, landing on his feet, crouched. The papers stacked around Ren's legs shifted and scattered. She watched him nod at the phone, thank whoever was on the other end, and hang up.

"Well?" she said. "I take it you got some news?"

There was something about his pose that reminded her of Spider-Man.

"Was everything you found at Crow Creek analyzed?" he asked. "All the sherds?"

"Yes. Why?"

"Did you find any red-slipped brownware?"

"You're going to torture me for a while, aren't you?"

His expression didn't change. "Red-slipped brownware?"

She was willing to let him enjoy this, whatever it was. He did have a gift for analysis. She thought he had his own visions that took shape in the graphs and percentages. "Yeah," she said. "A decent amount. But they stopped making that by 1000 AD. It's a century off our time period."

Silas nodded but did not look discouraged. If anything, he looked like he might leap into the air again.

"The lab said six sherds from Delgado don't match the clay we've found around the canyon," he said. "Those sherds are red-slipped brownware, and we only found them in one room. It was the same room where we found the big sherd of your artist's bowl."

Ren stood and started to pace. Pottery was too valuable to be thrown away simply because it broke. The pieces of a bowl could be used for plates, for utensils, for cooking and serving. If a large bowl broke in half, each half could be reinvented as a new vessel, and if it broke into four pieces, all four pieces would find new life. There was no waste. And maybe a cooking bowl held more than pragmatic value. Maybe your mother passed down her favorite pieces, which her mother had passed down to her. You'd keep those pieces with you until they were worn to nothing but dust.

"Somebody brought their grandmother's china with them when they moved to Delgado," she said.

Silas was bouncing on his heels, wobbling on the sofa cushions. "Here's the other thing: The clay in the brownware had significant traces of antimony and arsenic. We haven't found deposits with antimony and arsenic within twenty miles of the canyon."

She stopped pacing. "That matches what we found at Crow Creek."

"Yes," he said.

"They were at Crow Creek first," she said, walking faster now, spinning around at the fireplace and heading in the other direction. "The artist and the parrot woman, Lynay and Non, moved from there to Delgado."

Silas had already told her he did not feel comfortable calling the dead women by first names. Now he frowned—winced, almost— but he didn't correct her.

"Maybe," he said. "I think it's safe to say we had a group of Mimbreños move from Crow Creek to the Delgado site sometime around or after 1100. The pottery we've found would suggest that, yes, your artist was among these women."

"And she came with the parrot woman," she insisted.

"No indication of parrot ceremonies at Crow Creek, was there?"

"She was with Lynay at Crow Creek," Ren insisted. "Lynay drew her bracelets."

"Please stop doing that," he said. "Can you just stick with 'the artist'?"

She held up a hand in acknowledgment. "That's where their paths first crossed," she continued. "I'm not saying that's where the parrot woman was born—she could have been anywhere before Crow Creek. But I'm saying she was there with Lynay. That doesn't explain the northern influence on the pots, but we'll figure that out later. Maybe the parrot woman worked with parrots in the north, and that same northern influence—either through the parrot woman or through a larger transplanted group—shaped Lynay's style."

He rubbed his forehead with the heel of his hand. His eyes closed for one, two, three seconds.

"Maybe," he said. "There are plenty of maybes."

"We're closer," she said.

"A lot of strands running through this thing, aren't there?"

"We're getting closer," she repeated, collapsing onto the arm of the couch and leaning against him. His shoulder was warm against her bare arm, and she felt a callus on his thumb as he rested a hand on her thigh. His breath smelled of orange juice.

She watched his face and knew he had drifted off to somewhere in the distance, that he was seeing masses of people, uncountable, crossing broad swaths of land and mountain. He wasn't seeing faces. He was seeing movements, swarms, the gathering of multitudes.

"Can I see your files on Delgado?" he asked, as she had known that he would. His eyes were bright. "This could be it. The first step toward proving a specific large-scale migration to the canyon.

Dating it. It could be the anchor for the whole sequence of occupations."

"I can find out where she came from," she said.

He focused on her. "It's a lot to hope for," he said. "One woman in the middle of thousands."

"That's the point," she said. "I'll get the files."

It wasn't that she didn't care about the larger movements, about the trends and causes and effects that intrigued him. It was her job to care. But she was pulled in a different direction, maybe not an opposite one but one marked by two precise sets of footprints and wide, dark eyes and dirty fingernails. She couldn't see past familiar faces to look for Silas's crowds.

She kept all her file folders in the china cabinet by the front door—she didn't have any china, and the shelves were the perfect size. She headed toward the front room, crossing through the doorway into the entrance hall. A beam of light reflected off the hardwood floor, and bits of dust danced in the air. Silas had left a pair of shoes and a white shirt by the door.

As soon as she rounded the corner and could no longer see Silas, Ren spotted Lynay sitting on the windowsill, crushing something in her hands. Or rubbing something slowly. She stood as Ren approached, and Ren could see that it was not clay on her hands this time. This was a dark, vivid red, and it was dripping onto the floor. Two drops, three drops, hit the floor with a heavy splish. It was a thick liquid.

The girl stepped on Silas's white shirt, the brown of her feet handsome and smooth against the ivory. One drop fell from her hand to her foot, running down her arch and landing on his shirt. The red spread across the white.

She considered calling Silas, but she kept silent. He wouldn't be able to see the girl, anyway. And she did not want him near Lynay. Not when the girl's blood-colored hands were spreading dark stains over Silas's shirt.

Lynay came closer with her red red hands outstretched, and Ren couldn't help but step backward. The girl was as calm and serene— and beautiful and bare-chested—as ever. She reached for Ren's face, and Ren stumbled. She fell backward, hitting her elbow hard on the floor and yelping in pain. Lynay and her dripping hands were gone then, of course.

Here and then gone. Always here and then gone. The girl was going to give her whiplash.


She wasn't sleeping. There were nightmares that she could not remember well, nightmares with running and bright sun and the sound of things breaking. Once she was walking through a canyon and saw her mother standing in a driveway. Her mother toppled over backward, straight-legged, and her head hit concrete with a sickening sound. Then her mother bounced up, smiling, because it had not hurt at all. And Ren knew it was not her mother at all but something wearing her mother's face. The bone-on-concrete sound did not leave Ren's head even after she woke up. She dreamed she and Silas had found an immense pear, shoulder-high, that was as lightweight as a beach ball. They dribbled it and rolled it, then tossed it back and forth. As it came toward Ren, it blocked out the sun.

Other times she was running and running, and there was the scrape of claws at her back, blood on the ground around her. Once she felt teeth sink into her forearm, and she screamed as she sat up in bed. She was tired of waking up crying, out of breath. It had been a long time since she had nightmares. Now she lay awake next to

Silas, staring at the ceiling, just as she used to during the long, wary nights in her parents' house.

She no longer wanted to make friends with Lynay. She was not curious or flattered. She was on edge. It rattled her, constantly rounding a corner and seeing the girl. After all this time trying to summon the right ghosts, she found she just wanted them to leave. She couldn't shake the sight of the girl's hands dripping red, even though Ren suspected the liquid was paint. Paint was a good thing for Lynay, right? She painted what she loved: her pottery. And the girl herself didn't seem threatening. She was as nonthreatening as a dead girl with red dripping from her hands could possibly be. Still.

Ren had not seen Scott since she left the site. She considered that the girl had managed to convince Scott to let her trade hauntings with him. Like switching seats on a bus. She stifled a laugh.

How long since she had sat beside him in the canyon? Eleven days? Twelve? He didn't usually stay away so long.

Silas shifted in his sleep, his hand landing on her hip.

He was an affectionate sleeper. She had given him two men's T-shirts—just solid colors, no logos—to add to his drawer full of typing-on-the-computer clothes. He didn't seem to care where they came from. She thought they were both left from Daniel, who never came back to claim anything.

Daniel. For months and months she had thought that she was happy with him. She realized now that she had not been. That seemed as if it would be an obvious thing: happy or unhappy. But it had not been obvious at all. She had not been happy with Daniel. She had not been happy with other men, either, although she had not been unhappy. They could not have made her unhappy because her happiness was unrelated to them, independent of them. They had been peripheral.

She watched Silas's face. The moon was bright and cast a light through the shutters. Eyelashes and soft lips and angled jaw and three eyebrow hairs that broke formation and pointed skyward.

She had done this with her mother once upon a time. Her mother tended to fall asleep early on the couch, while her father was still watching Johnny Carson. If Ren stayed quiet, sometimes her father would forget she was in the room and not send her to bed. She would sit with her back to the sofa—she was usually sitting on the floor, using furniture only as a backrest—and she would twist her head around and watch her mother sleep. Her mother's eyes never completely closed, and Ren could see the white slits of her eyeballs. Her mother had three freckles on her right cheek and a red birthmark just behind her earlobe. She had the silver shine of cavities in the left side of her mouth, bottom and top, but no silver at all on the right side. Ren had cataloged every line and curve of her face. Maybe that was some marker of love—a hunger for a person's smallest details, a compulsion to memorize the bits and pieces that came together to make the whole. How long since she had seen her mother's face? She couldn't remember, couldn't call up a clear image of her face, but she could see the cavities exactly, perfectly, and those freckles and the shape of her ear.

There must be a reason this girl was following her.

She was becoming more and more aware of a terror other than the nightmares. It was Lynay's fault. Lynay's red hands had clarified the parrot woman's words, and now the words were sharper things. Ren could no longer pretend she didn't understand the puzzle. While she lay in their bed, she would run the pads of her fingers over the curve of Silas's shoulder, pressing herself against him so she would feel the rise and fall of his chest. She loved the sound of his breathing. Sometimes she would position her face where she could feel his breath hit her forehead: She would register every inhale and exhale and try to lull herself to sleep by the rhythm.

He was a new and inexplicable thing, and there must be a price for having found him. She had been with him for nearly three months now, three months of long days and nights together. She had wondered if the down-a-rabbit-hole quality of the canyon had worked some sort of spell on them, made this connection seem stronger than it was. But they were out of the rabbit hole now. And even in the canyon, the early mornings and manual labor, the monotony and sore backs, the disagreements over explanations and evidence and which way to smooth out a wall did not lend themselves to facile relationships. He was a new and inexplicable thing.

The fear, also, was new. At first she had slept more deeply with Silas than she had since she was a child. For nights on end she had slept without waking once to the cry of an owl or the snap of a branch or the brief snatch of a song. Then the parrot woman spoke, and since her warning, sleep had ebbed and the fear had grown. At night it pulled at Ren, tugging at her thoughts when she closed her eyes. Her need for Silas pressed on her chest, and she kept one hand on him. She could not stop confirming his heartbeat. She lay staring at his face or the ceiling or the shadowed topography of the sheets, and prayed. Please live forever. Please be next to me, forever and ever without end, amen.

She was not used to these twists and turns her mind took without her consent. Scott used to tell her she had a mind like a moth, stopping for a second at one idea and then flying off again—"hither, thither and yon," he had said, which was ridiculous because what teenage boy used a phrase like that? ("Hither, thither and your face," she had answered.) But that was before she had trained her mind to be straight and tidy. She was normally very good now at keeping her mind on track—moving forward, never back. No tangents. Thinking only the thoughts that should be thought. Suddenly that had changed. Her mind was letting in all sorts of unwanted visitors. It was as if Silas had worked his way inside her head, and he'd left the door wide open behind him. Now Scott and her mother and Lynay and Non and anything else wandered in and took up residence.

Was Non's message a warning? Was that the same reason Lynay had paint-blood on her hands? Would something happen to Silas at the site? Or was it a threat? Did these spirits have a power that Ren had not suspected? Could they hurt someone? They'd never seemed like anything more than tricks of the light, shadows flashing across the wall. They were memories without substance. But maybe they were stronger than she had realized.

She had lost Scott, and that loss had burned out her circuits. His disappearance had been incomprehensible. At twelve years old, she could not compute it and had never anticipated it. But now she knew, lying warm next to Silas, that one day he would be gone, whether because of some young thing or because of a crash of metal and glass or because of bedsores and bony hands that struggled to hold a glass of water. He would be gone, and she would be broken beyond repair. She knew this after only months.

*You will lose him.*

It was the fear that made her know it was true. She recognized it and could not run from it. She would lose him. And she could piece herself together—she knew after Scott that no matter what happened, she could piece herself back together—but the cracks would be there, spidery and endless, all her pieces glued back in the right shape but never whole again.

She watched his face, and he wrinkled his forehead.

Someone was singing. A wordless hum, sweet and soft.

Lynay was standing on the rounded footboard of the bed, the balls of her feet balanced on the polished wood as if she were climbing a tree and pausing before leaping for the next branch. Her hands were stretched toward Ren, palms up, and they were pale in the moonlight, no longer covered in red.

Ren sat up, turning herself so that she partially blocked Silas. The small of her back was against his.

"I'm tired of this," she said, whispering, and part of her hoped that she was crazy, that this was a dream and not a thousand-year-old girl pantomiming in her bedroom.

"Ren?" asked Silas, smacking his lips.

"Go back to sleep," she said, trying to keep her voice light while she kept a careful watch on Lynay.

Silas rolled over without opening his eyes.

"Well?" asked Ren, still quiet. Lynay was looking at her with something like pity, something that could have been kindness or knowledge or judgment, depending on how the shadows from the moonlight fell.

Lynay looked to Silas, lying on his back. She stepped from the footboard to the floor, landing too easily, as if gravity had forgotten her. She was next to Silas now, his body separating her from Ren. She was so close to him that her stomach brushed against the mattress, or, at least, appeared to.

"Stay away from him," Ren warned.

Lynay did not stay away. She leaned down toward Silas's face. For the first time since Ren had seen her, the girl's hair was loose around her face. It was matted and very long, past her waist, like shallow waves falling. She raised her hand to Silas's face and did not touch him, traced the lines of his face in the air, the outline of his jaw and ears and nose and eyebrows.

Ren placed her own hand over Silas's chest, reaching through Lynay's dark hair and feeling nothing but air. Instead she felt Silas's breathing and his heart, still steady.

Lynay looked at Ren, and there was a raw longing in her eyes, but it did not seem to be longing for Silas in particular. It was not lust but something more general. There was envy as well. And there was pain. Her eyes shone, wet.

Silas stirred, muttering under his breath.

Lynay pressed her wrist to his forehead and held it there, skin touching skin, closer to a mother checking for fever than a lover showing affection. She leaned closer, and Ren knew the girl was about to kiss Silas. She would have been jealous if the girl had seemed more solid. Instead she thought of a succubus stealing life with a touch of her lips. Then, as Lynay tilted her head, her hair fell across Silas's face. He frowned and swiped at his nose, sniffing. The sound echoed through the room.

When Silas spoke, his voice was clear and alert.

"Who are you?" he asked.


Immediately after Scott's accident, her parents treated Ren as if she had nearly died herself, as if she had woken up in a hospital room bruised and swollen and asked for ice chips through cracked lips. As if they had hugged each other and wiped tears from their faces and had brought her home carefully wrapped in blankets and bandages and helped her from the car with their arms around her waist.

They were everywhere—sitting on the edge of her bed to tell her good night, handing her orange juice when she came downstairs in the morning, opening the front door just as her hand touched the knob on her way in from school. They wanted to talk. No, they wanted her to talk. For weeks, they would ask her precise and thought-ful questions about school and homework, gymnastics and friends and television. They would listen for as long as she could talk, and when she stopped, they would lean forward slightly, encouraging more.

She felt that she could not talk enough, could not fill up enough space with her words. The one thing they never asked her about was Scott. She did not want to talk about him, about the accident or about his absence. She deeply appreciated her parents' evasion.

Her first birthday after the accident, her thirteenth, fell in the midst of the attention and evasion. Ren's mother insisted on a dance-party theme. Anna had found a disco ball that actually worked and hung it from the den ceiling, so the dozen or so girls attending stood in clumps and swayed their shoulders to Michael Jackson. It was a small room, and the lights from the disco ball flashed large and fran-tic across the furniture and bodies and the backs of heads.

Normally mothers would stay in the kitchen, getting cake ready, stacking up presents, staying out of the way. Ren could not tell her mother that it was embarrassing to have her there, standing with all the girls, asking them where they got their earrings and if they watched *Miami Vice*, which she knew Ren loved. It did not reflect well on Ren that her mother did not know how parties worked. But it seemed to be okay. She apologized to Allison Shum and Betsy Sapp for her mother, and they both shrugged. "Don't worry about it," Allison said, whispering. "It's been a really tough time for her. We totally understand."

The girls were extremely nice to her mother and extremely nice to Ren. It was the first time she realized that Scott's death had made her somehow glamorous. There was some part of these girls that envied her.

At one moment during the party, her mother stood against the wall. She was not talking to anyone. Ren looked up and saw her standing there while the disco ball's lights hit her full in the face, her eyes disappearing behind spinning white squares. The light blinded her again and again. She smiled so brightly.

It all began to change.

Once Ren was trying to hang a calendar in her room, and she smashed her thumb with the hammer. The nail turned black with a pretty swath of blue. A few days later, after the novelty of the wound had worn off, she painted her nails with dark red polish. It took only a little time before the damage showed through again—the nail would not hold paint anymore. So the red flaked off, one chip at a time, until the bruise was obvious.

The same thing happened to her parents.

First her father put the coffeepot in the freezer. Ren was alone in the kitchen, staring at the toaster and waiting for the toast to eject. This was January. Her father walked through the kitchen door, straight to the coffeepot, and poured a cup of coffee in his beige mug. He left the coffee cup on the counter, carried the coffeepot to the freezer, put it on the top shelf, and closed the door.

Ren laughed; then her father turned around. His eyes were open but blank.

"Dad?" she asked.

Harold left the room, and she heard him walk up the stairs. He did not come back, did not stick his head around the corner, grinning, did not laugh from the hallway and tell her it was all a joke. She waited for a long time, hoping. Then she opened the freezer and found the pot precariously balanced on a bag of Tater Tots.

(Scott had loved Tater Tots, and no one could stand to eat them anymore.) She returned the coffeepot to its burner.

That was the first time she saw her father walk in his sleep. Her mother started locking their bedroom door after Ren found him in the front yard one night. He also started sleeping at odd hours, and sometimes when she got up to go to the bathroom in the middle of the night, she would hear a noise and find him wide awake, eating a sandwich or putting a golf ball on the den floor.

Her mother stopped appearing at supper. Anna would prepare a meal at some point during the day, leave it in the refrigerator or the oven, and put a note on the counter with instructions. Either Ren or her father would get hungry at some point and heat the dinner. They stopped sitting together at the table. Ren would eat in her room or at the kitchen counter, and her father would eat in the green recliner. Both Anna and Harold seemed to be working more and were rarely home before dark.

Later, months and years later, Ren would think that she should have asked questions in those early stages. Just once she should have asked what was happening. But she didn't. Parts of the day kept being chipped away—no more meals together, no more mother picking her up from school, no more riding in the back of her father's truck (which was clearly unsafe and he wondered why he had ever allowed it), no more laughter from the kitchen that pulled her downstairs, no more music playing too loud (she had to use headphones because they could not stand music coming from upstairs), no more wrestling. That was the most obvious thing— routines and habits were being taken away. But also parts of her mother were disappearing: the touch of her mother's hand against Ren's face in the morning, the way her mother had of biting her lip just before she laughed, the sound of her mother calling her name through the halls of the house, her mother's excitement over parties. While her father was sleeping, her mother was fading away.

What Ren felt at first was relief. That was why she did not ask questions. She had not liked her parents' constant attention after the accident. She had felt as if her face might crack and split open while they watched her and something winged might spring from her skull. She felt there was something inside of her, struggling, and her parents were watching for signs of it. And when they sat on the edge of her bed, listening, she felt the something pushing harder at her skin.

But the struggling winged thing did not occupy her thoughts very often. The truth of her life at thirteen was an obvious one. She did not want to spend time with her parents: No one she knew wanted to spend time with their parents. All those girls at her birthday party had wanted to be more grown-up, more independent, and Ren was the most independent thirteen-year-old she knew. There had been those months—during her parents' constant-attention phase—when she wasn't allowed to go anywhere or do anything. They wouldn't let her ride in a car with anyone but them. But then, one by one, the restrictions lifted entirely, without a word being said. She could stay up as late as she liked, and they did not ask if she had finished her homework. They no longer asked how her day went as soon as she walked through the door. She could go to the mall or to a sleepover any night she liked. Her parents always gave permission. Some days she would walk in from school and not see either of them until the next morning. Harold and Anna drifted through the house, insubstantial, as if they could walk through walls.

The old routine shifted into a new one day by day. She never had an awareness that fundamental changes were happening—only, looking back, that they had happened. By the time she understood the depth of the loss, it was too late. She had not seen the whole of the thing, only bits and pieces, and she had been trying so hard not to see anything at all.

She did eventually want the things she had been relieved to see slip away. But they seemed impossible to retrieve. As a small child, she had loved beach trips, which required enough planning and time that they did not happen often. She would lie awake in her bed after one of those trips, missing the sand and the salt and the lovely monstrous sound of the waves. But the memories were removed by more than time and distance: They were removed by complete foreignness. The strange perfection of the beach could not be anchored to her normal life by a single detail—even the color of the sky was different—so the beach floated away from her. After a day or two, it was hard to imagine it had been real, that water thick with salt could swell against you and send you flying— the sounds, the textures, the colors were so disconnected from Ren's bedroom that it seemed impossible the two experiences could exist in the same world, much less the same life.

Her memories were blurry, with large chunks—like most of her fourteenth year—missing entirely. She never knew whether she remembered blurrily or she had lived that blurrily. But there were some clear images.

Her fourteenth birthday. She was not sure that her parents would remember it. In the weeks leading up to the date, they had not said a word. She considered reminding them, but she wasn't sure she wanted them to invite anyone over. There was the potential for this to be much worse than the previous year's party. For one thing, she did not know how her mother might act. Anna's eyes were always swollen and tired, and Ren had almost started to believe her when she said her allergies were giving her trouble. She was often quiet, often absent, but sometimes aggressively sad. There was a good chance her mother might actually spend an entire birthday party in her bedroom or in the kitchen, but there was also the chance that she might burst into tears or sit silently in the middle of the room without speaking to anyone.

The party idea was unappealing, whether or not her mother was there. Ren was not fond of conversation. Sometimes in the middle of a sentence—hers or someone else's—she would drift off completely. She preferred reading alone in her room, with its light green walls like a forest. She could be sucked into her books, and time would stop completely. She had bought her own tapes, including some Dylan, and she could listen to them without feeling like she had stolen something of Scott's. Sometimes she would close her eyes with the headphones over her ears, and when she opened her eyes, Scott would be sitting next to her, eyes closed, as if he were listening, too. Sometimes he would do ridiculous dances and make her laugh aloud. He was nicer to her now that he was dead.

She did not remind her parents. By the day before her birthday, she had convinced herself that she did not want them to remember. It would be much easier not to deal with a birthday.

She woke up on December 13, and when she stepped into the hall, she knew they had remembered. She could smell that they had remembered—her mother had made orange cinnamon rolls. Those orange rolls took hours to roll out and then let rise, and her mother had always teased Ren for liking them only because they forced Anna to wake up at five a.m. to make them. When Ren breathed in the sweetness from the top of the stairs, she felt so full of love for her mother that her skin felt tight, as though if someone squeezed her she would burst like fruit. She took the stairs two at a time and ran into the kitchen.

There was no one there.

She walked slowly into the pantry, anticipating a surprise. Once upon a time, her parents were fond of hiding behind corners and springing out loudly. But they were not in the pantry.

There was a note in her mother's handwriting on the stove. "Happy Birthday, Rennie—Love, Mom and Dad."

The orange rolls were browning in the oven, a shade past perfect, so Ren took out the pan and set it on the stove. She went looking for her mother and found her on the back porch swing.

"The birthday girl," said her mother, smiling. She held out her arms, and Ren stepped into them. Her mother's arms were loose around her shoulders.

"I hope you don't mind that we didn't do a party," her mother said, looking out at the brown grass. "You didn't mention wanting one. We thought maybe you were at the point where it wasn't cool to have a party anymore."

"It's fine," Ren said.

"Your dad wants to take you out for a nice dinner."

"Great," said Ren. She sat next to her mother, trying not to rock the swing. "Aren't you coming?"

"We'll see," said her mother.

"Thanks for the orange rolls."

Her mother nodded slowly. Ren shivered, wishing for a coat. She noticed that her mother was barefoot.

"We didn't do anything for Scott's birthday," her mother said.

Ren didn't know what to say. Her mother never said his name.

"June twentieth," said her mother.

Ren wanted to say that she knew that, that she had known very well the day Scott's birthday came and went, but she had not said anything, because she had thought she was not supposed to say anything.

"We should have done something," said her mother. "I wanted to bake a cake, or maybe those strawberry cupcakes he liked, but your dad thought it was a bad idea. He said it would only remind us of things. You wouldn't have minded, would you, if we had made cupcakes?"

Ren shook her head, but her mother wasn't looking.

"Or maybe blackberry pie," said Anna. "He liked blackberry pie."

"He liked every kind of pie," said Ren. She wrapped her arms around herself, twisting her fingers in the sleeves of her flannel pajamas. Her ears were burning from the cold.

Anna's legs were bare, and her nightgown didn't quite cover her knees. She held herself straight. Her hands were in her lap.

"I think we should make a tradition on his birthday," she said. "Maybe plant something. Not that he liked gardening. But maybe we could plant something anyway."

"Maybe," said Ren. She scooted closer to her mother, who was much warmer than the wood of the swing.

Her mother looked over briefly, patting Ren's knee with two cold fingertips.

"I didn't have to do my homework in Mrs. Allen's class," said Ren. "You get a free homework night when it's your birthday."

Her mother nodded thoughtfully. "I need to get batteries for the radio."

The wind blew suddenly, and Ren closed her eyes against the cold. The swing rocked with the wind, and her mother lifted her feet off the ground.

"I took the rolls out of the oven," said Ren. "They were going to burn."

"Good girl," said her mother.

Ren went back into the house. She ate an orange roll, because they were not as good once they cooled. She got ready for school and went to catch the bus, and her mother was still on the porch. She wished her mother had picked another day to say Scott's name. And she wished there had not been orange rolls. If she had walked downstairs without the smell of them, she thought it would have hurt less.

Her father was late that night, and they went to the Italian restaurant down the street for an efficient meal. Ren did not particularly like Italian. When they came back home and she went to pour herself a glass of water, she noticed the pan of rolls still sitting on the stove. The rolls were hard and cold, and only one was missing.

This was her worst memory.

They did not want her to leave for college, which surprised her, because she thought they had forgotten she lived with them. Her mother asked if she would stay in town, go to the small private college in the city.

Ren had cut her hair to chin length; she missed being able to lower it over her face as she read or studied. "I don't want to go there," she said.

"Why?" her mother asked. She had been working in an artsy gift shop, one with handblown glass, endless wine stoppers, and purses made from bottle caps. She had a sheer scarf around her shoulders with flecks of silver.

"I just don't."

"But why?"

"I'd like to see something other than Indiana."

"You could always transfer. We'd love for you to stay around another year or two. You wouldn't even have to live at home. But it would be nice to know you were close."

"We'll see," Ren said. "I've got a list made up already. You're supposed to apply to several."

She thought her mother would ask her to name the other places, but she did not.

"Do you think you'll go into medicine?"

At some stage in elementary school, Ren had wanted to be a pediatrician. "No," she said. "I was thinking I might go into history. Or anthropology. Or psychology. Or sociology. I don't know."

"Like social work," Anna said.

"Not that kind of sociology. But big schools like Arizona have a ton of stuff I'm interested in."

"But why do you want to go so far away?"

Ren didn't answer.

"Why?" repeated her mother. She was toying with her scarf.

Ren shrugged. She felt something shoving itself up her esophagus, threatening to make her gag. She desperately wanted her mother to stop asking her, not to make her say the words that were crowding into her throat, and she also desperately wanted her mother to ask again so that there would be no guilt in answering her. If her mother asked three times, then surely, surely, whatever Ren said would be justified as an answer she was forced into giving.

Her mother did not ask again.

A week later, maybe two weeks later, Ren did not know that the thoughts that had gagged her were still lodged in her throat. She did not know it until her father walked into the den while she was watching *Wheel of Fortune*. Her father, who had taught her how to plant flowers and how to spread pine straw and how to jump in raked leaves. Her father, who had once let the pain in his shoulders flow into the ground and sky. Her father asked her the same question. He had obviously been talking to her mother, which surprised Ren. She didn't think they had conversations.

He held a crystal tumbler in his hand. The alcohol was beautiful as it rolled in waves from side to side.

"Why do you want to go so far away, Rennie?" he asked.

His face was relaxed and kind, and she'd forgotten whether that was how he used to look or whether it was the whiskey. She watched as her mother drifted in from the kitchen, appearing just behind her father's left shoulder. She couldn't see her mother's mouth, but her eyes seemed to be smiling.

"Because I feel like I might kill myself if I stay here with you," Ren said.

Her mother's eyes did not change. Her father did not say a word, but his entire expression shifted. He stared at her, and she thought of martial-arts movies where someone was beheaded in one stroke with a sword, but it took a moment for the head to fall off the neck. The look on his face was the look on one of those heads' faces. Severed.

She turned back to the television. He left the room. A second later, so did her mother. They made no noise. She kept staring at the television. The puzzle was a PLACE, and it had a T, two M's, and two O's.

Vanna turned over one S. Then one N. There was no P.

She had not meant to hurt them. It hadn't occurred to her that it was possible.

The tall red-headed guy asked to buy an A, which was ridiculous, because the answer was clearly Mount Rushmore. Ren considered that she hadn't ever thought she would kill herself. That was wrong, and she shouldn't have said it. What she had thought was that she might already be dead. That she had been in the car with Scott that day, and the reason her parents forgot about her was that she was a ghost, too. Or that she was somewhere in between living and dead, and that as long as she was in this house, she was stuck in limbo. She had to get out or she would fade into nothing like those dead or dying animals left in the middle of the road that somehow vanished from the asphalt after a day or two.

She and her parents never talked about what she'd said. She saw her father the next afternoon, pouring a glass of water, and he smiled and called her "my girl" and seemed to have forgotten about their conversation. They were all good at forgetting. It was in October of her sophomore year in college that her mother called her and said he had died suddenly. He had been driving home from work and crashed his truck into the side of a bridge. Her mother said he had had a heart attack while he was driving.

Ren wished she had told him she was sorry. She wished that she could have gone back to when she was six or seven and, as the girl she had been, talked to the father he had been. She had adored him once, and then he had disappeared—he disappeared so gently, while her mother disappeared so glaringly—and then he had been gone for good. He had been gone already, but she was surprised—inexplicably—by how different death felt.

Once she had gotten in an argument with a limp-haired little girl at school about whose parents were better. That girl's parents, it turned out, were both doctors. And they could ski. Ren had come home and told Scott about the argument, and he had said, without looking up from a stack of cards he was shuffling, "Nobody's parents are better than ours. Don't tell them I said that." Then he looked up and smiled, and they both knew this secret that was only theirs: That they loved their parents and were pleased by them but that it was not the sort of thing they would ever actually admit. And she knew Scott, and he knew her and she imagined she could actually see through his head into his giant-coiled-worm brain and it thumped like a heart and expanded in a great gray hello to her. That's how well she knew Scott in that moment.

Ren went to her father's funeral. It was her first funeral. After the ceremony was over, she and her mother and her grandmother and a preacher and two friends of her mother's stood by the graveside and watched as the coffin was buried. It was a metallic gray-blue color, with black handles, and Ren watched it, wondering what Scott's coffin had looked like. She also watched the buttons on her mother's navy blue blouse, which were silver and shaped like small crescent moons. Her mother's hand was on her shoulder, resting at first, and then leaning harder. Ren felt the weight increase, the pressure from her mother's palm forcing her to slope to one side, and she wondered if the buttons had been polished, because they gleamed like mirrors in sunlight, and it was an overcast day. Her mother bowed her head, and Ren saw a drop land on her mother's chest, right where Ren could see the outline of her mother's bra through the fabric. Then another drop landed, soaking into the material and spreading. As her mother cried, Ren watched her blouse.

And then she looked toward the sky with its wispy clouds and the ground with its neat green grass. The dirt was rich and dark where the casket was being lowered inch by inch. The ground was damp under her feet, and she saw blades of grass stuck to her black heels. Her grandmother was leaning forward onto the balls of her feet, keeping her high heels from sinking like golf tees. Her shoes were beige with a white stripe across the toe, and her legs were remarkably attractive for a woman in her seventies. There was a sneeze and several discordant coughs and her mother's soft crying.

Her mother used to call and call Ren at college to ask why she didn't visit more, why she didn't come by, why she had left. After the years of silence, all these words came pouring out over the phone. The same words, over and over again. Often Ren did not answer the phone. When she did, she would listen and nod and make agreeable sounds. She went home at Christmas only. She would not go home more often, and she would not answer her mother's questions, because she remembered the severed look on her father's face. No good came of talking.

Then one day, as Ren sat on her bed, listening to her mother's questions, she looked down at the phone and took a tally of herself. She decided that she wasn't angry, she wasn't sad, and she didn't feel anything at all.

So she told her mother, "You left first," in a calm, kind voice.

And then her mother stopped calling.

# eight

*Anthropologists have glossed over the mechanisms through which knowledge comes to our awareness. That is, we have studied what the knowledge is, but not how it is received and processed. Although we know that humans experience their world through many ports.*

—From "Perceptual Anthropology: The Cultural
Salience of Symmetry" by Dorothy Washburn,
*American Anthropologist*, September 1999

Driving made Silas think of his father, of road trips when his father would bark for the boys to be quiet in the backseat. His father loved to hear the sounds of the car. Silas, too, liked the hum of the engine, the clunk of ruts in the road. He liked the rhythm of it.

He and Ren had been on the road for more than an hour, headed back to the Crow Creek site. He was still mystified by the turn of events: Ren had gotten a phone call less than an hour after he'd asked to see her notes on the site. There'd been flash flooding, and a chunk of the cliffside along Crow Creek had washed away, exposing more walls. The owner had thought Ren might want to come take a look at the newly uncovered rooms. She did, of course, and so did Silas, no matter how bizarre the coincidence seemed. Ren had not acted surprised at all. She'd had another restless night, and he was beginning to think her insomnia was catching. His eyes were red and dry from lack of sleep.

His father believed strongly in keeping his hands at ten o'clock and two o'clock on the steering wheel, and Silas had his hands in those automatic positions. He looked away from the road and studied Ren, thinking that he enjoyed her face more now than he had that day he heard her speak in Albuquerque. Or the day she'd stepped out of her truck at the bunkhouse. He had a flash of her at the Cañada Rosa, talking about lava flows, chewing her lip as she pointed to the streaks down the canyon walls. Just as she was chewing it now while she looked out the window. She had a small straight scar along the line of her cheekbone—from hitting the edge of a glass table when she was four, she said—that enamored him. The insides of her thighs were incredibly soft.

He cataloged this list of her virtues in hope of smothering his growing frustration with her. She had been edgy throughout the drive—really, he thought, she'd been edgy for the last day or two. Something had clearly rattled her. She kept watching him. It was a different kind of watching than usual. He liked her typical watchfulness, the warm weight of her attention as he worked or talked or slept. She let him know she enjoyed looking at him. But this new watchfulness wasn't admiring. He felt like she was assessing him from a safe distance.

Now, as he drove, her eyes would flicker toward him, then away, slippery and unsettled. Her hand was steady on his leg, but he felt the energy running through her, crackling in the air around her.

"What is it?" he asked finally.

"Nothing."

Her shoulders were tense, and her back was straight.

He ran his tongue over his teeth. A few breaths later, he reached over and brushed his thumb along her jaw before returning his hand to its two-o'clock position. It seemed as if he was perpetually reaching for her, always trying to close some distance while she stayed frozen in place. They both listened to the sounds of the truck for a while.

"Are you ever going to tell me what I said that bothered you so much?" he asked. "You can't blame me for what I say when I'm asleep. It's my subconscious working out issues."

"You didn't say anything."

"Come on. Tell me."

"No," she said.

That's how it works, he thought: I ask you to talk to me, and you give me one syllable. One negative syllable. He didn't like the bitterness of the thought. He reached for his half-full Dr Pepper, popped off the plastic lid and straw, and dumped soda and ice into his mouth. He swallowed the soda and began to crunch the ice. Loudly.

"Fine," she said, after maybe one minute of chewing. He stopped crunching, rolling the ice over his tongue. Although she hated it when he sucked the ice, too. She said she could hear it bumping against his teeth.

"You said," she started. She licked her lips and started again. "You said, 'I love you, Esmeralda.'"

He glanced at her, unamused. "Funny. That is not what I said."

"Uh-huh."

"Seriously, what did I say?"

"'I love you, Justine'?"

"I'm not joking, Ren. Something's bothering you."

"'Clementine'?" she tried again. "'Lucille'?" She was smiling, but her eyes still slipped and slid toward him. He did not smile. He focused on the road. They drove on.

"My head hurts," she said.

He looked over, and her eyes were closed.

"My mother used to rub my temples like this." She lifted her hands and demonstrated. "She said the best thing was to go into a dark room and close your eyes. And if that didn't make it better, get in a cool bath. She would make me lemon tea while I was in the bath, but it had juice in it, too. Orange juice, or maybe apple. Last year I had a terrible migraine, the first I ever had, and I went through all that stuff she told me to do. But I couldn't remember what was in the tea. I guess it didn't matter—I couldn't have gone shopping for ingredients, anyway. But I'd like to have the recipe. It would make me feel better."

She opened her eyes. Silas didn't want to say anything, hoping if she forgot he was there, she would keep talking. She didn't.

"Ask her," he said.

"She said to have a spoon of honey, too," she continued. "She thought honey was good for everything."

"Parents know things like that," he said. "My dad always said for a headache you should dunk your head in a sink full of ice and water."

Silas had dunked more than his head in icy water. When he was eleven, the newspaper proclaimed January 4 to be the coldest day in a hundred years in Silver City, New Mexico. The creek by the house froze still and hard. Silas and Alex started by tapping a toe on the ice, pressing gently. The surface stayed smooth and opaque. They slowly shifted more and more weight onto their feet. Then they began creeping, inch by inch, onto the smooth expanse. Finally they concluded that the creek had frozen solid.

This led to a new game. The boys would take turns getting a running start and throwing as much weight onto the ice as possible. It was a long jump onto the ice, a tumbling pass. It was a test of brute force. They would see what it took to break open this unnaturally solid thing. They would crack it open and see its insides. (His memories of Alex always came back to action and doing. There didn't seem to be any memories of talking, no late nights huddled under the covers, whispering or plotting. His brother had their father's miserliness with words. Even now, Silas and Alex discussed sports, watched sports, and occasionally—with knees and backs permitting—played sports. Alex did not have heartfelt conversations. Silas remembered wanting to sometimes crack open Alex or their father, not to hurt them but just to see what they were thinking, to know what thoughts churned around inside their heads, never to be released. He craved words and stories and talking and laughter, and his mother, at least, helped fill the silence of the house.)

Both brothers soon forgot it was even conceivable for the ice to break. Silas found large, flat rocks and tied them onto the bottom of his sneakers with his shoelaces. He stomped across the ice. Alex retrieved a hammer from their father's off-limits tool shed, but the hammer barely nicked the gray glass of the creek. (Silas wondered now what Alex remembered of that day. He felt sure that if he asked him, Alex would talk about the bitter cold and the satisfying thwack of the hammer against the ice and how much he had wanted to beat Silas. Silas wondered why they had been so drawn to breaking things, why games were always about crashing and banging and knocking things—including themselves—to the ground. He could remember many times as an adult when the sight of frozen bodies of water had been blindingly beautiful, but he remembered no sense of the creek's beauty or any sense of the magic of the snow. He remembered wanting to blast snowballs against the walls of the house. Maybe an appreciation of beauty came along with puberty, timed with facial hair and the smell of sweat. But even now, these were the kinds of thoughts that his brother—and father, too?— would surely never have.)

They grew tired of the game and drifted back to the house. The next day, Silas was outside by himself; Alex had gone to town with their mother. Their father was chopping cottonwood for the fire, so Silas wandered down to the water by himself. It was early afternoon, and the sun was bright. The cold air bit into his skin, and the creek appeared solid. He followed its mild twists and turns, looking for signs of fish or other animals trapped in the ice. He had visions of fish stuck mid-swim, of water snakes frozen in S-formations. But he saw nothing other than clouded gray. When he stopped walking, he was nearly a mile from the house, far from the spot where he and Alex had played the day before. With no other entertainment presenting itself, he decided to have another go at the creek. As he left the ground, pushing off from the bank, his foot slid onto the ice. He knew he was in trouble then—he could feel that the ice had some give to it—but he was already in motion, in the air. He landed in the middle of the creek, and the ice gave way with a crack. There was the slightest pause, and then he was falling, like one of those clowns at the fair who plunge into a barrel of water when a baseball hits the right target.

He lost his breath to the cold, even with his head still above water. Then he was completely underwater, unable to move, feeling his feet hit bottom. He managed to push off, out of reflex, and his head broke the surface. It was not a deep creek, and he could surely stand up, but he couldn't make his feet and legs work. Burning, burning cold. He took a long second to try to breathe, only his face above the water. Then he fought his way out. He had a few feet to get to the creek bank, and the ice broke away from his hands when he tried to boost himself onto it. So he whacked at it with numb hands, knocking chunks away as he stepped heavily through the water, his jeans heavy weights. His could hear his teeth.

At the bank, he heaved himself out and lay sprawled on the dirt and weeds and pebbles. He was soaked, and he suspected the strands of his hair were starting to freeze. The day before, it had hit twenty degrees—it must be closer to thirty degrees now. Right around freezing, since the sun had thawed out the creek. But he thought he might not be able to walk back to the house. He could barely move, his skin was blue-tinged, and his shivering made it difficult to think.

As he inhaled, he could feel a sheet of ice forming on the inside of his throat, spreading down to his lungs.

Still, because there was no choice, he stood up. He took one step and then another, hunched over slightly, arms wrapped around himself. He tried to jog, to warm up, but he didn't have enough coordination for it. He stuck his fingers in his armpits and took short, measured steps. He tripped over a log and fell down, slicing his right palm, barely able to get his hands out so he wouldn't land on his face.

He found a rhythm and tried to think about anything but the cold. His parents would be panicked. They would rush him to the hospital, and that would be where the news cameras would find him. His father would hug him and ruffle his hair like Silas remembered from when he was very small. His father would probably say how proud he was, especially if there were newspaper headlines. He wondered if they would be able to get him on the six-o'clock news that night. He imagined telling the whole story to his teacher, Miss Whisenhut, who had blue eyes and black hair to her waist. He would tell her how he couldn't feel his fingers or his feet and how he thought his lips had frozen shut. He imagined Miss Whisenhut's arm around him and the curve of her breast possibly brushing against his head.

There—his house. The plain brown walls of it and the dirt drive-way. He saw his father, still chopping wood. He nearly laughed with relief. He made the last few steps to his father, close enough to feel the warmth rising off his father's wide back.

His father looked up from the wood. He did not put down the ax.

"Fall in?"

"Yessir."

"Better hurry with your shower. Your mother'll need help with the groceries."

"Yessir."

"Take your shoes off before you go inside."

"Yessir."

Silas walked into the house without another word. He took a shower, changed his clothes, and was rubbing a towel over his hair when his mother pulled into the driveway. He told her about the creek, but in his story, the fall through the ice and the walk home were only amusing things. He said he had imagined newspaper headlines: "Boy Narrowly Escapes Frozen Death" or "Boy Saves Own Life with Death-Defying Trek." His mother laughed, which was what he'd intended. Once the warm water had steamed away the chill from his skin and his blood and his bones, he could see that no one should brag about falling into a thawed-out creek. There was nothing heroic to it. It had been stupid and childish, and he had seen that written across his father's face. He hated to see the onset of his father's disapproval—he could see the lines forming, the forehead wrinkling and narrowing of the eyes and tightening of the mouth, before any of those small shifts had even taken place. He waited for the displeasure to take shape.

His father was a capable man whom other people flocked to if they needed help with tools or equipment, but he was an unflinching pragmatist. When it was time to kill the lambs, Silas's father used a pocketknife. He could lift a two-hundred-pound calf without making a sound. To treat poison ivy, he skimmed a razor across the entire length of his leg, cutting the top off the rash, then poured bleach over the open wounds. He expected competence from his sons, second only to his expectation of good judgment. "You'll grow up, and you'll be a good man or a bad man," his father had said. "There's nothing in the middle." Silas very much did not want to be a bad man.

He and Alex could both fish by the time they were six, and within a year or two after that, they could recognize the tracks of almost any animal that happened across the winding dirt driveway. Silas could change a tire long before he could drive. His father drilled him on multiplication tables and spelling words, emphasized the importance of saying "Please" and "Thank you" and helping their mother with chores.

His mother was just as competent as his father—she could wrap tamales as she made a pot of coffee, all the while asking just the right questions about Silas's homework assignments—but she had a joy about her. She made Silas's father laugh, a loud, coughing sound that seemed to surprise him each time it escaped from his mouth. Once his father laughed so hard he sprayed milk all over the platters of fried eggs and bacon and tortillas, and Silas's mother started breakfast over again.

Silas wanted to tell Ren these childhood stories, but the stories never came out as he hoped. They were so clear in his head, but they changed when they spilled out into the air. He would intend to capture his father's strength and goodness, but instead the stories captured something cold in the man, something Silas did not recognize. These stories of slaughtered animals and callused palms made people wince. Still, he could tell them to Ren. He could tell her any number of things. But he found that what he most wanted was for her to tell him something. Anything. For her to let her stories and her fears and whatever was bothering her at this very second spill out into the air. All she was giving him was ghosts. He needed something more substantial.

They were in the foothills of the Piños Altos Mountains, up above six thousand feet. They'd driven through Silver City half an hour ago, and since then, they'd seen only ranch land in the foreground and mountains in the distance. The asphalt highway had given way to a gravel road, and they hadn't seen another truck for miles.

After half an hour of gravel, Ren pointed to a blue sign nailed to a gatepost.

"Turn there," she said. "Lanark Ranch."

The land dipped and rose, with few trees, few houses, and endless blowing grass. They passed through two green iron gates with "Do Not Enter" signs, and when they came to a third, Ren gnawed her lip for a moment and peered across the fields. The rise and fall of the hills obscured the view. A small copse of juniper and scrub oaks, plus a few ash trees, paralleled a long line of barbed wire to their right.

Ren announced that they wouldn't be able to get the truck any closer to the site, so they pulled under the shade of a decent-sized oak and grabbed what they could easily carry. They walked along a rough path cut through the trees, passing close to the barbed wire and the juniper fence posts. They each carried a backpack and a duffel bag of supplies. Tiny talons from catclaw shrubs grabbed at the bags, at clothing, at the backs of their hands. They stepped over a single pile of hay-crusted horse droppings, and passed a tall dead yucca plant stooping like a sad long-haired woman. Already Silas could hear Crow Creek below them, a giddy sound with bubbling exclamations. It reminded him of high school girls during lunch period.

A flock of birds burst from undergrowth on the other side of the barbed wire, and Ren jumped, actually lifted both her feet off the ground, as she spun around.

"What is the matter with you?" snapped Silas.

"Maybe too much coffee," she said, looking at her feet.

"Right," he said.

When they came out of the woods, they were on a wide, flat plateau a few hundred feet above the water. It looked like it had once been good grazing land, but now it held only a few juniper and piñon and some particularly scraggly mesquite. The flat land dropped off suddenly, offering a view of the creek below. A trail wound down to the bank, through shrubs and cacti and stubby grasses.

Peering down, Silas could see the river terraces descending to the water. Grassy slopes and sandstone cliffs rose on the other side of the creek—despite its enthusiastic chatter, it was only a thin ribbon surrounded by sand and gravel and hopeful trees. The view was much better across the water: The willows and sycamores had turned white-silver in the afternoon sun, a fringe rising up against the vertical rock wall Silas faced. The rock was layered sandstone, the same distinctive outcroppings—Gila Conglomerate, the geologists called it. Some lips and ledges of it supported an occasional prickly pear or catclaw. From a distance the rock rippled, fluid as the water that had carved it. The sandstone cliff gave way to grassy, juniper-dotted slopes to the north, and farther along there was an impressive volcanic knob topping one peak.

Ren's feet crunched over the pebbles behind him, and he felt her hand at his waist.

"Turtle Rock," she said, nodding at the volcanic knob. He could see why the name had stuck. "People say the Apache kept the women and children up there when they went raiding."

Silas stepped away from her hand. They followed the perimeter of the cliff until they spotted where the ledge had buckled. The collapse had uncovered a row of walls—four walls, so at least two rooms—that had been buried completely. It was too late to set up equipment and start measurements. They began setting up camp before the sun set.

The process did not go as smoothly as they had hoped. The ground was hard and resistant to the tent pegs. One of the pegs was missing altogether, though they found a large rock to use as an anchor. And when Silas reached for his lighter, his pocket was empty. He decided it must have fallen out somewhere along the hike to or from the truck. A quick search turned up an old pack of matches in his jacket pocket. He left Ren unrolling the sleeping bags while he went searching for dead wood for the fire.

More out of curiosity than efficiency, he decided to try the trail down to the creek. He jogged the first few nearly vertical steps; then the ground flattened slightly. For the first few yards, he was on solid bedrock. Volcanic sandstone, he thought. The Gila Wilderness was once a huge volcanic cauldron—hot springs were still bubbling up all over the place. Eventually waters washed all the volcanic ash and debris down into what became the creek bed.

The bedrock gave way to more greenery as he worked his way down—the shrubs grew thicker, and he could see tall spears of yucca off to his right. He enjoyed the steep walk, enjoyed noting the level of each terrace, the change in the flora around him. He would be glad to start hacking at the earth tomorrow. He was ready to feel tools in his hand, to stretch a string taut for a measurement, to sketch a meter-by-meter map. Though he hadn't said anything to Ren, he was ready to be out of her house. He was ready to get away from her dining room table and his laptop. He had started to feel ungrounded in her space, especially as she put in full days at the museum and he drifted through her house while she was gone. He could forget at times, when he was comfortably settled into a routine of sifting through dirt and studying outcroppings of stone and scrubbing at sherds with a toothbrush, that it was possible to feel ill at ease or out of place. Not that he didn't make mistakes in the field. Not that he didn't guess wrong or miss connections sometimes. But he always fit. He knew the right steps. There was a flow and an order to things, and he was in it and a part of it, like the yellow lichen growing on the rock just in front of his foot or the willows below, drinking from the creek. When he was on-site, he felt only sureness.

Ren was not as easy, not as readable as a wall of rock or the layers of a trash heap. He lay next to her at night, but there was still this wide expanse of open sand and gravel between them, just as there had been in the early days of the canyon. The last few days had deepened this feeling of separation, but the separateness had been there all along. He had grown more and more aware of it. He did not know how to bridge it.

He had learned the basics of flint-knapping, of shaping rock into tools. More specifically, using one rock—a hammerstone—to whack little pieces off a second rock until you'd made a dart point or a knife or an ax or such. He liked shaping obsidian, although it inevitably made him bleed. But if you wanted to break obsidian, you needed a soft rock to use for your hammerstone. Too much force would shatter the obsidian.

He watched Ren, and it was like walking up to the sheer pink walls of the canyon, craning your neck and trying to comprehend the lines and scope and sculpture of this thing that you could never quite see all at once. Or watching just one small piece of that same rock in the palm of your hand, catching the sun and throwing off colors that were unnamable, until you realized that it had ceased to be a known object. To watch her and feel his reaction to her—it shook him.

The downhill walk jarred his knees. The trees grew bigger as he got closer to the water: The junipers towered thirty or forty feet above him. He worked his way down onto the last terrace before the floodplain. He found what he was looking for and made his way back to Ren.

She was watching for him when he reached the top of the trail.

"Why do you have dead sticks?" she asked.

"They're seep willows."

She nodded, obviously waiting for more.

"The Spanish called them *yerba de pasmo*," he said.

"Okay, herb," she said. "Herb of . . . what?"

"Chills. People used the leaves to make a remedy for chills. And I think they chewed the stems for toothaches."

"Do you have a toothache?"

"No. The dead sticks are perfect for roasting marshmallows."

She raised her eyebrows. "We have marshmallows?"

"*Sí.* Lucky for you, I packed the groceries."

Night fell, and the temperature dropped. They'd brought sandwiches but needed a fire for warmth, and they took their time cooking and savoring the marshmallows. The melted sugar and the heat and the view of the stars left Silas content and lethargic. Ren was pressed against his side, and he felt affection return full force, trumping frustration. It was difficult to stay angry with her when she had marshmallow, inexplicably, in her eyelashes.

The thought made him swipe at his beard; he located a sticky patch and scraped at it with one finger. Then he could feel her eyes on him again, and when he turned, she looked away. He felt his contentment evaporating.

"Why do you keep looking at me like that?" he asked again.

"I'm not looking at you."

"Do you think I don't know when you're looking at me?"

"Obviously you don't."

"Aurenthia," he said, exhausted.

"I'm not looking at you. Not at you."

He caught the distinction. "So what are you looking at?"

A pause. "Nothing."

He stood, twisting at the waist, popping his back. She seemed startled by the sudden movement.

"You're a terrible liar," he said. "And you're driving me crazy."

She only looked up at him. He made one last effort.

"Tell me what's bothering you," he said evenly.

Objectively, he couldn't help but be fascinated by the workings of her face in the firelight. She wanted to tell him. She wanted him to leave her alone. She didn't want him to be angry with her. She was pissed off that he was pushing her. Her jaw and lips moved, just tiny pulses of movement, and her eyes slipped and slid.

"This will be a mistake," she said. But now her gaze was steady, holding his, and he knew he had won. He sat beside her again.

"What will be a mistake?"

"To tell you."

"Try it," he said.

She didn't pause at all, and later, when he thought back on it, he was impressed that once she made up her mind, she didn't flinch.

"You saw Lynay the other night," she said. "Or maybe you just felt her."

"What?"

"Lynay. At my house. In bed two nights ago. She was leaning over you, and her hair brushed against your face. It made your nose itch, and you sniffed. Then you said, 'Who are you?'"

He kept his face empty as his mind whirred. So this was what she had been watching and waiting for: this moment of revelation when he would show that he did not believe in her ghosts and never had. He looked at her as intently as she looked at him, the blue-black sky around her face, and knew she had been preparing for him to fail her test. Or for her to fail his. He wasn't sure which.

"I told you it would be a mistake to tell you," she said.

"I didn't say anything," he said.

"Exactly."

"I know this won't really raise the level of our discourse," he said, "but you're being such a girl. Quit reading too much into a few seconds of silence."

"You don't have to pacify me," she said. "You don't have to believe me. But you asked me what happened, and I told you. So don't blame me for this whole awkward situation."

Her jaw was jutting slightly, and her eyes looked too big for their sockets.

Silas shifted slightly in the dirt. He felt a rock digging into his thigh. The truth was that he did not believe in actual ghosts that wandered around sites and haunted lovely archaeologists. He did not believe that spirits mimed little dramas, trying to get someone to pay attention. He did believe in spirits, but he believed these spirits were subtle, prone to whisperings and nudges and inspirations. Intuition.

"You know about Eilean Donan, the Scottish castle?" he asked.

Now she looked less defensive, more annoyed. "What?"

"In the early nineteen hundreds, a stonemason in Scotland claimed to have had a vision of the Eilean Donan castle as it had been in the fourteenth century. The castle was in complete ruins by that time. But it was rebuilt according to the stonemason's vision, and when the actual plans for the castle were found years later, they matched his vision down to the slightest detail."

She looked less annoyed.

"And there was a geologist who found a fossil, some sort of prehistoric fish," he continued. "Agassiz was the man's name. He couldn't figure out how the fish had looked, the bone structure was so bizarre. Then he had a dream for three nights in a row that showed him the fish, and he finally sketched what he saw in his dream. It matched the fossil perfectly."

"So what are you saying?" she asked. "You think I'm daydreaming?"

"No," he said. "I think you've seen something, understood something. I think your ghosts are your subconscious trying to give you clues."

He believed that dreams and visions were the hippie cousins of the scientific method. He believed there was value to them. He believed that knowledge could bend and twist itself into surprising shapes. He did not believe a bit of subconscious knowledge could tickle his nose.

"You think I'm imagining it all," she said, matter-of-factly.

"No. I believe you've seen something that I don't," he said. "I believe there's something here. I believe your ghosts are a manifestation of your insights."

"You don't think she's a figment of my imagination?" she asked.

"No," he said, and meant it.

"Okay," she said, and meant it. "I'll take that for now. But you're wrong: She's not just an idea. She's too annoying."

He looked at her and thought how much he loved her face.

*She woke him, whimpering, as she sometimes did. Monster dreams, he called them. He had nightmares himself occasionally, but hers always took the form of a child's terrors—witches, werewolves, vampires, dark shadowed things under the bed.*

*He slid a hand down her warm arm as he shushed her, whispering, "It's a dream," in her ear.*

*She was instantly awake, breathing heavily. "Oh. Thanks."*

*"Vampire?" he guessed. The last one had been a werewolf climbing in through her bedroom window, and she had known it had already eaten her parents.*

*"Witch," she said, speech sleep-slurred. "I was hiding behind Dad's recliner, and she was coming for me, so I jumped out and grabbed her, and when I put my fingers in her mouth, she bit me."*

*"Well, honey," he said, "that's what you get if you stick your finger in a witch's mouth."*

*She snorted, stretching her arms, then rolled over to wedge her head under his chin.*

*He wrapped both arms around her, warding off witches. He pressed his cheek against her hair.*

*"The monsters are always in your house, aren't they?" he said.*

*She didn't answer. He assumed she had fallen asleep again.*


He had seen another site suddenly revealed like this, bared to the fresh air after a layer of earth had washed away. That had been an untouched site, a huge site, maybe as big as any Mimbres village ever found. The pueblo had been built near a big seep at the meeting of a side canyon and the west fork of the Mimbres River.

The site was a treasure. Hundreds of rooms. The secrets they could hold, the details of architecture and diet and social structure, of trade patterns and spirituality and health. The entire pueblo had been covered and hidden for centuries, no hint of it above the surface. It was located in an alluvial fan, where water had washed down a slope and spread several feet of silt and gravel—alluvium—over the once surface-level village. So it all disappeared under the dirt. Then arroyos had cut through the land, and the walls had started to show themselves.

The pueblo was found in 1989, just months before the burial laws banning the destruction of burial sites went into effect, and Silas had come out to the site only because his professors had mentioned it. He was a college kid with no experience. But he got directions and drove himself down the narrow county road. He was careful and quiet, staying on the right side of the "No Trespassing" signs, peering over barbed wire to get a look at the edges of the walls. He knew the site would take years, and that maybe if he played his cards right, he could be a part of the excavation. He could help uncover an entire world.

Then the bulldozers had come. The owner of the land needed money, and Silas understood that. These were the same people, with the same set of problems and fears, he had grown up knowing. The ranchers who came to drink coffee with his father were just like these men along the Mimbres. They had their land and not much else. So if they found out that suddenly a patch of dirt that happened to hold a bunch of old bowls could be worth tens of thousands, maybe hundreds of thousands, of dollars, they cashed in. Those bowls could mean sending kids to college, a new roof, retirement. And they were only talking about digging up a bunch of old bowls and old houses and old bones.

He had once heard a preacher say that because these bones weren't Christian bones, they didn't have to be counted as human. They deserved no more care than rabbit or coyote bones.

Silas came back after the bulldozers had come, after the earth had been torn up and pushed around. There were bodies scattered through the backfill. He could see the bones piled up in the dirt— ribs and mandibles and tibiae and patellae, skulls. Tiny bones of children and infants. And mixed in with the bones there were river stones from the walls, wooden posts from the ceilings. When he got closer, close enough to smell the freshly churned earth, he could see teeth scattered through the dirt, canines and molars and incisors. Some black-and-white sherds. There had been whole bowls, of course, but they were gone now.

The neighbors said that the art dealers had lined up along the barbed-wire fence, yelling out offers as the bowls were pulled from the backfill. They could be handed a bowl then and there, a successful deal made, and they could walk off with their bowls and leave the bones behind them.

Later a group of archaeologists had still excavated the ravaged site—there were still burials and a few stray walls left in place. They found the faunal remains of domesticated turkeys—a first. But Silas never worked at the place, never even tried to arrange an assignment. He hated the thought of bones out of place, scattered and left behind. Even now, if the images surfaced, if he pictured it all in his mind, the memory made him tired.

Ren wasn't awake yet, and the sun was just coming up. Silas had needed to pee, and now he stood outside their tent and watched the light spread across the sky, spilling warm over the flats. He twisted to the side and cracked his back. He rubbed his hands over his rough cheeks. He could feel bits of Gila Conglomerate in his beard. He would make coffee later. Now he wanted to rinse off, to wash the grime off his hands and feet and face, at least, and get his thoughts together.

He couldn't find soap. He must have forgotten to pack it.

He started down the trail, which felt slicker and less stable to his sleep-sluggish feet. He skidded right away and righted himself quickly. He brushed against a branch of honey mesquite—which had more substantial claws than the catclaw—and scraped his arm. No blood. Something small moved in the brush—probably a bird. He paused but couldn't see anything. He started down again. He made a point of concentrating on his feet, watching the trail instead of the sideoats and blue grama and juniper reaching toward him. There did seem to be an awful lot of honey mesquite on this trail, though. And something else was rustling off to his left. Something bigger. Maybe a rabbit. He looked toward the sound and noticed a clump of whisklike snakeweed mottled green and brown—good not just for snakebites but as a cure for joint pain, his mind supplied.

He remembered one of his last arguments with his ex-wife—they rarely even had arguments, that's how much distance had accumulated between them by the end of the marriage—when she kept insisting that they were fine. The marriage was fine. She was happy, he was happy, everything was wonderful. And he said, "No, it's not." He said, "I'm not happy. And you can't really be happy. Shouldn't we at least try to talk about this?"

Tina said, "Since when does the man want to talk about relationships? Isn't that supposed to be my line? There's nothing to talk about."

He hated not talking.

He tried to keep his mind on his footing.

But then there was the most amazing rock lichen underneath a mesquite bush. The lichen's bright yellow and rust-orange paint splotches covered the entire rock, impossibly bright. He wondered if he was wrong, if it actually was painted, but no, that was ridiculous. He stopped and looked, bending sideways at the waist, so when his foot slipped on a smattering of pebbles, his balance was off. The trick to falling was to let your feet go ahead and slide forward and just sit down into the fall. Scraped hands and a sore butt would be the worst of it. But one leg went out from under him, and he was slamming onto the ground flat on his back, too fast, too hard, head snapping forward and then back onto solid rock. And then he was not aware of anything.

❖ ❖ ❖

The light was too bright. Sun in his eyes and a headache. And he was lying on the ground. None of this made any sense at all. Why would he be lying on the ground? He had been tired earlier, not quite awake. Maybe he lay down here on this trail? He shifted, and his head throbbed. *Oh*. The pain made it all clearer. That sonofabitch lichen.

He heard Ren's voice above, calling for him. He sat up, wincing.

"Here," he yelled, and his voice echoed around his skull unpleasantly. "I fell down."

He still couldn't see her, but he could hear her steps coming quickly. He wondered how long he had been lying here and how long she had been calling.

"You okay?" she called.

"Yeah. I tripped on a rock," he said.

He saw her feet and then her face as she leaned over him and her hands landed on his shoulders. He was still lying flat, so her face was upside down. He expected to find her rolling her eyes, teasing him. At Cañada Rosa he had fallen into the stream several times, his toes slipping off the rocks, soaking his boots.

She was not laughing. A tear hit his cheek.

"You're crying," he said.

"No, I'm not."

She straightened, then knelt beside him, her hands still on him. He was at a loss for a moment, watching the tears stream down her face and splat on the dirt.

"Yes, you are," he finally replied.

She raised a hand to her face, touching her cheek lightly, like checking to see if paint was still wet.

"I don't cry," she said, looking up at him. "I really never cry. Not ever."

He cocked his head. There had been a touch of pride in her voice.

"You're crying," he said again.

"I heard you leave the tent," she said. "And I heard the grass rustling down here. Then you yelled."

"I don't remember yelling."

"Well, you yelled, and so I got up and came out here and called for you. And called and called. So I started down here, still calling. And I couldn't see anything, but then I saw your foot and the blue of your jeans on the ground. And you weren't moving at all, and you didn't answer me. Then I got close enough to see that your eyes were closed. There's some blood on this rock, and you still didn't answer me."

"Was I out more than a few seconds?"

"It felt longer than that."

"Do we have any Tylenol?" he asked, trying to raise his head and finding that movement was easier if he kept his eyes closed. "It's just a little slice off my scalp, but I might have a serious bump."

"You looked dead," she said.

This stopped him. "I'm not. Not remotely dead."

"Maybe it was a mistake coming out here," she said, lowering herself onto a rock. She had not bothered to button her jeans. He braced one hand on her knee and pushed himself into a sitting position.

"Because I tripped?" he asked.

"You could have been really hurt."

His thoughts did not seem quite clear, so he tried to carefully consider what she was saying. It didn't make sense.

"I fall down all the time," he said.

"Still."

He ran both hands over his scalp. Everything felt normal, other than the one missing chunk. He wiggled his toes and his fingers, flexed his legs and arms. He took his time, taking inventory of muscles and joints and bones.

"I've broken both arms," he said. "I've gotten a few concussions, sprained my left ankle seven—no, eight—times. Let's see. Dislocated my shoulder. Did I tell you about that time I killed a rattlesnake with a can of ravioli? You and I would be working in a bank if we wanted to sit at a desk all day. What's got you so disturbed?"

"I'm not disturbed," she said, as a tear slid into her mouth.

The only sound was the rushing of the creek.

"You are definitely disturbed," he said calmly, but his words were clipped and tight. "And it's not just me falling down. Something's worrying you."

He could feel an ant bite starting to sting on his hand. His head hurt.

"You scared me," she said finally, running a hand across her face. She looked as worn down as he felt. "I had a few seconds where I thought you were lying dead right in front of me, gone, and the idea of losing you terrified me. Okay?"

He looked down to take a breath. She was right, he noticed—there was blood on the rock where his head had landed. He shifted his eyes to her face. She was trying to stop the crying, desperately trying to not look disturbed at all, and he wished he was still unconscious and could wake up and start the whole scene again. He did not like this place. He did not like how tense they had been ever since they got in the truck and headed to this hillside. He had thought the edginess was her fault, but now he wasn't sure. There was sadness on her face, and he would swear there was love there, and the tamped-down terror she'd admitted. He wished they were back in the canyon, back in their little side-by-side rooms where he could hear her bare feet padding toward his bed after she'd changed into that blue T-shirt with bear prints.

"I'm sorry you thought I bashed my brains in," he said.

She smiled, weakly.

"I like your brains," she said. "In your head, specifically."

They got to their feet together, and he felt reasonably steady. Other than a headache, he felt perfectly normal. After a few steps up the hill, a few steps behind Ren, he thought even the headache wasn't as bad as he had thought. Maybe he wouldn't even bother with the Tylenol—it was only a bump.

He hummed, some lyric on the edges of his thoughts. The tune was there, barely, and he felt like he could tease the words into focus. A girl and a car. Summer. Something about a girl and a car and summer.

*"Barefoot girl sitting on the hood of a Dodge,"* he sang softly.

And, amazingly, Ren picked it up, her hand in his. *"Drinking warm beer in the soft summer rain."*

He paused, keeping hold of her hand, so she turned back. She had a pretty voice.

"Springsteen," she said. "Scott used to sing it all the time."

"I don't know what made me think of it," he said. "I don't even know the name of the song."

"'Jungleland,'" she supplied. They started moving again.

"Oh." He dodged a catclaw. "Who's Scott?"

She had been scrambling up a patch of gravel, bracing one foot against a rock, but she stopped. She was frozen with one foot and one hand touching the ground, like a sprinter just leaping off the starting block.

"Who's Scott?" he asked again.

For a moment, she actually did not know the answer to the question. Her mind was filled only with panic, with the desperate need to undo her own words. She didn't know how she could have gotten so lax, so unguarded, that Scott's name would fall out of her mouth. But there was no choice, no way to back up. She spoke around the panic.

"My brother."

She started climbing again. He did not.

"You said you didn't have any siblings."

She was still heading up, and she found that it was easier to speak if she focused on her feet. She would continue to let the words fall out, and she would stay as far away from them as possible. "I don't," she said. "Not now. He died when I was twelve. In a car wreck. He was seventeen."

"You had a brother who died?"

She would not slow down. "He died when I was twelve. I don't talk about him much."

He was not behind her anymore, so she did look at him, briefly. More words, he needed more words. "It wasn't a lie," she said. "I just don't talk about him."

Mercifully, he did not say more. She was allowed to stop talking. Which was good, because she was having trouble breathing. She swallowed again and again, trying to clear her throat.

Those few details that she had blurted out to him—the fact that Scott had existed, the fact that he had died, the way that he had died—had taken everything she had. She had thought the words would choke her, but they hadn't, and she had handed her brother over to Silas. It felt like she had run a long way—exhausting, depleting, but with a trace of adrenaline.

Now he was silent, surely realizing how much it had cost her. He knew her, and he was the only one who ever had. She looked back at him, grateful, but the look on his face puzzled her. He looked hurt, which she assumed must be because of the bump on his head.

He did not say anything else, because he couldn't think of what to say. She had a brother—someone she had played with and eaten breakfast with, someone who surely tormented her and called her insulting names. A brother. A brother who had died in a terrible sudden way that surely made her cry even if she never cried. She had never mentioned him.

Silas had told her dozens of stories about Alex. He had told her dozens of stories about everyone and everything—he loved her, and he wanted her to know him, because how could she love him back if she didn't know him? And how could he love her properly if he didn't hand over all these things? When she listened to his memories, she became a part of them. She stood there next to him when he was mesmerized by his first puppy, stoned in his undergrad dorm, half dead from dehydration in Peru. Each story pulled her deeper into his head, and he wanted her there.

His head throbbed. He hadn't known about her brother. He hadn't known until the last twenty-four hours that she thought a dead woman's hair had tickled his nose in his sleep. He had not known her spirits were so tangible. When he considered these ghost stories of hers intellectually, blocking out his attachment to her, they defied belief. He did not want to hear more of them. The woman who told them was a stranger.

And the omission of a dead brother was malicious. She had told Silas that she loved him. But if she loved him, and if she also loved Scott (which she must have, because you had to love your brother even if you hated him), then she would have shared Scott with Silas. She would have trusted him. It would have been proof of her own feelings.

Her silence seemed to be proof of something else, but he didn't know what. He thought it must somehow reflect on him.

# nine

*The emergence theme involves the passage between lay-ers or worlds through an opening or portal; the Mim-bres symbolized the portal by the kill hole in mortuary bowls ... [as well as] by the slab-lined rectangular hearth and the hatchway into the house.*

—From "Architecture and Symbolism in Transitional Pueblo Development in the Mimbres Valley, SW New Mexico" by Harry J. Shafer, *Journal of Field Archaeology,* Spring 1995

Ren did not like the feel of the air at the site. In the two days since Silas had knocked himself unconscious, a pair of Silas's socks had vanished, along with Ren's bug spray. They both showed up in the backseat of the truck, which was odd but understandable—their backpacks might have been unfastened. Then the keys to the truck, which they both knew had been zipped in the side pocket of Silas's backpack, dropped off the face of the earth for nearly twenty-four hours. Just as the sun was going down on their third day at the site, Silas found them in the pocket of a sweatshirt he didn't remember wearing. He'd misplaced his watch last night and still hadn't found it.

Now, on the third full day at the site, things were not merely disappearing—they were breaking. The sole had come off her right boot as she was making her way down to the creek. The blade of the pickax had come loose from its handle, sailing over Silas's shoulder and into the mesquite below. It decapitated several blades of grama grass before it lodged in the dirt. Not an hour later, when he flipped open his pocketknife, the catch had misfired and the blade sliced a gill across his thumb. He said he was always accident-prone, and that was true.

But still, she did not like sharp blades flying through the air. The ground under her seemed suspect. It was as if everything was coming loose around her, as if nothing was anchored. She or Silas could topple off the cliff at any moment. And as keys and watches blinked in and out of existence, as Ren felt the last of her careful barricades disintegrating, Lynay was becoming more and more concrete.

On the night they arrived and set up camp, the girl had been lingering around their campfire, holding a basket of bright yellow star-shaped flowers. She made no noise as she walked, and she'd been inching toward Silas. Ren had noticed her several times around the edge of camp, always with flowers.

She watched the muscles in Silas's forearms as he dug, shirt-sleeves rolled just below his elbows, and she liked the pale strip of skin where his watch had been. She remembered nipping the tan lines there once and tasting dirt. She shifted her gaze to his face—he was overly focused on digging. She could not make him understand that she never mentioned Scott, that she had not said his name to anyone alive in the last nineteen years. She could not say it. She had learned not to say it. She had learned to defend against the past, because it would swallow you whole if you let it.

It made no sense to her why he would presume that her speaking—or not speaking—of Scott had anything to do with him. He didn't know anything about Scott, didn't know anything about the years before and after his death. He had a brother of his own, and he had parents who never forgot about his existence, even if his father seemed to be a bit of an asshole. He was judging her as if his personal experience gave him any idea of her own. He did not know enough to have an opinion.

But she had hurt him. The guilt was, so far, trumping her sense of righteous indignation. And underneath the guilt was a fear that she was wrong, not just about this but wrong on some fundamental level. Maybe the ghosts were a punishment. Maybe the threat to Silas was some retribution against her. Maybe the ghosts wanted something she wasn't giving them, and if she could interpret the signs right, she could save him.

Despite her wandering thoughts, she and Silas were working quite efficiently. Perhaps they should try not talking more often. She could see frustration in the lines of his body and the set of his face, but if anything, he was digging faster, moving more dirt.

The placement of the rooms made it difficult. She and Silas were perched precariously on the side of the cliff, with very little room to maneuver. It wasn't a steep drop—the worst that could happen was that they would slide a few feet and skin their elbows or knees—but the incline made climbing in and out of the pit difficult. She couldn't relax into the site.

They'd found three rooms, and at the base of a wall in the first room they'd found what was left of two infant burials and an older child's burial. The bones had been scattered, which was common with the bones of children, so easily disrupted or carted away by predators. If there had ever been pottery with the burials, it had been stolen or destroyed over the course of centuries. These were thousand-year-old babies, nameless and unknowable. She and Silas covered them and moved on to the next room.

The dirt was dry and clumped, and her hands were rubbed raw from breaking it down. She banged one stubborn clump against the side of the screen, and a layer of dirt fell away. She brushed her thumb over the remaining rock. Babies. She hated finding them, although on a site of any size you were bound to find plenty of infants. It was more common to find juvenile burials than adult burials. Early death was a trend in most nonindustrial societies, and the prehistoric Southwest was no different. Infants, toddlers, children, teenagers barely out of childhood—they were more vulnerable. The thought of tiny fragile bones made Ren screen more carefully.

They discovered the cluster of bodies late on their third day.

"Human bone," said Silas, and the words brought Ren to his side immediately.

The skeletons lay, en masse, against one wall. An adult, probably female, pieces of a bowl lying around her skull and spine. There was another adult, probably male, buried a foot away from her, slightly lower in the dirt. Both skeletons showed signs of arthritis and vitamin D deficiency—the male's humerus bone was curved like a bow. They had not been young when they died. The end of the man's femur was nearly touching the woman's tibia.

Slightly farther out from the wall lay another adult—most likely male—and two babies, one perhaps a toddler.

Silas had uncovered those three almost simultaneously—the toe bone of the man, the rib of the toddler, the skull of the infant. A piece of pottery lay next to the head of the adult, and a bowl broken into two pieces lay over the toddler's face. A turquoise stone, no bigger than Ren's thumbnail, rested among the toddler's ribs.

"The family plot," Silas spoke into the quiet air.

For a long time, they looked at the bones. Ren put her hand on the baby's skull, just resting it there. There was the usual sadness of finding bodies, but there was much more than that. She felt a recognition, a flash of familiarity. Not as if she'd seen this before, but as if she'd been expecting to see it.

"Yes," she said, and the anticipation spread through her bloodstream.

Ren reached for her camera, but the lens cap was jammed. She worked a nail under the edge of the cap, and the nail broke off below the quick. The lens cap still didn't budge. So Silas went back to the tent for his camera while Ren whisked and scooped and tidied the floor of the hole, cleaning up the outline of the skeletons. She bided her time and focused on the aesthetics of the photos, and only when they had snapped every angle did she reach for a sherd. She wanted to savor this. She wanted to appreciate every detail, every tense muscle and scrape of a tool.

She started with the bowl lying in pieces around the adult female next to the wall. Something had disrupted the burial—maybe a later occupant had dug into the grave—and she could tell immediately that at least one section of the bowl was missing. She spat on the largest of the pieces and wiped away as much dirt as she could. She couldn't tell what the design had been, but it was abstract and geometric. It was solid artistry, almost textbook.

Silas's shadow fell across her hand, and she could feel him looking at her, maybe for the first time all day.

"This is a traditional southern slip," she said. "Everything about the sherd is typically southern, typically Mimbres. And the brushwork doesn't seem right to be Lynay's." At the moment, she didn't care how he felt about her referring to ghosts by name.

"But there's something similar about it," she continued, "something in the alternating thickness and thinness of the lines, how some of these curves flare out at the end of a stroke. I don't know. Maybe this artist and Lynay had a teacher in common. Or maybe it's only the style of this community."

She reached for another sherd, this one not as big as her hand.

"Ren," said Silas.

She looked up. Silas was kneeling, brushing around the head and shoulders of the adult buried with the two children.

"Another bowl," he said.

During the first assessment of the remains and throughout the photos, it had been impossible to tell how much of a bowl remained with this burial. Only the one piece had turned up on top of the skull. But Silas had seen another edge of pottery, and he'd brushed away dirt until he had uncovered the C-shaped lip of a bowl.

As Ren scooted to his side, he worked one gloved finger under the lip of the bowl, and it popped free, as if it were glad to escape. It was nearly three-quarters of a bowl, and even with a layer of dirt, the curve of the vessel was vivid with images. She and Silas looked at each other, eyes wide. It was an owl-and-parrot design in the shape of a star—owl next to parrot next to owl next to parrot, joining in the center of the bowl with a knot of talons. The talons were intertwined, indistinguishable, impossible to tell which claw belonged to which bird. She knew it was Lynay's hand that had painted it.

"This is hers," Ren whispered. She breathed out, letting her shoulders sag. All of this, every second of the last three months, had been about finding this bowl or others like it. Finding another link to her artist. And now she was holding that link in her hands, feeling the coolness of the clay and the dryness of the dirt. She had thought the art would lead her to the artist. In this case, though, it seemed to have been the other way around.

The bowls had connected her to Silas, too. He was leaning in close to the skeleton, his forehead over the forehead of the skull.

"Young guy," Silas said. "The basilar suture isn't totally closed, and that should happen sometime between seventeen and twenty years old." He rocked back on the balls of his feet. "No sign of osteoarthritis. Not much wear on the molar."

"She could have known him," she said. "He could have been family or friend."

He frowned. "Or just someone who happened to have one of her bowls passed on to him."

She did not feel like the push and pull of an intellectual argument. She wanted to feel this, not think it. She was tired of thinking. She moved to the bowl over the head of the toddler, briefly touching the turquoise stone before she lifted the ceramic pieces away from the bones. It was a simple bowl with an unending circle. A single, gently curving line spiraled down to the center of the bowl, where the line thinned until Ren could not see its ending point.

"This one's also hers," she said.

"You're sure," said Silas. He was not asking.

"It has the polished slip," she said. "Two bowls of hers, buried together, with a young adult male and two babies. A family."

"A potential family unit without a mother and wife, you mean."

She leaned in closer to him, her knees starting to ache from crouching. "That actually is exactly what I mean," she said.

He refused to continue her train of thought, though he nodded. He stood, taking off his gloves and boosting himself up to the edge of the pit. His feet dangled. She stood as well.

"Let's say I go along with you, for the sake of argument, and say that these people are part of the artist's family," he said. "They could be any members of her family. This guy could be a father or a brother or a cousin."

"If it were her father and he died that young, she wouldn't have been able to paint a bowl," Ren said. "It must be a contemporary— brother, husband, cousin, brother-in-law—could be any of the above. But why a parrot on his burial bowl?"

"The woman liked parrots," he said.

She shrugged that off, returning to what interested her more. "Back to your point—this is a family missing a wife and mother."

"Was that my point or your point?"

"Her family," she said. "This is her family. Her husband. Her babies."

"That's a huge leap," he said, climbing out of the hole altogether.

"The man and the babies are so close together," she said, following him. "The same level exactly, and grouped a little apart from the older man and older woman. The adult male and the babies must have died around the same time."

"What about other burials on the site?" he asked. "Did your other excavation turn up any signs of mass deaths—epidemics or violence? Malnutrition? An odd number of juvenile deaths?"

"Not at all. There were actually fewer juvenile remains than we would have expected. Whatever killed these people, I don't think it was on a mass scale."

"So maybe the artist had a brother and a couple of nieces," he said. "And they all ate the same bad meat and died. And she provided bowls for their burial. Or maybe she did that for her next-door neighbors. The bonds of this community could have been as strong as family bonds. You can't identify these bodies based on her bowls."

"Listen to me—this makes sense," she said. She drummed her

fingers on her thighs, unable to keep still. "Assume that if Lynay was this man's partner, his wife, that she was around his age—not much older, at least. So she was still young when she lost them all. Late teens, early twenties? And her whole family is gone. Maybe that's her mother and father against the wall over there. So she's got no one. What better time to leave, to pull up and try another beginning?"

"She could have had other children," he said.

"She could have. But I don't think she did."

"Why not?"

"Because she left. She picked up and went to the Cañada Rosa. We know that. And you're quicker to leave if you have nothing left."

He was standing now, pacing along the edge of the cliff. "Why does it have to be so personal? So specific? Why not look at the more logical possibilities—weather, drought, hunger, sickness or fear of sickness. Her moving as part of a larger migration. These are reasonable explanations, and you're dismissing them outright."

She gritted her teeth, clamping down hard enough that it almost hurt. He saw only what he wanted to see. He stood there, watching the bones, and he refused to see what they really meant. The two of them had been steered here, led here, and even the rains and floods had helped them. He was looking so hard, focusing so intently, that he couldn't see the truth of it all.

"I know you want bigger patterns, a bigger piece of the puzzle to fall into place for your canyon," she said. "You want to connect some of the dots. But what I'm looking at, what I've held in my hands, is personal. It's one woman. This bowl sat in her lap, and she stared at it while she painted these scenes on it. That's not the big story you want, but it's important. To make one woman's story real—to flesh out the life of someone dead for centuries—that's worth something. Even if it doesn't tell you about social networks and large-scale abandonments."

He exhaled loudly. "It's a story. That's what you're telling me: A story. A fantasy. No more than that. You're not pointing to clay composition or slips or even parrot feathers now—you're not reading the information. You're spinning a story."

"And so are you," she said, her words nearly overlapping with his. "That's what we do all day long."

"You are not making her real," he said. "You're making her up."

She was silent then. The frustration ebbed, and a kind of shame took its place. He had lied. "You never believed me," she said quietly.

"That is not what I meant," he said, exasperated. "I think you're brilliant. I think you're incredibly empathic and you can read sites like no one else. It's a kind of creative intelligence I've never seen. And yes, I believe you can see something. I have no idea what that means, but I believe you can see this girl. But I do not believe you can create some entire life story for her based on looking at unmarked graves. You're overreaching. We need to get back to the data and listen to what it tells us."

She felt something shut down inside of her, and her insides went cold and blank. He had not believed her, not really. She had handed over not just Scott but herself, and he had turned away.

"Okay, let's talk about the data," she said.

"Don't do that," he said.

"What?"

"Turn off."

She thought of her mother banging on her bedroom door, the hard sound of her mother's palm striking wood. She called Ren's name, sounding tired. Hurt. "Rennie, don't do this," she had said. "Talk to me. Please talk to me. Come downstairs."

When had that been? After Scott? Ren could see her purple toe-nails hanging off the edge of the bed as she waited for her mother to go away, could see the poster of a sky-high British castle on the back of her door. She must have been a teenager. But that didn't make sense, because her mother was the one who shut herself in her bedroom. Her mother was the one who had turned herself off. Her mother never wanted to talk. She was remembering wrong.

"It's fine," Ren said to Silas. "It's really fine. I understand what you mean. I see your point."

"You do not see my fucking point," he said, quietly and with care-ful pronunciation. "You do not see it at all. But you've decided to end this conversation, and on top of that, you're going to try to make me feel guilty for trying to address something that is a very big deal."

"You haven't talked to me for the past two days," she said. "And you want to talk about ending a conversation? You say this is per-sonal for me when you're the one who's so pissed off? You're pissed off because of our personal relationship. Don't let it carry over to the site."

"Even if we didn't have a personal relationship," he said, "we would still have a disagreement over this professional point."

She did not like the sound of the phrase "if we didn't have a per-sonal relationship." She chose to ignore it.

"You don't get to set the rules," she said. "Talk when you want to talk. Keep quiet when you want to keep quiet. Make up your mind. You get in one of your moods where everything is so terrible and awful, and you stew over things and make yourself miserable and expect everyone to just put up with it. I'm not going to this time. I'm not playing along."

He frowned. "This isn't about a bad mood."

She considered walking away, but then she would also have to walk away from the site. She had no intention of quitting work for the day. They stood awkwardly, and Ren imagined they were both assessing whether to continue the argument or, if not, how to get back to work as smoothly as possible.

"Maybe this would be a good time to keep quiet," she said. "Finish the work, deal with this later."

"I prefer to deal with it now."

"I don't even know what you want! You want me to focus on the evidence? Okay. You want me to keep my thoughts on Lynay and Non to myself? Okay."

"I don't want you to keep your thoughts to yourself," he said. He winced, and Ren wondered if his head was hurting. "I think I've made it clear that I want the opposite of that. But I want you to look at the evidence and acknowledge that there are many different ways to connect the dots. Many possible outcomes, many possible scenarios. You could be right. But don't limit us to only one possible answer."

For the first time, it occurred to her that maybe this was how she would lose him—he would force her to choose Lynay or him. He would ask impossible things of her, and then he would leave.

She smoothed the loose bits of hair back from her face, took her time answering. She tried to make her voice calm. "I just want to tell their story. They deserve that."

"What if it's the wrong one? What if you tell the wrong story because you're so eager to fill in the gaps? What if there is no right story? What if we can't know it?"

She could not believe that. She could not believe that there was no right answer, not when the right one had been tagging along after them from her kitchen to their campsite.

Her voice wasn't calm anymore. "What if you won't see the right story because you enjoy the puzzle so much? Because you like the possibilities more than the reality?"

"That's idiotic."

"Yes, it is."

It was not a good way to end. But they were upset and exhausted, and neither one of them enjoyed fighting with each other, not when it felt more personal than professional. They went back to documenting the site, tense but trying. More photos, then covering the remains with a few inches of dirt for the night, then cleaning the sherds for better, high-resolution close-ups. They did not touch at all, even as they bent and reached across the narrow pit. Ren considered the string she had felt stretched between her and Silas— even through the cool blankness that filled her head as she worked, she could still feel the string, twisting unpleasantly somewhere around her kidneys.

Late in the afternoon, she heard the high grating sound of a spade hitting rock, and, almost simultaneously, she heard Silas grunt. He had been tidying up the edges of the walls. She turned just as he turned to her, still only a foot away from each other, even after all the distance of the day, and there was a gray shard of rock embedded at the end point of his eyebrow, jutting from the soft skin just above his eyelid. He was blinking blood out of his eye already.

He cursed and ripped off his gloves, then reached for the bloody shard. She batted his hand away.

"I can see it," she said. "You can't."

The rock hadn't penetrated deeply—it fell away with the lightest of pulls. But as soon as she removed it, the blood flowed freely. He was trying to pull his T-shirt off, looking for something to wipe the blood.

"Keep your head back," she said. "At least keep the blood out of your eye."

He looked toward the sky, and the blood ran down his temple and into his hair. She shrugged out of her linen shirt, handing it to him. She considered handing him her T-shirt as well, but with a swipe or two at his face, he looked much better.

"I hit the rock just wrong with the blade," he said. "Like a truck throwing a rock into your windshield. I never saw it."

"It missed your eye by maybe an inch," she said.

They didn't work much longer. He wanted to rinse the blood out of his hair, so she pulled out cans of soup while he was down at the creek. The sun was setting when he returned, and they ate quietly. It was not exactly uncomfortable. At one point, she touched his thigh, but she could not read his reaction, so she withdrew her hand. It was hard to tell in the firelight, but she thought his cut had scabbed over already.

For a little while after dinner, Ren tried to read by firelight, but soon she put down her book and watched the flames instead. Silas was asleep, propped on his elbows with his head dropping forward, when Lynay appeared with her basket of luminous flowers. They looked like moonflowers, but they were the wrong color, too yellow. She approached and pulled out a single flower, holding it between her thumb and forefinger.

Silas stirred, smacking his lips, and the girl and her flowers were gone.

"I'm going to stretch a little," said Ren, not sure if he heard her. "Just loosen up my legs before we go to bed."

She walked away from the campfire, into the small copse of trees. She had no idea how to ask Lynay to reappear. She didn't know her rhythms or preferences, unlike with Scott. She could feel him nearby at times, could anticipate his snatches of song just a second before he started singing them.

He used to sing in the bathtub, actually under the water—she could hear the gurgling from her bedroom. She would press her ear to the door, and the wood was cold but she could hear the wet melody very clearly. He told her it was how mermaids sang. His hair was dripping down his forehead and his collarbone poked sharp through his skin and he held a towel around his waist with one hand. And she called him a mermaid and he got flustered and said only girls were mermaids. But he was not happy when she called him a merman, either.

It had been weeks now since she'd seen him. She missed him. It was not a slow ache of missing but a sudden stab in the gut. She wondered if she'd ever said aloud that she missed him, that she wanted him back. That it sucked to have him gone. Did she ever say that to her parents? Did they say it to her? Did she whine or beg or scream with the unfairness of it, and did they nod like they agreed? She didn't remember it happening, but maybe it had. She tried harder to remember, tried to summon images that were obscured. She closed her eyes and breathed in the smell of the night—the woody smell of the fire drifting, the slight scent of freshwater, the deep, cool smell of trees and decomposing leaves. She began humming about Lily and the Jack of Hearts, about girls playing a game of poker backstage. Her thoughts drifted, and when she opened her eyes, Lynay was sitting cross-legged with a half-empty basket of glowing flowers next to her. Her hands were clean, not a trace of clay on them.

"What are the flowers for?" Ren said. She thought they were beyond polite greetings.

Lynay was moving the bright blooms, one by one, to her lap.

"These are the best flowers to use," she said, and Ren was proud that she didn't even flinch at the sound of the girl's voice. It was an unexpectedly high voice, more child's than woman's. It had never occurred to Ren that the girl would actually answer her.

Lynay lowered her chin, looking up at Ren so that the whites of her eyes reflected in the moonlight. "You must pick them at the right time—they only open at night so that the right moths will find them. And they close as soon as the sun hits them. But it will be dark on the climb into the next world, and in the dark, these flowers will open and light the way. You put them on his eyes so he will see clearly. They will shield him from creatures we are not meant to see. The petals over his mouth keep him from speaking and drawing any attention to himself. He'll want to move swiftly and silently into the next world."

"They're for a burial," said Ren. She wanted to move back to safer ground, away from talk of other worlds.

The girl went on. "Cover his ears with them, too, so that he will keep your voice in his ears and take it with him. Take more flowers and thread them through his fingers—bind his hands with the stems to keep him still until the time is right for him to climb up out of the darkness. And the flowers will be a remembrance. He may bring them with him and plant them and remember you always."

"No," said Ren, dirt and dry air catching in her throat. "That will not happen. That is not going to happen. Whatever you want, I'll give it to you. But leave him alone."

"I do not want him."

Ren sat on the ground in one collapsing motion, knees bent to the side. "Then why are you here?"

The girl was still looking at the flowers. "Because you will lose him."

"What can I do?" Ren asked. The words repeated themselves in her head over and over. She could smell the flowers now, a thick, sweet scent like magnolia or honeysuckle. These were some version of moonflowers she had never seen.

"I thought my fingers would smell like death," Lynay said. She had emptied the basket, and now her lap was full of flowers. "Like sickness. His skin smelled of damp and sweet rot at the end. But, do you know, my fingers smelled of starflowers. They bring the guides to you, the ones who will show you the way onward and upward."

Ren watched the sky and listened to the girl's voice.

"He was the first," said Lynay. "My man. Then my boy died. Then my girl. The only girl ever of mine. I filled them full of flowers, wrapped around their wrists and knees, around their throats, the little holes in their bellies like vases. Toes wound with vines. I covered them with flowers until they would have lit the dark like small moons. Listen to me: It's very important that you treat the dead correctly, that you prepare them to climb up. You must use the right flowers or they won't find their way."

Ren no longer watched the sky. She watched Lynay's face, and she saw the same expression she'd seen as Lynay watched Silas sleep, as she reached for him. The same sadness, the same affection and longing. It hadn't been about Silas, Ren realized. The girl was seeing someone other than Silas: She was seeing a man who had slept beside her, breathing warm and even, someone whose face she used to touch and had not been able to touch for a long time. Not a threat—a remembrance.

Then Lynay covered her face with her hands, and, after a short while, wet tracks ran down her wrists. Ren felt her own eyes fill. The girl stirred strong emotions in her. She felt the pain rising off the girl's skin like a fever. She wanted to run from her.

Through the shadow of the juniper, Non appeared, hair pulled back severely with a long thin piece of white bone that flashed bright. It was the first time Ren had seen her since their meeting in the canyon, but the strength in her shoulders and her legs, the easy way she moved—Ren could not mistake her even though the feather skirt was covered in shadow.

Non was looking down, already reaching toward Lynay as she walked, and her face was hidden. Ren kept still. Lynay gave no sign that she heard or saw the other woman until Non touched her shoulder. Ren had not noticed it before, but Non had beautiful hands. They were elegant and well shaped, and they moved from Lynay's shoulder to her forehead. She brushed the back of her hand against Lynay's skin as if checking her temperature. Then Lynay's arms lifted, and Non helped the girl to her feet, lifting her easily. Lynay, still weeping, wrapped her arms around the older woman's neck. There was no sound at all now, other than night birds and insects and gurgling water.

Ren watched the two women moving toward the trees, determined to keep her eyes on them so she would catch the moment that they vanished. The girl was boneless, her feet stumbling, her head propped against the parrot woman's shoulder. The parrot woman herself was straight and steady, and kept one arm tight around Lynay's bare waist. They did not disappear—they passed through the shadows, under branches and around thin trunks, fading from sight as naturally as any two people wandering through the woods.

Ren couldn't help but follow their path for several feet, examining the dry, undisturbed dirt where Lynay had sat, where her tears had fallen, where two sets of feet had stepped. All was smooth and blank.

Silas's voice was too close when he spoke. She jumped.

"She was here, wasn't she?" he said.

She turned quickly. She wondered how long he had been next to her.

"No," she said, automatically. "Yes."

He turned, walking back to camp, and she followed. He pressed his hand against the base of his skull as he walked, and she wondered if he'd had headaches since his fall.

"So what do you think she wants?" he asked, over his shoulder.

"Wants?" she repeated.

"Well, isn't that what spirits do? Pass along messages to the living?"

"I don't know," said Ren.

"There must be a message," said Silas.

The fire was low, the embers brilliant red-orange. It put off a pleasant heat as they settled in on their blankets.

"I can't tell when you're joking sometimes," she said.

"Yes, you can. You can tell."

"Then I don't think you're joking."

"I'm not."

"She didn't want to stay here in this place," she said, and even as she said it, she wondered why she was speaking. He did not want to hear what her ghost told her.

But he was apparently willing to regard this as a game of hypotheticals. He rolled his neck from side to side before he answered.

"Why do you assume she was running away from something?" he asked. "As you've said, there was no sign of sickness or drought here. What if she didn't want to escape at all? What if she was running to something? A better water supply, more fertile soil? Maybe she left with a new husband or went out looking for a new husband."

"She would follow the parrot woman," Ren said. "If Non wanted to go, Lynay would follow."

"Why would you think that?"

"They were family. Maybe not technically. But they belonged to each other." She thought of elegant hands on a warm forehead. She thought of Non supporting Lynay's full weight.

Silas leaned closer to the fire.

"What do you want, Aurenthia? What do you want to go back to Valle de las Sombras and tell your museum? What are you looking for?"

"My artist."

"Her bowls? What she's left behind? Or a living, breathing person? Because we can't find that. We can't construct a whole person. It's hard to know anyone," he said. "Even if they're still breathing."

"I know you."

"You're getting there," he said.

"You know me."

His exhale whistled through his teeth. "Why didn't you tell me about your brother, Ren?"

The change of topic made her freeze. He had been angry with her for days, even angrier with her today over her interpretation of the remains, and for the past few minutes it had been as if none of the harsh words and cold silences had happened. She had relaxed into his voice and the nearby warmth of his body again, enjoyed the back-and-forth of the conversation. His question hit her with a physical force.

"It's not easy for me to talk about Scott," she said, finally. "It's not something I do."

"You've never wanted to talk about him?"

"No," she said. "Not really."

He scooted closer to her, but for once his closeness did not feel reassuring. She felt hemmed in. "Tell me something about him," he said, conversationally.

"Like what?"

"Anything. A story."

"What kind of story?"

"Oh, I don't know," he said. "Tell me about a time he got in trouble with your parents."

She thought of her mother and father and her and Scott wrestling on the kitchen floor, his face laughing up at her, her mother's head on her father's chest. She shook her head.

"Come on," he said.

"Why are you trying to push me into this?" she asked.

"I don't want to push you."

"That's what you're doing."

"Okay," he said. "I'll stop pushing."

She did not like his tone. It was as empty as his face. It hinted at the end of something. He looked at her, right in the eyes, long enough that she blinked and looked away. She wished she could take back the blink. It seemed like an admission.

"If nothing changes between us, this isn't going to work for me," he said. "I don't like that idea. I do love you. But if you keep making me work so hard to reach you, eventually you'll bleed me dry."

She wondered if this was what it sounded like when a man broke up with you. That didn't seem like the right term—"break up" was what you said in high school or college. But she wasn't sure what other term was appropriate.

"Are you breaking up with me?" she asked, and as stupid as the words sounded, she was glad she'd said them. She needed clarification.

"No," he said. "I'm predicting a possible outcome."

And then the conversation was over, which was what she had wanted in the first place. He didn't push her anymore. She didn't throw her arms around him and plead that she didn't want to lose him, although she could imagine that scenario in a movie-screen sort of way. She could imagine explaining everything to him, telling the stories he needed to hear, but it didn't seem as simple as just speaking, as opening her mouth and moving her jaw, letting her tongue touch the roof of her mouth in the patterns that she recognized as speech. She didn't know how to say the memories. She didn't even know how to think them.

They put out the fire and joked as they settled into their tent. Silas was affectionate and relaxed, as if giving voice to his unhappiness had released the unhappiness itself. But she couldn't shake the feeling that she had broken something permanently.

She woke in the night and stared at the stars. She didn't know what had woken her. Out of habit, she listed for the sound of Scott's singing, just in case. But he had not returned. She rolled over and propped herself on her elbow. Silas was snoring, but it was the soft, companionable kind. It was almost musical—in, out, a slight whisper on the exhale.

She felt hot and fuzzy-headed, and her mouth was dry.

It was like time had shifted, but neither Lynay nor Non nor Scott was there. It was only Silas. His wrists and fingers relaxed on top of the blanket. He was not often physically relaxed—usually the lines of his arms and the set of his shoulders were tight with tension, and he rolled his head from side to side to loosen the muscles. There was the softness of his mouth, the vertical wrinkle between his eyes. The thickness and length of his eyelashes. She loved the parts of him and the whole of him, and she watched him with no sense of purpose or time or place. There was only the watching.

She shut her eyes and lowered her head to his chest.

This was the thing she realized. That it was a staggering, unfathomable thing to want no one other than the one she had. To mentally scan the whole endless world, considering all its potentially brilliant, beautiful, perfectly unexplored loves, and to know that even their imaginary possibility fell short of this man sleeping under the curve of her elbow and knee, breathing against the weight of her fingertips.

She was terrified.


*"Reet. Snoke," he said, falling into sleep.*

*She pressed against him until she could feel his breath hit her face.*

*"Snoke," she agreed.*

*He smacked his lips together. "Dar."*

*"Mmm-hmm."*

*"Nematode."*

*She inhaled the breath that he exhaled, and it warmed her throat.*

*"Cartilage," he insisted.*


*He fell asleep with her head on his chest, her forehead against the roughness of his cheek. She lay on her side, and he lay on his back—she slid her palms under his shoulders. His left knee was raised, pointed at the ceiling, and she tucked both knees under his leg, anchoring it.*

*Eventually they would peel away from each other, facing outward and sliding together again. Their spines pressed together tight as chopsticks. They shifted and rearranged and woke touching in the morning, sometimes only the ball of her foot brushing against the arch of his or his fingers resting on her hip bone.*

The stars were winking and flashing the next night. As they watched, Ren asked Silas to tell a story. He did not mention the irony of her wanting him to tell stories. He seemed to have one waiting on his tongue.

"The First Woman made the sun and moon out of quartz," he said, "but after they were set in the sky, she noticed all the sparkling bits left over. So she decided the dust could be made into extra lights for the night sky. But before she sent the new stars into the sky forever, she said, 'These are what I will use to write the laws for all people for all time. Only what's written in the stars can be remembered forever. Such things can't be written on the water, because water is always shifting, and they can't be written in the sand because the wind will blow them away. You can't write the truth in the earth—it's always changing its shape.'"

AFTER SHE JOINED WITH Little Owl, there were four planting seasons with nothing but happiness for Lynay. When she thought of those years, she saw them as sudden movements—climbing in and out of their new home, chasing after the wobbling walking baby, Little Owl hooking a quick, strong arm around her waist. And dancing on the stone square, knees high, hips twisting, the large rabbit bowl on her head.

She was the giver in the dance of the bowls. It was her most important dance. In this public way, she would choose the woman for each bowl. Now at times a woman might come to Lynay asking for a particular piece, devastated that a family bowl had been broken, and Lynay might decide to do this for the woman. In that case, the bowl's ownership would be well known from the first time she took a ball of clay in her hands. But usually each bowl would be an unexpected gift and a blessing, and the women in the village would line the plaza, singing and swaying like willows, and she would lift a bowl in both her hands, upside down, over her head. The dome of the bowl mirrored the dome of the sky overhead, and the bowl contained a world just as the sky contained a world. Lynay had created each small world of animals and water and air and sky and spirits.

She lifted her eyes to the world she had created, pausing. The singing grew louder, and the women began to move as one, a wall of trees bending to the right, then the left. Lynay lifted one foot and took a single step, as confident as the First Woman, who always knew the right path. This first step was always a trick. The maker never walked directly to the chosen woman. As in life, it was always a convoluted migration before reaching the chosen destination.

So Lynay would stop and start, turning, swaying and circling from the waist, legs lifting high and slow and steady with each step. The stones under her feet still held some heat from the day, and her heels were warm. Turning, halting, jerking to the west and then to the north, always with a firm grip on the bowl, she danced until finally she reached the woman she had intended. Lynay lifted the bowl, and the woman held out her own hands, and the world of the bowl was transferred to its new owner. The women screamed, high and happy, still swaying. The chosen woman joined Lynay in the circle, setting her own rhythm as Lynay reached under a cloth and drew out the next bowl. Then it was quiet again, with the soft whispering singing and movement of the trees, and Lynay lifted the bowl to the sky.

The rabbit bowl had been her final bowl on the spring after she had accepted Little Owl. She had joined the rabbit perfectly to the bowl—everyone had said so. The praise had made her realize that her other works had not been sufficient. She had made many other bowls since she had matured as the village's maker. She had not tried rabbits, but she had crafted many designs of water and sun—not as they looked to the eye but as they felt on the skin—and the women whirled around her, with her jars and bowls on their heads.

Another bowl from another year: a never-ending circle, flowing. This was the bowl she made after the coming of her little girl, who caused her to bleed more than she should have, who left her weak for many days, wrapped in skins, shivering. But Lynay was strong, and she did not stay weak for long. She painted a bowl later, a bowl with a waxing and waning ribbon of blood that ran out into the universe without end.

She still loved the parrots, and she saw them constantly under her brushes. But there were everywhere patterns. Bird notes were sharp points like beaks. The small dashes in a mist of rain floated in the air. The wind came in long curves. She caught the golden squares of a turtle's shell and the layers of feathers on a heron. Sometimes she would stare at small things and then see them grow on the clay—the very center of a flower, the endless straight lines on a blade of grass, the loops in a single piece of bark. Everywhere patterns.

The ache in her knee was growing worse. Sometimes walking down steep slopes bothered it, and she had learned not to straighten her leg completely. But for the most part she could ignore the complaints of her knee once she was outside of her rooms, moving and warm. She also had three teeth pulled, and her head went black from the hurt of it. But that pain was short-lived.

It is possible those years were not so happy. Perhaps she never got used to the weight of his body on hers. Perhaps he did not smile often or refused to warm her cold feet in the creases of his knees. Perhaps he lost interest in her once he had won her. Perhaps the baby was sickly and never grew as fat as it should have.

Or perhaps she and her man and her baby were contented. Food and water were plentiful. She held two more babies inside her, but they were taken from her early, before she ever felt them pat her stomach in welcome. But the baby girl grew taller and walked and attempted to run. She always grabbed at the turquoise pendant around Lynay's neck, and five times had broken its cord with her grip.

They had not yet decided which name to use for her.

The fourth year after her joining, there was death, all at once. First a boy, the fourth child that had budded inside her, born early and never even uttering a cry. Then the baby girl lost her breath. She died during the night, also without a sound. They buried their daughter with her one small bowl. There were weeks that passed, each day growing hotter. Then her Little Owl caught a fever so that his face beaded with sweat—which she had never seen on him—and his body trembled. No barks or buds would soothe him. And he was gone. She covered him with flowers and his bowl, and the dirt fell over him. As winter approached, his brother caught a sickness of the stomach and passed blood instead of food. Blood poured from him and drenched his blanket and his sandals, so his shaky footsteps left prints of blood. The dirt was put on him. Even one of the birds died—Early Waking tottered from her perch, could not hold on to the dead branch where she normally performed her acrobatics. The bird could not even close her beak around a branch. Non noticed this early one morning, and by the evening the bird was dead.

All this happened within two seasons, in between the planting and the coming of the cold. There were whispers that everyone was growing weak because there was not enough meat, because the land was drying up. There were whispers that more babies were dying without taking breaths, that more mothers were dying from too much blood gone, that children were weaker and not growing as tall. Lynay did not care about the whispers. She had no space in her head for whispers.

Non was still there beside her, of course. She had lived with Lynay and Little Owl. It seemed as if she had always been there. But then after the deaths it was only Non and Lynay left in their rooms. And there was silence between them for some time, but not a long time. Non was never without a plan.

One morning, after they had all died, Non shook Lynay awake. This was not uncommon, because Lynay had stopped waking with the sun—she could not calm her mind at night and lay staring at the dark sky, and when her eyes finally closed, it was as if they were sealed with packed mud. She could barely pry them open. She rarely felt any awareness until she felt Non's hands on her shoulder.

So she blinked at Non on this morning, trying not to remember the feel of Little Owl next to her. Non told Lynay that she would return to her own people. She said that Lynay should stay and find refuge with her brothers, marry one of the men among these families. Lynay was young still and pretty enough—strong, anyway, and from a good powerful line, and she would be sought after.

Lynay sat up, fully awake. She said she would not stay. She said she would go wherever Non went, that she would be her daughter now and would never leave her.

And then Non told her a story of what happened to her own daughter:

"The ones who hold the rain would not listen to me," she said, the room still chilled from the night. "They would not listen to anyone. And so the wise ones decided that we must give them a child, must woo them back to us. And because my daughter was of the strongest blood, they asked me to give her with my blessing. And I did. She was seven years. She walked to the circle of men who had come up out of the ground, and two of them took her hands—she was washed and combed and wore a soft cloth that covered her, and she wore the pink stone bracelets she loved. They took her below, down the ladder, into the room of the chosen, which even I had not been allowed to see. I heard soft chanting. I couldn't hear her voice, and I never heard a scream or even a cry. She didn't make a sound. She must have been afraid; she must have felt alone. But she didn't call out for me. The men came up after a short time had passed. I saw the stone knife with blood later, and I knew they had taken her head and buried her body only.

"I could not forgive myself. I went cold inside. I had handed her over. I had let them have her. We could have run, or I could have argued with them—I do not know if they would have forced me if I hadn't agreed to give her to them. And even after her blood soaked into the ground, the rain still did not come. I knew they blamed me still. But they would not say so. They needed me. Men cannot understand the parrots. They need them for the offerings, but they cannot speak to them, cannot know them. And I lost interest without her next to me."

"So you shut the door? You blocked out the voice?"

"I tried," Non said. "I tried to block out everything. I tried to stop hearing and feeling the parrots. And there was no rain. So perhaps I did shut the door."

"And then?"

"And then they asked me to leave. I was allowed to take only one male and one female bird with me, though they all would have come with me. You'll think this is unfeeling of me, to talk of losing a bird now when I have lost so much more." She ran a hand over her face, lingering at her mouth. "You must know that I adored my sons. I am empty without them. But the loss of Early Waking was more than the loss of a bird. I will never have the parrots surround me again—there will be no mating. I am no longer their keeper. It is as if someone took away your clay and told you to live in some other way."

Lynay placed her hand on the floor. "But if you shut the door on the top of your head, you wouldn't miss them."

"You cannot shut it. If you try, the voice will come in other ways. And those ways are not always pleasant."

Lynay did not believe her.

They were not the only ones talking about leaving. The creek continued to contract. The turkeys had vanished, along with the rabbits. Corn had grown tougher, and the kernels had no juice to give. A few—two family groups—had left already, headed south. In truth, the dryness and the hunger and the worry and even the sicknesses somehow comforted Lynay: She was not alone in her suffering. It was a widespread pain, even if the others' pain was different from hers. In those months she could not have borne to see others contented and unscarred.

But most of the others still felt too bound to Women Crying to cut their feet loose from the ground and move on. Lynay and Non did not feel bound. Lynay felt sometimes as if she might float away like a strand of corn silk caught on the wind.

Sometime later, the two of them headed east, following the water for a little while, then filling their water jars and trusting that the trails would take them where they wanted to go. Non knew the way.

As Lynay left, the memories fell at her feet, the memories of her life at Women Crying. Bits of silver falling from the cottonwood, flashing. Spine from a cactus in the soft skin of her arm. The smell of sweet hot cornmeal as she unwrapped the folded husk. Mother's hands washing her hair, rubbing at her scalp. Non's hands on her face after the dirt was shoved over her mother. Clay on hands. The bowls—rabbit, trickle of blood, owlet locked with parrot, the parrots that were not only parrots but Non herself.

They walked and walked.

The bird added a new word to its vocabulary. He knew all the family names, as well as greetings and good-bye, yes and no—though these were often not used correctly—pretty and water and toy and nut. He called for Little Owl and for the baby girl and for his own mate. He is gone, Lynay would say. She is gone. Over and over, he asked for Early Waking, calling her name as if it were a question. And nearly as often, the bird called "Little Owl Little Owl Little Owl" as steady as water dripping drop by drop and hitting the ground. He had been a young bird when Little Owl was born, and Non said he considered the boy his hatch mate. Little Owl Little Owl Little Owl Little Owl. Lynay kept telling the bird that he was gone, that they were all gone. She thought the sound of the name would drive her mad.

Somewhere along the journey to the new place and the new water, the bird understood. He was silent for nearly an entire day. Then he landed on Non's wrapped wrist and said, "Gone." Throughout the long, dry walk over the canyon walls, he repeated Gone Gone Gone. And, as if reminding itself, the bird would announce Little Owl gone. Little Owl gone. Early Waking gone. Gone. Gone. Gone. Gone. Gone. Gone. Gone. Gone. Gone. Gone.

And they walked. Lynay's heels split open and bled, even though her skin was as hard as the ground they walked on. They talked as they walked, and Lynay realized that Non did not want to go back to her old home, even though her parrots were there, or at least they could have been. She did not want to walk where her daughter's feet had walked and feel the absence of those footsteps.

Lynay understood this. She also had liked the idea of a place where she did not recognize any of the footsteps. She told Non she would follow her to whatever place Non chose. She did not care about place. She cared only about Non.

And Non chose a lovely place, a place she had visited before she was grown, where she had spent several seasons. It was a great ditch in the earth filled with all things green. Life was everywhere, and on their first day descending the mountain, Lynay saw a rabbit frozen still by a water shrub. The creek had enough force to knock the sandals from your feet. The people had welcomed Non, even without the possibility of more parrots. And they welcomed Lynay as well.

But Lynay proved Non wrong. You could close the door on the top of your head—you could close everything. You could prevent anything from getting in. She had twenty-one years when they took their first downhill step into the canyon, and she did not dislike their new home. She no longer cried. She smiled and nodded. A few men wooed Lynay— one who was tall, one who had a scar down his thigh, and one who never showed his teeth when he smiled. She agreed to join with the one who had the scar, because she liked how he looked at her. Over time she created a new person who looked like her and spoke like her, and she lived inside that person's skin. She grew to think of the skin as her own, except sometimes at night when everyone else slept, she could feel her other self shifting and stretching and remembering inside her tidy, comfortable skin.

She did not let her new man or her new family inside that skin. She smiled and nodded, but her head was sealed tight. She had brought powdered clay in the bottom of her basket, clay from her mother's favorite bend, where the tall grasses grew. She left the gray powder dry and untouched, hidden behind one of the two bowls she had brought with her. They were the bowls her mother had used for mashing and kneading. Lynay had taken none of her own work with her. She had no use for it. Her hands were clean here in the new place, with nothing but fine layers of cornmeal or dust darkening the creases of these brand-new knuckles.

# ten

*Representation vessels are rare reflections of Mimbres conceptions of society—as it actually was, or as an idealized version of what it should have been.*

—From "Picturing Differences: Gender, Ritual and Power in Mimbres Imagery" by Marit K. Munson, *Mimbres Society*, 2006

It was parrots that brought them back to Cañada Rosa. Ed and Paul grew tired of waiting for Silas and Ren to return, and they started taking down a few of the outlying rooms, along the perimeter of the rooms where the parrot woman had been found. A few meters below the surface they found a handful of effigies—small clay parrots—three whole sculptures and pieces of another two. These were abstract, hastily formed pieces, but the shape was unmistakable. There were no bowls or sherds that pointed to Ren's artist: Still, there were parrots.

Twenty-four hours after they hung up with Ed, Ren and Silas were headed back to the canyon. There was nothing that had to be finished at Crow Creek, nothing that couldn't wait weeks or even months. They had reached the floor level of all five of the newly exposed rooms, had found what bodies there were to find, and had found the bowls that were with the bodies. They found another two bowls that Ren felt sure were Lynay's, although these didn't have macaws on them. Her style was still distinctive.

On the drive back to Cañada Rosa, something had settled between Silas and Ren that was neither comfort nor discomfort. They spoke and still made each other laugh, but the smooth rhythm they normally had, the ease in each other's company, felt shaken. Ren wondered if all she needed to do to restore the rhythm to what it had been was to invoke Scott. If she opened her mouth and the right words fell out, would the tightness at Silas's mouth loosen? She could tell him about when Scott tried to cut a hole in his bedroom window with their mother's engagement ring while she was in the shower. Or when he gave her a rabbit for her sixth birthday. The dog killed it the next day.

On the other hand, she wondered if the canyon itself might smooth things between them. Perhaps mere geography, the creek and the soil and steep rock walls, would recenter whatever was destabilized. She would wait and see. Her own rhythms pushed her to wait.

The drive was not a long one, and time passed quickly. Ed must have heard the truck coming up the road: He was waiting outside as Silas pulled under the shade of a walnut tree. Ren opened her door before the truck had completely stopped.

"Welcome back," Ed said. His T-shirt read "PETA—People Eating Tasty Animals." His khakis were smooth, with crisp pleats.

Ren looped an arm around his neck. "I hear you've been busy."

"Doogie Howser here found the good stuff," Ed said.

Paul jogged through the doorway and stopped slightly behind Ed. "I don't understand that ancient pop-culture reference," he said. "Hello again."

Ren smiled and reached out to lay her hand on Paul's shoulder, and he stepped into her touch. He lifted his own hand as if he would return her gesture, but he stopped short of touching her, leaving his hand floating awkwardly for a moment. Ren was more interested in the hand that she couldn't see—the one behind his back. Silas was beside her now, giving and receiving his own thumps on the back.

Ren kept her eye on Paul's hidden hand.

"What do you have there?" she said, once the hellos were completed.

He looked as if he might like to tease her, to prolong the suspense—as Ed or Silas would certainly have done—but he couldn't resist showing her. He uncurled his fingers, revealing a small clay parrot, no more than two inches long. It had no feet, and its tail was broken off. The point of the curved beak was gone. The shape of the bird was crude, asymmetric, and unsure. If it weren't for the long lines of its body and the few millimeters of its tail, Ren would have wondered if it was meant to be a turkey or a wren or maybe even a duck.

"Isn't this what you found at Crow Creek?" prodded Paul. "When you found the bowls?"

She lifted the tiny bird with her thumb and forefinger, dropping it into her own palm. The bottom of the parrot was smooth and worn, and seemed to fit her hand. She couldn't help but imagine it had been held often, rubbed down by another set of hands.

"No," she said. "It's not like what we found. It's similar in some ways, but this is smaller. And the wings here are painted on, not shaped into the clay. It's . . . sloppy."

"There has to be a connection," said Ed. "Like Silas keeps saying, there's no trace of parrots in the canyon. The only connection is that woman's skirt and your artist's bowls. Who else would be making parrots?"

Ren worked her lip with her teeth and brought the clay bird closer to her face. "Where are the others?"

"Inside," said Paul.

They all followed him back to the lab. The parrots were sitting neatly together in a cardboard box, washed and dried. Ren held each figure in turn, studying the paint and the shape of the beaks, the design of the wings. None of the tails looked right—they didn't hang properly from the bodies. They were shortened, fanlike, dropping no lower than the parrot's belly. Nothing about the design looked familiar to her. But Ed was right: The chances of someone else shaping parrots in this canyon, meters away from Lynay, with no connection whatsoever, were unlikely.

Silas plucked one parrot from the bunch, cradling it in one hand. "Cute little guys, aren't they?"

Ren picked up another parrot, and the movement took her closer to Silas. He did not lean toward her, didn't reach for her hand, but he didn't step in the other direction, either.

By the next day, after digging several more rooms, Ren was even more puzzled. She sat at the edge of the Delgado site, with the brown tips of her fingers aching for water. The sky was an unbroken sheet of blue. They did not fit, these parrots. There had been none around Non's grave. None at the burials at Crow Creek. No direct connection except the effigies she had found with that first set of nesting bowls that started everything. And why weren't there more bowls here? If Lynay had any hand in these clay parrots, where was the evidence of her other work?

They had found four more batches of parrots in four unconnected rooms—a harvest of clay birds from the dirt. Yet there seemed to be no rhyme or reason to them: Some were crude, and some were surprisingly well formed. Some were painted down to the tiniest detail—multicolored eyes, wings with individual feathers, textured beaks. Others had two dots for eyes and a slash of paint for wings. Some were naked clay, baked and bare.

Ren had arranged them in groups, divided into separate boxes, depending on where they had been found. They were bizarre decorations to the site—cardboard nests filled with small birds pushed up against screens and buckets and tools. But Ren couldn't see them in their neatly categorized boxes. Now she had the birds spread around her in the dirt, examining them en masse. Nineteen of them.

"Well?" asked Silas. He had found a piece of charcoal as big as his thumbnail. They could surely get a date from it and isolate when one of these rooms had been in use.

"I don't know," she said. "It's not her. It doesn't make any sense that it would be her. Where's the skill? Where's the sense of perspective? These aren't done by anyone with artistic talent."

"Maybe her style changed. Maybe they were supposed to be abstract."

She didn't bother to answer.

He shook gravel from his glove. "Maybe your artist was teaching someone else. Maybe she had a daughter."

"There are too many of these things, by too many different hands," Ren said, noticing that he always said "artist" instead of "Lynay." He could not dispute the existence of an artist. "It would make sense if she were teaching a child, but then why would we find parrots in five different rooms? And this many surviving figures? There could have been hundreds of them if this many are left."

"Still looks like children to me," Silas said.

"So she had five children, and they all lived in separate rooms?"

He dropped the charcoal into a clear plastic vial and snapped on the lid. He walked back to the stack of paper bags and fished for the black pen in his pocket.

"Fine," he said, as he wrote. "Say it's not her. Could be other people from her village at Crow Creek. Or even a completely unaffiliated group. Another group from the north, maybe."

They'd found plenty of sherds, just no more of Lynay's. Ren lifted one open-beaked parrot. A tongue was painted inside the beak. She liked these figures, liked the smallness and simplicity of them. You could fit two or three of them in your palm and feel them jostle together like marbles. They were solid and warm, as if they had tiny clay hearts beating inside them. And Silas was right—they undeniably had the feel of toys. She was sitting among a flock of children's playthings. She stared at a particularly fat bird with stunted wings. It looked like a chicken. She tugged it through the dust by its stub of a tail, then spun it in a slow circle. These parrots could have taken flight, danced through the air in little hands. They could have had names and tiny rock eggs and nests of twigs packed tight by dirty fingers. She drew a line in the dirt, added branches and leaves, and sat the fat bird on its perch.

But the parrots did not fit. She could not make sense of them. For all of Silas's demands that she focus on concrete proof, all their data supported her view of Lynay and Non's life story. These clay parrots did not disprove her theories, but they complicated them. Had there been another artist at work? Was there some broader connection to parrots here in the canyon? Were there other forces at work, maybe from the northern pueblos, as Silas suggested?

She thought of her mother banging on her door, trying to talk to her. That also did not fit. But she believed it was true. She had poked at the edges of the memory and found it to be sound. Other strands of that day had risen to the surface. She thought the door banging had happened on a weekend when she had wanted to go hiking with a friend—but which friend? She remembered not having friends during those years—and her mother had told her no. Ren had already bought new gold-rimmed sunglasses for the hike, and this was part of her resentment. It was possible her mother told her no because she wanted Ren to stay in the house that day, to spend time with her parents. Ren thought this was both impossible and correct. She could not remember if she answered her mother, if she had opened the door and let her mother sit next to her on the unmade bed, or if her mother had given up and gone back downstairs.

She had expected to see Scott somehow, now that she was back at the canyon. This was where she had left him. But he had not shown himself.

She added two more birds to her dirt branch.

By the time the four of them made their way down the elk trail just before sunset, they were balancing boxes of parrots and sacks of sherds. Paul had found half of an impressive Tularosa bowl, and Ren had added one more clay bird to their collection. No one had a free hand, which made for a careful pace downhill. They stopped halfway down on a plateau to catch their breath and re-situate their packages. Silas convinced Ren to give him one of her boxes. Taking it from her, he ran one junipered finger up the inside of her arm: The familiarity of the trail and the view and his touch and the evergreen scent made her eyelids heavy. Across the canyon, the shadows on Mantilla Butte made the rock look slick and wet. The air had cooled, and the birds sounded excited.

Starting back down the trail, she had both arms wrapped around the box she held, though she was ready to shift it to one arm if she felt her feet slipping. Silas was in front of her, and when the path curved just right, she could see Paul even farther down the trail. Silas disappeared behind a wide shrub, and when he reappeared, two other figures were pulling even with him, not on the trail but in the dry, waving grass. Ren squinted. She kept looking, straining her eyes, long after she had realized the two climbers were female and bare-legged. They were a few yards to the west of Silas, but none of the men paused.

It was Lynay climbing up the trail, Non slightly in front of her. They ascended slowly—fifty yards from Ren, then forty. They were bending under the weight of the baskets on their backs. Each held one hand above her head, balancing other baskets that nodded slightly with each step the women took. Ren scrambled to get closer, not caring if the others noticed where she was going. She cut across the side of the slope, angling to intersect with the two women.

Now she could make out more details. These were traveling baskets the women were carrying, not just wood-gathering baskets— large, faded by sun, with frayed edges of yucca flapping. They were baskets that signified long distances being crossed. A distance as far as Crow Creek.

Ren checked behind her, glancing down the trail. Silas didn't seem to have noticed that she had left the path. No one had noticed—they were too intent on their footsteps. She kept moving.

She could not see their faces clearly, but she could see the tired slump of Lynay's and Non's shoulders, and how their feet barely cleared the ground as they walked. Their hair had blown free of its moorings, strands whipping around their faces. Their legs were caked with dirt and mud, not merely a layer of dust but a coat as thick as a layer of brown paint. As exhausted as Lynay looked, as worn down by her load, what struck Ren was that the girl should be carrying more. She could not possibly have fit more than a few bowls in those baskets. Where were the others? If Lynay and Non were entering the canyon for the first time—as the baskets and the hard lines of their faces and the dirt covering their hair and skin suggested—where were the years' worth of bowls from Crow Creek?

Lynay must have left them behind. All those bowls not yet found. The thought made Ren kneel, ignoring the popping in her knees. Whatever the girl had created at Crow Creek, whatever images of birds and sun and ceremony, must have been stolen or crushed or lost over the centuries. Ren had searched the site, sifted uncountable mounds of dirt, and she felt sure she had found all there was to find. There must have been so much more. She had held out hope that there was still a body of work lying in wait, a great cache of painted pottery that documented an entire lifetime, an entire people. Even if Ren was unable to read it.

But the girl had not brought them with her. She turned toward Ren, and her face held nothing, not even fatigue. She had left them behind, the bowls and the bodies. She left the turquoise necklace on the little girl. She left the flowers over the faces of her children and her husband. She left the graves of her mother and father. She left the ledges of sandstone and the yucca that seemed to grow everywhere. She took nothing but what she could carry.

Ren lost sight of the two women for a moment; she squinted and wondered if she had seen shadows or cholla or something else inanimate and manufactured a vision out of it. Maybe she was so desperate to have her questions answered that she was hallucinating her ghosts now. But no, if she had imagined the women, she would have imagined them loaded down with bulging sacks of Lynay's bowls. And she would have imagined them strong and contented, not muddy and defeated.

She spotted them. Not too far away. She adjusted her angle slightly so that her route took her just down the hill from Non and Lynay, who had not acknowledged her. She could have jogged and caught up with them in five or six steps. Instead she kept a slight distance and fell into step behind them. Lynay obscured the view of Non, but Ren could stare straight at Lynay's wide shoulders and thin waist and absorb details that she had missed when she'd been distracted by the girl's large eyes and quick-moving hands. Now she could see the line of Lynay's spine visible under her thin brown shawl woven with strands of red. She wore one shell bracelet, as white and smooth as Non's two bracelets. She was favoring her right foot. Ren noticed how Lynay followed Non's path exactly. Every loop around a cactus, every step over a boulder. If Non stepped on the left side of a dead branch, Lynay did not step on the middle or the right. She put her foot where Non's had stepped. And it was a good thing, Ren thought, because the girl seemed past thought. Lynay moved mindlessly. She stumbled over a rock, jerked forward, then righted herself, her motions as loose as a puppet's.

Gradually, Ren closed the distance between herself and Lynay. She tried to place her feet where Lynay's had been. She noticed the difference in the girl's pace and Non's sure feet. Non did not hesitate, did not check the angle of the sun or look for signs along the trail. She seemed to know where she was going. Maybe she had been wrong, Ren thought. Maybe the women had not come to warn her or threaten her. Maybe they were retracing their own paths, over and over, and she was only observing.

Non ascended a slab of rock in three steps—wide step to the left, smaller one to the right, pushing off on the last left step to get to even ground. She stopped, turned—not looking at Ren—and held out her hand to Lynay. Lynay followed, left, right, left, and briefly squeezed Non's hand when she reached the top of the slab. Non touched the younger woman's chin with her thumb and forefinger, narrowing her eyes as she read Lynay's face, surely catching the exhaustion and the soreness and deeper things. They held hands for two more steps, three more steps, Ren counted, before Lynay let her hand drop to her side again. Non reached back once more and ran a hand over Lynay's hair.

Lynay's feet landed like falling things, with a surprising impact on each step. She had a deep scrape down her calf muscle, the edges of skin swollen around it. Dried blood dotted her brown leggings. As Ren looked closer, she could see other signs of sharp edges. The layer of dirt had smoothed over other cuts, but touches of red-brown streaked the mud on her legs. The path had left its mark on her skin.

"Lynay," Ren said. Then louder: "Lynay."

The girl paused at the sound of her name, just a small second of her foot hovering before it landed on the dirt. She did not turn around.

Why did they make it so hard? Ren wondered, still plodding through the grass. These dead women interrupted her work and plopped themselves down in the middle of her site; they made themselves at home in her living room; they lounged on her bed. They inserted themselves into her life, and then they did their best to ignore her. Ghosts were frustrating, moody creatures. They exhausted her.

"Lynay," Ren said again, soft as toes on gravel, knowing she already had the girl's attention. She did not want to draw Non's attention. Non might make another proclamation, another terrible decree.

Now Lynay turned her head, only a twist in Ren's direction.

Ren had to ask, had to hope that she had misunderstood all the clues. "What about the bowls? Your work?" she said.

Lynay answered Ren as if she were a very young or very stupid child. "Some things I did not want to carry."

Ren kept looking at the dried blood on the dirty skin. Lynay's bowls did not reflect this canyon, or an entire people, or a merging community. Lynay had been painting with traces of the north back when she was at Crow Creek, when no other potters had shown any sense of the world ruled by Chaco. But Non had brought the other world to Lynay. And Non had brought the girl to this canyon. She had shaped the routes Lynay would take. While Ren had thought she was tracking the intersection of civilizations caught in the clay, she was following one girl and one woman, and they had let her catch them.

Ren knew the answer to the next question before she asked it. "Why did you come here?"

Lynay did not slow down. She looked straight ahead at Non. "She is all I have left. She holds everything. Little Owl and my children and my mother and myself—they are all alive in her head."

Ren stopped moving. She let the women draw away from her: Lynay never looked back. She stumbled again, but Ren felt confident if the girl fell, she would fall forward. And surely Non would catch her.

"Ren!" Silas's voice carried up the slope. She couldn't see him.

"Ren!" he called again.

"Coming," she called back.

She leaned down and let go of the box in her arms, coming back to the present. Her feet hurt. Her biceps were burning from holding the same position, even though the clay wasn't that heavy. When she looked behind her, she could not see Lynay and Non, either. She did not want to follow them, anyway. She wanted to get off this mountain. She wanted to laugh at Ed's jokes and make fun of Paul for drinking beer and feel Silas's thigh next to hers. The sun would disappear soon—she could already see the pale parenthesis of the moon shining.

She grabbed her box and started downhill. She looked down into the canyon, at the steep slide of green and brown, and thought of falling, of how easy it would be to roll pell-mell over the rocks and ledges, in and out of the arroyos, to gain speed until she hit the bottom.

That night, while she was splashing water on her face at the bathroom sink, she saw Scott in the mirror.

"You're back," she said.

He nodded.

She turned to face him, resting the backs of her thighs against the counter. Until weeks ago, maybe days ago, she would have sworn Scott would never leave her. He had died, and even that had not forced him away. But she had spent the last few weeks without him, and she had begun to question his permanence.

"I thought maybe you left," she said, a little resentfully.

"You keep bringing me back," he said.

His voice sounded just as it always had. She swallowed. His words seemed to have dried up any words of her own.

"You haven't talked to me since I was thirteen years old," she said, finally. "That summer. In the kitchen—do you remember? I was trying to make popcorn with powdered sugar on top like Mom used to do."

"I remember."

She was reeling from the sound of his voice. "So why are you talking to me now?"

"Because I shouldn't see you anymore."

The bathroom counter was cold and hard under her hands. She could feel a slippery patch where water had dripped from her face. She tightened her grip. "You're the one haunting me."

"No," he said. "I'm not."

"You are a ghost," she said, slowly, precisely.

She thought of him, fading over the years. He had seemed completely concrete that first day he appeared on the edge of her bed. She had seen him and heard him and felt him, his shoulders as bony as ever under her hands. She had felt his breath on her forehead. His T-shirt had felt like it had been washed a hundred times. The sheets had been bunched up under his legs. And then for some reason, in the days and weeks after that, she couldn't touch him anymore. By the time a year had passed, he had stopped speaking. She saw him less, and even when she saw him, he didn't stay for long. He was often no more than hum, a song. He had hardly any substance at all. She had told herself that this was the way of ghosts, because, after all, he was the only ghost she knew. She did not want to question it. He was a gift—that he was with her at all was the best gift of her life. That he could stay with her and nothing ever changed. No matter how close he had seemed to evaporating altogether, he always came back.

She let go of the hard, wet counter and stepped toward him. She did not try to touch, and he did not flinch away from her. She studied his face. Strong jaw, never a trace of stubble. Thick, straight hair falling over his forehead. Dark eyes. Her mother's nose, straight and fine. She knew that face as well as she knew her own. Better. His face had never changed, never showed a single month or year. When she looked at her own face in the mirror, she was thirty-seven. When she looked at his deep-set eyes and too-long hair, she was twelve. Always twelve.

His hand lifted, pausing in the air not an inch from her cheek. His nails needed cutting.

"You can't touch me," she said.

"No?" he asked, moving his hand halfway across the inch of air separating them.

She stepped back, pressing herself against the bathroom counter again. The room was small, and she could hear Silas banging around in the kitchen. The toilet was running. Her dead brother was going to touch her face.

"No," she said, arching backward, her skull tapping against the mirror. Suddenly she could not bear the thought of his hand passing through her. The thought of feeling nothing but air—it made her throat close.

"Look, Rennie," he said, and he lowered his threatening hand, lowered the fingertips with loops and whorls of fingerprints still on them—should ghosts have fingerprints?—and pointed to the mirror.

Her position was awkward, still leaning backward, cheap laminate edge sticking into the small of her back. She twisted her head and looked at the mirror. She hadn't seen the two of them together since he died. Now she saw herself, shadows under her eyes from too little sleep, hair messy, flustered and even panicked-looking. Beyond her, she saw her seventeen-year-old brother, and she loved him and wanted him to tell her how pretty her voice was, and she wanted him to laugh at her jokes, and she wanted to take his hand in her right hand and take her mother's hand in her left hand, and they would swing her up the stairs like they sometimes did at bedtime.

It was different to want this in her child's thin chest, as she looked at her own face, at the faint lines around her eyes. It was different to think these thoughts and, straightening, look directly into his eyes. She should not be able to do that—the top of her head should just reach the vaccination scar on his shoulder. She looked down, away from him, and saw her toenails, which were painted and should not be. She should have scabs on her knees that were not there.

She saw herself, and she saw him. He was young, and she was not. He should not be here.

"I didn't mean to," she said.

"I know."

She could feel the weight of her mistake, hovering nearby, ready to descend. She had done this somehow. She had kept him here, not even out of love but out of need.

"Did you try to leave?" she asked.

He sat on the closed toilet. His knee jangled as he spoke. "All the time."

"And you couldn't?"

He shook his head.

She wished she was not having this conversation in the bathroom. She leaned against the door, angling herself toward him so that she was not watching herself in the mirror. "Why didn't you tell me? Why didn't you tell me it was my fault?"

"It wasn't your fault. You just wanted me back."

"That was all it took? Me wanting you?"

"Your wanting comes out in unexpected ways."

This brought out another thought so sudden and clear that she half expected to see it flicker back at her in the mirror. "It wasn't Silas. It was you."

He didn't answer.

"It's you that I'll lose. That's what they wanted to tell me." The relief made her laugh. She'd had it all wrong. There was no threat, no warning, no danger. Silas was safe. And her brother was staring at her like she was an idiot. She licked her lips.

"Lynay and Non," she said. "They told me something."

He cocked his head.

"Wait," she said. "Did I bring them here?"

"What makes you think that?"

"Duh," she said.

He lowered his chin and looked up at her from under his hair. "People don't say that anymore."

She rolled her eyes.

"Duh," she repeated. "I'm the one they're showing themselves to."

"So?"

This was the Scott that she remembered, really. The annoying one. "Did I magic them here just by wanting to see them?"

He rested an arm on the sink. "You think some dead girl has nothing better to do than be your guiding spirit? She's got her own things to deal with."

He was infuriating. She remembered when she'd asked him what the capital of China was and he said Anchorage and she wrote it down on her homework and then her mother told her never to listen to Scott when he sounded totally sure of himself. He never lacked confidence, even when he should.

"Why can't you ever admit when you don't know something?" she said. "You're not even making sense. You just said that I forced you here. That you didn't want to be here."

A softening of his face. "I never said I didn't want to be here with you. I said I knew I should leave."

"Then why are Non and Lynay here if I didn't bring them here?"

He shrugged.

"Aren't you supposed to be wise and all-knowing now that you're dead?" she asked.

"Your mortal mind would shatter from the depths of the wisdom I can impart."

"You are full of crap."

He laughed and flipped his hair out of his eyes. "You love me."

"Always," she said. She loved his hair. "I thought you were a gift, you know. I thought that the fact that you came back to me was a gift from God. You coming back, keeping me from being alone in that house—it was the best thing that ever happened to me."

"Really?" he said.

"Well," she said, "maybe not."

"Ren?" called Silas. He was just outside the door. "You okay? Ready for bed?"

"Yeah," she said, the relief hitting her again full force. Silas's voice was cheerful and strong and safe from harm. "Coming."

"Bye, Rennie," said Scott, and he touched her face as gentle as a song.

She told him good-bye and meant it.


*"You're snoring," she said, ramming her shoulder into his.*

*"Sorry."*

*He did not roll over, and she knew the silence would not last. She elbowed him when he started again.*

*"You're still snoring," she said.*

*"You used to like me," he said, rolling over to his side.*

*"I still do. When you're not snoring."*

*"I'm not listening to a word you're saying," he slurred. "You treat me like a dog. A dog you'd rather kill and eat."*

*She got up to use the bathroom, and when she came back, shivering at the chill in the air, she slid under the covers with one lunge, curving herself close to him to soak up his warmth. He murmured, nothing intelligible, and his hand landed on her thigh. He always reached for her when she climbed back into bed, whether he was awake or not. Now, as his hand settled on her cool leg, he frowned in his sleep. He began rubbing his palm against her skin briskly, as if he were hoping to start a fire. When her thigh had warmed to his satisfaction, his hand stilled. He leaned in to her body.*

*"You're a gift," she said in his ear.*


Silas insisted on showing her the warm spring that fed the creek. It took half an hour of driving and another half an hour of hiking to make it there. They didn't bother with bathing suits: From their vantage point, they would see anyone approach from a mile or more away. The source of the entire canyon's water supply collected in a pool no more than twenty feet across, then trickled down the rocks farther into the canyon. The water was only waist-high, so they had to bend their knees to properly submerge. The sun reflected off the water and onto the juniper, running through the branches like an electrical charge.

Scott was gone. Ren did not miss him. She felt closer to him than she had in some time, really. He had left all his songs in her head. After the skin on their toes and fingers had crinkled, Silas said he needed to cool off, and Ren walked to the edge of the pool, toes sinking into algae, stumbling on an occasional rock. The view was impressive. The water fell like a ribbon down the hill. Something splashed a few feet behind her. A short branch bumped against her arm.

"What are you, twelve?" she called over her shoulder. "Stop throwing stuff at me."

Another splash. Then another. She swiped at the branches at first, shoving them away, making a face at Silas. He shrugged, both hands hidden behind his back. She turned back to the view. The branches continued to float past her, and she stopped trying to avoid them. They collected in the water around her, and as she got used to the rhythm of splashes, she stopped noticing them. The warm water lulled her. Suddenly a hand clasped her ankle, tugging just enough to make her lose her balance and tumble forward. She fell facedown and came up sputtering.

Silas was behind her, water dripping into his eyes, pleased with himself.

"Apache duck hunting," he said.

"What the hell are you talking about?"

"That's how the Apache hunted ducks."

"I'm the duck?"

"Yeah. You're the duck."

She splashed him, using both hands. "What are you talking about?"

"There were these shallow residual lakes left behind after the Rio Grande flooded," he said, spitting out water. "And there were these ducks that would gather in the lakes. They looked like very tasty ducks to the Apache. The ducks, of course, were highly suspicious of anyone coming close to them. The Apache would try to creep close enough to them to shoot or catch them, and the ducks would

just swim to the other side of the lake. So the Apache started floating a bunch of big gourds out into the water, and the gourds would
drift just like the ducks were drifting. If the ducks had drifted to one
edge of the lake, the gourds drifted over there, too. The ducks got
used to the gourds and stopped paying attention. But then the
ducks started disappearing one by one: A man would wade into the
water behind the gourd, using the gourd as camouflage, walk up to
a duck, grab its foot, and pull it under."

He was so damn pleased with himself. She sprang up and out,
her hands landing on his shoulders with all the force of her weight,
and pushed him down into the water. He didn't go under as she had
hoped—he twisted and wrapped both arms around her waist, trying to flip her under instead. She took him with her, arms wrapped
around his neck and legs around his waist. She started laughing
while she was still underwater, swallowing great gulps.

As they both surfaced, an image of her mother, unexpected,
flooded into her head. Her mother teaching her to dive, to wrap her
toes around the concrete edge of the pool, to raise her arms over her
head so that they touched her ears. Her mother's arm had been firm
across Ren's belly button, showing her how to curve into the water.

"You're smiling," he said.

"So are you," she said.

"But you're smiling at something that's not going on in this pool
right now."

"It's nothing," she said, still smiling.

She watched his mouth tighten into a firm line, and something
pulled sharply at her insides. She bent her knees and sank lower
into the water, up to her chin.

"I was remembering swimming lessons," she said.

His mouth softened. "How old were you?"

"Six, I think."

"Were you any good?"

"I was a very good floater."

This intrigued him. "Let's see."

So she showed him her dead man's float and her jellyfish and her corkscrew. Her mother had shown her that one. Face half in, half out of the water, she felt her hand scrape against algae, and she felt her leg brush against Silas. Another memory rippled past—one afternoon in high school. Her mother had been in an unusually good mood, a playful mood, the kind of mood that Ren's memories told her had not existed after the accident. Ren had come through the front door after school, and as she started toward the refrigerator, she heard her mother's voice calling "Marco" from somewhere upstairs. It was a favorite childhood game, one her mother had loved to play in the house as well as in the pool. Scott had loved it, too. Ren had felt the pull of the old response: She'd called "Polo" and sprinted into the kitchen on her tiptoes. She'd heard her mother coming downstairs.

"Marco," Anna had called.

"Polo," Ren had answered from the kitchen before creeping into the dining room, hoping to make it upstairs while her mother was in the kitchen.

She'd turned the corner to find her mother waiting for her at the bottom of the stairs.

"Gotcha," her mother had said, grinning. There had been no sadness on Anna's face, and she had reached out one graceful hand and run it through Ren's long hair.

Ren couldn't remember what had happened next.

She closed her eyes and stood up. She staggered away from Silas, steps heavy in the water. "Hey," she said. She turned toward him and made a show of putting her hands over her eyes.

"Marco," she announced.

She heard splashing and attempts at quiet.

"Polo," called Silas from somewhere behind her. She leaped toward the sound of his voice.

It was early when Ren heard the gunshot. There was only pink in the sky—no sight of the sun itself. The birds were loud and short-tempered. She had lain awake for hours in the middle of the night, and obviously Silas had decided to let her sleep when he left their bed.

Just one gunshot.

She was swinging out of bed as she woke, already throwing the sheets back before she even remembered where she was. She did remember Non's threat, though, which had resumed its status as a threat as soon as she heard the shot. She had been wrong. She had left Silas to the ghosts.

She threw open her door, striding into the kitchen in nothing but her T-shirt, which she tugged down nearly to her knees. Noises echoed around the walls of the canyon, whether a birdcall or a car door slamming or a gun, and it was hard to place the sound. It could have been fifty yards away, or it could have been a mile.

"Silas?" she called. Louder. "SILAS?"

Nothing.

Then Ed opened the screen door, pretended not to notice her lack of pants, and pointed toward Santina Canyon. "He said he wanted to go for a quick climb. Didn't sleep well, wanted to burn off some nervous energy, get his head straight. He left half an hour ago."

Ed was reaching for his windbreaker. Ren had already grabbed both hiking boots before she remembered she needed jeans first. She ran back into her bedroom, leaving the door cracked.

"By himself?" she called.

"Yes, by himself."

"With a gun?" She hoped it had been his gun, not someone else's.

"He never goes up through the canyon without a gun."

She wiggled her heels into her boots as they were headed out the door. Paul rounded the corner of the building, picked up speed, and caught up with them as they started jogging toward the canyon.

"Who was that?" he asked, out of breath.

"Don't know," Ed said. "Could be Silas was just trying to scare off a snake."

They had walkie-talkies in the bunkhouse, but Silas hadn't taken one. No one ever remembered to take one. Ren resisted the urge to call his name again. It would do no good until they had climbed into the mouth of the canyon.

They stalked through the wide patch of grama grass, under the branches of the wild walnuts, sped up and jogged down the gravel path to the canyon. They drew closer and closer to the sheet of rock with its carved-out handholds. There was nothing but rock in front of them—no movement, no sound other than the crackle of gravel under their own feet. They all called Silas's name.

"He's still up there," said Ren, even though they all knew it. "He'd have to have come past us otherwise."

They scaled the wall one by one, limbs still stiff from sleep, Ed going first and Ren going last. Ed was surprisingly agile, and Paul—in the middle—was surprisingly nervous. "Heights," he said.

"Never seems to bother you hiking up to Delgado," said Ed, pushing off with one leg, heaving with both his arms, and hoisting himself onto the flat rock at the top.

Paul wasn't taking his eyes off his fingertips and their tight grip in the handholds. "It's different," he said.

"Come on," said Ren. Her hand was inches below Paul's boot, and she was itching for the next grip. "Look straight ahead of you and focus on one hold at a time."

Silas would surely guess they had heard the shot. He would know they would worry. If he were okay, he would have headed back to the bunkhouse, surely. They should have seen him by now, scrambling down an incline, easing through a fissure, head peeking over the rock wall to ask them what the hurry was.

There was only one path to follow once they reached the entrance to the canyon—the rock closed off all other options. A path of pebbles and struggling weeds wound through boulders and towering rhyolite. The rocks climbed to the sky. The three of them passed through the first natural amphitheater, welcoming the air and light as the rock opened wide around them. A few steps on flat, easy ground, then they climbed the four steps up to the next level of the canyon.

Five minutes later, stepping into the second circular room of rock, they saw the blood. A thin trail of it ran across dirt and rock, past a catclaw, and then nothing. It was still wet. There was more rock than dirt, making it impossible to decipher footprints or other signs of movement. It was a quiet space. Nothing unusual but the blood.

Squatting on their knees, the three of them looked for a trail that wasn't there. They called Silas's name again, separately, overlapping, sometimes in unison, a rhythm like church bells. Once Ren thought she heard a response, one syllable on the wind, but then there was nothing. The tall, narrow walls did strange things to sound. She suspected the rock might be swallowing up their voices after they echoed around this one chamber, not letting them escape into the air.

"He's fine," said Ed. "He's walked through here a thousand times."

No one answered him. There was nothing to say. There was only watching and searching and moving one foot after the other. More long minutes of walking. Maybe ten, maybe twenty. The pink of the sky had fallen away to solid blue. They walked until the canyon walls widened and shallowed, more the height of a house than a skyscraper. For the first time, there was a glimpse of the world beyond Santina Canyon: The yellow-green fields on the other side of the canyon stretched out to the smooth sky. Some of the ledges and openings led out to those fields eventually. Their one passageway had expanded to several possible routes, none visible for more than a few yards before the rock concealed them. Ren, Ed, and Paul checked their watches, picked a direction, and agreed to meet in an hour if no one heard or found anything.

"He's fine," said Ed, as they divided. This time Ren and Paul nodded.

On her own, Ren tried to fight back the panic. Now she needed words, needed a way to drain out the fear. She did not know which would be worse—to find him or not to find him, and she did not want to think about the possible scenarios. So she talked to Silas as she walked: "If you hurt yourself, you should have stayed still and waited for us to come. You should have stayed back there by that bloodstain. Then we would have found you. But that might not be your blood—it could be some sort of animal's. So where's the animal? And if it was an animal, why was there a gunshot? And why didn't you come back? You should stay where you are, right now, just stop moving. And yell for me. Or fire the gun. Just let me know where you are."

She thought the thought as loudly as she could: Let me know where you are. She picked up her pace, nearly running through the canyon. She slipped occasionally, and her ankles threatened to turn. The altitude defeated her, leaving her gasping, and she slowed again after not even a quarter of a mile. She called his name. This time she did see movement, a flicker to her left. She turned, mouth open and ready to speak.

Lynay was picking her way down stair steps of boulders. Ren ignored the girl, refused to even look at her. She took long, strong steps up and over the rocks, putting distance between herself and the ghost. She did not look back again.

The next time she called his name, there was an answer.

"Ren?"

It was clearly his voice. And he did not sound weak or wounded. She heard him but could not see him. She made it around another bend, scrambling up an incline, pushing past a mushroom-shaped outcrop. And he was there. He was limping. She couldn't speak.

"Hey," he said, smiling but surprised. "What are you doing up here?"

"Gunshot," she said, wondering why she was not running to him. She felt unsteady.

"Oh," he said. "Wow, I forget how sound carries. I thought I heard voices a minute ago. I thought I was starting to hear your ghosts."

She threw her head back and yelled, "Found him!"

There was no answer from Paul and Ed, although she hadn't expected one.

She was close enough to touch Silas now, and she did. She put both hands firmly on his chest, and she could feel the beat of his blood pumping. He covered one of her hands with his own, but the gesture seemed more out of habit than comfort.

"Crazy javelina," he said, breathing unsteadily. "Came running out of the bushes back there, not five feet in front of me. Those things are mean as hell."

He looked at her face fully, carefully, for the first time since she had appeared. His hand tightened around hers.

"I scared you," he said. "Sorry about that. I didn't think about you hearing the shot. No problem, though—could have been one if I didn't have a gun. I don't know that I'm as good at javelina wrestling as I once was."

That was her cue to smile, but she did not.

He nodded toward his ankle, lifted it, and winced. "It ran off back that way, squealing like a, well, like a pig. But I tripped over my own feet when I was backing away from the thing, and I twisted my bad ankle. Slowed me down. I can't make the climb down with this—not that last bit down the rocks. I was heading the long way, out the other side of the canyon."

She nodded, trying to keep her face under control.

"Ren?" he asked.

"I thought the ghosts were telling me I was going to lose you."

He sobered. "They said that?"

"I misunderstood. I think I misunderstood."

The wrinkle between his eyebrows deepened. "But now you're wondering whether or not you're going to lose me?"

It sounded stupid to her when he said it aloud. Hell, it sounded stupid when she said it aloud. But she could still taste the panic and the tears in her throat. She shrugged.

He had pulled up his khakis, and she could see his swollen ankle—no sign of bone, thick as his calf, flushed and soft-looking. She wished for a glimpse of the curve of his arches.

"You are," he said.

She tilted her head to meet his eyes.

"What?"

"You are going to lose me," he said. "Or I'm going to lose you. That's the way this works. It's got to end someday. I wouldn't mind that day being fifty or sixty years from now, but it will end, and one of us will be in god-awful pain."

"Fifty or sixty years from now?"

"That's my general plan at the moment."

She digested this.

"Would that be okay with you?" he asked.

"Yes." She reached to a waist-high outcrop of rock. It was rough and warm against her hand.

"Good." He shifted more of his weight to the bad ankle and took a step. "Walk with me?"

She matched his pace, staying close in case he stumbled. He walked slowly, not exactly limping but treading carefully. She found herself still looking, above and below, watching for snakes, for rocks, for any manner of thing that could bite or sting or smash.

He reached one hand behind him without slowing, and she allowed him to pull her closer. He looped an arm around her shoulder, leaning on her slightly.

"I don't plan to die today, Ren," he said. "Stop looking for omens. Look at me."

She did, still moving forward, trusting she would not step wrong. She took in the curtains of eyelashes and the gold flecks in his eyes, the beard that needed tidying up, dirt on his face, thick hair, and soft mouth. He smiled, flashing the crooked edges of his teeth. She liked the way he looked at her. A bee or wasp buzzed past her face and drew her attention. She could hear its hum.

Ed and Paul. She had forgotten about them.

"Stay here," she said, easing away from him. "Let me go tell Ed and Paul that I'm going the long way with you. They can head on back. Maybe they can at least bring one of the trucks up to the fields and save us a little time."

"I'll keep going," he said over his shoulder. "I have a feeling you'll be able to catch up with me."

She worked her way back through the canyon and called out occasionally, but she couldn't find Paul and Ed. Why hadn't they brought the walkie-talkies? Why hadn't they brought water, for that matter? She hadn't noticed her thirst until she saw Silas, but once the fear was gone, thirst had replaced it. Just one good cool mouthful of water, just enough to wet her tongue—that's all she needed. Or a pitcherful, maybe, enough that she could drink it gulp after gulp and let it run down the sides of her mouth. She needed water. Her lips were dry; her skin was dry. Even her eyeballs were dry. Just looking at the dirt made her thirstier.

She licked her lips and swallowed, making her way to the agreed-upon meeting place. She did not have too long to wait before the two men appeared, almost at the same time, from two opposite directions. They were breathing heavily, and the relief washed over their faces when she told them Silas was fine.

Once she had sent them on their way, she turned back to catch up with Silas. He was moving slowly, but still he had maybe a half-hour head start on her. She needed to hurry. She would find him, and then they would, eventually, find water. Although now that Silas had been out of her sight for this long, some of the earlier groundless fear had crept back. He was fine. It was only a twisted ankle.

Thoughts of his swollen ankle seemed to tamp down her thirst.

She retraced her steps, setting a quick pace, but without the desperation to it that had driven her an hour before. Focused on steps and drops and turns, she saw only the rock in front of her. She pictured Silas's slow, one-sided gait and looked forward to making her way through the rest of the canyon more slowly once she reached him.

Then she stopped altogether.

Lynay was sitting in the dirt, surrounded by clay parrots, like a child with rubber ducks in the bathtub. Her face had a joy to it that Ren hadn't seen since she first saw the girl cutting her hair off at Crow Creek. But it was clearly an older face. An older body, too, with a softness to it, lacking the long lines and sharp angles of youth.

Lynay moved one parrot slightly, leaving a trail in the dirt. "Come sit next to me."

"I'm sort of in a hurry," said Ren.

Lynay smiled, and Ren realized she was smiling back. She looked toward the dirt.

The parrots rested on their bellies, and finally Ren could see the logic behind the truncated tails. If they had been a realistic length, the figures couldn't have stayed upright. They were designed to be handled and posed.

Giving in, Ren lowered herself to the ground, her right knee nearly touching Lynay's left one.

"He's safe, you know," said Lynay, and Ren thought again of Lynay standing over Silas sleeping, not seeing him, not wanting him, but wanting a man long dead. She thought of Lynay dripping blood-paint on Silas's shirt, of the blades flying at Crow Creek, and she thought maybe none of it had been a warning. Maybe she had been so sure of the answers that she had made all the pieces fit. Maybe sometimes tools broke and skin bled for no reason other than a loose screw or a slippery rock.

Or maybe the ghosts had been at work. Maybe they wanted to

sharpen her fear, because it was the fear that made her feel more. It was feeling—the love and the fear—that left her wide open and reachable. And they had wanted her to be reached.

"I know," said Ren.

"He won't always be," said Lynay.

"I know."

"The knowing can be a good thing. The knowing can deepen it all, make you see clearer." Lynay reached for one parrot, skimming her fingers over its smooth head. "I did not make these. For a long time, I did not make anything. I did not want to see anything under the surface. All the patterns flattened themselves out like a chunk of ice melted. I had a man here"—she noticed the lift of Ren's eyebrows—"yes, another one, and I had two children who lived. But I still managed to keep everything flat."

She lifted the parrot, cradling it in her hand. "I did not touch the clay. For years. And then"—she turned over the parrot, and Ren could see the shallow imprint of a small thumb on its belly—"and then there was a girl."

"Your daughter?"

"No. Someone else's daughter." She raised her face to the sun. "She had an aunt across the canyon who worked with clay, so she knew how to make a simple bowl, a small jar. And Non had told her that I was a maker. She begged and begged, and eventually I agreed to pull out the powder and turn it to clay. We made parrots that day. And the day after. And then more children came. Girls, and even some boys."

Ren stretched out one finger toward a parrot and found that she could touch it. It felt just as concrete as the ones she had collected in cardboard boxes. "And you showed them all how to work the clay?"

"Yes. They asked."

"And then you started making bowls again?"

"I did. I ran my hands through the patterns again and let them sift through my fingers until I plucked out the ones I wanted. And it felt good to feel the clay again. Each bowl, each second of wind and sun. I'd forgotten how it could feel."

"I've only found one bowl here."

"Just because you can't see them doesn't mean they aren't here," Lynay said, and there was teasing in her tone. Ren had never heard any lightness in her voice.

Ren nodded. She dug the toe of her boot into the dirt. "Are you here?"

Lynay lifted her chin and didn't answer.

Her hands were covered in clay again, the color etched into her knuckles and under her nails. Her shoulders were straight. She smiled, and Ren couldn't remember seeing the girl's teeth—small and worn—before the last few moments.

It struck her that maybe this girl did not need her to solve a mystery or to avenge a wrong or to spell out a name that had been forgotten. Lynay needed clay in the creases of her skin and hot ground under her feet and the touch of Non's hand and children clamoring for small parrots.

"Why me?" Ren said. "Why did you come to me?"

Lynay tossed the parrot once, lightly. "I liked the way your hands moved and the way you touched the dirt. I liked how you closed your eyes when you waded in the water. I recognized the patterns in you."

"I thought you wanted me to tell your story." She felt embarrassed to say it.

"Yes," Lynay said quickly. Eagerly. "It's a nice thing to be remembered. But I have many stories."

"And are they like the bowls? Where I may never get to them?"

"There's a pleasure in the looking, isn't there?"

Ren half stood, exasperated. "Then why have you gone through all this if you won't tell them to me?"

The sun was in the girl's eyes. She lifted a hand to shade her face. She took her time answering, and when she did, she sounded amused again. "I can't tell you all my stories, of course. I don't even know all of them. But you can look and listen, and we will see how it all shapes up."

Ren smelled juniper in the air. Now she did stand, brushing the dirt from her hands and the backs of her thighs. She looked down at the top of Lynay's head, with its black shining twists of hair, and Lynay craned her neck to meet Ren's gaze.

"You also have many stories," Lynay said. "Perhaps you will tell them sometime."

Ren turned away. Two steps forward, and then she rounded a boulder. She didn't look behind her. She wanted Silas, separate from all signs and portents. She wanted to stay wide open, and if ghosts came, fine. But she wanted other things more. Once the walls of Santina Canyon shallowed, she could see the outline of the larger canyon, see the ledge where the Delgado site began. Lynay was likely there. And perhaps more bowls were there as well. She would see. She would look and listen.

The rock under her feet was the color of a child's eraser. It was shot through with mica or silver or starlight, and it sparkled as she moved. The peaks and valleys of the canyon were shadows of purples and pinks and blues, and the sky still had rose streaks in it. She could smell the soil, could smell the chill of the night evaporating into day.

Silas. He was there ahead, drinking water from a Gatorade bottle.

"Hey," she called.

"Hey yourself." He wiped his mouth.

"You have water?"

"You don't?" He handed it over to her. "What kind of morons come up here with no water?"

"I barely remembered to put on pants," she said. She cut her eyes at his expression.

Something in the canyon had erased the pain from Lynay's face. Whatever she had left behind her at Crow Creek, she had brought along the pain. Maybe it was the husband or the children who had siphoned out the sadness. Maybe it was miles and years. Maybe she poured the loss and the pain into the pottery itself until it all drained out of her, or perhaps the unfamiliar soil soaked it up and channeled it into succulent roots and cactus spines.

These were fanciful thoughts, Ren knew. She would not get an answer to this question. Not just one certain answer. She hoped she would see Lynay smiling again, running or laughing or tossing sun-warmed parrots. She hoped she would learn more of her stories. But she would not try to raise the ghosts from the ground—they could come to her if they liked.

"I missed you," Silas said.

She rubbed her hand along his shoulder blades and kissed his chin. The sweat mark on the front of his shirt was shaped like a cat.

She wondered if Lynay had ever asked Non to remind her of Crow Creek, to tell her stories of days she was too young to remember. Ren could see a picture of them, of Lynay and Non, one that was much less concrete than the visions that had walked and talked in front of her. She pictured the older Lynay, the one she had just seen, with children of her own around her, children she could lift with one arm so they could wrap their legs around her waist. She saw the children sleeping as Lynay leaned against Non's side, and the fire caught the gray in Non's hair. Lynay would lay her head on Non's lap, and Non would stroke her hair and run rough-soft fingers over her forehead and tell her stories of the things that used to be. And Lynay's face would show that there was a pleasure to those stories after a while. She would listen to the stories, and she would start to see patterns, multiple patterns, designs she had not seen at first. The patterns were not simple, but they were beautiful. The television would cast a shimmering light on her face as her mother touched her hair. She would lean into the sleepy-safe feel of her mother's hands, and she would wish desperately for this to go on and on for always.

Ren lay her head against Silas's arm, and she meant to speak of Lynay. Instead she slid her fingers against his and saw that her hands were long and elegant, like a pianist's hands or an artist's. She thought how much she would like to taste her mother's orange rolls, and how Silas could scrape the icing from the pan. She thought of sitting with him on the back porch swing.

And she told him, "My mother's name is Anna."

# acknowledgments

First and foremost, I'd like to thank Karl Laumbach, archaeologist and storyteller extraordinaire. I'm convinced there is no detail about New Mexico archaeology that he does not know and no story that he cannot spin. Without him, there would be no Cañada Rosa in this story, no Lynay and Non, no intersection point between Mimbres and Northern Pueblo cultures. I went to Karl as a blank slate, and he resurrected a world for me. Thanks also to Toni Laumbach, who knows everything anyone could ever want to know about ceramics. Karl and Toni both answered endless questions with patience and amazing detail. They astonish me. The archaeological knowledge here is theirs, not mine. Any mistakes are mine alone.

Important bits and pieces of this story came from a variety of people and places. Thanks to John Fitch, another expert and a charming character in his own right. To Earthwatch and all the archaeologists and staff in the excavation at the Cañada Alamosa: Michael Wylde, Morgan Seamont, Dean Hood, Marc Bacon, and Delton and Mary Lou Estes. To Denny and Trudy O'Toole—your hospitality made all this possible. John Herzog gave a lesson on Ruth and Naomi at just the right time. The Reverend Shannon Webster complicated the story of Ruth in interesting ways. Sandra Sprayberry helped point me in the right direction on Native American legends. I found myself thinking fondly of Santina Lonergan, a lovely lady whose name I borrowed for a canyon. My dad, Donny Phillips, will notice that I've purloined a story or two of his, and I appreciate my brother Dabney's letting girls write on him in middle school.

As helpful as all the living, breathing sources were, I found these published works to be crucial: *Mimbres Society,* edited by Valli S. Powell-Martí and Patricia A. Gilman; *Mimbres Classic Mysteries: Reconstructing a Lost Culture Through Its Pottery* by Tom Steinbach, Sr.; *The Chaco Meridian* by Stephen H. Lekson; *Collapse* by Jared Diamond; *Painted by a Distant Hand: Mimbres Pottery from the Southwest* by Steven A. LeBlanc; *Anasazi America* by David E. Stuart; *Book of the Hopi* by Frank Waters; *Navajo Folk Tales* by Franc Johnson Newcomb; and *Captives and Cousins: Slavery, Kinship, and Community in the Southwest Borderlands* by James F. Brooks. I found the following articles particularly relevant: "A Mimbres Burial with Associated Colon Remains from the NAN Ruin Ranch, New Mexico" by Harry J. Shafer, Marianne Marek, and Karl J. Reinhard, *Journal of Field Archaeology*, vol. 16, 1989; "Prehistoric Macaws and Parrots in the Mimbres Area, New Mexico" by Darrell Creel and Charmion McKusick, *American Antiquity*, vol. 59, 1994; "New Interpretations of Mimbres Public Architecture and Space: Implications for Cultural Change" by Darrell Creel and Roger Anyon, *American Antiquity*, vol. 68, 2003; and "Social Organization and Classic Mimbres Period Burials in the SW United States" by Patricia A. Gilman, *Journal of Field Archaeology*, vol. 17, 1990.

Thank you to Fred, who reads everything I write first and last. Much appreciation to my agent, Kim Witherspoon, for her insight and for making business calls much more enjoyable than they should be. To my editors, Sarah McGrath and Sarah Stein, who, thank goodness, saw the things I didn't. Thanks to Rose Marie Morse for her editorial scalpel, to Jamie Roberts for her sharp eyes and smiley faces, and to Debbie Ashe for not trying to be nice. And extra thanks to my friend Ceridwen Dovey, who reads as brilliantly as she writes.

**Gin Phillips** is the author of the Barnes & Noble Discover Award–winning novel *The Well and the Mine*. She lives in Birmingham, Alabama.

# ALSO AVAILABLE FROM GIN PHILLIPS

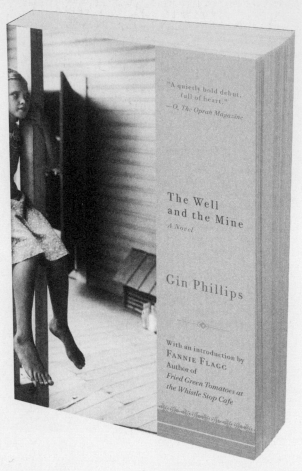